Where's My Mother's Leg?

A Dark Comedy

DAN DISTEFANO

For rights, media & contact visit www.WiseMediaGroup.com/dan

ISBN 978-1629671789

Interior Formatting by Brian Schwartz
Cover Design by Tatiana Vila

Rev 6.9

DEDICATION

To Dianne

Without your inspiration
this book would never have happened.

Table of Contents

SUNSET AT SEA BREEZE

Sea Breeze was one of the premier skilled nursing facilities in Los Angeles. It was on the Westside of LA where the cars are expensive and the houses are big. The facility was a magnificent three-story Spanish Colonial perched on a bluff above the Pacific Ocean. It was where the wealthy came to recover from their stroke or triple by-pass, or when their dementia made it impossible for them to live safely at home any longer.

A woman's pleasant voice came over the intercom. "Mr. Russo, please go to nursing station one, Mr. Russo, to station one."

Ned Russo was in his fifties. He was about six feet, with a full head of neatly trimmed salt and pepper hair. He had whiskey colored eyes, smooth olive skin and gleaming white teeth. He was fit and damn good looking by anyone's description. He was impeccably dressed in a Ralph Lauren suit, white shirt and cranberry-colored silk tie. His gait was straight and his walk purposeful. He could easily be mistaken for a successful politician or a captain of industry. He was smiling as he walked toward station one. And why shouldn't he? Ned was the administrator of Sea Breeze. Today, like so many other days had been without incident. In the almost three years Ned had worked here it afforded him the opportunity of becoming a 'gentleman administrator', a man who came to work late, lingered over lunch, and went home early. But as Albert Einstein once wisely said, "The only constant in the universe is change."

Ned walked down the newly carpeted hallway toward station one. He passed by a nurse, Gloria. She was in clean, neatly pressed scrubs that matched the color of the Pacific. She smiled and greeted him politely, "Good morning, Mr. Russo."

"Good morning, Gloria," Ned said as he smiled to her.

When Ned got to the nursing station there were two women, a physician, Dr. Douglas Brant, and a patient in a wheelchair. The patient, John Lite, a man in his seventies, was attached to an IV. The two women, Mr. Lite's wife and daughter, were astonishingly well dressed, and dripping with expensive jewelry. The older of the two women, Mrs.

Lite, who looked to be in her sixties, was grilling Dr. Brant, "How long will he last if you put him on hospice?"

"But your husband's not ready for hospice," Dr. Brant answered.

Mr. Lite's daughter, who was in her late thirties, entered the conversation. Her tone was decidedly insincere. "My father wouldn't want to live like this. He really wouldn't."

"Why don't you come into my office? I think this conversation would be better suited in private," Ned interjected in his best diplomatic tone.

The older of the two women immediately turned her attention to Ned. "Who are you?"

"I'm the administrator."

She looked at Ned's gold-colored I.D. badge that was pinned to his lapel. "Ned Russo. Are you Italian?" she said in a high-pitched, gravelly, voice that was pure Brooklyn.

"Yes. Very," Ned smiled hoping to gain control of the conversation.

"Oh! I love Italy," the older woman responded.

Dr. Brant turned to the man's daughter as if appealing to a judge for an eleventh hour stay of execution. "Your father had a stroke and a recently discovered prostate cancer. But at this point neither are life threatening."

Ned realized anyone within earshot suddenly became aware of this poor guy's medical dilemma. The older woman didn't seem to care who was listening. Ned looked at the old man in the wheelchair, his eyes revealed that he knew his fate was being discussed and he wasn't happy about the direction it was headed. Ned could only imagine what was going through the poor man's head as these two women who were standing right next to him were trying to have a doctor put him down like a race horse with a broken leg.

"We really should talk about this in my office," Ned urged.

Generally, when these kinds of conversations about how long someone might live take place, Ned would go through a box or two of tissues trying to console the family, but not this time. These women seemed annoyed that their husband and father was still at Sea Breeze rather than in a cemetery.

"How long is he going to be alive?" the older woman asked the doctor.

"I can't answer that. I have no idea," Dr. Brant responded.

"What the hell kind of a doctor are you?" the older woman shouted angrily.

"I'm an oncologist not a fortuneteller."

"What if you just took Daddy off the IVs?" the younger woman asked.

"Are you kidding? I can't do that," Dr. Brant said.

“Well I can. I’m his wife and I have the power of attorney. That gives me the right,” the older woman growled.

“Don’t you want to think about this decision for a few days?” Ned gently asked.

“No. I really want to put him on hospice,” the older woman insisted.

“Cuz we want my father to be pain free,” the younger woman added.

“I understand pain pills are paid for by the hospice company, right?” the older woman inquired.

“Maybe you ladies don't understand exactly what hospice is,” Ned said.

“I know exactly what it is,” the older woman said condescendingly.

Dr. Brant finally decided to end the discussion, “I'm sorry. Your husband is not ready for hospice. And I'm not going to write an order that says he is.”

“Then you're fired,” the older woman said turning to her daughter, “Come on, we’re leaving.”

As the women walked off down the hallway, the older woman shouted to Ned without turning around. “And you administrator, we’ll be back with another doctor. Make sure my husband is either here or dead when we come back! Don’t send him to the hospital.”

Ned, Dr. Brant, and the poor bastard who was married to that shrew and that witch of a daughter were left there to digest what had just transpired.

“That was amazingly awful,” Ned muttered.

“It certainly was,” Dr. Brant responded.

Mr. Lite, the poor bastard sitting in the wheelchair, attached to the IV, grunted in agreement.

And then, the pleasant woman’s voice announced over the intercom “Mr. Russo, you’re wanted in your office.”

Ned’s office was big and furnished with expensive antiques that were also throughout the rest of the facility. He had a picture window that looked out over the ocean. Waiting for him, was Robert Shipp, a VP of the corporation that owned Sea Breeze and numerous other nursing homes across the country. Robert was older than Ned. He had snow white hair, manicured fingernails and wore a very expensive hand-tailored English suit. Robert was sitting in one of the two chairs in front of Ned’s desk. Ned was surprised by Robert’s unannounced visit. Unannounced visits by corporate VPs, in Ned’s experience, never came to any good.

“Robert, this is a surprise. What brings you down here?” Ned asked.

“Ned, I’m afraid I have some bad news. We’re going to let you go,” Robert delivered the news like a doctor without bedside manner telling a patient to get his affairs in order. It hit Ned like an unexpected punch in the gut. “Let me go? Jesus, why?”

"Ned, since we went public, all the board cares about are the current numbers and yours' haven't been very good lately," Robert said bluntly.

"Ok, I had a less than expected quarter," Ned conceded.

"And unfortunately this quarter isn't looking any better," Robert interjected.

Ned slumped into his expensive ergonomic office chair. He knew it was useless to explain. Robert Shipp was just the well-dressed messenger boy sent to execute the orders of the board of directors.

"How long have I got?" Ned asked.

"Until Friday."

"That's tomorrow! Are you fucking kidding me?" Ned responded as if he received a second blow to the midsection.

"Why don't you take the rest of the day off," Robert offered.

"That's really generous. Fuck you, Robert!"

Within an hour Ned had cleaned out his desk and left Sea Breeze. He was too angry and hurt to call the facility's department heads into his office and have a wake for himself. He would call each of them within a day and tell them how much he enjoyed working with them and how much he would miss their company. For Ned it wouldn't be just a departure speech, wherever he worked Ned always grew to love his staff. They always became a surrogate family to him and parting was always difficult.

Ned was in shock. He was embarrassed and hurt to his core. He believed he had given Sea Breeze his all and made a positive difference in the lives of the patients. As he drove across LA, east toward his home in Pasadena, his pain evolved into anger. With every mile it grew. When he got home, he pulled off his suit and threw it on his bed. He put on a pair of shorts and spent nearly an hour taking out his anger on the heavy bag he had hanging in his garage. When his hands got sore and he had worked up a soaking sweat he took a shower. Then he called his ex-wife, Katie. Ned hated texting. He was relieved when he got her voice mail. The shock of losing his job was still too intense, too painful. He wasn't ready to tell her what happened. Ned did his best to sound normal, "Katie, I've got to cancel lunch tomorrow. Sorry. Something came up. I'll call you in a few days."

Ned sat in his house, staring out the window thinking about his next move. He was beginning to face the reality that he had just lost his job. Ned made a second call to one of his best administrator buddies, Andy Silver.

"Hello, Ned!" Andy said answering the call.

"Andy, guess what? I got fired today."

"What? Holy shit!" Andy responded shocked.

"How 'bout you meet me at Smitty's I could use a drink," Ned said.

Smitty's was a popular after-work Pasadena watering hole. The food was better than average, especially the meatloaf, and they made their own potato chips. That was a big plus for Ned. He got there before Andy, sat at the bar and ordered a Grey Goose martini with Sicilian olives. A few minutes later, Andy came in and sat on the stool next to Ned, "How are you doing, buddy?" Andy said empathically.

Andy and Ned had been friends since they took the state administrator's licensing exam together years before.

"I've been better," Ned said. He was doing his best the shield his feelings of hurt and rejection.

"What happened?" Andy asked Ned, then he looked over to the bartender, "Can I have a draft beer, please. And more chips."

"I didn't make them enough money," Ned said.

"Fuck them! You were doing a great job. Good surveys, happy patients. What the fuck do they expect?" Andy said.

"More money," Ned said bluntly.

"Well, fuck them," Andy said.

"Yeah, well, in the meantime, you know of any nursing homes that need an administrator?"

"I know of a couple of places that are looking," Andy said.

"Andy, I need a job. I have a family to take care of. I don't want to let them down," Ned said.

"I know. There are a couple of places but none of them are Sea Breeze."

"That's okay, long as I can pay my alimony," Ned said jokingly.

Later that night after Ned got home, Katie called. When Ned saw her name on his cellphone his first thought was not to answer. He was too embarrassed, but he knew sooner or later he would have to explain what happened. He took the call. She got right to the point.

"Ok, tell me what's going on?" Katie asked.

Ned sighed with relief. "You are psychic. How could you tell?"

"I'll call you in a few days," she said imitating his voice. "That isn't you."

"I got fired," Ned responded.

Katie was shocked, "What? Why? You were doing so well there."

"The corporation had a different view of my performance," Ned said wryly.

"I'm sorry. What are you going to do?" she asked.

"Katie, there's six hundred nursing homes in LA. I'll get another job.

NOT ON THE WESTSIDE ANYMORE

It was about eight in the morning when the GPS led Ned into the heart of Koreatown and to his new job as the administrator of Central City Convalescent Hospital. Ned pulled up to the stop sign near the corner. He looked around the neighborhood. It was old and rundown. Across the street from the facility, a man had a food stand on the sidewalk where he was selling coffee and tacos to men who looked like day laborers. There was graffiti sprayed on the block walls and buildings that surrounded the hospital. A young black girl in a short skirt and fake fur jacket was leaning against a nearby parking meter. It was obvious to Ned what line of work she was in.

"Hi," she said as she moved closer to Ned's SUV, "Wanna date?"

Ned shook his head no. He turned right at the stop sign and another right into the driveway that ramped down into the underbelly of Ned's new job. A painted sign on the metal gate at the bottom of that driveway read: CENTRAL CITY CONVALESCENT HOSPITAL. The sign was dirty. The letters were peeling off. Ned pressed the button of the electronic gate opener. The heavy iron-gate creaked and groaned as it slowly rolled back on its track. Ned pulled into the parking area. It was dark. Half the florescent tubes in the ceiling fixtures were out. There were puddles here and there caused by dripping, leaky pipes that crisscrossed the ceiling. Ned looked around at the garage. The sounds of gulls and splashing waves that was so much a part of Sea Breeze flashed through Ned's head, "I'm not on the Westside anymore," Ned said reluctantly.

Ned drove down the center of the garage until he found the spot labeled: ADMINISTRATOR. There was a beater pick-up truck parked in that spot. There wasn't a vacant parking space anywhere to be seen. Ned parked in the middle of the garage blocking the beater truck, shut down his SUV and got out. He was wearing his blue suit and silk cranberry tie. He pulled his Ghurka briefcase out of the back seat. Katie had given it to him when he became the administrator of Sea Breeze. He walked toward the stairs at the back of the parking area. Two Hispanic kitchen workers were sitting on a bottom step. Their aprons were stained and they were drinking beers out of brown paper bags. The two guys seemed a little annoyed to have to move so Ned could climb by.

"Good morning. Do you work here?" Ned asked.

One of the two workers glanced up at Ned, "Yeah," said the guy closest to Ned, "...in the kitchen." That same kitchen worker took a swallow from his beer.

"Hey, man," the other guy said to Ned, "you know you blocked that truck."

Ned glanced back over his shoulder, "You're right, I did."

He continued by them and up the stairs. He pushed open the security gate at the top. He was greeted by the stench of three over filled dumpsters about ten yards away. Ned could see that their contents were medical waste, used diapers and rotting food, "Oh, my God," Ned blurted out as the stench from the dumpsters crept up his nostrils. A large rat stopped his foraging on top of one of the garbage piles. The rat sat up on his hind legs and looked at Ned. They stared at one another for a second. Then the rodent seemed to raise his little paw and held out his little rat digit as if his were giving Ned the finger. The rodent disappeared back into the depths of the dumpster. Ned continued on into the facility.

WHERE'S MY MOTHER'S LEG

Ned walked through the facility. He passed by a series of nurses who acted more like robots than angels of mercy. The facility smelled foul. He found his way into the lobby and went up to the reception window. There was a young man who looked to be in his twenties sitting at the desk in the reception cubicle. The young man was flipping through a Vogue magazine. He was wearing bright yellow kitchen gloves and had ear buds that were blaring Ranchera music into his head. Kitchen gloves? Ned wondered. Ned stood there for a few seconds hoping to get his attention. It didn't work. Then, Ned gently tapped on the cubicle window. In addition to the gloves, Ned noticed that the young man had a man-bun and had shaved his eyebrows and then used an eyebrow pencil to draw them back in. The young man was unreceptive to Ned's tapping. The Mexican music that was blasting into his ears was so loud Ned could hear it standing on the other side of the glass. Ned rapped on the window again, this time a little harder. Still there was no response. Then Ned used his fist. That got the young man's attention. He looked up. "Yes, can I help you?" he asked, suddenly flashing a bright smile. The young man gave Ned the once over. The suit, cranberry tie, expensive briefcase didn't seem be belong in Central City. "You look like you're lost," the young man said in a thick Mexican accent.

"I'm not," Ned responded.

"Are you sure you're in the right place? Great suit, by the way," The young man said.

"Yes, this is where I'm supposed to be. Can you tell me where the administrator's office is?" Ned asked.

"We don't have an administrator. We haven't had one for…" he thought about it, "…I guess about two months now."

"I'm the new administrator. They told me at corporate you'd have the keys to my office?" Ned said.

"Oh, wow!" The young man quickly opened a drawer at his reception desk and fumbled through it before pulling out a large key ring with lots of keys on it. He held the ring out to Ned. "Here you go."

Ned looked at the dozen or so keys, "What's your name?'

"Jose, Jose Medrano."

"Jose, which is the key to my office?"

"Oh, I'm sorry. I'll show you." Jose got up from his chair. Ned saw that his chair had a toilet seat protector on it. "Jose, excuse me for asking but why are you wearing kitchen gloves?"

"This is a hospital. Too many germs. I don't want to get sick. They're the thickest gloves I could find and still be able to work my phone. Do you know how many germs are on a phone? Lots." Jose replied with a degree of certainty.

Ned nodded in agreement then pointed to Jose's chair, "And the same is true for that seat protector?"

"Yes. I'm still looking for something better than a toilet seat cover. I think the paper's too thin."

"I see," Ned said. "You know, that seat protector and those gloves can only do so much. I don't know how to break it you, but there are far more airborne germs floating around here than what you'll sit on or touch."

"I didn't know that," Jose responded uncomfortably surprised.

Ned pointed to the ring of keys Jose had given him, "Which one is the key to my office…"

"Sorry." Jose took the ring back with his gloved hand fumbled through the keys until he found the right key. He took it off the ring and handed it to Ned. "This one's the master."

Ned looked at the remaining keys left dangling on the ring, "What are the rest of the keys for?"

Jose looked at the ring and then shrugged, "I don't know. They've always been there."

"I'm Ned Russo. Please take off those ear buds."

Jose yanked the buds out of his ears.

"Thank you," Ned said as he walked across the lobby to his office. Suddenly, Ned heard an old woman crying, "Mama. Mama." The sorrowful sound was coming from a patient's room right across from Ned's office. Ned stuck his head into the room where he heard the moaning. There, sitting on a bed, was an old Korean woman. "Mama, Mama." She just sat there, her eyes closed, rocking back and forth. "Mama, Mama."

Ned walked out of her room back into the lobby. Sitting there in a wheelchair was a skinny, little man in his fifties. He was holding a bucket of candy bars on his lap. He was doing his best to speak to an older woman with a blank expression on her face. She was sitting next to him on one of the lobby chairs. The man's speech was so slow and so slurred that his words were almost unintelligible. "Buy some candy" the man struggled to get those words out. But it didn't matter to the woman she just sat there and stared out into space. There was a weathered, old, black lady sitting in her wheelchair looking out the lobby window. She was carrying on a conversation with no one. She kept kicking the window like the little kid who kicks the seat in front of him on an airplane. Ned went up to the woman and put his hand on her shoulder, "What's the matter? Can I help you?" Ned said hoping to console the woman.

"I wouldn't get too close to…" Jose called to Ned from his cubicle, but he was too late. The old lady suddenly spat a glop of saliva onto the leg of Ned's Ralph Lauren suit. Ned was caught completely off guard. Before Ned had a chance to react, the old lady spat a second glop that landed on Ned's other pant leg. He jumped back before the woman could get off a third volley. Ned looked around for something to clean off the spit but there wasn't anything available. Ned took out the expensive pocket square from his suit jacket and dabbed the glops from his suit. He looked to the reception cubicle and saw Jose was trying to cover up his snickering. "Sorry, I tried to warn you," he said somewhat apologetically. Ned stood in the lobby of the facility. He looked down the hallway taking in the robotic nurses and his new patients who seemed oblivious to their surroundings and finally the large wet spots of spit on his suit. Disgusted, he took the pocket square he used to clean off the spit and threw it in a nearby trashcan. Maybe an orange vest at Home Depot might be a better option, he thought to himself.

Ned walked to his office and was about to stick the key in the lock when he heard, "You look like you could be the administrator. They change so damn many of them in this place. Are you the administrator?"

Ned turned to see a black woman, hands on her hips, standing behind him. "Yes," he replied.

"Well, I need to talk to you," the woman said.

"What can I do for you?"

The woman was big, about six feet and sturdy. She was maybe fifty with a lot of miles on her. She was in a smart-looking print dress and sported a large, brimmed hat, the style ladies wear to Churchill Downs on derby day. "Where's my mother's leg?" she demanded to know.

"Your mother's leg? Ah-huh," Ned was set back on his heels by the question. "Isn't it on your mother?"

"If it was, why in the hell would I be asking you where it was," the woman snarled.

"Good point," Ned conceded. "I just got here. Can you give me a few minutes? I promise I'll find out," then Ned asked the woman as politely as he could, "Any other parts missing?"

Sometimes Ned couldn't help himself. There was a little bit of a wise-ass inside him. The woman straightened herself as tall as she could and glared at Ned, "Are you fuckin' with me?"

"Absolutely not. Under the circumstances, don't you think it's a legitimate question?"

The woman seemed puzzled by Ned's answer. Then she added, "I don't want to be sittin' my ass out here any longer than I have to. I have business to take care of."

"I'm sure you do. If you could just give me a few minutes, please," Ned responded.

Ned turned from the woman and was about to use the master key to open the door to his office, but the door was slightly ajar. Ned pushed the door open further. What greeted him was a sight far more surprising than he could have ever imagined. There, sitting in Ned's office chair, at the administrator's desk, was a stark naked man. The man's clothes and a soiled diaper were in a pile on the floor next to Ned's chair. The man was sixty-something. He was fumbling through the top drawer of the desk. He stopped what he was doing when he saw Ned standing in the doorway and greeted him with a smile. "Hi, I'm looking for a pencil. I can't find one," he said in perfectly calm, sentient voice. Ned's frustration with the parking garage, the smell of the facility, the spit on his suit all came out of Ned at once like the eruption of a volcano. "What are you doing in my office in my chair with no clothes on?" Ned screamed.

"I don't like to wear them," the man said calmly. As the man rummaged through the drawer, he found a pair reading glasses. He put them on. "How do they look?"

Ned turned and screamed, "Jose!"

Jose heard Ned shout and quickly scrambled from his cubicle. Ned just stood in the doorway of his office. He was fuming. He knew if he moved another inch toward the naked man he might end up doing something really stupid.

Jose ran across the lobby to Ned's office. "What's the mat…," Jose instantly realized why Ned was screaming. "Oh wow! That's Mr. Beatty. He doesn't like to wear clothes," Jose said.

"He told me. I don't care who he is, get him out of here!" Ned screamed.

Then Ned pointed to the pile of clothes and soiled diaper on the floor. "And pick that up," Ned's voice quaked with anger.

"I don't want to touch it," Jose cried out.

"You're the one wearing thick rubber gloves. Pick that mess up before I kill him!"

Jose grimaced and carefully picked up the mess on the office floor. He winced as he held the clothes and the soiled diaper as far away from him as his arms would allow. "What do I do with it?"

"I don't care what you do with it. Just get it out of here! And then get him and that chair out too," Ned continued his voice still quaking with anger.

"There, I found one," Mr. Beatty proudly held up a pencil he found in the desk drawer.

"And throw away those glasses!" Ned screamed.

"Well, since you're going to throw them away, I'll just keep them," Mr. Beatty said.

"I have to cool down. I'm going to take a walk around the block," Ned said as restrained as he could be under the circumstances. As Ned stomped out of his office he yelled to Jose, "You make sure my office is clean and I have another chair before I get back."

"Yes. But I don't know where to get another chair. I never had to do that before."

"Find a way."

Ned stormed out the front door and took a turn around the block. Every alley in the neighborhood was littered with homeless encampments. Their tents, numbering in the dozens, were everywhere. And at the end of each row of tents was a pile of garbage. Ned knew every aspect of Central City was as far away from Sea Breeze as the Earth is to Mars. He was suddenly overwhelmed by the task he was now facing.

A few minutes later Ned cooled down enough to returned to Central City. He entered his office and closed the door. Gone were Mr. Beatty, his clothes, the soiled diaper and his office chair. Now free of naked patients, Ned looked around his new headquarters. It was cramped. The décor consisted of two ugly chairs for guests. A window that looked out on the front of Central City where he could see that the old woman who spat on his suit had just spat on the window again. There was graffiti sprayed on a section of the building right below some words written in Korean. There was an ancient wooden desk and a bookshelf full of binders. Some of the binders had spines with dates from the last century. There were cigarette burns on the edge of the desk put there from a previous administrator. The office chair that Mr. Beatty was sitting in had been replaced. The replacement was from the same period as the desk. The leather arms were pretty much worn through. Ned sat in the chair. It creaked loudly. Ned got out of the chair and pushed it back and forth trying to find the source of the creak, but couldn't. He gave up and sat back down. On the wall directly in front of him were two TV monitors with eighteen pictures on each monitor. This was Central City's security system. From his creaky office chair Ned could watch his patients fall out of their wheelchairs, get into fights in the dining room, or watch his nurses talking on their cell phones rather than attending to their patients.

"What did I get myself into?" Ned muttered aloud. "No wonder this place hasn't had an administrator in two months," Ned said as he looked around his new office. "How did I end up here?" Ned sadly lamented.

But in his heart, Ned knew exactly how it happened. Those last months at Sea Breeze were not his best financially. Without realizing it, he had taken his eye off the ball. He was two years out of his divorce, from Katie, his second wife, and while his divorce by all measurable standards was a walk in the park, it was still traumatic. On top of the divorce, that year during his annual physical, his doctor found a spot on his lung. The big 'C' and Ned never even smoked! Even though Ned's cancer was described by his doctor as 'garden variety,' it still scared the shit out of him. No amount of "you're cured" spoken by his doctor could convince Ned that he was totally free of the disease. Regardless of what he had gone through or what he thought of Central City, Ned was going to do his damnest to make this place a winner then leverage his performance to get a better job.

THE ARMY YOU HAVE NOT THE ARMY YOU WANT

Ned picked up the phone and punched the button for reception.

"Yes, Mr. Ned," Jose answered.

"Jose, that black woman with the hat who was sitting in the lobby, who is she?"

"Latrina Watkins, her mother is a patient here. She was sent out to the hospital yesterday," Jose replied.

"And where's her mother's leg, do you know?"

"No."

"You have any idea who might?"

"Probably Violet. She's the DON."

"Where's her office?"

The DON (Director of Nursing) was the top medical position in a skilled nursing facility and was number two in the chain of command.

Ned walked down the hallway to Violet's office. He passed by the Activities Calendar for the month that was posted on the wall. It was a three foot by four-foot piece of butcher paper that was made up to be a calendar. Its purpose was to inform and excite the patients of all the interesting things that would be happening on a day by day basis that month at Central City. Ned stopped and took the time to see what was up-coming. Bingo was played every day. It was followed closely by Keno which was played every night. There were a couple of cracker and cheese events. There were Korean religious services even though there weren't very many Koreans in the facility. There was a Baptist Evangelical minister who was coming by to baptize and do some saving. There was coloring, lots of coloring. And there were endless hours of watching television. At the end of the month there was a special treat for the patients, Harmonica Mike and his dancing dog.

"That should be a show stopper," Ned muttered.

Ned continued on toward the back of the facility. He almost passed by Violet's office. She had found the most out of the way place where she could hide from the toils and troubles of the hospital. Violet's office was tiny. It was a converted closet set up next to a bank of patient showers. As he got close to Violet's office, Ned heard a patient yelling. The screams for help were coming from one of the showers. Why would anyone want an office next to that? Ned wondered.

On a narrow door next to the shower room where the yelling was taking place was a placard with the letters DON embossed on it. The letters were painted the same color as the door so they were easy to miss. There were a number of patients sitting outside the shower room. They sat in plastic shower chairs. They were covered in thin, white, cotton ponchos. The patients were waiting to take their turn in the shower. For many patients, the twice a week shower was like going through a car wash. One by one the process was repeated on each patient whether they liked it or not.

First in the shower line was a reluctant Hispanic gentleman. In addition to the poncho, he was wearing a straw cowboy hat. "Pendajo!" he cursed at the CNAs as he tried to get out of the shower chair, but the nurses held him down.

"This gentleman doesn't like to be showered?" Ned asked the CNA standing behind his shower chair.

The Hispanic gentleman turned his rant on Ned. "Pendajo!" he screamed and thrusts his finger at Ned as if it were a weapon. The nurses were quite unaffected by the man's rants.

"He hates it. Are you the new Administrator? Jose said a new one came today is that you?" one of the CNAs standing behind the Hispanic gentleman asked Ned.

"Yes, you can call me Mr. Ned or Mr. Russo," Ned looked at the I.D. badges of the two CNAs holding the Hispanic gentleman, "Jennifer and Louise, I'm sure I'll be seeing lots of you," Ned said smiling at the CNAs.

The shower door opened and a CNA rolled an old lady out of the shower. Louise and Jennifer rolled the cursing Hispanic gentleman in. He continued to scream and curse, "Pendajo!" at the nurses. But his screams fell upon their deaf ears as the nursing assistants, called CNAs, positioned him in the shower. They stripped him of his hat, the water was turned on and one nurse washed him as the other held the old man in his shower chair. The whole process took seconds. Ned thought about saying something to the CNAs about handling that old man. He could have told them that with a bit more kindness maybe he might behave better, but since it was his first day he decided he would wait. Ned looked at the line of waiting patients in shower chairs and the CNAs standing behind them. The nurses were chatting to each other or paying no attention to the poncho covered patients waiting for their turn to be rolled through the process.

Ned knocked on Violet's door. It opened. Violet's office was just big enough to fit a child-sized desk and chair and one folding chair for guests. There were papers scattered on her desk along with three or four binders. It was obvious her office was not set up for meetings. There were no windows, just a small fan that blew the air around in that tiny space. The focus of the room was a plastic Baby Jesus wearing a crown. He was decked out in a purple robe. The Baby Jesus was on a shelf on the wall above her desk. There were two nearly expired votive candles burning, one on either side of the statue. Jesus held the earth in one hand and seemed to be giving a blessing with the other. Ned thought given the condition of this hospital, it would have been more appropriate for Baby Jesus to be wearing a housekeeping uniform and holding a bottle of cleaning solution.

Ned stood in the doorway. He got an immediate bad vibe from Violet. But she did manage to fake a smile to greet him. "Hello," she said tepidly.

Violet had been the DON at Central City for going on thirty years. She was comfortable. She didn't want anyone to rock her boat. She liked the fact that there was no Medicare in the facility. There was a whole lot less paperwork that way. She wasn't worried about making numbers. Her job was secure. Violet had achieved sacred cow status long ago at the corporation. She saw administrators come and go. They rarely lasted more than a year. But she stayed on. Violet was in her sixties. She was plain and did nothing to improve her looks. No makeup. No stylish clothes or haircut. She was wearing a stained lab coat that was hiding a faded blue dress. But her eyes expressed her feelings beautifully and they telegraphed the message to Ned that he was just a temporary annoyance.

"I have a woman outside my office wondering where her mother's leg is. Do you know where it might be?" Ned asked.

"It's in the social services office. We don't send prosthesis out to the hospital with patients. The hospital ends up losing them," Violet curtly responded.

"Smart. I'm Ned Russo."

"I know. You're the new administrator. They called from corporate yesterday," she said.

"And you are…?

"Violet Tomas."

"Nice of them to let you know I was coming. Didn't you tell the staff the facility had a new administrator?" Ned asked.

"No, I thought you might want to do your own introductions."

"It might have been nice to give them a heads up," Ned commented.

"I didn't think it was necessary," Violet said.

"Ok…I'll introduce myself," Ned said. He looked around her tiny space. "Couldn't they find you a better office? This doesn't seem fitting for the DON."

"I'm happy here," Violet said curtly.

"Well, if it makes you happy. I think I'd be a little cramped. Listen, I'm going to call a meeting of all the department heads, so I can introduce myself. Say in thirty minutes. Is there a conference room in this place?"

"Over by station one," then she added. "I've got a lot of paperwork I've got to do so I won't be coming. Besides, we just met, and I think I already know you," She pushed out another false, friendly smile.

"I think it's important that you be there," Ned gently urged.

"I'll do my best," she said.

The very first meeting with her new boss and she's setting terms? That took balls, Ned thought.

Without realizing it, Violet had just pressed the absolute wrong button in Ned. There was a certain kind of woman that Ned could not abide. It went all the way back to his mother, Rose. At least that's what a series of shrinks told him. The first few times a shrink told Ned that his mother had damaged his psyche he walked out of their office. By the fourth or fifth shrink, Ned began to wonder if there was a shrink conspiracy or perhaps they were right.

Ned's mother was one of those women who ran things. Everything. Not with an iron fist or her force of will, but she always came in through the back door of every problem. She wore out her adversaries like a man using up a bar of soap. Every day a little bit more would disappear until the resistance to whatever she wanted, was gone. Rose had worked as a secretary in a high school, back in a time before women became assistants. At some point she decided being the school secretary wasn't good enough for her. She wanted to run the school. So she went to work on the school principal, Chauncey. He was a homunculus man at the end of his educational career. He was counting the days until he could take off his bow tie put down his briefcase and go fly fishing. He was easy pickings for Rose. Little by little she nibbled away at his duties, the small things at first. She created the schedules he was supposed to create. Soon she took over the small discipline problems, then the bigger ones. Next the teachers began to come to Rose to solve their problems. Within six months she was the vice principal of the school without the official title. She made it so easy for Chauncey to relinquish power to her. By the time fishing season opened, she had complete control in that school. It got to the point where she would even cover for Chauncey, taking his calls from the Superintendent of Schools so Chauncey could sneak out early or come in late especially on those really good fishing days. But Rose's all-time best bit of manipulation was 'playing dead.' When Ned was a child and somehow didn't comply with whatever she wanted at the time, she would feign death. Generally, she'd collapse into a chair, have her arms drop to her side and not breathe for a few seconds. When she really wanted to pull out the stops, she would fall to the floor. Splayed out like a murder victim until God miracled her ass back to life. Then she would explain to poor, frightened Ned how his bad behavior caused her trip down the River Styx. And it was only after she explained to God that if she were able to return to life Ned would be a better boy and listen to his mommy. Ned was so traumatized and so afraid if he didn't do exactly as she said she would actually die and it would be his fault. This worried him so much he used to chew the collars on his shirts. It's no wonder shrinks told Ned his mother had fucked him up. She did.

At the time, seeing his mother pop back to life seemed perfectly believable to Ned. After all, he was in Catholic school and that whole religion is based on people coming back from the dead. He heard it day in and day out from the nuns and the priests. So he guessed it had to be true. By the time Ned reached the age of reason, he realized he was being conned by his mother and the church. But by then, the damage was done.

Unfortunately, Violet didn't realize her attitude toward Ned set off deep seated issues in him. He bristled at women who had authority and flaunted it, or worse, tried to manipulate him with their power. Violet was throwing down a gauntlet right at Ned's feet. Violet was showing Ned who was really going to be the boss of this skilled nursing facility. And regardless of his title, it wasn't going to be Ned.

Ned smiled back at Violet, but the course of their relationship was now set in stone.

"I can appreciate how busy you are but I think the first meeting of the department heads and the new head of the facility should include the Director of Nurses. I'll see you in thirty minutes." Ned turned and left Violet's closet office.

For as much as Violet pressed the wrong button in Ned, he had done exactly the same thing to her. Violet was a woman who was used to having Central City run the way she wanted it run. She had managed to get the corporation used to this facility being a financial dog. It was in a bad location, full of bad patients. Violet got points for just sticking it out. After all, who else would go down there? She had made a cocoon for herself at Central City. She had wrapped herself in failure and made corporate believe she was doing them a favor.

The root of Violet's attitude at Central City was her home life. She had a son who was on drugs and in and out of rehab. Her husband was an abusive drunk. He was one of those little men who blamed everybody for the fact that he was a failure. So he found solace in a bottle and then he took his failures out on Violet and their son. After years of battling her son's and husband's addictions, Violet was burned out. And now along comes Ned, another arrogant administrator that was going to demand much more than she was able to give. Her well was dry. She didn't have the energy or the inclination to help turn Central City around. She liked it just the way it was.

On his way back to his office, Ned passed by the woman with the large brimmed hat in the lobby.

"You find out where my mother's leg is?" she asked.

"In the social service's office. If you want, I'll get it and you can take it with you."

"What the fuck am I gonna do with a leg in my car? You just make goddamn sure you don't lose it. This motherfuckin' place has lost every other fuckin' thing I brought in here." With that pronouncement the woman stomped out of the facility. Ned looked over at Jose who was watching the exchange from his reception cubicle. Jose raised his penciled-in eyebrows, grimaced and shook his head. Ned walked over to him. Ned saw that now in addition to the kitchen gloves and toilet seat cover Jose was now sporting a surgical mask. Ned wondered if he could make enough comments about the germs in Central City to force him into a hazmat suit.

"Jose, can you get all the department heads in the conference room in say thirty minutes."

"We don't have a conference room," his muffled voice replied.

"The DON told me over by station one?"

"Oh, that's the Media Room."

"Ok, the Media Room, fine. Can you please get the department heads over there in thirty minutes. And have the Dietary Super bring coffee and cookies or pastry, please."

"We don't have a Dietary Super. He quit three weeks ago."

"Who has been running the kitchen?" Ned inquired in disbelief.

"Some of the dietary supervisors from the other buildings come by and do the ordering and stuff."

"And that works?" Ned asked.

"Not really well. We're always running out of things."

"Jose, can you do me a favor and please get rid of that mask. You're going to scare the b-jesus out of everyone who comes in here."

"But what about the airborne germs?"

"I'll pay for your lung transplant should you need one. Now lose the mask, please."

Jose reluctantly removed his mask.

Ned entered his office and closed the door behind him. He flopped down in his chair. Within minutes there was a knock on Ned's door, "Come in," Ned said.

The door did not open. "Come in," Ned repeated in a louder voice.

Still, the door did not open, but there was another knock. Ned got up and opened the door. The man in the wheelchair holding the bucket of candy Ned saw earlier was in his doorway. Something slow and unintelligible came limping out of his mouth.

All Ned could reply was "I'm sorry, can I help you?"

The man repeated his speech, several times before Ned was able to decipher what he was saying.

"I am Steven. You want to buy some candy?"

It was clear Steven was a stroke victim. After all that work Steven put into trying to communicate Ned decided he should at least buy something. Ned looked in Steven's bucket. "I'll take a Snickers."

With his good arm, Steven picked up a Snickers bar and handed it to Ned. Ned took out his wallet and handed a 'five' to Steven. "I don't have anything smaller. You have change?"

Steven took the five dollar bill from Ned and rolled his wheelchair out of the office without saying another word. Ned realized he had just been hustled.

Ned deliberately waited thirty-five minutes before he walked down the hall and entered the Media Room. Almost all the department heads were gathered there. Almost all, the most important member of the team, Violet, was missing. Ned looked around at his new department heads. The kitchen staff had brought coffee and a bag of chocolate chip cookies. Some of his department heads were drinking and munching away. A few had the courtesy to wait for Ned to get there before they began. As Ned looked around the room he knew no matter how good he was at his job it was the people in front of him that had to get the job done.

In his tenure as an administrator Ned had encountered many different styles of managing. Experience taught Ned the best way to manage was by getting out of his office and walking around the hospital. He actually tasted the tasteless hospital food and tried to improve it. He got to know the patients and the staff. He made sure the diapers he bought would actually fit the patients, ensuring that what filled the diapers stayed in the diapers. He criticized people for doing a bad job in private and praised those that did well in public. He hated firing people but from time to time knew it was the only solution to a problem. The key to Ned's success would be to make sure his department heads also succeeded.

His new department heads were an interesting looking bunch. Most didn't look very professional. Maybe if they were dog groomers. But this was a hospital. The group sitting before him wouldn't exactly instill confidence to a concerned family that granny would be safe and smell pleasant on Sunday when they came by, out of guilt, to take her out for a ride.

"Good morning and hello everybody, I'm Ned Russo, the new administrator."

Ned waited for a reaction. There were a couple of muted "good mornings." He continued with his standard first day speech. "I've been in this business for some time and I know each facility has special challenges. You folks know this facility. I'm going to need your help to make it successful. I'd like to know what you feel are the biggest challenges we're going to face?"

"We can't keep an administrator." Dylan said. He was a black man about forty-five. He had a shaved head, earing and a goatee.

Some of department heads quietly chuckled at Dylan's comment. Then he added, "The last one was here two days and the one before that lasted two weeks."

"Any idea why they left?' Ned asked.

"They saw this place as a dog, a real loser and ran outta here as fast as they could."

"Why do you think that?" Ned asked.

"No parking, shitty neighborhood, bad patients, terrible survey."

"I can't do much about the parking or the neighborhood, but I think I can help with the patients and I know I can improve the next survey."

"That's if you're still here," Dylan remarked.

"I believe any facility can be a winner or a loser. It depends on the staff's attitude and that starts with the people in this room. We're in charge, if we have a positive outlook about our facility and our patients that will filter down through the staff to our patients," Ned said.

"Not these patients. Most of them are street people," Dylan said.

"Street people are still people. And they will react to kindness. We can start by putting smiles on the faces of the nurses. If we smile and treat our patients with a little dignity instead of seeing them as problems they might act differently," Ned said.

"Maybe," Dylan said skeptically.

Sueann Stennis, the Business Office Manager. Spoke up. She was a plain looking woman in her mid-forties.

"We have zero communication between the departments," she said, "I'm supposed to send a census report to corporate every day by nine. I'm always late. Here we are nine-thirty and I don't know who was admitted or discharged yesterday."

Freddie, the medical records director, a nervous little man, fumbled and stumbled before blurting out, "I'll have your report in about an hour."

"See what I mean," Sueann said reluctantly.

"I'm sorry, you know it's the nurses," Freddie said apologetically to Sueann.

"That doesn't do me any good, Freddie. You're not the one getting the unhappy phone calls from corporate, I am," Sueann said.

"Why can't we have that information on time?" Ned asked Freddie.

"The nurses don't complete their charting," Freddie said.

Casey, the Assistant Director of Nurses broke into the conversation, "Most of the charge nurses are new. They're still learning the system.

They're very slow. We don't spend enough time training them." Casey was in her late fifties. She had green eyes and that milk-white Irish skin.

"Don't they get orientation?" Ned asked.

"Yes," Casey responded. "But not enough. They get a week if they're lucky. Most of these nurses are right out of school they need at least two weeks to get comfortable with their patients."

"Even two weeks isn't really long enough to throw a new nurse on the floor," Ned commented.

Sharon, the activities director poured herself a cup of coffee. "Would you like a cup?" she asked Ned.

"Yes, thank you. Milk no sugar," Ned responded.

"Sharon, you're the activities director," Ned said reading her name badge.

"That's right," she responded with a thick Caribbean Island accent. She was a black woman in her forties.

"I saw the activities calendar and I noticed the patients mostly play bingo," Ned said.

"That's all they want to do," Sharon responded.

"Have you tried to introduce some new things," Ned asked.

"Lots of t'ings but they only want to do is bingo."

"You know these patients, but I'm going to work with you and see if we can come up a few more exciting activities," Ned said. Then he added turning to Benito the maintenance man, "Since you're in work clothes I bet you're the maintenance super."

"I working here almost thirty years," Benito answered proudly in a thick Mexican accent.

"That's an accomplishment," Ned said.

"Especially in this place." Dylan commented.

"Benito, please get two floor fans for every hallway. Big ones. Then put them on and leave them on until this place airs out."

"The fire marshal no like fans in the hallway. This a big violation," Benito warned.

"The fire marshal doesn't have to live with the smell of this place. Also, how 'bout you paint the entrance gate, replace the burnt out light bulbs in the garage, fix the leaky pipes and add another garbage pick-up day. And after you do all that can you do me a big favor and get the squeak out of my office chair? It's already driving me crazy," Ned said.

"That chair squeak for long time. But I try to fix for you." Benito said.

"Thanks. I would appreciate it. Now let me tell you a little bit about me. I'm here because this place needs an administrator. It's my job to make it successful. If I don't do that somebody else will be giving you this speech in a few months..."

"Or sooner," Dylan interjected.

"That's right, or sooner…But I don't intend to fail or leave until the job's done. I don't expect to turn this place around all at once. I believe in small daily successes. That's how all of us are going to change this facility. The daily success for today is tomorrow dress like professionals. No jeans."

"What about on casual Friday?" Dylan asked.

Ned thought for a minute, "Ok, jeans on casual Friday," then Ned added. "That's enough for our first meeting. I'll come by and meet with all of you individually, but right now I want business office, admissions, and the Medicare coordinator to stay. Oh, can someone bring me last year's survey."

The rest of the department heads left the room. Eileen, the medical coordinator, Dylan and Sueann remained.

Ned sipped his coffee, "Tell me how you handle the inquiries?"

Dylan responded. "I get a call from a hospital discharge planner. They send over the paperwork. Soon as it comes in I give it to Sueann," Dylan said.

"I run the eligibility to see if the patient has Medicare days. If they do I get it to Eileen," Sueann said.

"If it gets to me I check the cost of the meds and any special equipment," then Eileen paused.

"Then…?" asked Ned.

"I give it to the DON and wait," Eileen said.

"Wait, for what?" Ned responded.

"For a yes or no to see if we can admit, sometimes an hour, sometimes all day," Dylan added.

"What about giving it to the ADON? She can make a decision," Ned said.

"Violet makes all the decisions on who we admit here," Dylan said.

At that moment Violet entered. "Hope I'm not late?" she smiled.

Ned sensed Violet deliberately waited until the standup meeting was over before she made her grand entrance. She knew it was giving him the finger and it had the added benefit of flaunting it in front of the other department heads.

"No," Ned returned her smile. "You're actually just in time. We were discussing the admissions process and how we can improve it. Dylan said it sometimes takes an hour or more for you to turn inquiries around?"

"That's true. At times I'm very busy," Violet responded.

"I'm sure everybody's very busy, but if we're going to be successful we need to turn every inquiry around in fifteen minutes...or less," Ned said.

"That seems a little ambitious," Violet chuckled as if Ned proposed the impossible.

"No, it's not. It can be done it's just a matter of coordination," Ned said.

"I don't believe I can assess a patient's needs or their profitability accurately in fifteen minutes," Violet responded.

"The ADON and I can be part of the admissions team. We can turnover inquiries much faster that way. I've done it before," Ned said.

"I don't know if I'm comfortable with that," Violet said.

"Why wouldn't you be?" Ned asked.

"You're not a nurse," Violet responded.

"But I am the administrator," Ned said.

"That's an interesting proposal. Let me think about it, excuse me, I have a lot to do," Violet forced a smiled and left the room.

"You won't be the first one that tried to speed things up around here," Dylan said.

"I can't speak for anybody else. But I know if we're going to succeed the key is more Medicare. And that means turning around inquiries faster," Ned said.

"We don't get a lot of knee and hip replacements down here. It's all psych, and Violet turns most of them down." Dylan said.

"That's going to have to change. I want to see every inquiry that comes in here. At the end of the day it's my decision not hers."

Ned understood the bravado of his statement was one thing, having it become the hospital policy would be quite another.

MEET AND GREET

Ned went up to the reception window in the lobby.

"Jose, do you know a lot of the patients here?"

"Most of them," he answered.

"How 'bout you introduce me to a few of them?" Ned asked.

Jose was delighted to get out of his cubicle and show his new boss around. He took Ned down the hallway by one of the nursing stations.

"Good morning," Ned said as he passed by the members of his new staff. They all smiled and returned the courtesy. "Good morning."

Halfway down the hallway Jose stopped outside a patient room, "You remember Mr. Beatty, you met him this morning in your office," Jose said.

Ted Beatty, naked again, got up and greeted Jose and Ned. He was only wearing the glasses he had taken from Ned's desk.

"Hello," Mr. Beatty said. Then he added, "I'm glad you have cooled down. If you're in charge you should never display that kind of emotion."

"Thanks for the advice," Ned responded.

"I know these things, I used to be in charge of the Cocoa Puffs division for General Mills."

"And I bet when you were on charge of Cocoa Puffs you probably wore clothes," Ned said.

"Only in the winter. It gets mighty cold in Minnesota. Since I moved to California the weather is much milder and I don't have to wear them."

"Well, even in California we have a long standing tradition of wearing clothes," Ned answered.

"I can appreciate the tradition but I still don't like to wear them. The fabric irritates my skin. I rash easily."

Ned turned to Jose, "Maybe we can have the laundry wash his clothes with milder soap."

"We've tried milder soap, special fabric conditioner, we even tried baby shampoo. Nothing worked. The rash is invisible. Mr. Beatty just doesn't like to wear clothes."

"Why don't we get Mr. Beatty into a hospital gown. It's loose enough that it shouldn't irritate his delicate skin and there's the added bonus that Mr. Beatty's private parts aren't on display for everyone in the hospital to view," Ned said.

There was a young, CNA who was in the hallway stuffing dirty linen into a rolling hamper. Ned called to her, "Can you please get a hospital gown on this gentleman?"

"That's not my patient," the CNA responded cheerfully.

"Excuse me," Ned was taken aback by the CNA's answer.

"That's not my patient. I only do this side of the hall," she smiled.

"Does that mean if he fell you wouldn't help get him up?" Ned asked.

"No, that's different," she responded.

"If you took a wider view of your responsibility you might realize that helping him up from a fall and getting him into a gown are all part of taking care of his needs. We don't want him to catch cold now, do we?" Ned said.

Ned and Jose continued down the hallway. Ned heard heavy labored breathing. He looked into a room to see a very obese man, almost six hundred pounds, splayed out, lying on the bed. Even though it was a bariatric bed, it was clearly too small to accommodate his size.

"That's Jonathan Bell. The poor man never gets out of bed. The nurses call him Big-Balls. I think he's really depressed. All he does is eat and watch TV," Jose said.

Ned entered Bell's room. He was asleep. He had a BiPAP covering his mouth. It forced air down his throat to keep it from collapsing. Ned saw that there were blocks of wood instead of caster wheels on his bariatric bed. There was a trapeze above his head that was there to help him adjust himself.

In another room was an elderly Korean woman, Ying Kang. She was on a walker. She looked to be deep in her seventies. She was combing her hair.

Ned knocked on her door and announced himself, "Hello."

Kang put down her comb and was stuffing a bunch of over ripe bananas into her small closet. The closet was already filled with other over-ripe fruit and it was a breeding farm for thousands of fruit flies. When she opened the closet door the flies scattered throughout the room, but the woman didn't seem to be bothered by the insects.

"No, no, no!" Ned said as he took the bananas out of the closet.

"We can't have fruit in the closet. See..." He indicated all the buzzing flies. "...insects, bugs."

Kang was immediately offended. "My fruit! My..." She grabbed the bananas out of Ned's hand and began to give him a tongue lashing in Korean. Whatever she was saying, Ned judged from the dower look on her face it wasn't pleasant.

Ned turned to Jose, "Can we get housekeeping to clean out her closet."

"She won't let anyone near her closet. She gets very combative," Jose responded.

Kang ripped the bananas from Ned and threw them into the closet then slammed the closet door closed. She used her closet key to secure the lock. Feeling her stash was safe, she balled her fist threatening Ned. "You no touch!" she said. "Me go churchee. You no touch!"

With that declaration Kang wheeled her walker out of the room.

Suddenly, there was a horrific scream that rolled down the hallway like a giant flame-ball of ignited gas. The scream consumed everything in its path. Ned reacted immediately. He rushed to the sound of the screaming. Jose followed but at a much more leisurely pace. The screaming was coming from a patient's room. Ned expected to see blood on the floor or worse. What he found was a tiny, toothless, ancient black woman sitting in a wheelchair. When Ned came face to face with Hattie Oaks, she stopped screaming.

"Who the fuck are you?" she asked.

"Hattie, be nice. This is our new administrator, Mr. Russo," Jose said.

"Why are you screaming?" Ned asked the tiny woman before him.

"Because everybody in this place is an asshole," she responded.

"Does that mean you have to scream?"

"I like to scream," To prove her point Hattie let out another blood-curdling scream.

"Please stop," Ned cringed.

"Then go get me some potato chips."

"I will if you promise to stop screaming."

"All right," she said. Then she added, "Hurry the fuck up with those chips."

Jose and Ned left Hattie's room and walked further down the hallway. "This is my favorite patient, Doctor Zucker. He used to be a professor at USC," Jose said.

"Why is he here," Ned asked.

"He has advanced dementia, but he's a sweetheart," Jose answered.

Ned knocked on the door then he and Jose entered the room. Dr. Zucker instantly reminded Ned of Albert Einstein. The doctor was deep into his seventies. He had a thick moustache and needed a haircut. He was sitting up in his bed reading.

"What are you reading?" Ned asked.

Zucker looked up at Ned then down at the magazine. "I don't know," he said then he chuckled. "I can't remember much lately. I think that's why I'm here."

"What kind of a doctor are you?"

"I'm a doctor of biology. I teach at USC. At least I used to."

Ned noticed a stack of Scientific American magazines on his bed side table. "And I see you like to read scientific journals."

"Oh yes, but I can't remember what's in them," Zucker laughed.

"How did you end up here?" Ned asked.

"I'm not sure."

"Well, it's not important. I'll tell you what, Doctor Zucker, next time I go by a magazine stand I'll pick you up a couple magazines."

"Can you get me a Playboy. I like the pictures."

"Me too!" Ned smiled.

They both laughed. As Ned turned to leave the room an Asian girl in her twenties entered the room. She was holding a box of almond cookies and a vase full of flowers.

"Are you here to visit Dr. Zucker?" Ned asked.

"Hi, Jose," she said

"This is Amy Lee, she comes to visit Doctor Zucker almost every day," Jose said.

Ned extended his hand to her. "I'm Ned Russo, the new administrator."

She politely took his hand then put the vase of flowers on the bedside table. "How are you feeling today?" she asked Zucker.

"I think I'm fine," the doctor responded.

"Are you a relative?" Ned asked her.

"I'm Doctor Zucker's grad assistant."

"That's very thoughtful of you to come by so often. I'm sure that's a great comfort for Doctor, Zucker, Ned said then he turned to Jose, "Why don't we let Amy and the good doctor visit," Ned said then he and Jose left the room.

They continued down the hall. Ned stopped in front of the Director of Staff Development's office. "I'm going to talk to the DSD," Ned said to Jose.

"I'll be in reception if you need me," Jose said as he left.

Ned knocked on Milaney's door and then walked in. She was sitting at her desk. The place was a mess. It was a disaster of papers, folders, binders, chocolate bar wrappers, memos from corporate, and a backpack. There wasn't even a place to sit down. The one chair had piles of dog-eared, coffee-stained papers on it. Milaney was digging through a drawer looking for something.

"What are you looking for?" Ned asked.

"The in services for the fire drills. I was planning to have one today," she responded.

She kept moving the stacks of papers on her desk looking for the fire drill in service sign in sheets.

"Have you been at Central City a long time," Ned asked.

"About a year," she responded.

"And how long have you been a DSD?"

"Central City is my first time."

Milaney kept searching through the piles on her desk.

"I'll tell you what. Let's have that fire drill at two. I'll get to meet the line staff and I'll see how they respond."

Milaney stopped digging through the piles on her desk. "Yeah, that's fine."

"I'll see you at two," Ned said as he left her office.

As he walked out of her office, he watched her return to shuffling through the stacks of paper. She was completely unorganized. The job of DSD was all about organization. Ned felt Milaney couldn't organize a birthday party for a five year old let alone keep detailed records for hundreds of employees for years.

Ned returned to his office picked up the phone and called Jose.

"Yes, boss," he answered.

"Did you get housekeeping to clean out that fruit fly farm?" Ned asked.

"They're working on it," Jose answered.

"And how about the potato chips for that screaming woman?"

"I'll take care of that myself," Jose responded.

"Does she scream often?" Ned asked.

"All the time," Jose responded.

"Doesn't her screaming bother anybody?" Ned asked.

"It bothers everybody," Jose answered.

"Please, take care of the chips. Oh, and make sure Mr. Beatty is wearing a gown the next time I see him," Ned hung up the phone.

What is it about this place? Ned thought to himself. Everybody can see it's in trouble but won't lift a finger to help change it. He slumped down in his chair. It creaked. He thought for a minute and wondered how corporate would respond to what he was about to do. If Ned was going to succeed, he had to get traction right away. He knew corporate had a clock on him. Regardless of how hard it was to get an administrator into Central City, corporate wasn't going to wait but so long before Ned would be in jeopardy. After ginning up a little courage, he picked up the phone and punched in the number for corporate Human Resources.

A pleasant female voice answered. "The Mersh Management Group, how can I direct your call?"

"Can I have..." Ned looked at a name in the corporate information binder that was on his desk.

"Carlos in HR, please."

A second or two passed as the connection was made.

Discussion about replacing people on the first day was radical. Corporations didn't like radical.

"Hello, Carlos, HR."

"Carlos, this is Ned Russo at Central City."

"The new guy! Isn't this your first day?" Carlos answered enthusiastically.

"It is."

"I didn't think I'd hear from you quite this soon," Carlos chuckled.

"Well, I thought about waiting a week or two and how that would be a little more politically correct but that would just get me deeper into a hole. I need a Dietary super and a DSD."

"We've been looking for a Dietary super for a while. Milaney not working out for you? Jesus, you just got there!" Carlos said.

"She's not ready for a building this size. I think she's weak."

"She is. But good DSD's are hard to come by. We go through almost as many as we do administrators. Especially at Central City," Carlos said jokingly.

"Is that supposed to make me feel good?"

Carlos laughed, "Don't take it personally."

"I won't. Look Carlos, I have a lot to do over here. I need some help."

"I know. I'll see what I can turn up for you. Hang in there."

"Thanks."

Ned hung up the phone. His mouth was suddenly drier. He didn't know if Carlos would help or not. All he could do was hope for the best.

Freddie entered Ned's office. He was visibly nervous. He was holding a binder. "Here is last year's survey." A little drop of sweat ran down the side of Freddie's cheek.

"Freddie, calm down. I'm not going to bite you," Ned said.

Freddie chuckled but he acted like he was locked in a cage with a hungry tiger who asked him if he wanted to stay for lunch.

Ned grabbed the survey binder. He flipped through it. There were a lot of deficiencies.

"Can I go?" Freddie asked.

"Yes, you can go. Hey, Freddie, you're going to give yourself a heart attack. Calm down."

Freddie nervously chuckled again and backed out of Ned's office, smiling and nodding his head all the way out. Ned went back to studying the survey. He flipped through the pages just counting up the number of deficiencies Central City had received. What Ned saw wasn't good.

The survey was the hospital's yearly report card from the State of California. The state average was thirteen. Central City had more than forty. The deficiencies were in all departments. But by far the worst part of this horrible survey was devoted to the dietary department. Central City's kitchen was a hair's breadth away from being shut down. Ned knew that when the state came back for their next inspection, the kitchen better be perfect or they would get shut down.

Ned was suddenly interrupted with shouts of anger.

"I'm going to kick your fucking ass! I swear to Christ I'm going to kick your fucking ass!"

"Bring it on you stupid red neck!"

The shouts came from the lobby. Ned left his office and ran toward the yelling. His years of experience told him that the volume of the shouts, and colorful language was the prelude to violence.

When Ned got to the lobby, he saw about thirty patients in wheelchairs. Steven, the candy seller, and the Korean woman, who was raising fruit flies, were among the group. It was almost time for lunch and the patients began herding outside the doors to the dining room. In the middle of this herd of the elderly was an old, skinny white guy. He was standing up out of his wheelchair. He was so skinny that his belt didn't hold up his pants and the back of his pants were down below his backside. He was holding the front of his pants up with one hand, and he balled his fist, threatening the black gentleman sitting in a wheelchair in front of him.

"You old black bastard, I'm going to kick your ass," the old white guy threatened.

"Yeah, go ahead try it!" said the black man.

"Don't do it!" Ned screamed.

Everything then moved in slow motion. But Ned was too far away to stop what happened in the next second. Ned watched as the old white guy punched the black gentleman square in the face. Blood shot out from the black man's nose in all directions.

"My nose! My nose! That son-of-a bitch hit me!"

"Too late!" came out of Ned's mouth.

Nurses came running into the lobby from all directions. Suddenly, there was chaos. The closest patients, all in wheelchairs, tried to flee the altercation but only managed to slam into one another. It looked like bumper cars at an amusement park.

A female patient at the far end of the lobby suddenly began to shake violently. She fell out of her wheelchair and onto the floor. The excitement and chaos of the moment brought on a seizure. Amazingly, nobody ran her over. Ned shouted to one of the nurses, "Help that woman!"

Ned pushed his way through the gaggle of wheelchairs. He grabbed the old white gentleman who was ready to throw his next punch and forced him back into his wheelchair.

"Leave me alone or I'm going to kick your ass too!" the old white guy yelled at Ned.

He tried to hit Ned but since Ned was behind him, he couldn't. All the old white guy could do was flail his arms and scream. "I'm going to kick your ass you son-of a bitch!" his arms swung wildly in the air but no blows landed.

More nurses rushed into the lobby. Two of them attended to the woman having the seizure on the floor.

"Get these people out of here," Ned yelled.

The nurses began to back the wheelchairs out of the lobby, and at that point Jose opened his cubicle window with his gloved hand and asked, "Do you want me to call 911?"

"Yes!" Ned yelled back as he held the redneck down in his wheelchair.

A nurse worked her way through the wheelchairs and pushed a towel against the nose of the bleeding black gentleman.

Some of the wheelchair bound patients wanted to get into the dining room. After all it was time for lunch and they didn't want to miss lunch or lose their special place at their special table. The 'it's-time-for-lunch-bunch' patients began to argue with the nurses about being backed out of the lobby and away from the dining room. The fact that there was a woman thrashing about on the floor and a nose spurting blood did not seem to influence their time schedule. The 'its-time-for-lunch-bunch' tried to roll through the wheelchair traffic jam making it worse. They bumped directly into the group that wanted to escape the wildly swinging old white guy and the bleeding black patient.

"Please, get these people out of here!" Ned commanded for a second time.

Ned had his hands full holding the redneck down in his wheelchair and not getting punched himself. More nurses arrived and began to back the patients out of the lobby. Many of the patients resisted. Thankfully, Ned heard the sound of sirens as a fire truck pulled up in front of the hospital. It was followed by a 911 rescue vehicle.

Normally, two or three 911 rescue personnel would enter the hospital. But today was different. It was training day. So, half a dozen fire fighters and paramedics flooded the lobby. Followed by two fire fighters pushing a gurney and a third crew carrying emergency medical equipment. This whole circus of life-savers was followed by a fire captain. The captain was in his late fifties. His best fire-fighting days were behind him. He had a gut that hung over his belt and a full head of dyed blond hair. He also had a miserable disposition. That was obvious by the snarl on his face.

Jose yelled out of his cubicle window to the rescue personnel. "Over here!" He used his brightly colored kitchen glove to point to the woman who was having the seizure on the floor.

All of these additional people added to the confusion of thrashing, bleeding and wanting to eat lunch. More nurses and some department heads arrived in the lobby. They began to try to reassure patients that they indeed would get lunch. Two nurses pushed their way through to Ned and the bleeding black patient.

"Put a one-on-one with our puncher, and get the bleeder to a nursing station," Ned gently ordered. One nurse took the old white guy and another nurse took the bleeding black gentleman in opposite directions. The nurses pushed them through the herd of wheelchairs. As the old white guy was rolled away from the lobby he continued to rant, "Where're you taking me? I'm not through kicking that old bastard's ass!"

"We're going to your room. It's almost time for lunch. Don't you want lunch?" the nurse said to him in her most soothing tone.

For the first time during the chaos Ned was able to take a sigh of relief.

"I called the police," Eileen said.

"Thanks," Ned responded.

Though it was chaotic, the mini-crisis Ned had just gone through had a few positives. The response of the staff was quick and attentive. They handled the moment as best it could be handled. For the first time since Ned drove in this morning, he was really pleased with the staff's response. Ned stood in the middle of the lobby and surveyed the aftermath.

Maybe this isn't the worst hospital in LA. Its close...but maybe it's not the worst, Ned thought.

The one glaring negative in this adventure was the DON. The key player in this opera never took the stage. Violet never bothered to show up.

Moments passed the yelling subsided. The paramedics got the woman having the seizure onto the gurney and safely out of the facility. The combatants were out of the lobby and were being tended to. Those waiting for their lunch began to roll into the dining room. Normalcy was slowly beginning to return. The fire captain was the last of the rescue team to leave Central City. As he was leaving, he turned to Ned. "Are you in charge of this place?" he asked.

"Yes," Ned responded.

The fire captain pointed his finger right at Ned, "I'd wrap my shit a little tighter if I were you."

Then the fire captain left the facility.

Two female Rampart Division police officers arrived and entered the lobby. The taller of the two, Officer Ramos, had short hair and was wearing Oakley sunglasses. She took the glasses off and tucked them into her breast pocket. They were both all business.

"You're a little too late to the party. We got everything cleared up. But I do need your card for my incident report," Ned said.

"What happened?" Ramos asked.

"A couple of my patients had a disagreement. But it's all settled."

The senior of the two female officers took out her card and handed it to Ned.

"Officer Ramos, thank you for being so prompt. I have the feeling I'll be calling you again."

The officers left.

"I need to go to the bank," An elderly black woman announced. Ms. Thelma was in her eighties. She had kabuki make up on her face and an orange wig. She was wearing a man's suit jacket that was at least ten sizes too big and she was dragging a very large suitcase.

"Why do you need to go to the bank?" Ned asked.

"I need to get some money so I can go shopping for clothes."

"Don't you have clothes in the suitcase?"

"No, there's only ball gowns in there. I need to buy some casual things."

"Only balls gowns? Honey, why don't you have lunch now and we can discuss a shopping trip later," Ned said sporting his best administrator's smile.

"I don't have anything to wear to lunch."

"But you look just fine."

"You think so?" Thelma blushed.

"And I love your hair."

"Thank you," Thelma said very pleased.

Sharon, the Director of Activities, approached and saved Ned, "Ms. Thelma, we'll take you shopping after. Come on let's go have lunch now."

Sharon took Thelma by the arm and escorted her and her suitcase into the dining room. Thelma turned out to be the period at the end of Ned's first morning on the job. He turned to Milaney who was helping one of the patients to the dining room.

"Let's cancel that fire drill. I think we've all had enough excitement for today."

"Thank you! That's a good idea," Milaney said.

Ned took a deep breath. He decided after the excitement of the fight in the lobby, he could use a breather. He went out onto the non-smokers patio. There, sitting by herself was an elegant old white lady. She was tiny and delicate. She was wearing navy blue slacks and a red silk jacket. The jacket had two large gold embroidered elephants on it. Most of her face was concealed by a wide brimmed straw hat. She was reading a book and smoking. Ned walked over to her. "Excuse me. This is the non-smokers patio. You shouldn't be smoking here."

She looked up from her book. She had bright, sparkling eyes and pale white skin. She smiled at Ned. "I know" she said. "But where they let you smoke here all the patients are daft. I can't endure one bloody minute with them." She held out her hand to Ned, "Maggie Pembroke."

Ned took it. "I'm Ned. Are you English?"

"Does it show?"

"What are you doing in California?"

"It's a long story. After the little buggers threw us out of India, I was there during the war you know, I grew so fond of the sun, and England is so bloody damp and cold, so I moved here. You Yanks are a bit rough around the edges, but still tolerable," she smiled.

"Why were you in India?"

"I was a corporal there in the English Army."

"No kidding!"

"I was Mountbatten's personal driver," she said proudly.

"Lord Mountbatten, the one in the Royal Family?" Ned responded incredulously.

"And he would have been King of England too if the IRA hadn't blown him to bits."

"Maggie, you are a very interesting lady. I can see I'm going to have to get to know you better."

"That would be lovely."

"India, is that where you got that jacket?" Ned asked.

"It was a gift from Mountbatten."

"I'm impressed," Ned said. He didn't believe a word Maggie said, but she was charming and a welcomed relief from the other patients he had met.

"Have I impressed you enough so I could have a little spot of gin…? I do so miss it," she said. Maggie held up her fingers to indicate the tiny amount that would satisfy her.

"I haven't had one since…" she rummaged through her mind. "…bloody hell, I can't remember when."

"Maybe we can arrange that," Ned smiled at her.

"Plymouth Gin please." She thought for a second, "They still make it, don't they?"

"Yes, they do. I drink it myself."

"It's easy to see you are a gentleman of breeding."

"Thank you, Maggie. Why don't you finish your cigarette and not light up another one."

Ned left Maggie and walked around the facility until he found the Social Service office. Grant, the Social Service Director, was working on his computer. "Are you completing the abuse report?" Ned asked.

"I'm working on it right now," Grant responded.

"I want you to put the officer's card with the file." Ned handed Ramos' card to Grant.

"What do you want to do with Alex Conner? He's the guy you were holding down in the wheelchair," Grant asked.

"Oh, the old white guy, can you get him out of here?"

"That will depend on his insurance. If he only has medical insurance nobody will take him."

"Can we find out?" Ned asked.

"Dylan will know."

Ned picked up Grant's phone and pressed the intercom. "Dylan, please call the Social Services Office."

The sad truth is that the care patients receive in nursing homes is dependent on their insurance. Without Medicare, or decent HMO insurance, getting even a dangerous patient out of a skilled nursing facility is at best difficult.

The phone rang, Ned took the call. It was Dylan. "Hey, what kind of insurance does Alex Conner have?" Ned asked.

"He's Medicare."

Ned thought for a moment then he turned to Grant. "Has Conner ever hit anybody before?"

"No."

"How many Medicare days does he have left?" Ned asked.

"Lots. We just got that guy a couple of weeks ago," Dylan responded.

Ned pondered his next move, "Ok. Dylan, call one of your doctor buddies and get a three day observation hold on Conner. Get him stabilized and tell the doc we'll take him back."

"What about Baker? He's Medicare too. But he needs a qualifying stay," Dylan said.

"Is he the guy that got hit?" Ned asked.

"Yes, they're in the same room and haven't gotten along since Conner moved in," Grant said.

"I'll get nursing to send Baker out and get an X-ray. Let's make sure he doesn't have a busted nose. When he gets back we'll put them in separate rooms," Ned said.

"We'll send Baker to Good Sam. I'll call and make sure he stays there three days," Dylan assured Ned.

"Ok. That's our plan. Thank you gentlemen," Ned ended the call and left Grant's office.

PRISON MEAT

Ned walked back toward his office through the dining room. It was as if the excitement that took place but a few minutes ago never happened. There was no chatter about it between the patients. The patients who could feed themselves were eating. Those that couldn't were being fed. All of the patients were wearing bibs. Table manners were generally overlooked.

Ned turned his attention to the food and observed that lunch was decidedly unappetizing. It consisted of beige colored chicken. On beige rice covered with a beige cream sauce. All of it lumped onto a beige plate. On the side of this sumptuous feast was also a beige cookie seated on a smaller beige plate. There wasn't a hint of color in the entire meal. Ned imagined the prisoners at San Quentin were enjoying a better dining experience. He stopped by one of the patients, an old Hispanic gentleman wearing a Dodgers baseball cap. The man wasn't eating he was just looking at his food.

"You're not eating," Ned commented.

The patient looked up at Ned, "I'm not hungry."

"Can't say as I blame you. Do you mind if I take your tray?"

"Won't they give you one?" the old gentleman asked.

"Probably, but I want to borrow yours."

Ned slid the tray off the table and carried it back to the kitchen.

Mealtime in the kitchen of a nursing home is a blur of movement and a riot of sound. There, sweaty employees work like crazy to get tray after tray loaded with the right meal consistency and out to the patients.

Ned entered the kitchen. He carried the tray of bland beige food and placed it on the dishwashing table. There was a scraper, cleaning dirty plates and a dishwasher, operating the dishwashing machine. Ned took the plate of bland chicken off the tray and carried it to the tray line person and the cook.

"Regular, double portion," the tray line person called out.

The cook filled the plate with an ice cream scoop of rice.

Ned interrupted the progress of these two workers, "Hold on."

The cook and the tray line person suddenly came to an abrupt halt. The faces of the entire kitchen staff were befuddled. It was as if the assembly line at Ford suddenly lost power and stopped. Ned held out the plate he took from the old gentleman and showed it to the cook and tray line person, "Why is everything on this plate monochromatic?"

"We don't use that here. That's mostly in Chinese food," the cook responded with positive authority.

The cook, Calvin, was a black man about forty. He had a number of prison tattoos. He was wearing a red T-shirt and jeans. The tray line person looked no better. He was wearing a green gas station shirt with his name embroidered above the pocket: 'Tyrone.' He was also wearing a baseball cap turned backwards. The rest of the kitchen staff was also eclectically attired. Collectively, they looked like they had been grabbed off the street an hour ago and asked to serve lunch.

"The colors, everything on the plate is beige," Ned said.

The cook looked at the plate and then Ned, "So?"

"Don't you think we have an obligation to make the food enjoyable?" Ned asked.

"Enjoyable?" Calvin responded. He had no idea what Ned was talking about.

Ned looked around the kitchen to the rest of the staff for an answer but all he got back were blank stares.

"We're just following the menu," the cook said.

"I appreciate that, but from now on we're going to make their dining experience something they look forward to," Ned said.

"How are we going to do that?" the cook asked.

"Let's start with what's your name?" Ned asked.

"What's my name got to do with it?" the cook responded.

"Nothing, but I'd like to know who works for me."

"Calvin."

"Thank you, Calvin. Now, you eat with your eyes before you taste the food. Don't you agree?" Ned asked.

"I guess so," Calvin had no idea what Ned was talking about but felt he better go along with him.

"Good. We're making progress."

Ned smiled at Calvin. "Now, can you add some food coloring to that sauce?" Ned pointed to the beige sauce. "I want it dark brown. Can you do that?" Ned asked.

"Yeah."

"Let's do it," Ned responded cheerfully.

Calvin scrambled through the kitchen, found a bottle of dark brown food coloring took it off the spice rack and added it to the sauce turning it from beige to deep brown.

"Better," Ned remarked smiling.

"Now, Calvin, use the scoop and draw a squiggle on a clean plate with the sauce."

"A squiggle?" Calvin said now completely confused.

"Give me a scoop," Ned gently commanded.

Calvin handed the scoop to Ned. He took a spoonful of the newly created dark brown sauce and drizzled it on the clean plate in the shape of a Z. "That's a squiggle," Ned said.

"That looks like a 'Z'," Calvin said.

"You can call it anything you want. Just make sure it's on every plate. Now add the chicken and the rice on top of the sauce," Ned commanded.

Calvin complied.

"Do we have dried parsley?" Ned asked.

"Yeah, we have some," Tyrone answered.

"Go get it, please," Ned said.

Tyrone left his post as tray line person and went to the spice rack and grabbed a gallon container of the dried parsley.

"Sprinkle it over the top of everything."

Tyrone sprinkled the parsley all over the plate as Ned ordered.

"Wonderful!"

Ned took the plate and held it up to the staff to see. "See the way this plate looks? That's the way every breakfast, lunch and dinner that comes out of this kitchen will look from this plate forward. Every plate is going to have a garnish and be as appealing to the eye as to the palate."

At the dishwashing station someone mumbled a Spanish curse word under his breath, "Pendejo."

Ned recognized the dishwasher from his encounter when he first came into the parking lot.

"I know enough Spanish to understand what you said. I'll let it go this time. Next time I'll fire you. Comprende?"

Ned looked around the kitchen hoping the staff would get what he was trying to do. They didn't. Most of them nodded in agreement but Ned knew they just didn't get it. Whether or not they understood, Ned was going to make sure his instructions would be followed. Ned handed the newly constructed lunch plate to Tyrone and turned to Calvin.

"Do we have a pastry bag and decorating tips?"

"I think so?"

"Find them. If not, buy them. Tomorrow we decorate."

Ned walked over to the dishwashing table and removed the tray card from the plate he took in the dining room. He handed it to Tyrone. "Make this patient up a new tray."

As Ned started to leave the kitchen, he suddenly stopped and turned back to his staff. "The uniform for this kitchen, starting tomorrow, is a white polo shirt and black pants."

"I ain't got anything like that," Tyrone said.

"Then after work today go buy it. You all have a fifteen dollar budget. Bring me the receipts. This is a hospital kitchen not a gas station.

And no more turned backwards baseball caps. Hairnets are the state regs. Follow them."

"What about me?" Calvin asked.

"You can wear a cook's uniform and hat. You have a chef's hat?" Ned asked.

"Yeah, somewhere."

"Wear it tomorrow. One last thing, I need a couple of bags of potato chips," Ned said.

Tyrone ran to the pantry and returned with three bags of chips. He handed them to Ned.

"Make sure we always have plenty of these on hand."

Ned walked back into the dining room. He stopped in the middle of the room. "Ladies and gentleman, starting breakfast tomorrow. I promise we will be serving more enjoyable meals."

A couple of the residents clapped. The rest just kept on eating. His declaration went generally unnoticed.

Ned then went to Hattie Oak's room and gave her the bags of chips. "Here you go. You don't

scream and I'll make sure you'll have all the chips you can hold."

"Good," she smiled a toothless grin at Ned.

As Ned started leave her room, Hattie reached into her bedside table at took out a stick of deodorant. She called out to him. "Hey!"

Ned stopped and turned to Hattie. She handed the deodorant to Ned.

"This is for you."

"Thank you, Hattie. No one ever gave me deodorant before."

"Don't think anything of it. I like you." she smiled at Ned.

"Now get the fuck out of here and get me a nurse. I have to take a shit."

Ned went back to his office. Lyle Ellis, the VP of Operation for the corporation, and the man who hired Ned, was waiting for him. Lyle oozed upper management, power tie, Rolex watch. He was ten years Ned junior and had a swagger about him that projected success.

"I just wanted to stop by and say welcome aboard," Lyle said as he extended his hand to Ned.

Ned took it, "Thank you."

"I heard you've already had a busy morning," Lyle said.

"Very busy," Ned responded.

"Central City has lots of challenges, but I'm confident you can handle it," Lyle said.

"I appreciate your confidence," Ned responded.

Ned knew he was hired because they were desperate. Ned took the job without even taking a walk through because he needed the money.

"Ned, the best advice I could give you is work on improving the Medicare and make sure you have a good survey. They had a tough one last year."

"I looked through it, I know," Ned said.

"Have you met your DON yet?" Lyle asked.

"Yeah," Ned said.

"Be careful of her, she has a lot of friends at corporate."

THE FIRST REPORT

Ned got home that first night from Central City about six-thirty. He was exhausted. He picked up a tray of sushi on the way along with a six-pack of Tsingtao beer. He stripped off his spit-on suit and tossed it in the mesh bag that was headed for the cleaners. He sat down in front of the TV, cracked open the tray of sushi, and one of those Chinese beers. He tried to find something to watch on cable. The best he could do was 'Die Hard' which he had seen at least ten times. As Bruce Willis was jumping over the side of the building wrapped in a fire hose…Ned's phone rang. It was Katie.

"So, how was your first day?" she asked.

"Better than I could have ever imagined," Ned stated wryly.

"That bad, huh…" she responded.

"A patient spit on my favorite suit."

"Your Ralph Lauren? You love that suit!"

"That's the one. Another patient was naked sitting in my office chair. Oh, and there was a loaded diaper on the floor next to him."

"Eeeeow…" Katie cringed.

"The DON and I instantly hated each other. And I had to break up a fight in the lobby. I'd say it was a spectacular first day."

"Maybe you ought to apply at the Post Office. I hear they're looking…"

"I already came to that conclusion. I'm going to give it a week. Then if it doesn't work out, I'm going to see if I can become a barista at Starbucks."

EVEN A BLIND LADY CAN THREAD A NEEDLE

It was day two of Ned's administration at Central City. He pulled up to the stop sign the corner of the facility. The cute black girl from the previous day was once again leaning against the building having a cigarette. She smiled at Ned. He smiled back. He turned right and drove down the ramp and into the parking garage.

Benito had re-painted the lettering on the entrance gate. The leaky pipes weren't dripping any longer and all the garage lights were working. There was a new sign above Ned's vacant parking space written in large letters: ADMINESTRATER. The sign was mis-spelled but at least his maintenance supervisor had gotten the message. Ned parked and got out of his vehicle. Gone was the blue suit. It was replaced with chinos, a white shirt and a black sweater. He grabbed his old briefcase, not the Ghurka, and followed the same route through the garage he had taken the day before. The two kitchen workers he had passed the previous day were again on their break. They were properly attired and were sitting on empty milk crates by the stairs. This time as they saw Ned approach they stood up. They were sharing another beer from a brown paper bag.

"Good morning," one of them said to Ned.

"Good morning," Ned replied.

Then Ned pointed to the brown paper bag. "I won't look today but tomorrow if that turns out to be a beer, you're both fired."

The two kitchen workers stood there in stunned silence.

Ned walked by them and climbed the stairs.

Benito was putting a non-slip tape strip onto the stairs.

"Good morning, Mr. Ned," Benito said as he moved enough for Ned to get by.

"And good morning to you, Benito, I like what I see."

Ned climbed over where Benito was working. He climbed to the top of the stairs and pushed open the security gate. Ned looked toward the dumpsters. Their lids were closed. The rat Ned had seen the previous day feasting on the pile of garbage crawled out from under one of the dumpster lids. The rat looked at Ned.

"See, I told you your dining days were over. If I were you, I'd find another place to live."

The rat looked at Ned and scrambled back into the dumpster. To Ned's right were the wheelchairs. They were now covered with a tarp. All neatly lined up in a row. The housekeeper that was yammering away on his cell phone yesterday, was now busy hosing off the sidewalk.

Ned entered the hospital as he had the day before. The noise level was down. The smell had improved dramatically. Benito had placed floor fans in the hallway and they were doing their job venting the facility of that nursing home smell. Ned passed a couple of nurses. They were wearing lipstick and their scrubs were clean and pressed.

"Good morning, Mr. Ned," a nurse smiled.

"Good morning," Ned smiled back. Progress was being made.

Ned walked down the hallway toward his office when he heard yelling. "Get out of here you little bitch!"

The yelling was coming from one of the rooms nearby. The yelling was followed by a CNA, Sharnise, running out of the room. Sharnise was a cute, young black girl with a head full of gold nylon braids woven into her coal black hair. A second later a glass of water followed Sharnise out of the door. The plastic eight-ounce glass hit the floor. Water sprayed. The glass bounced along the floor. Ned caught it with his foot.

"Well, at least you didn't get hit," Ned smiled and remarked to Sharnise.

"Would you please get a towel and get the water picked up before someone ends up on their bottom," Ned gently ordered.

"That woman is impossible," Sharnise responded as she pulled a towel out of a linen closet and dropped it on the wet floor.

"What's her problem?"

"She hates everything."

"Everything? I think I need to have a chat with her."

Ned looked at the name plate on the door: DORIS HANDEY. He entered the room. The head of Miss Handey's bed was raised up forty-five degrees. She was a woman in her fifties. Her clouded eyes gave away the fact that she was blind.

"Did you just come back in the room," Handey barked.

"Miss Handey, my name is Ned Russo the new administrator."

"Let's see how long you last."

"What seems to be the problem?"

"This hospital. There isn't one goddamn thing about it that's any good."

"I'm sorry to hear that."

"What do you want?"

"I want to see if there's anything I can do to make you happy."

"Yes. Get out!"

"I'm sure I can do better than that."

"No, you can't. Just get out."

Ned suddenly realized that on Handey's bedside table was an orange hazmat medical waste box. He carefully picked it up and discovered it was full of finger lancets.

"Why do you have a box of lancets by the side of your bed?" Ned questioned.

"I do my own finger sticks. I'm an RN."

Ned's voice got measurably more demonstrative. "No. You're a blind woman and patient in this hospital."

"I can take care of myself!" she replied angrily.

Ned grabbed the box off the side table and walked out of the room.

"What are you doing?" she screamed after Ned.

Handey's water pitcher followed Ned out of the room. It banged off the door and landed on the floor. Sharnise was still mopping up the glass of water thrown at her.

"When you finish mopping the water thrown at you, would you please get mine?"

Sharnise smiled. "She didn't like you any better, huh?"

"Charming woman, isn't she?" Ned said to Sharnise.

"Fuck you! Bring back my box!" Handey screamed.

"I see there's nothing wrong with her hearing."

Ned headed to Violet's office. Even though he smiled at Sharnise, the incident with Handey had really angered him. Ned hurried to Violet's office and was about to pound on her door when he regained his composure. Ned knocked instead.

"Come in," Violet said.

Ned entered her office. When she saw that it was Ned, she turned her attention to adding notes to a patient's chart. Ned put the orange hazmat box of lancets on Violet's child-sized desk. "Did you know this box of used lancets is in Handey's room?" Ned asked.

Violet stopped, looked at the orange box then returned to writing her notes, "She's been a patient here for years and she's an RN," Violet said dismissing Ned's comment.

"Yeah, she told me," Ned responded.

"She checks her own blood sugar. It helps her psychologically. She has a sense of control," Violet said.

"Does she have a braille meter she can use to read her numbers?"

"I personally check the readings. There's never been a problem."

"Don't you think leaving a box of used lancets in her room is inherently dangerous?" Ned asked.

Violet stopped her writing and turned to Ned, "Don't tell me how to care for my patients," she bristled.

"I'm not telling you how to care for your patients, I'm discussing policy and procedure," Ned said.

"If you try and change things in this facility all you're going to do is create problems," Violet responded.

"For you, or for me?" Ned responded.

He took the box of lancets from Violet's desk. "I don't want to see a sharp's box in her room again," Ned said. He turned and left her office.

Ned went back to his office. Ned was furious. He slammed his office door so hard it brought Jose out from his cubicle to see what had happened. He went up to Ned's office door.

"Mr. Ned, are you ok?" Jose asked.

"I'm fine," Ned snapped back, but his anger bled through in his statement.

Ned paced around his office trying to cool down. "Damn that woman," he yelled aloud.

Jose decided to leave well enough alone, and went back to his cubicle.

Ned stopped, thought for a moment, then drew a deep breath and took his cell out of his pocket and punched in Lyle's number.

"Ned!" Lyle's cheery voice responded as he answered the call.

"How big a problem you think we'd have if DHS found a box of used lancets on a blind lady's side table?"

"Does Violet know about this?"

"She's known about it for years. What is it with this woman?" Ned said coming a little unglued.

"Calm down. I can hear how pissed off you are."

"No, you can't. I'm reigning most of it in."

"I know she's a problem. But we have a political mine field to navigate with her."

"What does that mean? Lyle, she's a bad nurse. You're lucky she hasn't brought this place down on top of you already."

"We'll get rid of her."

"When? It's my license hanging on the wall."

"Look, we've got to be careful how we move her out."

"Why?"

"She's been there forever. She has proven loyalty to Mr. M. That counts to him. Now you have to trust me on this. She'll go. I promise. But we've got to do it right."

Ned realized he was just told to shut up in the nicest way possible. Pushing the issue any further would only make him a barking dog.

"Just stay calm and play head's up ball. We'll get rid of her," Lyle said.

Ned got control of his emotions, "I'm going to trust you on this, Lyle."

"Don't worry I understand the problem and it'll get solved."

Ned knew he really had no choice but to listen to his boss.

“I’ll make it happen,” Lyle said reassuringly.

“Lyle, I'll tell you what scares me the most. Not what I find, but what I don't find,” Ned said.

The call ended. Ned was no fool, he knew if it came to blows Lyle would throw him under the bus so fast, he wouldn’t even feel the wheels that would crush him.

That night Ned took out his frustrations on the heavy bag hanging in his garage. He punched the bag until his hands hurt and he worked up a soaking sweat. He took a shower. He had a martini and watched Bruce Willis jump off Nakatomi for the eleventh time.

A VISIT TO THE FUNNY FARM

The next morning Dylan stuck his head into Ned's office. "You want to go see a couple of potential patients?"

Ned answered Dylan almost immediately. "Yeah, that sounds like a good idea."

Dylan drove. Ned sat quietly. Dylan turned down the smooth jazz on the radio and turned to Ned. "I heard you came up against Violet over Handey."

"That didn't take long."

"There are no secrets in Central City."

"I would categorize it more as a difference of opinion about patient care," Ned sighed then added, "Why won't corporate hold her accountable?"

"They don't. No matter what happens it's always the administrator's fault."

"That's reassuring."

Dylan pulled his car into the parking lot at Rothman Community Hospital. He knew the parking attendant. They exchanged a few words in Spanish. Dylan parked and he and Ned entered the hospital. The security guard at the entrance signed them in and issued visitor's passes. They got on the elevator went to the sixth floor. The door opened on to the psych unit.

"Welcome to the funny farm," Dylan whispered Ned.

There were maybe two dozen patients wandering around. All had expressionless faces. Most were in untied hospital gowns. Their backsides were prominently displayed. Others were partially dressed. Some had shoes with no laces, others with non-slip hospital socks. They hardly spoke to one another. A few talked to themselves. Mostly they just wandered around in large circles. One of the male patients came up to Dylan and Ned. "Can I have a cigarette?"

"Sorry man, don't smoke," Dylan replied.

"My father came by and gave you cigarettes for me."

"No man, he didn't. He probably gave your smokes to one of the nurses."

The patient shuffled off.

All the patients appeared to be in a stupor. It was the drugs. To keep the patients from doing unimaginable things, psychiatrists made sure their patients were slightly more active than cabbages. This is easily accomplished with a myriad of powerful psychotropic drugs. The sixth floor was Aldous Huxley's vision of the new world. There were no problems. Everybody was on Soma. Just in case the Soma didn't work, and to keep order, should a patient get out of hand, there were two very large security guards standing nearby. They were leaning against the nursing station chatting about sports. The guards were dressed in black jumpsuits, just like guards in a prison. They had handcuffs, pepper spray and batons. The desk they were leaning against was a four-foot high barrier that spanned nearly the entire length of the room. Behind the desk, safe from the patients, were the nurses, doctors and discharge planners. The desk was the 'no man's land' that kept the sane from the insane, hospital business taking place on one side, oblivion on the other.

Dylan and Ned walked up to the desk. The doctors, nurses and discharge planners all greeted Dylan. He took a handful of Central City promotional pens out of his pocket and placed them on the desk. "I know you folks can always use more pens," Dylan said.

"Thank you, Dylan," came from one of the nurses.

"Dylan, you're here to see Mr. Tower," Sophie, a discharge planner said.

"Yeah."

"Follow me."

Sophie came out from behind the desk and walked down a hallway that led off the lobby. Dylan and Ned trailed behind. Sophie was in her thirties, cute with short dark hair. She was wearing jeans and a blue smock.

"This is Ned our new administrator," Dylan said.

"Hi, Ned," Sophie said, then she spoke to Dylan, "Mr. Tower is generally pretty calm. You're not going to have any problems with him."

They all entered a patient room. Sophie raised her voice as if she were talking to a nearly deaf person, "Hello, Mr. Tower."

Mr. Tower was curled up in his bed. He was an African American man in his fifties. He was wearing a hospital gown. His room, like all the others in the psych unit, was a step up from a prison cell. There were two beds in the room. The other bed was empty.

"Mr. Tower, these men are here to see if you want to move to their facility."

Asking a patient 'if' they wanted to move was just a ruse. They were going out one way or another.

"Can I smoke there?"

"Yes, and we provide the cigarettes," Dylan answered.

Sophie turned to Dylan. "He really won't be a problem."

"What about the other half of the deal?" Dylan inquired.

"She's in the day room."

Sophie led Dylan and Ned down the hall to a day room. There were a number of patients watching a soundless TV. None of the patients seemed to care. Sophie pointed to a seventy year old woman sitting in a chair staring out the window.

"That's Miss Flowers. I really need to find a placement for her. If you help me, I promise you another Medicare."

"Does she have behavioral issues?" Ned asked.

"No, she's been quiet since she's been here," Sophie answered.

Dylan looked at Ned. He was waiting for a decision.

"Ok, we'll take the package," Ned smiled.

"Great. I'll send them over later today."

Their business concluded for the day, Dylan and Ned got back on the elevator and left the sixth floor. "You do a lot of business with her?" Ned asked.

"Not as much as I'd like to," Dylan responded.

"Why did you bring me over here?"

"I wanted to see if things were really going to change. I've heard a lot of bullshit from other administrators but nothing ever changed."

"How did I do?"

"You passed."

"And if I failed?"

"I was gonna put in for a transfer. I'm tired of working my ass off givin' away all the fuckin' Medicare to our sister facilities."

"Is that what you've been doing?"

"Ever since I came to Central City. I was going to give you six months but when I woke up this morning and said fuck it! I decided you had two weeks."

"Figure I wouldn't last two weeks?" Ned asked.

"Somethin' like that."

The elevator doors opened. Standing in the lobby was Dr. Kovani. He was an elegantly dressed man who had a full-head of long silver hair and a thick trimmed Van Dyke beard. Dr. Kovani was the head of psychiatry for the hospital.

"Dr. K, I want you to meet out new administrator, Ned Russo," Dylan said with enthusiasm.

Ned extended his hand to Kovani.

"Dylan is a good man. He helps us out a lot," Kovani said in a thick Persian accent.

"I'm going to make sure that he keeps on helping you," Ned said.

"Listen," Kovani said, "I have a new patient. Medicare. No strings on this one. He's a paraplegic. Twenty-nine years old."

"Young patients are very difficult. Does he have one hundred days?" Dylan asked.

"Yes, but he's difficult," Kovani said.

Dylan turned to Ned, "That's Doctor Kovani's way of warning us this guy is a ball-breaker."

"If we can't handle him can I send him back?" Ned asked.

"Absolutely," Kovani quickly responded.

"Send him over," Ned said.

Kovani smiled, "I'll have Sophie send you the paperwork." Kovani got on the elevator.

Ned and Dylan got off.

"Two psych Medicare in one day. If you're trying to impress me, you're doing a good job," Dylan said smiling at Ned.

WE DELIVER

The ride back to Central City was as quiet as the ride to Rothman but the weight of the air in the car was much lighter. Dylan found a different radio station. The cool jazz was replaced with pop. He was happy with Ned's first test as the admissions officer in chief. Dylan pulled his car into the parking spot in the Central City garage.

"You earned your pay for today. Why don't you go have lunch on me," Ned said as he was getting out of the Dylan's car.

"Not a chance. I want to be here when Violet finds out you accepted three psych patients."

"You expect all hell to break loose."

"No question about it."

As Ned walked back to his office, he nearly bumped into a Domino's pizza delivery man coming into the facility. The Domino's man was carrying three giant pizzas.

"Excuse me. Where is Johnathan Bell's room?" the pizza delivery man asked.

"Come on I'll show you." Ned Led the Domino's man to Mr. Bell's room.

"Mr. Bell, this man is here with your pizzas."

"Put them down right here," Bell said indicating his bedside table. The Domino's man complied. Bell used the trapeze above his bed to pull himself up. He took his wallet out from under his pillow and paid the pizza man in cash.

"Thank you," the delivery man said enthusiastically, eyeing his tip. He left Bell's room.

"That was nice of you to buy pizza for the staff," Ned said.

"They're not for the staff. I'm going to eat them."

"You're going to eat three giant pizzas by yourself?" Ned was a bit stunned. Then he added,

"I buy three large pizzas for the whole shift."

"Well, I'm hungry."

"Please excuse me for saying this, but three pizzas isn't hungry, it gluttony."

"I don't remember asking your opinion."

"I know the food here isn't the best, but come on…three pizzas?"

"My eating habits are none of your business."

"Mr. Bell, you are morbidly obese. You are on a bariatric bed that's held up with wooden blocks because you blew the wheels out and you need a trapeze to adjust yourself in that bed. You're not hungry, you're eating out of habit."

Bell's mood changed. He suddenly got angry. "I don't want to talk to anybody including you. I just want to enjoy my pizza, ok?"

Bell was sentient, alert and completely sound of mind, if Bell wanted to eat himself to death Ned knew that was his choice.

"Listen, if you need a case of Coke to wash those pizzas down, let me know. I'll have someone pick it up for you." Ned turned and left Bell's room.

Ned went back to his office and checked his email. As he scrolled through them, he discovered a report that would be important to his survival at Central City, the overtime report. He opened the email and discovered the dietary department was so far beyond the budgeted work hours, it was as if they were cooking for all of Koreatown. Ned left his computer and went to the kitchen. He knocked on the door. Nobody answered. He could see two dishwashers on the other side of the glass but they pretended not to hear Ned's knocking. He used his master key to open the door.

"Who's in charge here?" Ned asked.

There was a pause before the cook, Calvin, who was sweating as he was cooking at the stove, looked sheepishly at Ned. "Ain't you?" Calvin responded.

"I'm in charge in the big sense but you're...never mind." Ned realized an explanation would be useless.

The kitchen was a financial disaster. Ned knew it would take more than a squiggle of brown sauce to bring it into compliance. Ned counted noses. He discovered there were four people working in the kitchen. Ned checked the schedule that was posted on the wall. There were only three scheduled to work. He turned to the staff. "Three people are scheduled. There are four of you. Who's not supposed to be here?" Ned asked.

Calvin pointed to one of the dishwashers. "That's Mamook. He's deaf. He comes in whenever he wants to wash dishes."

Ned studied the schedule. Mamook's name wasn't on it. "He's not even on the schedule...anywhere!" Ned said incredulously.

"Being deaf and all, he doesn't pay attention to the schedule. So we gave up a long time ago trying to tell him when to come in. So he just comes when he wants."

"And he comes a lot?" Ned asked.

"Oh, yeah, he comes all the time. I don't think he has much else to do."

Ned looked over at Mamook, who was unaware of the conversation going on around him, he never looked up from his dishwashing.

Ned had a soft spot in his heart for workers with disabilities. In Ned's experience worker's with disabilities were better than average employees. He appreciated them for wanting to be functioning members of society. Mamook seemed to be no different.

"Calvin, since there is no supervisor it falls to you and the other cooks to make sure the kitchen runs smoothly. That means you're supposed to watch things like the schedule. That means you are in charge."

"Does that mean I get a raise?" Calvin asked.

Ned ignored Calvin's query about finances. "Has anyone tried to communicate with this guy, Nanook? Is he an Eskimo or something?"

"His name is Mamook. I don't know about the Eskimo part he's from some African country. I didn't know they had Eskimos in Africa."

"They don't. Come on, someone must be able to talk to him," Ned said.

"We can't, he's deaf," Calvin said.

"How about writing something on a piece of paper?"

"He can't read," Calvin said.

"How do you know? Did you ever try?"

"Like I said, he's deaf."

"That didn't stop Helen Keller," Ned said.

"Does she work here?" Calvin asked.

"I wish she did," Ned responded.

TOM WOLFE WAS RIGHT

Ned hadn't seen his mother, Rose, in weeks. He gave himself the excuse that it was job hunting and then the new job. But that was only partially the truth. It was hard to drive across town, LA traffic was awful. It was a lot easier to visit her when he was at Sea Breeze. Even then seeing Rose had become a bit of a punishment. Ned and Rose would have the same conversation every time he was there.

"What did you have for dinner, Ma?" Ned would ask looking for a way to start a conversation.

"Meat," she would respond. Then she would add, "You know that nice lady who sat next to me at bingo…she died."

Ned didn't want to hear it one more time. But he knew there would come a day in the not too distant future where he wouldn't have to make the trip anymore. He decided it was time to visit his mother.

Assisted living facilities are different from skilled nursing. It was more like living in a hotel with some nursing thrown in. Where Rose was living was no Sea Breeze, but it was pleasant, new and clean. She had a small room, her TV, bed and bureau, her rocking chair and lots of pictures of her family were there to remind her of home. Ned and his brother had shipped some of her belongings out from Rhode Island when they moved her to California. The facility had fitted out the bathroom for old people complete with lots of grab bars and a higher toilet seat. And she had sort of a kitchen. It had a microwave Rose would never use. She had gotten to the point it was too complicated. And there was a small refrigerator. Ned kept it stocked with lemon flavored bottled water and rice pudding. This was a woman who used garlic on just about everything but birthday cake now it was rice pudding. In her younger days, Rose was the woman that had poisoned the well for every other woman in Ned's life. But at the end of the day she was still Ned's mother and for all the damage she caused in his life he still loved her.

"Is your brother Mike coming this weekend?" Rose asked.

"No, Ma. Mike lives in Rhode Island."

"Oh yeah, that's right. Well, is he coming this weekend?"

"No Ma, Mike will probably come next summer."

"That's a long time from now. Gee, I haven't seen him in a couple of years."

"Ma, Mike was just here last month," Ned said gently.

"Oh, yeah, I remember."

But she didn't. Ned was watching her intellect fade with each visit. Ned and Mike decided to move Rose to California a couple of years ago. It was at the advice of her physician who told them that if they didn't move her soon, she wouldn't be able to go. Transplanting Rose to California seemed logical since Ned was in the old people business. The issue of money never came up. It was a bit of a pinch for Ned. Mike was the more successful of the two. He was a small town lawyer in Rhode Island. Both Ned and his brother partially subsidized Rose's assisted living cost because they knew it was what their father would have wanted. And Ned idolized his father.

John Russo had been gone now seven years. John watched one of his close friends, Jimmy Fazio, spend the end of his life in a nursing home. They had grown up together, been army buddies. At the end of his life, Jimmy had dementia. As the dementia worsened eventually John's friend didn't recognize anybody. It got to the point where John couldn't go see him; it was too hard. After Jimmy's death, John made Ned promise he would never put him in one of those places, no matter what.

John was a plumber. His fingers were like sausages and his hands rough as cactus. When Ned was a boy, John would take him to work with him on a Saturday. Ned thought his father was the toughest man in the world as he watched John solder pipes together by using his finger to stir molten lead. Ned just knew any other human being would have their finger burned off by the bubbling metal, but not John. Ned would watch in awe as his father would drop small ingots of lead into a cast iron bowl. When the lead melted John would wet his finger and dip it in the molten metal. Then he would drip the liquid lead into the pipe joints soldering them.

John was a quiet man. He worked like a plow mule so his sons could go to college. That was an opportunity John never had. But he was determined his sons would get an education.

"Don't work with your backs. After a while they're going to break. Push a pencil." He would say that over and over to Ned and Mike.

When Ned and Mike were on the high school football team, John, after a hard day's work, would come by their practices. He would park his truck just off the road. He never came onto the field. John would stand on the outside of the chain link fence and watch them practice. He would never say anything, just watch. And after a few minutes he and the truck would be gone. Ned came to realize it was an act of unspoken love for his sons. One of Ned's great regrets in life was that he never told his father how much he loved him.

At the end of some of those 'working' Saturdays' John would take Ned to Raffalo's for a bowl of tripe. Raffalo's was a neighborhood working man's bar. The men would laugh boisterously, drink beer and eat tripe with crusty Italian bread. John would give Ned a glass of beer and tell Ned not to tell his mother. It was their secret, Ned loved those Saturdays. One day, long after Raffalo's and John were gone, Ned was watching a cooking show on TV. The chef cooked up Italian style tripe. It brought back all those fond memories of all those Saturdays with his dad at Raffalo's. Ned ran out and bought the ingredients to cook up a pot of what he hoped would be happy moments from his past. But it turned out to be just a bowl of red sauce with the chewy lining of some cow's stomach. Tom Wolfe was right. You can't go home again.

The last few years of his life, John had Parkinson Disease. A man who could stir molten lead with his bare finger had to have his meat cut for him because his hand shook too much. One day he fell and broke his hip. He knew Rose couldn't care for him from this point forward and he would have to go to a nursing home. He just shut down. Five days later he was gone.

Soon it would be Rose's turn. In their weekly conversations when Mike would call Ned to see how Rose was doing, Ned would report how she slipped a little further away. At first they both secretly hoped she wouldn't last long enough to have to be put in a nursing home. But they could never talk about such things. Ned had terrible guilt about those thoughts. But as she slowly slipped further and further into that strange abyss that so many old people enter, the guilt faded. Ned and Mike could talk about it openly. They would joke about their mother and their mother's plight. About her current state and how she used to be, the good times and the bad, her attributes and her faults. She had plenty of both. It was almost as if they had a weekly wake for Rose. In a way, Ned felt it prepared them for what was inevitable.

BED BATH FOR A BEHEMOTH

One morning, as Ned was making rounds, he heard laughing coming from Jonathan Bell's room. Ned peaked into the room. He watched as two young, Hispanic, CNAs gave him a bed bath. It looked like a humiliating experience for Mr. Bell. His huge bulk filled the entire bariatric bed and the two nurses struggled to move his extremities so they could give him the most minimal of cleaning. The CNAs were chatting away in Spanish not paying attention to Mr. Bell or the experience he was going through. They used a washcloth and a body cleaning product to clean him. They made no real attempt to wash his massive body but simply dabbed Mr. Bell here and there. Bell said nothing but the look on his face as he endured the two nurses giggling and yammering away was pure agony. Ned felt sorry for Bell. He decided then and there Mr. Bell's experience was going to be a teachable moment for his staff. He went to the nearest nursing station and spoke to Carmen, the charge nurse. She was nearby, busy passing medication and wasn't paying attention to the Spanish and the laughter coming from Bell's room.

"Do we have any empty beds around here?" Ned asked.

Carmen pointed to the room across the hall. "That one, the 'A' bed is empty."

Ned picked up the phone and pressed the intercom button.

"I want all nurses to come to room fourteen now, please."

Ned left the nursing station and went to room fourteen. He stripped down to his boxers and got onto the bed. An old woman in her eighties took note of Ned's arrival. She was in the 'B' bed. She pulled herself up to get a better look at Ned. "Finally, a decent roommate."

One by one the nurses filed into the room. They were thunderstruck to see Ned, stripped to his skivvies lying there. There was giggling and sighs of shock. Within seconds the rumor mill spread throughout the facility. Mr. Ned was naked in room fourteen. Everybody came, even the deaf dishwasher, to see what was going on.

"If you're not a nurse go back on the floor," Ned said.

Half the onlookers groaned, but left the room.

"You two...," Ned pointed to the CNAs who gave the bed bath to Mr. Bell. They were both inexperienced and new on the job. "Give me a bed bath."

The two CNAs stood there frozen in place their mouths open in shock. The rest of the nursing staff equally stunned, looked on.

"Come on…what are you waiting for?"

"But you're the administrator," one of the chosen CNAs said.

"No, right now I'm a patient. So give me a bed bath."

Sippie stepped in front of the two CNAs. "I'll do it."

Sippie was a tall, slender and pretty CNA. She was black woman in her thirties. She was eager to get the opportunity to get her hands on her boss.

Carolina Calder, one of the bolder of Ned's CNAs commented. "And I'll bet you'll enjoy it too. Mr. Ned, Sippie usually charges her customers but she wants to give you a freebie. You should take it," Carolina said wryly.

Some of the CNAs giggled. Rumor was Sippie's other job was as a prostitute.

"Thank you, Sippie. But I want these two ladies to do it," Ned said.

The two CNAs skittishly approached Ned. Without saying a word, they put the body cleaning product on their washcloths and were about to start Ned's bed bath.

"Aren't you going to close the privacy curtain?"

"You don't have to. I want to watch," said the old lady in the 'B' bed.

One of the CNAs pulled the curtain halfway closed while the other began to give Ned the same type of cleaning they gave Mr. Bell.

"Aren't you going to speak to each other in Spanish? Or how about a giggle and laugh?" Ned asked.

The CNAs said nothing. They gingerly used the washcloth and went over his arms, his legs, chest, feet and face. When they finished they backed away from the bed.

"Are you finished?"

"You didn't wash his balls," Carolina said cracking a smile.

"That's right. And when they were washing Mr. Bell's, they chatted in Spanish."

Ned turned to the CNAs. "Do you think it's possible he might have thought you were making fun of him?"

The two CNAs were silent.

"I'll tell you what else they didn't do. They didn't use soap and warm water and a towel to dry me or Mr. Bell."

Ned turned to the rest of the nurses gathered around him. "From this moment forward, I don't want any patient washed with this stuff."

Ned took the bottle of body cleaning liquid and tossed it in the waste basket. "It's a harsh chemical. You leave it on the skin the patient will end up with a rash and then a bed sore. You will use soap and warm water and you will wash each patient from head to toe. You will not speak a foreign language in front of the patient. You will respect the patient's dignity by closing the curtain."

Ned looked into the eyes of the nurses gathered around the room. "Everybody understand that? The next nurse who doesn't wash a patient properly gets a three-day vacation with no pay. Now all of you get out of here so I can get my pants back on."

"Don't put your pants on for me," came a comment from the woman in the 'B' bed.

"Sorry honey, maybe after I get to know you better," Ned said. Then he winked at the woman in the 'B' bed.

THE ANGEL OF DEATH

The following day Ned decided to come in earlier than usual. He learned over the years just changing his routine by as little as fifteen minutes could give him an eyeful of insight into the workings of his hospital. As he walked down the hallway toward his office, surprised CNAs scrambled to suddenly pay attention to their assignments. It was obvious his staff had been caught off guard. But Ned said nothing. He just kept walking knowing his showing up early would reverberate through the building.

Ned got to his office, turned on his computer and went over the previous profit and loss statements. They were mostly loss. His task was to find a way to turn Central City around. There was a knock on his door. A blonde woman holding two Starbucks Grande Lattes didn't wait for Ned to open the door she just pushed open the door.

"Hi. I'm Karen Stoble."

"Good morning," Ned replied a little startled.

Ned was surprised by this woman's boldness. She handed him one of the coffee drinks along with a couple of packets of sugar. "Hope you like a latte. There's no sugar in it. But I brought you a couple just in case."

"No sugar is the way I take it," Ned responded.

Karen Stoble was an attractive blond in her late forties. She was wearing a tight black dress and stood tall in a pair of stiletto heels. Her hair and makeup were perfect. She had sales written all over her. She was kind of woman who didn't take 'no' for an answer.

"I'm the marketer for Pacific Hospice. People die at all hours. I've always got to be ready. Did Lyle tell you I was going to come by?"

"I think he mentioned something about it."

"Ok, here's the deal. You know there's like a thousand hospice companies in LA. But you guys only do business with us. Why? We're owned by corporate."

"Lyle explained that arrangement."

"Great. That will save me the whole have to do business-with-corporate-partners-bullshit."

Ned let her run on as he sipped his latte.

"Here's the good news. I'm going to get you the best rate every time I can. And none of this two year, three year nonsense eating up one of your Medicare beds. I need two weeks to make a buck. Tops, that's it. If they're not dead in six months we take them off. How's that sound?"

Karen smiled and looked Ned right in the eye.

"Perfect," Ned smiled at Karen.

"All right, I need a male bed. Pancreatic cancer. Maybe a month, no more," Karen said.

"When do you want to send him over?" Ned asked.

"Today, I'll set it up with the hospital."

"Where's he coming from?" Ned asked.

"Good Sam," she replied.

"Try and get him here on the day shift. At least I know they'll find a bed for him that way," Ned said.

Ned always felt hospice was a bit of a sham. All hospitals and nursing homes could give a dying patient palliative care. That meant keeping the patient full of morphine and comfortable until they died. Hospice companies did the same thing but would send in a girl with a guitar to sing to the patient. The same effect could be reached with headphones. And if you piped in Gregorian chant the patient lying there in their drugged induced state might think they were already in heaven.

"Now I want something from you," Ned said.

"What?" she responded as she sipped her latte.

"Every time you come to see me you bring me a latte and I get to rename you the Angel of Death."

"I like that! Beats what a lot of other people call me."

They raised their lattes to seal the new partnership.

Later that day, some unfortunate patient from Good Samaritan Hospital would be taking his last ride in an ambulance to spend his final days in Central City. He, or his family, didn't know it but his passing, something that should have a bit of reverence attached to it, became part of the daily workings of profit making within the healthcare industry. Good Samaritan opened up a bed for a more profitable patient. Central City got a better hospice rate and Karen Stoble got a commission. And Ned felt he got a hospice partner. Karen was the way Ned liked to do business. Fast with a minimum of negotiating. Ned could tell he was going to get along just fine with her.

Karen released a long forgotten fond memory for Ned. It was her style of negotiating. It was a memory of his father, John, and the way he would negotiate to buy his new Chevy every three years. John never believed he should spend what he called family money or money for Ned and Mike's college fund to buy a car. To John, a car was a luxury. If he wanted a new one it was up to him to provide for it. He would work as many second jobs as he could to save up the needed cash. And on the day, and it was always the last Saturday of the month, when John knew car sales quotas had to be met, then he would strike. To Ned's delight, through all his formative years, he would accompany his father in the car buying adventure. The way John would work was to appeal to the dealership's instant gratification for money. John would fill a sock with the cash he determined he would spend for his new vehicle. Then he and Ned would go to a dealership, meet with a salesman and John would say exactly what he wanted and how much he was willing to spend. Then he would put that sock full of cash on the salesman's desk. Oh, how Ned would delight when he saw the greed in the salesman's eyes light up at that that sock full of cash. John was cagey enough to leave a little corner of a hundred dollar bill sticking out of the top of the sock. There was no negotiating. There was no test spin. There was no haggling over the price. John would point to the car he wanted and present a take it or leave it offer. There was always the "I'll have to ask my manager…" John was ready for that. He just sat there like Sitting Bull, stone-faced, expressionless. The whole time that sock full of cash sitting there on the salesman's desk. Ned couldn't remember a time when he and John didn't leave the dealership in a new Chevy.

LOVE AMONG THE RUINS

Ned saw Mamook, the deaf dishwasher, over by the time clock. He was punching in for work.

"Mamook!" Ned yelled, forgetting Mamook was deaf.

His deaf employee clocked in and started to walk toward the kitchen. Ned chased after him. He caught Mamook from behind and tapped him on him shoulder. Then Ned spoke to Mamook with a combination of sign language and the 'me Tarzan you Jane' form of English.

"Mamook…"

Mamook stopped and turned to Ned.

Ned pointed to his wristwatch, "I need you to set a time to work," Ned almost yelled. He pointed to the time clock, "Make schedule, you understand?"

"You don't have to shout when you talk to me. I'm deaf not hard of hearing. Besides, I can read lips," Mamook replied in that deaf person's odd tone but in perfect English.

"How did you know I was shouting?"

"Everybody shouts at deaf people. They think if they talk loud enough maybe we can hear them."

"Well, don't I feel just the stupid one," Ned laughed and patted Mamook on the shoulder.

Mamook took out a pen and piece of paper and wrote down the number.

"This is my hearing-impaired phone number. You can always leave a message."

"Thank you, this makes life a lot simpler."

Ned shook Mamook's hand and his employee went to work.

Ned went back to his office and started to work at his computer when Dylan stuck his head into the room, "I have a Medicare. One hundred days at USC Medical. He's a deal of course."

"How bad is the other half of the deal?" Ned asked.

"A four hundred pounder, but he has Medicare," Dylan said.

"We already have one of those, Mr. Bell. Is this guy really four hundred pounds or is the hospital shaving the truth?"

"I'm betting they're definitely lying about his weight," Dylan added.

"Assuming he's way more than what they say, do we have a bed that can hold this guy?"

"I'm sure Benito can dig one up somewhere at the warehouse."

Ned had been down this road many times before. He knew acute hospitals often shaded the truth about patients they knew were difficult to discharge. A five hundred pound patient would be almost impossible for them to move to a skilled nursing facility. Patients that heavy needed all kinds of special care. There was also a good chance a nurse working with a morbidly obese patient could be injured and end up with a huge workers' comp case. If Ned accepted this patient, he was, in poker terms, drawing to an inside straight.

"I already showed the Medicare to Eileen and the business office. They're fine with him, but they're also worried about his weight," Dylan said.

"If we take the deal will you be able to get rid of him?" Ned asked.

This was the key to the deal for Ned. The Medicare was three months and maybe seventy grand. But this patient could cost a fortune in the long run.

"If we don't use up all his Medicare, eventually I'll get rid of him. But it'll take work," Dylan said.

"There's always an administrator out there hurting for Medicare, that's my bet," Ned said. Then he added, "Ok, tell USC I'll take the deal but I need time to get him a bed and I want two Medicare up front and the promise of a third within a month."

"That takes stones. I don't know if they'll go for it," Dylan responded.

"Then they can keep their patient where he is at five grand a day. Don't worry, this guy isn't going to fly off the shelf," Ned said.

Dylan was skeptical but went along with Ned's hunch. He took out his cell phone and called the discharge planner.

Ms. Flowers and Mr. Tower, the patients Ned had accepted from Rothman, had been in Central City long enough to adjust to their new surroundings. For most patients, those first few days are always the most difficult. They are generally disoriented. It is the most likely time they fall or try and run away from the facility. Ned decided it was time to see how his new patients were doing. He went out onto the smoker's patio to check on Mr. Towers. Sharon was lighting his cigarette. Mr. Towers was wearing a smoker's apron. Sharon handed him a can of Coke.

"How's he doing?" Ned asked.

"Long as I give him a cigarette and Coke he's happy."

"What about Ms. Flowers?"

"That one is something else. She has fallen in love with Mr. Imo," Sharon said.

"The little old Japanese guy? I thought he was demented?" Ned asked.

"He is. But that doesn't stop her."

Sharon took Ned to the back of the activities/dining room. Ms. Flowers was sitting as close to Mr. Imo as she could get. He was oblivious to the fact that she was there or holding his hand.

"Hello, Ms. Flowers," Ned said.

She didn't answer.

"Does she talk?" Ned asked Sharon.

"Not yet."

Ned sniffed the air, "What's that smell?" Then he sniffed Ms. Flowers, "It's coming from her,"

Ned recognized the scent, "Old Spice! That's after shave," Ned said incredulously.

"I know. She found a bottle of it somewhere and wears it all the time."

"That's harmless enough. Just make sure she doesn't drink any of it."

THE WEIGH IN

Ned was in his office listening to the weekly weight report from Claudia, the RNA (Restorative Nursing Aid). She was a pretty, Hispanic woman who had been at Central City for twenty years. It was her responsibility to check the weight of all the patients. The weight of a patient was critical to their health.

"Mr. Bell gained seventeen pounds this week," Claudia said.

"In one week?" Ned said.

"He eats pizzas every day, Chinese food, hot dogs and his regular food. We can't even weigh him any more with the scale. We have to use a tape measure and guess. He probably weighs more," Claudia said.

"Did we order a psych consult?"

"He refused."

"I better talk to him," Ned said.

Ned went to Mr. Bell's room. He was watching TV. There were four empty pizza boxes on his bedside table and Chinese take-out cartons in his trash.

"Mr. Bell, do you know you gained seventeen pounds this week?" Ned asked.

Bell didn't answer.

"Are you trying to eat yourself to death?"

"If I am, it's none of your business."

"If that's your goal, you're doing a good job. Do you think you need to talk to someone?" Ned asked.

"By someone you mean a shrink. I don't want to talk to some shrink," Bell responded.

"Look, it might help," Ned said trying to cajole his patient.

"I've been in three nursing homes for the past five years. I've talked to I don't know how many shrinks and I'm sick and tired of it. They don't help. My life is eating and watching TV. That's all. And I'm ok with that. I appreciate what you're trying to do, but I'm not interested," Bell turned his attention from Ned back to the television.

"But, Mr. Bell, you really are eating yourself to death," Ned reiterated.

Bell turned and looked Ned straight in the eye, "I don't care! Now leave me alone."

Ned knew the conversation was over.

COME TO JESUS MEETING

The delicious fumes from the taco stand across from Central City had been tempting Ned since his first day there. But he was always to occupied and never got around to trying the vendors food. The smoke from the beef and pork the vendor was grilling filled the air with all the flavors of the best Mexican food had to offer. Ned had heard the 'buzz' going around the facility that the vendor's tacos were fabulous. Ned watched out his window as the vendor served up tacos to a couple of Ned's nurses.

Dylan came into Ned's office. "Have you tried that guy's tacos yet?" Ned asked Dylan.

"Not yet. Guess what? Remember the fat guy from USC. He showed up with sepsis. He ended up on a trach. Now he's in intensive care. They don't think he's going to make it."

"Did we lose the other Medicare?" Ned asked.

"No! USC was so happy we were willing to work with them on the fat guy, they are sending us a Medicare anyway," Dylan said.

"No kidding!"

"And here's the best part, we're now on their first call list. You know how much easier that makes my life?" Dylan said.

Making USC's first call list was a big win for Ned.

"I want to celebrate. Let me buy you a taco," Ned smiled.

Ned and Dylan walked across the street to the taco stand. Carolina and two other female CNAs were there ordering beef tacos.

"Their tacos are on me," Ned said to the vendor.

"Thank you, Mr. Ned," Carolina said.

"You're all worth it. I know how hard you work."

"That's true, especially me," Carolina joked.

"Give us each a couple of beef tacos too."

The taco vendor made the carne asada order for the CNAs and Ned and Dylan. He handed the tacos out. Ned paid for all of them.

The CNAs took their tacos back to Central City. Ned and Dylan ate theirs by the vendor's stand.

"Everything I heard about this guy's food is true. This taco is delicious," Ned remarked as he finished his first taco.

Dylan was watching as an ambulance van pulled up in front of Central City. "I got a call from Sophie this morning. I think that's Kovani's paraplegic," he said.

The rear doors opened up and the lift gate came down. As the attendant came around to the back of the van to help his passenger out, a young man in a wheelchair came rolling down the metal ramp on the back two wheels.

"Oh, I hope you're wrong," Ned muttered.

Ned's years of experience had taught him this patient was going to be trouble.

Juan Estrada was in his late twenties. He was an ex-gang banger who was shot during a street battle with a rival gang. He was angry at the world and was going to do everything he could to prove it. Estrada rolled himself into Central City. Ned and Dylan left the taco stand and followed him. By the time they entered the facility, Estrada was in the lobby speeding around some of the wheelchair bound patients like a skier going through a downhill slalom course.

"Would you mind slowing down please," Ned said to Estrada.

"Why?" he answered back.

"Because you might hit somebody," Ned responded.

"No chance of that," Estrada said.

Just to prove his point, Estrada pulled a 'wheelie' and darted between two patients. "See!" he exclaimed.

"I want you to please slow down," Ned said this time more forcefully.

Estrada reached up over his head and gave Ned 'the finger' through his fingerless leather glove. Then he sped out of the lobby down the hall.

Ned went to Jose's window. "What room is he in?" Ned asked.

"He's in room ten." he responded.

Violet was in Jose's cubicle collecting her mail as she watched Estrada's wheelchair demonstration. "It was a bad idea to accept that patient. He's dangerous. He's going to hurt one of the patients," Violet said to Ned.

Ned ignored Violet's comment and spoke directly to Jose. "Call Grant. Tell him to meet me in Mr. Estrada's room. Tell him to bring an IDT form so we can have a record of the meeting with our new patient."

Ned followed Estrada down the hallway and entered Estrada's room. Mr. Estrada had just lit up a joint. "Hey man, what do you want?" Estrada said to Ned.

"Let's start by giving me that joint and whatever you used to light it," Ned said holding out his hand to Estrada. Juan took another deep hit from the joint. He squeezed off the burning end of the joint and flicked it onto the floor. Then Estrada popped the rest of the joint into his mouth.

"See, no joint," Estrada said with a smirk.

He handed Ned the lighter. "You can have this one. I'll just get another."

"I can see you're one of those people that I'm going to have to do battle with…aren't you?" Ned responded.

"No. Just leave me the fuck alone and we'll get along just fine."

"Can't do that as long as you're a patient here," Ned said emphatically.

"Sure you can," Estrada responded.

"We're going to have to come to an understanding, you and me, let's call it a come to Jesus meeting."

"I'm not religious," Estrada said.

Grant entered the room holding a clipboard with the hospital IDT form attached to it.

"This is Grant, head of Social Services. He's part of your care team. He has an IDT form. The form is going to explain the care we have planned for you. So here it is, you don't bust my balls with that wheelchair, you do what the nurses tell you to do, and I get you an out-on-pass so you can go around the corner and smoke your weed," Ned said with a smile.

"What if that doesn't work for me," Estrada defiantly responded.

Ned turned his attention to Grant. "Write down that I explained to Mr. Estrada he needs to operate his wheelchair at a much slower and safer speed in the facility, and that smoking banned substances is against hospital policy."

"I'm not going to stop smoking weed for you, asshole," Estrada insisted.

"I didn't say you had to stop smoking weed. I said you have to stop smoking weed in the facility."

"I'll think about it," Estrada said.

"Think about this, tough guy. You don't stop smoking weed in this hospital, I promise your stash will magically disappear."

Ned turned to Grant. "I imagine we can find two or three dope smokers among our staff that might like a little free weed."

"More than two or three probably," Grant replied grinning.

"And if you don't slowdown in that wheelchair around the old ladies it might disappear as well."

"Fuck you! You can't steal my chair," Estrada screamed at Ned.

"Who said anything about steal? I said it would magically disappear then it would re-appear when I kick your ass out of here. And in the meantime, I would be glad to provide you with a wheelchair that has a hard time simply rolling," Ned smiled at Estrada.

"Fuck you! I'm calling the Department of Health!"

"You need the number?" Ned asked.

"Grant here will swear that whatever you tell them is a lie. That's why he's here."

"I'm leaving!" Estrada screamed.

"You know where the door is. Feel free to go."

Ned pointed down the hall, "But if you decide to stay you're going to have to clean up your act."

Ned turned to Grant again, "Write that we had a successful first meeting with Mr. Estrada. That he agrees to what we're asking him to do but he refuses to sign the necessary form until he consults with his legal counsel."

"Fuck you," Estrada screamed as Ned and Grant left the room.

Ned knew Estrada wouldn't be leaving. He had far more freedom at Central City than he had in the acute hospital. Ned and Estrada would be stuck with each other temporarily until Ned exhausted Estrada's Medicare or Estrada did something so outrageous that Ned would have to return him to Dr. Kovani.

As Ned and Grant walked away from Estrada's room, Grant turned to Ned. "Did you get a chance to look at his face sheet yet?"

"Not yet."

"Make sure you read the part about suicidal tendencies," Grant said.

"Order a psych consult for Mr. Estrada. I want it in the chart, just in case," Ned said.

"I already did," Grant responded.

Ned walked back toward his office. Violet was in the lobby with two LVNs.

Violet walked over to him. "My nurses are very unhappy with the patients you're admitting and that patient specifically. He's too young for this facility," Violet spoke loud enough so the two LVNs in the lobby would hear the conversation.

"I can appreciate the fact that some of these patients take more attention. I'm going to arrange for more training for the staff," Ned responded.

"I don't know more training will be enough," Violet said.

"Well, why don't we try and see."

"There's talk of nurses quitting," Violet warned.

"I'm sorry to hear that. Perhaps, if you send the unhappy nurses to see me I could explain my strategy going forward."

"I don't think that will help."

"You know, Violet, I don't think anything I suggest will help. But it isn't going to change what I have to do."

Ned walked away from the conversation and into his office.

Violet had carefully crafted the conversation with Ned to show herself as 'the good guy' to the nurses. She knew the nurses were listening and that they would gossip about the tension between the DON and the Administrator. Violet might have been lazy but she understood the culture she built at Central City and also how the politics at corporate worked. She was positioning herself to gather enough support from the nursing staff that when she made her move against Ned she would be victorious. Just as she always had been in the past.

TIT FOR TAT

Ned sat down at his desk and opened his emails. There was one from Carlos in HR. The message read: Call me!

Ned pulled out his cell phone and punched in Carlos on the speed dial. He answered.

"Ned, I might have some good news for you."

"I could use some."

"I think I have a solution to your DSD problem," Carlos said.

"That sounds good."

"There's a DSD at another facility the administrator wants to term. If you take him, she'll take Milaney in trade and put her on the floor behind a med cart."

"Hold on, you want me to take some other administrator's dump and in turn she'll take mine. Did I get that right?"

Carlos laughed, "That's the deal. We have an HR problem with Milaney. She has no write-ups in her file, if we term her, she'll file a lawsuit. They all do. Look. So we give her a transfer and a raise. She's happy, you get a new DSD and corporate doesn't get a lawsuit. It's a win-win for everybody."

"I love the way you guys think. Don't solve the problem, just move it to another facility."

Ned hated it but he knew that was corporate group think. Corporations would rather pay out a few bucks than risk tens of thousands in court. It was smart business.

"Tell me about this guy you want to pawn off on me?" Ned reluctantly asked.

"I think he's perfect for your facility," Carlos said.

"I bet. That's why he got dumped by the other administrator because he's perfect," Ned said wryly.

"I said he's perfect for your facility. Getting moved has nothing to do with his work performance. Truth is he's good at his job, neat as a pin, detailed, but no personality."

"He sounds like a robot."

"He kind of is. I know the problems you're having with Violet…"

"My dirty laundry already drying out at corporate?" Ned asked.

"There are no secrets. Ned, I think he's what you need to calm things down at your place. No bullshit."

"All right, send him over," there was hopeful resignation in Ned's response.

The following morning Ned got to work extra early. Like five in the morning early. He had a bad night. His looming staff problems were invading his sleep.

When he entered the hospital, the nurses were surprised to see him.

"What are you doing here this early? Your wife throw you out?" an older female CNA jokingly said to him.

"A long time ago," Ned responded as he continued toward his office.

As he walked by one of the nursing stations, he saw another young female CNA with her head down on the counter. She was sleeping soundly. Ned stood over her for a few seconds hoping she would wake up. She didn't. "Hey," Ned said.

She didn't move.

"Hey, wake up," Ned yelled.

The CNA snapped her head off the counter. See saw Ned standing above her on the other side of the counter. "Shit," she muttered.

"I expect a little cat napping on the 11-7 shift, but you were into a full snore," Ned said.

"I've got three jobs twice a week," she responded unapologetically.

Ned interjected, "And I'm number three? That doesn't make me feel very special."

"I gotta sleep someplace," she responded.

"How about sleeping on your other job? Clock out and go home."

"Am I fired?" she asked.

"Not this time. Tell your charge nurse to come to my office."

Skilled nursing is a business that pays its most important people, the CNAs, starvation wages. To make ends meet, many CNAs must work two, and for some, three jobs.

Ned was unlocking his office door when the charge nurse, Filbert, came up behind him. Filbert was a middle-aged Filipino man. He was nervous as he approached Ned; he knew what was coming. "Mr. Ned, you wanted to see me?" Filbert asked.

"The next time I find a CNA asleep like that on your shift, I'm going to fire you," Ned said.

"But…" Filbert began to protest but Ned cut him off.

"You're the charge nurse. That means you're in charge. Unless you forgot we're in the life and death business. You're not just here to push a med cart and hand out pills. Your job description dictates you check on your patients…and your staff."

"Yes sir, sorry sir. Do you want me to write her up?"

"No. Write yourself up. And bring the write-up to me before you clock out today," Ned entered his office and closed the door in Filbert's face.

Later that morning the shift changed. The 11-7 nurses clocked out and the 7-3 nurses arrived for work.

Ned's phone rang. It was Jose. "There's somebody here to see you. He said Carlos from HR sent him."

Ned went out to greet his perspective new DSD.

"Mr. Russo," the young man said as he stood up.

Anthony Prada was about thirty. He had very short hair and was clean shaven. He was wearing pressed teal colored scrubs. He looked more like he had been sent from the Marine base in Oceanside than from HR.

"Yes..."

"I'm Anthony Parada, Carlos from HR sent me to speak with you about the DSD position."

"Yes. Call me Ned. Come in."

Ned led Anthony into his office. "You want coffee or anything?" Ned asked.

"No thanks," Anthony replied.

"Sit down."

Anthony sat erect in the chair. Hands folded in his lap.

"Let me get right to it." Ned sat on the edge of his desk. "Carlos said you're a detail guy. True?"

"Pretty much," Anthony answered.

"To be a successful DSD I think you have to be the kind of guy that goes through the pepper for the fly shit," Ned said.

"Pretty much."

"If we get together, tell me how you would run the CNAs?" Ned inquired.

"I'll come in early twice a week and late twice a week to make sure I monitor all the shifts," Anthony responded.

"What about weekends and in-services?"

"I'll have an in-service schedule posted and I'll come by as needed on a weekend to check on things. I'll keep an in-service log in my office for you to see and be sure all the mandatory in-services are given as required by the state."

"What about scheduling?" Ned asked.

"I like to schedule a few extra CNAs. Then if there are call offs that will keep the overtime to a minimum or to none at all."

Scheduling the nursing staff is the juggling act each skilled nursing hospital must perform daily to keep the state happy and not have the corporate bean counters unhappy.

"Last question. What about discipline?" Ned asked.

"The CNAs will complain that I follow them around too much," Anthony said.

"Is that how you got in trouble at the other building?" Ned asked.

"Pretty much."

"We have a lot of work to do to get this place straightened out."

"I've heard," Anthony remarked.

"From who?" Ned asked.

"Everyone else who works in this company."

"Is that so," Ned said.

"Can I speak freely?" Anthony asked.

"Please do," Ned said.

"Central City is the worst hospital in the chain. Nobody wants to get near it," Anthony said.

"Well, that's why you and I ended up here. Isn't it? It's a facility full of misfits," Ned said.

"Pretty much."

"I've known you all of five minutes and I don't think you're a misfit and I know I'm not. So how about we prove everyone wrong," Ned said confidently.

For the first time in the conversation Anthony smiled.

"The DSD's office is a disaster. God knows when you start digging back there what you're going to find. You think you can straighten it out? More importantly, do you want to?" Ned asked.

"Yeah."

"Don't say much do you?" Ned asked.

"No need to," Anthony replied.

"You have any questions of me?"

"Not now."

"All right, when do you want to start?" Ned asked.

"Right away."

"That's good for me." Ned held out his hand. Anthony shook it. The conversation concluded Anthony got up and left Ned's office.

Ned took out his cell phone and called Carlos in HR. Carlos answered. "Sorry to call you this early but I just met with Anthony," Ned said.

"Well, what do you think?" Carlos replied.

"He's not exactly a talker," Ned said.

"I told you. But believe me he's what you need over there," Carlos said.

"And what about Milaney?" Ned asked.

"It's already in the works. She'll be gone in a couple of days," Carlos said.

"Have you talked to her yet?" Ned asked.

"Yes."

"She's ok with the move?" Ned asked.

"I don't think she was wild about it, but we gave her a good deal," Carlos answered.

"Anthony wants to start right away. That work for you?" Ned asked.

"That's fine. He's already left the other facility."

"As far as Milaney's departure, I want to give her next couple of days off with pay," Ned told Carlos.

"That's fine. See, I already solved the first of your problems." Carlos said.

"This was the easy one. The big one is going to be a lot harder," Ned said.

"Oh you mean the DON. You're right," Carlos chuckled. "The Violet situation will be a lot harder."

"Yeah, it sure will. Thanks, Carlos for getting on this right away."

"No problem. I don't want to be looking for a new administrator for that place till at least Christmas," Carlos joked.

"That's what I like confidence," Ned answered wryly.

The phone call ended. Jose came into Ned's office and handed him a note the RN super from the 11-7 shift had left for him. Violet wouldn't be coming to work today was the entire message. Ned crumbled the note and tossed it in the trash.

About ten o'clock Ned was going through the dozens of emails he got every day. He kept looking out his window watching for Milaney to enter the facility. As he kept looking, he saw Michael Weller, one of his patients, drive his electric wheelchair out the front door of the facility and disappear down the street.

Weller was a former inmate that some judge saw fit to release from prison early, like so many other prisoners, he found his way into the skilled nursing facility system. True, he had some physical limitations, but nothing that needed skilled nursing. Ned could never grasp how a man could go from a prison cell to a nursing home.

A few minutes after Weller, Ned watched Ying Kang, the fruit fly farmer, push her walker out the front door of the facility. She saw Ned was watching her through his window.

"Churchee, churchee," Ying called to Ned. She smiled and waved.

Ned gave the woman a big smile and waved back.

As Ying continued down the sidewalk she passed right by Milaney who was walking toward the front of Central City. Ned went out to the lobby to greet her. Milaney was heading for the time clock when Ned intercepted her. "Milaney, can you come to my office for a minute," Ned said. She followed Ned to his office. He pointed to a chair for her to sit down. "I understand you talked to Carlos in HR."

"Yes," she sighed.

"Are you ok with the move?" Ned asked.

"I really didn't want to go back on a med cart, but I need a job."

"Carlos told me they gave you more money, right?" Ned asked.

"Yes."

"And I hope you're happy with that?"

"Yes, they were generous," she said.

Ned thought for a bit then he spoke to her sincerely. "Milaney, Central City needs a lot of changes to be successful. It's been sideways for a long time. I don't like replacing people. I've been replaced and I know it hurts," Ned said.

Milaney grimaced and held back tears, "It does."

"But the truth is, sometimes it's got to be done. I'm glad that we were able to work things out for you."

Milaney smiled, "Me too."

"When are you supposed to report to your new facility?" Ned asked.

"Next Monday."

"Then go home. Take the next couple of days off. I'll pay you for it. Get ready for your new job."

Ned took her hand and smiled at her.

She smiled back. "Thank you, you're very kind," she said.

"If it ever comes up, you can say you got tired of being the DSD and wanted a change. I'll back you up."

She smiled and nodded positively at Ned, "Thank you," she said.

"You have a son, right? How old is he?" Ned asked.

"Nine," she responded.

"Does he like to go to the movies?" Ned asked.

"Very much, he loves super heroes," Milaney said.

Ned opened his briefcase he took out two gift card movie passes.

Ned always kept a supply of various 'gift cards' handy. He handed them out to reward the employees who did him favors or earned recognition.

"Here, take your son to see a super hero today," Ned said with a smile.

Then Ned put his hand in his pocket and pulled out a twenty dollar bill and put it with the tickets. "And young kids always want to eat, so get him a bucket of popcorn."

Milaney was caught off guard by the offer, "I can't take..." she said.

Ned stopped her, "Sure you can. I have a connection. I know a guy who knows a guy."

Ned pushed the tickets and the twenty closer to Milaney, "Come on take it. I'll be offended if you don't."

"Are you sure?" she reluctantly asked.

"Very sure," he responded.

Milaney was pleasantly surprised by Ned's gesture. She took the tickets and the twenty from Ned. "Thank you, very much. My son is going to love this!"

"Send me a selfie from the movie lobby."

Milaney wasn't happy that she lost her job, but Ned had made it as painless as possible. She got up and gave Ned a big hug as she left his office. She walked out of Central City for the last time. Ned watched her walk down the sidewalk and away from the facility. Before she disappeared, she looked back at Ned who was standing in the window. She smiled and waved goodbye.

COOKING KIMCHI

Sharon, the activity director, came into Ned's office. "Look at this."

She held out an empty pint bottle of very cheap vodka. The kind that comes in a plastic bottle.

"I found it in Shelia Moran's room."

"How did she get it?" Ned asked.

"Somebody brings it in to her. She never goes out," Sharon said.

"Let's go have a talk with her," Ned said.

Shelia was on the smoker's patio puffing away. She was sitting in a wheelchair a cigarette in one hand a can of Coke in the other. She was wearing a baseball cap covered in rhinestones.

Ned took the empty bottle of vodka from Sharon and held it out to Shelia. "This yours?" Ned asked.

She moved her head within inches of the empty bottle. "Nope," Shelia grunted.

Shelia was an African American woman deep in her sixties. She was almost blind and she had most of her tongue removed, thanks to cancer. From her decades of smoking, her voice sounded like a lawnmower. Understanding her was at best difficult.

"Yes, it is, I found it in your closet," Sharon spoke up.

"I don't care where you found it. It's not mine," Shelia said.

"Come on, Shelia, who brought you the booze?" Ned asked.

Shelia looked Ned straight in the eye. "I ain't no snitch," she grunted.

"Snitch? This isn't San Quentin," Ned said.

"If you don't tell us, I won't give you anymore cigarettes," Sharon warned.

"Like I said, I ain't no snitch."

Ned turned to Sharon. "Let's go, Shelia's not going to give up her bootlegger."

"Damn right, I ain't," Shelia said defiantly.

They started to walk off the patio. "Ok, Shelia, have it your way. Your smoking privileges have been revoked until you tell me how you're getting this rot-gut in here," Ned said.

Shelia grunted after him. "I need to quit anyway."

Ned was back in his office about a half hour later when his phone rang. It was Jose.

"I think you better come out here," he said.

Ned got up and walked out into the lobby. Suddenly, it hit him. It was the pungent smell of something burning, something rotten. And whatever it was it smelled really foul.

"What is that?" Ned asked wrinkling his face from the odor.

Jose's gloved hand opened the reception window. "It's coming from room five, the Korean guy."

He fanned his nose with his gloved hand and quickly closed the reception window.

Ned went to room five. On his way through the lobby, he saw Ms. Flowers take out her breast and put Mr. Imo's hand on it.

"Jose," Ned called out.

"Yes, boss," he replied from his cubicle. His nose pinched with his gloved hand.

"Call a nurse and get Ms. Flowers covered up. And then find something else for our lovers to do, please."

"Ok," Jose answered chuckling and choking from the smell at the same time.

As Ned got closer to room five, his nostrils filled with the pungent odor of Kimchi and something else he couldn't identify. When Ned reached the room, the door was closed and smoke was coming out from under it.

"Holy shit!" Ned exclaimed.

The horrible first thought that went through Ned's mind was the Korean guy in room five was burning and his roasting flesh smelled like kimchi. Ned quickly pushed open the door and entered the room. The first thing that hit him was the smell. "Oh, God that's awful," Ned blurted out.

The smell and the smoke were coming from a pot sitting on top of a hot plate on the bedside table. The horrible smell almost made Ned gag. The occupant of room five, John Kim, was sitting in his wheelchair huddled over that pot. Mr. Kim was stirring his pot and adding in some green colored powder to it. The powder hissed and threw up a cloud of green smoke. The smell in the room worsened.

Mr. Kim always wore camouflage with Korean insignia, which Ned guessed was from the Korean Army. Which Korean Army Ned wasn't sure. He was a patient at Central City while he was being treated for brain cancer at Good Samaritan Hospital. He was a disagreeable enough fellow that his family didn't want to take care of him. Unfortunately, his radiation treatments had burned off the hair from the sides of his head. Ned believed it burned his brain too. What was left was a tuft of hair on the very top front of his head. It made him look like a weird Asian-Mohawk warrior.

"Thank God it's not you that's on fire," Ned said to Mr. Kim.

Kim looked up at Ned. “Fire? There’s no fire. I’m making medicine for the cancer,” Kim responded.

Ned rushed over to the sliding glass door at the far end of the room. He threw open the door just in time to prevent the smoke detectors and the sprinklers from creating a watery mess. Had he been a couple of seconds slower, Ned would have had a load of explaining to do to that unfriendly fire department captain as to why a patient was cooking inside his room. Not to mention the sprinklers flooding the entire facility. Ned grabbed the towel Mr. Kim had on his bed, and flapped it over the green smoke rising from the cooking pot. Ned’s flapping directed the smoke out through the open glass door and onto the patio where other patients could get a snootful of Mr. Kim’s toxic smelling concoction. In a matter of seconds, Ned’s towel flapping cleared most of smoke out of the room.

“What the fuck is that smell?” came a shout from a patient’s room across the patio.

As Ned kept flapping the towel he yelled back, “Sorry, we’re fixing the problem right now. Sorry.”

When Ned felt enough smoke had cleared out of room five, and he felt safe the sprinklers wouldn’t go off, he stopped flapping and turned his attention to Mr. Kim.

“Now, what do you think you are doing?” Ned asked rhetorically as he decided to flap the towel a few more times, just for insurance.

“I told you, making medicine,” Mr. Kim said angrily.

“You know you can’t cook in the room,” Ned said as he pulled plug out of the wall on Mr. Kim’s hot plate.

“Nobody told me,” Mr. Kim responded.

“I didn’t think anybody had to but I’m telling you now.”

“The food you have here is shit. I need to eat good food to get better.”

“Whether you think it’s shit or not, you’re not going to cook in the room.”

Ned took the pot off the hot plate with the towel and carried it outside and put it on the patio.

“Hey! Don’t touch that! It has special herbs from the doctor.”

Watching Ned take his cooking pot made Kim mad enough that if he could have gotten out of his wheelchair and stopped Ned physically he would have. Ned put the pot of whatever it was safely on the patio. Then he went back through the sliding door into Mr. Kim’s room and out into the hallway to call for help.

“Can I get a couple of CNAs in here,” Ned yelled.

He went back into Kim’s room. “Mr. Kim, you have broken about every fire ordinance in Los Angeles. Luckily, you didn’t burn down the building. But I’m sorry, the cooking has to stop.”

"No, I need to eat this kimchi. This is special. It's from the best doctor in Koreatown. Very special!" Kim did his best try to convince Ned of the magical powers of his concoction but Ned wasn't buying any of it.

"You can eat all the kimchi you want. I'm guessing Mrs. Paul's or Campbell's makes a delicious version of kimchi. Korean cuisine is very in now. I'll have the kitchen stock it for you."

"Mrs. Paul's, Campbell's?" Mr. Kim was befuddled by Ned's statement. "Are you shitting me?"

"No, I'm not. I'm sure it won't be as good as homemade, like Chef Boyardee isn't really Italian. But's that's the way it is," Ned responded.

"What's that smell? I think somebody shit on the patio," came a shout from another room.

Mr. Kim yelled out through his sliding glass door, "Fuck you!"

"This place is a fucking dump," came another shout.

"It's being taken care of. I promise. Sorry," Ned yelled back at the voice from across the patio.

Two CNAs entered the room. Others watched from the safety of the hallway.

"Yes, Ned," Sippie said in a low, slow, sexy voice.

Ned was surprised to hear his first name come out of Sippie's mouth. He knew that's how romantic rumors got started. Sippie was the tall, good looking CNA that volunteered to give Ned the test bed bath. No one else in the facility would have the audacity to call Ned by his first name. But right this minute Ned needed to deal with Mr. Kim. He would deal with Sippie's name calling later.

"One of you please get Benito to put a floor fan outside this room and blow that smell out of here."

"You go," Sippie said to the other CNA, "I'll stay here with Ned."

"Sippie, go on the patio and take that pot of whatever it is, and pour it in the toilet, please."

"Hey, I told you there are special herbs I got from the Korean doctor in that soup. I paid a lot of money for them," Kim said his voice getting angrier.

"Next time, please have the magic soup at the doctor's office," Ned said. Then he added, "Sippie, after you clean out the pot bring it to my office."

Sippie started to move toward the patio. Suddenly, Mr. Kim took a street version of a taser out from his camouflage jacket and brandished it at Sippie and Ned. They both jumped back. Kim fired the taser. It made an electric crackling sound and a large blue and red spark jumped out from the business end of the weapon.

"Don't touch my medicine," Kim said.

Sippie screamed and jumped behind Ned, taking the opportunity of holding tightly onto his waist.

Kim pressed the trigger on the taser again and a second electric crackle came out of the weapon along with another large blue and red spark.

"Well, what do we have here…" Ned said rhetorically.

Sippie screamed again and scrunched herself closer behind Ned. She sheepishly peeked over Ned's shoulder at Kim.

Mr. Kim continued to brandish the weapon.

"Give me that taser," Ned said in as low and commanding a voice as he could muster.

"You're not gonna take my medicine," Kim said defiantly.

Ned's voice deepened and his eyes narrowed, "Mr. Kim, you have brought a weapon into this facility. If you had bothered to read the admission papers, it clearly states weapons are not allowed in a skilled nursing facility."

"I didn't read. And I'll use this if you touch my kimchi." Kim pulled the trigger and another crackle and blue spark leaped from the taser.

Ned moved in closer to Mr. Kim and pointed his finger at him, "Not only am I going to take that pot of stink you made and flush it down the toilet, but I'm going to take that taser too."

Ned moved still closer to Mr. Kim, Sippie still clinging to his waist. The finger Ned was pointing at Mr. Kim became an open palm, "Now put that thing in my hand."

There was a long moment when nobody moved.

Ned moved closer to Kim then he said as threateningly as he could. "I swear to God, I'm going to call the cops and tell them you've got a gun. And then while the cops are beating the tar out of you I'm going to eat a ham sandwich. If you don't want me to do that, put that thing in my hand. Right now!"

Seconds went by with Ned staring at Kim, Kim holding the taser and Sippie holding onto Ned.

"Sippie, tell Jose to call the cops," Ned commanded.

Sippie gingerly worked her way out from behind Ned and out of Kim's room. Kim's eyes followed Sippie out of the room. He realized Ned was holding all the cards and he slowly put the taser in Ned's hand. "That's my property," Kim said as he was complying with Ned's order.

"Not any more it's not," Ned responded.

"I'm gonna want it back," Kim said.

I'll return it to you the day you leave here," Ned said then he added, "Which is going to be soon."

Ned put the taser in his pants pocket.

Kim laughed. "You better be careful with that thing in your pocket. It might go off and fry your dick," Kim said.

By now a large group of patients and staff were gathered outside room five. Benito arrived and turned on a large floor fan. He pointed the fan directly into Mr. Kim's room. In a few minutes the smell of Mr. Kim's medicinal cookout was gone. Casey, the ADON, came by and shooed everyone away. "Ok, everybody let's clear the hall."

She looked in at Ned, "That was a close one. I thought he was going to stick you with that thing."

"Me too," Ned responded.

"Better take that thing out of your pocket," Casey said pointing to the taser, "It might go off."

"Don't worry, I have no intention of getting that kind of an injury."

Among the group that was gathered outside room five was Violet. Her displeasure with the incident was showing on her face. She scowled at Ned but didn't say anything. Ned looked at her. When Ned came out of the room she turned and walked away. Ned watched her walk down the hallway. Ned knew patients like Kim were the fuel Violet was throwing on the fire with the nurses at Central City. The more difficult the patient the more it played into Violet's hand. Ned was sure every nurse in the facility would know about Kim's taser by the end of the day. Violet would see to that. Ned knew he had to win over the nurses. Going head to head with her was never going to work. Violet was always going to position it like she was on the side of the poor, overworked nurses. Ned was the outsider trying to make a name for himself by working the nurses to death. Ned needed allies in the nursing department. But who?

As the incident ended, Ned found Sippie and brought her into his office. "Sippie, first, thank you for helping me."

"You're welcome, Ned," she said.

"Second, please don't call me Ned. You can call me Mr. Ned or Mr. Russo or Boss. Calling me by my first name will give people the wrong idea, ok?" Ned asked her politely.

She smiled at him. "Anything you say, Ned." Then she added, with as invitational a voice as possible, "Anything." She left his office.

FINDING A FRIEND

Ned sat in his squeaky chair and put his feet up on the desk. He thought about the power structure in the nursing department. Ned had to find a nurse he could bring over to his side and at the same time influence enough of the nursing staff to tip the balance of power to Ned's way of thinking.

He thought about Eileen the Medicare nurse. She was the most attentive to detail but didn't interact closely enough with the rank and file nurses. Then there were the 3-11 and 11-7 RN supervisors. Ned quickly ruled them out. He needed a day shift nurse. That was where most of the action took place in any hospital. One of those nurses would be the logical choice. Ned thought for a bit more and then picked up the phone. He pressed the button for reception. "Yes, Boss," Jose answered.

"Jose, who do you think is the most liked nurse at Central City?"

"I don't know, there's a lot of them," he responded a bit confused by the question.

"I want to know who YOU think is the most liked nurse," Ned pressed him.

Jose thought for a second then said, "Casey Flynn."

"Why?" asked Ned.

"She's never in a bad mood. And no matter what, she'll always help you. That's the way she is with everybody."

"Thanks," Ned hung up the phone.

Ned went to the metal filing cabinet in his office. He found the drawer marked Department Heads and Senior Staff. He pulled out Casey Flynn's folder, brought it back to his desk and began to read. He read the comments Violet had written about her. What he found was standard stuff, nothing glowing or negative. She was a transfer from another facility, Violet didn't hire her. All the comments written by Violet were right down the middle of the road. Then Ned had a thought. He went back to the file drawer and flipped through the folders until he found the files for all the RN supervisors Violet had hired. Unlike Casey's file, the comments were outstanding. Violet had gotten them each raises. It seemed the only thing these RNs couldn't do was raise patients from the dead. Ned returned the folders to the file cabinet.

Now Ned at least had an idea as to how he could move against Violet. He knew where there was a possible weak link in the nursing chain Violet had forged in her years at Central City, Casey Flynn. The question Ned asked himself was how to get her over to his side. Ned decided before he attempted to bring Casey to his point of view, he was going to do a bit of research.

Ned made rounds. As he walked around Central City he casually asked some innocuous questions about Casey to floor nurses. Lots of floor nurses. He went to the house keeping staff, medical records, activities and maintenance people. He even went into the kitchen and while pretending to need a cup of coffee, found out how the cook felt about her. All the responses he got were genuinely effusive.

Casey Flynn, the ADON (Assistant Director of Nurses) at Central City was the most liked staff member in the facility. Hands down. And the most important group of all, the nurses, loved her. Casey was their mother, their sister, their friend. She covered up their little nursing mistakes, and praised them when they deserved it. Rarely, did she punish anybody. The nurses would go to her office to laugh or to cry. When the nurses needed time off or just time to decompress, she arranged it. For the nursing staff, Casey was the most important person at Central City. It became clear, Casey was the obvious choice if Ned was going to win the war with Violet.

Ned went to Casey's office. He knocked on her door.

"It's open," Casey said.

Ned entered, "Got a minute?"

Casey was seated at her desk. She was going over a patient's chart. There were a number of other charts piled up next to the one she was working on. She put down her pen sat up in her chair. "Yes..."

Casey's office was Spartan but friendly. It was at least five times as big as Violet's. Unlike most of the offices in Central City, it had a window. Ned guessed at one time this was the DON's office. But Violet moved to that broom closet so she wouldn't be bothered by anybody. It was obvious Casey had all the meetings with patients, and family and staff there. Casey's office had two chairs separated by a small round table. Her RN nursing diploma was hanging prominently on the wall behind her desk. It was encased in a gold-painted frame. You couldn't miss it. She was obviously very proud of her degree. There was a blooming orchid plant on top of a small refrigerator next to her desk. There was also a jar of jelly beans and a big box of tissues. Ned could tell she used her office a lot, unlike Violet who hid out in hers.

"What can I do for you?" Casey asked.

"I need your help," Ned said.

"Oh? How can I help you?" she quickly responded.

Ned pointed, indicating he wanted to sit in one of the chairs, "Mind if I sit?"

"You're the administrator," she said.

He sat down and looked at her refrigerator, “You have any water in there?”

“I think so.”

She opened the refrigerator and pulled out a bottle of sparkling water and handed it to Ned.

“Thanks,” he said. Then he added, “Who do I see to get a refrigerator like that in my office?”

“Benito, but you didn’t come in here to ask about refrigerators. Did you?”

“No,” Ned said.

“I'd like to talk to you about how this place operates.”

“That’s a strange question. You’re the administrator. Isn’t that what administrator’s do?”

Ned took a deep swallow from the bottled water, “Yes. But to run a facility effectively an administrator either has to bring the culture to the facility or adapt to the culture that’s already in place. And the culture in Central City is Violet.”

Casey sat there for a few seconds deciding if she was going to end the conversation or not. “I get the feeling this conversation is going to get difficult,” she said.

“I don’t think so. I have no intention of putting you in a difficult position,” Ned said.

“I already am,” she responded.

She thought for a moment, “Mind if we talk outside. It's time for me to have a cigarette. It’s a bad habit I can’t give up.”

“Sure,” Ned got up.

Ned and Casey left her office walked down the hallway toward the back door of Central City. Casey put her hand in the waist pocket of her white nursing skirt. She pulled out a lighter and pack of cigarettes. Ned noticed that there was also an airline sized bottle of vodka in her pocket as well. Ned didn’t say anything about the vodka. Casey lit up her cigarette before they had even cleared the doorway. She took her first drag on that cigarette as if she were kissing her true love for the first time in a month. She led Ned to a corner of the facility where old wheelchairs and other dated mechanical hospital paraphernalia ended up instead of being tossed into the dumpster.This was Casey’s personal smoking spot. She even had an ashtray sitting on a window ledge. It was already full from the previous cigarette breaks she had that day.

“You have some habit,” Ned remarked looking at the full ashtray.

“I’ve been trying to quit for years,” she said.

“What’s the longest you’ve ever quit?” Ned asked.

“About a month. But I gained ten pounds and had the disposition of an alligator. So, I gave that up. You ever smoke?” she asked.

"Not cigarettes. But I've had a joint or two in my day," Ned responded.

Ned took a deep breath as he stepped away from the 'smoking conversation' and got into the meat of why he wanted to talk to her, "Casey, I know I'm the latest administrator in a long line of administrators here. But I want to succeed. And I'm going to need your help to do it."

"Isn't this a conversation you should be having with Violet?" she asked.

"I tried to, but it went nowhere. I'm not going to win over Violet to my point of view. You know that. She's set in her ways. She's not going to change," Ned said.

"Why did you come to me?" she asked as she took another drag from her cigarette.

"You're the best liked nurse at Central City."

"Who told you that?" Casey asked.

"Everybody," Ned answered.

"That's flattering but I don't know that it's true," Casey responded.

"I think the staff recognizes that you love what you do. And they know they can trust you. That makes it true. I hope I can trust you as well," Ned said.

"I love being a nurse. My mother was a nurse. It's all I ever wanted to do since I was a little girl," she said.

"Then help me make this the best hospital in LA," he said.

"That's not going to be easy," Casey responded.

"I agree. But I think it's possible," Ned said.

"I still think you should try and talk to Violet," she said.

"My plans for Central City involve far more work for Violet. She's used to keeping this place full of empty beds and no Medicare. More Medicare means more work and more responsibility. More of everything she hasn't done for years. She's not going to help. I'm going to have to work around her."

"She's the DON. How are you going to do that?" Casey asked.

"That's why I need your help."

Casey took another drag from her cigarette, "And what do you want from me?"

"Just be fair. And understand my job is to bring Medicare into Central City. That's why I was hired. You don't have to be disloyal to Violet."

"And how am I fair to you and not disloyal to her?"

"That's going to be difficult for you. But I think you're smart enough to understand the demographics of this hospital have to change whether it's me or the next administrator. Sooner or later you're going to have to choose."

"And how do I know you won't fill every bed with a problem and then move on?"

"I promise I won't bring in any patients in here the staff can't handle."

"They're going to need training," Casey emphasized.

"I'll get it."

"You brought in a couple of tough patients already."

"But the staff handled them. I think given half a chance they'll be able do a lot better than what they've done in the past," Ned said.

"You may be right," she answered.

Casey didn't say anything else. She just kept smoking her cigarette.

"Please think about it," Ned said.

Ned decided to leave Casey out behind the hospital.

"Think about it seriously, Casey," Ned said.

He went back inside the facility. Ned knew as soon as he was out of sight Casey could have a nip from the little bottle of vodka she had in the pocket of her nursing uniform. As he closed the door behind him, Ned gave one more look over his shoulder. Casey was sipping the vodka from that little bottle. Trusting her would be another big gamble. But again, Ned didn't really have any better choice.

Ned went back to his office. He picked up a bag he had brought with him to work that day. He took the bag, left his office and went by nursing station one and grabbed two plastic cups off the med cart. He went out onto the non-smoker's patio. Maggie Pembroke was sitting in a chair reading a book. Ned put the bag on the table next to her.

"What are you reading?" Ned asked.

"A bloody romance novel, it's as close as I can get to the real thing."

"Can't find anyone in here?"

"They're either half dead or balmy."

"Considering the sorry state of your romantic prospects in Central City, which I must apologize for, I have decided to enhance your psychological wellbeing."

Ned opened the bag and took out a pint of Plymouth Gin, a lime and a bottle of Fever Tree Tonic. Ned handed her the plastic cups. "Would you please hold these, Maggie?" Ned asked as he used his penknife to cut the lime in half.

Maggie watched Ned assemble the libations. She was as delighted as a child being handed a Christmas present by Santa himself. "And look at that, Plymouth Gin. You are a darling boy!"

Ned completed the gin and tonics and they 'clicked' the plastic cups.

"Cheers!' Ned said.

She sipped her drink. It was heaven! "Oh… that is bloody wonderful!"

Ned sipped his drink. "This is our little secret, Maggie. If one person finds out about this..."

"My lips are sealed," she said with a smile. She drew her fingers across her lips as if she were closing a zipper.

When they finished their cocktails, Ned left Maggie and made rounds. As he was heading into the dining room he passed by Dr. Zucker's room. The door was open. Amy Lee was visiting. Ned knocked on the door and entered. "Hi, Dr. Zucker, and Amy," Ned said.

"It sounds like you know me but, sorry, I can't remember who you are," Zucker laughed.

"I'm Ned the administrator."

"Did you meet Amy? She's one of my students."

"Grad assistant," she gently corrected him.

"Yes, we met," Ned said.

"Since I'm going to be here 'til I get better, Amy is going to get me a few things that I need. Isn't that sweet of her?" Zucker said.

"Just sign it. I'll fill in the rest," Amy said as she handed Zucker his checkbook as innocently as if she were giving him a girl scout cookie.

"What do you need? Maybe I can help," Ned said to Zucker.

"I don't know, I forgot." Zucker laughed.

"I'm going to get him a few personal things I know he likes," Amy said.

"That's very kind of you," Ned said.

"I'll stop by later, Doc, I'll let you two visit," Ned left Zucker's room.

A red flag went up for Ned. He was always a bit suspicious when it came to a patient with cognitive problems signing a blank check. There were too many stories of that kindly old nurse who took care of Uncle Buddy with those warm, soothing, genital-rubbing baths for years who made him cookies and along the way managed to clean out Uncle Buddy's bank account. And after he passed-on that kindly cookie-baking care giver presented a new will to Buddy's children that turned over his house to her. Ned decided to keep a watchful eye on Dr. Zucker's friend, Amy.

Walking back through the dining room, Ned was stopped by the miracle of salvation that was taking place right in the heart of Koreatown.

"You are saved! Praise, Jesus!" The black minister proclaimed as he saved one of Ned's patients by pouring water over their head.

The minister had set up a portable piece of the Jordan River in the middle of the dining room. The river was a fiberglass tub about four feet by four feet by a foot deep. It was about half full of water and had a plastic palm tree attached to one of the corners. Along with the plastic palm, there was an almost life-sized mechanical John the Baptist. John was actually a repurposed Santa Claus that was stripped of his red coat and made to look like the desert prophet. The mechanical John "Ho-Ho-Hoed" and waved one of his arms whenever the minister saved another soul. The whole process of salvation was quite entertaining.

"In the name of Jesus I baptize you!" The minister proclaimed.

"Amen," sputtered out from the few wheelchair bound patients in the line gathered there to be saved.

As a safety precaution, Sharon positioned two CNAs close by the tub. They were firmly holding onto the just saved and the about to be saved patients. Their job was to prevent the patients from falling, thus insuring the miracle of salvation rather than a broken hip and a trip to the hospital.

Ned watched and realized that for as absurd as the whole plastic Jordan River saving extravaganza might seem to a casual observer, for the patients, it was in its own way the possibility of hope. Most of Ned's patients knew Central City was the last part of their journey in this life. For them, the notion that they could shed the trappings of a nursing home for a better existence was too delicious an idea to relinquish.

"Where did you find this guy?" Ned asked Sharon.

"He's been around for years. But John the Baptist is new," she replied.

Ned watched the minister pray, pour water and save another patient from eternal damnation.

"You want to get in line?" Sharon asked Ned.

"No, I'm afraid if I get saved by that guy, Jesus might just strike me down dead. I was raised Catholic. Even being in the same room with him puts me in danger," Ned said.

Ned wondered if maybe he should get in line and risk the wrath of the Catholic Jesus. He knew he needed a small miracle to bring Casey over to his side and solve his problems with Violet. Giving up on the saving, Ned headed back to his office. As he walked by a nursing station he saw one of his old doctor buddies from the Westside, Dr. Pierre Melville. He was sitting at the station signing charts.

Dr. Pierre Melville was one of those rare doctors who at his age, deep in his sixties, hadn't burned out. Physicians who worked the nursing home circuit weren't the plastic surgeons from Beverly Hills. That group fixed noses and enlarged breasts for the big money. That group of doctors drove Mercedes. The nursing home circuit doctors were more the Toyota or Ford guys. Ned chose to call them lunch-pail-docs.

Pierre hardly looked like a physician that could make even the lunch-pail-docs team. His hair was too long and hardly combed. He always wore a shirt that looked like it was never pressed since the day he bought it from the outlet store. His tie was loosened with the last six lunches he had eaten proudly displayed on it. But in truth, he was a hell of a good physician. He had earned his degree at the Sorbonne in Paris. He graduated first in his class. His practice included a large number of patients that no one else would touch. Either they were without good insurance or they were serious behavior problems. The first time Ned went to Pierre's office, when he started at Sea Breeze, he saw a plaque on the wall in his waiting room naming him one of the best one hundred physicians in the United States. The honor was given to him by American Medical Association. Dr. Pierre Melville was the kind of doctor that ends up with a street named after him for all the good works he had done in the course of his career.

"What are you doing on this side of town?" Ned asked.

Dr. Melville looked up from his charting. He was surprised and happy to see Ned. "Ned! I could ask you the same question," the doctor responded. His speech was accented with a thick combination of Israeli and French.

"I decided the sea air in Santa Monica wasn't good for my asthma. I decided to come down here and breathe in some car fumes. They get somebody to replace me over there?" Ned asked.

"Yeah, a young guy, he's a new graduate out of USC," Melville responded.

"How's he doing?" Ned inquired.

Melville shrugged, "He hasn't taken me to lunch so I haven't graded him yet."

"How long have you been here?" Melville asked.

"Since I left Sea Breeze. How many patients you have?"

"I think five," Melville responded.

"You have three, Doctor Melville," the charge nurse sitting next to Melville responded.

Pierre shrugged his shoulders, "Then I have three."

"You want more?" Ned asked.

"That would be nice."

"I'll get you a few more patients. That will make the trip down here a little easier to take."

"Are you looking for patients?" Melville asked.

"Always, especially if they're Medicare," Ned responded.

"I have one ready to come out of the hospital. They don't want him back in Santa Monica."

"How come?" Ned asked.

"He doesn't like to pee in toilets he prefers the corner of whatever room he's in," Melville said with a smile.

"Does he have any Medicare days left?"

"Yes. I think so."

"Anything else I need to know about this guy?" Ned asked.

Other than the peeing problem, he's not going to cause you any trouble."

"The peeing problem will be enough. If he has days, I'll take him. And thanks. You need a coffee or anything?" Ned asked.

"No, I'm fine," Melville said.

"Come back here at lunch next time and we'll go to the best Jewish deli in the city," Ned said.

"I know, Langer's, best pastrami west of New York," Melville added.

"I'll buy," Ned said as he walked down the hall toward his office.

Langer's Deli had been an LA landmark since 1947. It's an old world Jewish deli. Those that care about gastronomy, like Ned, say the #19 is the best sandwich in the world.

EX WIVES MAKE THE BEST FRIENDS

After work Ned went to meet Katie at Smitty's. She was at the bar waiting for him. Katie was Ned's age with natural platinum hair that she kept short. She had flawless skin and an athletic body that easily made her look just this side of forty. Ned stayed in the doorway for a moment and watched Katie. He always saw her as beautiful. Ned knew the greatest mistake of his life was mucking up his marriage and letting her go. He slid into the stool next to his ex, gave her a kiss on the cheek and grabbed a handful of the house chips. Ned signaled to the bartender. "Grey Goose martini, three Sicilian olives."

"How's the new job?" Katie asked.

"Not as good as the old one, but it'll do for now."

"Koreatown? What did you suddenly develop a taste for kimchi? Why did you go down there? It's like homeless central."

"I have bills to pay. You ought to know, you're one of them."

"You know I would have waited if you got in a bind."

"I know that. But do you think UCLA would wait for our daughter's tuition? I didn't want to have to explain to Amelie she'd be going to Pasadena City College this semester. This job came along and I took it. It's only temporary. How's the bank treating you?"

The bartender brought Ned his martini. Ned took a sip and ate one of the olives and a few chips.

"They keep threatening to send me to Santa Barbara to run Ventura County."

"Will that be a big promotion?"

"No, it's more a horizontal than vertical move."

"Yes, but you can live on a boat in the harbor. Doesn't that sound romantic? Just make sure it's big enough so I can come up and visit you on the weekends."

"Living on a boat sounds like when we went 'glamping' and you rented that giant silver potato…"

"You mean the Airstream trailer."

"Remember how that turned out?"

"We dumped the trailer after two days and stayed in a hotel. It was a learning experience. We learned 'glamping' wasn't for us."

"No thanks. I'm going to stay in LA," Katie said.

"Are you hungry? I'm going to get the meatloaf," Ned said.

"You always get the meatloaf. Why don't you branch out I heard their pot pie here is delicious."

"Katie, there's only one pot pie on this planet worth eating and you make it."

FRIDAY PHONE CALLS ARE THE ALWAYS THE WORST

On the following Friday, Ned answered a call from Jose. "Boss, you have a call from corporate."

Ned pressed the button on his phone, "Ned Russo."

"Ned, this is Saul."

"Hi Saul, what can I do for you?"

I wonder if you could bring Sueann Stennis down here to corporate.

"Sure, when?" Ned asked.

"Now."

Ned looked at his watch. He knew a Friday afternoon at three o'clock come to corporate meeting was trouble. "Ok. I'll be right over."

Ned ended the call with Saul and punched in Sueann's extension. She answered, "Business office."

"Sueann, I just got a call from corporate. Saul wants us to come to over, now," Ned said.

"Why?" she asked.

"I don't know. I'll meet you in the garage. I'll drive."

Along with Jesus, Ned had always had bad luck on a Friday. But when he thought logically about it, he came to the conclusion that he hadn't been at Central City long enough to be fired. But still, going to see the chief financial officer at the end of the work week had to be trouble. He picked up his keys, took the sports jacket he kept hanging on the back of his door, just for these impromptu meetings at corporate, and headed for the parking lot.

When they pulled out from the underground parking garage at Central City Sueann was quiet. Ned could sense maybe she was even a little nervous. Ned had no clue what he was heading into. He didn't like that feeling at all. "You have any idea what this is about?" Ned asked Sueann.

"No," she didn't say another word for the entire drive.

Ned pulled up to the parking attendant's booth. It was filled with dense white smoke. The sliding door opened and Chang, a Chinese gentleman, poked his head out of the cloud. He was puffing away on an electronic cigarette. With each puff, he put a new cumulus cloud into LA's atmosphere.

"Hi, I'm Ned Russo from Central City. We're here to see Saul."

An arm came out of the white smoke. "Park over there," Chang said. Then the arm disappeared back into his smoke-filled booth. Ned parked in one of the few spaces marked for visitors. They got on the elevator and went up to Saul's office.

Saul's office was the antithesis of Ned's. The furniture was new, Danish Modern. There were two leather and chrome chairs in front of his glass and chrome desk. Lyle was sitting in of one the chairs. "Thanks for coming over on such short notice," Saul said with a smile.

Lyle turned in his chair and spoke to Sueann, "Sueann, I wonder if you could give us a couple of minutes. Why don't you get a cup of coffee in the conference room. Jeanie will show you where it is. Ned and I have a couple of things to go over."

"Ok," Sueann said with a kind of nervous smile. She left Saul's office.

When Saul was sure Sueann was out of hearing range, Saul's voice deepened. His brow furrowed. "We have a problem. Central City's patient trust accounts are well…fucked up."

"What do you mean?" Ned asked. There was part of Ned that was relieved. Whatever the issue it probably didn't involve him directly.

"Money is missing," Saul responded.

"Are you talking about mistakes in accounting?" Ned asked.

"No. It's bigger than that," Lyle said.

"There's a paper trail of court dates and meetings with conservators, family members, purchases of personal items like TVs and computers for various patients. There's a couple of pre-purchased burial plots, a full on funeral service, and even an after the funeral party at the Rib Shack," Saul said.

"I know that place. It's down by USC," Ned interrupted.

"None of which happened," Lyle said.

"Not even the funerals? Are you absolutely sure?" Ned asked.

"We're sure. When we got a feeling something was wrong a few months ago, we had a forensic accountant go through Sueann's books. She did a great job creating all the necessary paper. All of it was bullshit. And none of my people caught it," Saul said.

"Hold on. Are you saying she embezzled money?" Ned caught himself. "I sound like an idiot. Of course, that's what you're saying."

"It looks that way," Saul responded.

Ned was thunderstruck, "Wow!"

"This has been going on for years," Saul said.

"How many years?" Ned asked.

"About twelve," Saul responded.

"Twelve! And you guys didn't catch it?"

"She was very good at cooking the books, and she was a trusted, long term employee. So nobody looked very hard. What can I say, we fucked up," Saul said.

"Well, I guess that trusted, long term employee thing worked out. How much are we talking about?" Ned asked.

"About a hundred and fifty," Saul said.

"Thousand!" Ned blurted out.

"She's been taking it in drips and drabs," Saul added.

"A hundred and fifty thousand! Are you kidding me? You see how she dresses? It's obvious she's not spending it on clothes. I'm used to the kitchen staff stealing a box of chicken wings or a tub of ice cream now and then, but a hundred and fifty K…Jesus!" Ned was incredulous.

"Now we need your help," Saul said.

"My help? Don't you have a policy about stealing somewhere in the employee handbook?" Ned asked wryly.

Lyle interjected. "We would like to keep this a Central City problem."

Ned slid back in the Danish Modern chair, wanting to escape what he knew was coming. "Why do I get the feeling I'm not going to like what's next," Ned said.

"We got our heads together with the attorneys and feel we have come up with a solution that we think will work for everybody," Lyle handed Ned a document. "Take a look at it. I think you'll agree this is the best solution."

Ned began to read the document. It became obvious what was going on. The corporation wanted this whole embezzlement thing to go away. If an employee was stealing money for a decade and the people that were supposed to catch it didn't in all that time, the corporation looked like idiots or worse. Maybe they were hiding something, or a lot of somethings. And maybe some ambitious Department of Justice investigator would start to go through the books in every one of the corporation's other facilities. Just having the DOJ around for months snooping into everything would give everyone at corporate a wicked case of hemorrhoids. Sooner or later the DOJ would find something. After all, there is a little dirt under every corporation's fingernails. The perfect solution was to have Sueann pay back everything she had stolen, interest free. Then she would resign, quietly, of course. The corporation would back-fill the missing money. Sueann would even get a tepid letter of recommendation so she could move onto her next job and start stealing there, preferably in another state. Everything would be nice and neat and no one the wiser…no one but Ned.

Ned finished reading the document. He looked over at Lyle.

"Don't you agree this is the best way out for all of us…even Sueann. We don't want this to become fodder for the LA Times. Get her to sign it, Ned, and we'll all move on." Lyle got up.

"I'm going to see Mr. M now. I'm going to tell him this problem has been solved, by you," Lyle smiled and pointed his finger at Ned. "I promise you this won't go unnoticed by the people upstairs. You'll get a lot of points for making this work," Lyle left the room.

"The ball's in your court," Saul said.

The corporation had just put Ned right in the middle of a very awkward situation. Here he was, the ink was hardly dry on his new contract and he had to cover up misappropriation of funds made by the business office manager. Ned could almost see the state regulation where it's clearly written that misappropriation of funds must be reported to the DHS. After all, it is a crime. Ned toyed with the idea that he could always say "no." This wasn't his mess why should he have to clean it up. Then his car payment, mortgage, Amelie's tuition and the rest of his monthly nut got the best of him. He had bills to pay and he didn't want to lose a job he just started. How would that look on his resume? Ned could see himself at his next interview trying to explain to some version of Lyle how he did the noble thing and threw his previous employer under the bus. That would be a real plus to get a job. Ned would carry corporate's water because he really didn't have another choice. If he didn't, they would just get somebody else to do it. And then they would decide Ned wasn't a team player.

Ned left Saul's office and walked to the conference room. Sueann was sitting at the far end of the large table sipping a latte. Concern was written all over her face. Ned smiled and said nothing to her. He went to the expensive, restaurant quality, latte machine that was set up in the corner. He really didn't want to drink anything but he was buying himself a little time. He was deciding how to present the offer Lyle had given to him to pass onto Sueann. Then the espresso machine turned against him. It was one of those complicated machines that could make as many variations as a Starbucks by just pressing the right series of buttons. Ned struggled with the choices until he found latte. The whole time he fumbled with the machine, he was trying to figure out how he was going to get this conversation with Sueann started. He kept smiling as he looked over to her.

"These things are complicated aren't they?" he said.

"You need help? I know how to make it work. I have one just like it at home," she responded.

Ned now knew where some of the stolen money went. Suddenly, the machine came to life.

"Ah, here we go," Ned said.

His cup filled and walked over and sat down next to Sueann. He sat there for a moment going through his next move like Bobby Fisher planning his checkmate at one of his matches. Ned decided to use one of his favorite tricks when trying to illicit the truth out of one of his employees. It was a law school trick his brother Michael taught him.

"Sueann, do you know what makes a good lawyer?" Ned asked.

"No, I don't think so," she responded somewhat nervously.

"A good lawyer never asks a question he doesn't know the answer to."

"Oh, that's smart. But if he already knows the answer, why would he ask the question?"

Her response caught Ned off guard. "Uh…it's a tactic lawyers use to get to the truth. Now I'm going to ask you a question, a very important question. And I want you to be honest with me."

"All right," she said nervously.

Ned took a deep breath, "Did you ever take money from the patient trust accounts?"

Sueann blanched. Her eyes glazed over and her mouth dropped open. Finally, she spoke, "No, I would never…"

Ned cut her off, "Sueann, Saul says that you stole thousands of dollars. They have proof and are ready to prosecute you. Do you understand what that means? You'll be looking at a lot of jail time."

"Oh my God!"

"Did you take the money?" he asked her again firmly.

"No," she fired back.

"They hired an accountant who went through your books. He said you've been stealing money for years. Is it true?" Ned growled at her like a prosecutor grilling a reluctant witness.

"Yes," she started to cry. "I'm sorry," and then she sobbed.

Suddenly, gone was Ned's Javert. The evil French investigator was instantly replaced by the kindly bishop who gave the hounded Jean Valjean the candle sticks which was the break he needed so he wouldn't end up back in that horrific French prison. Ned fumbled through his jacket pocket and pulled out a crumpled tissue. He handed it to her, "Here."

She took the tissue and dabbed her eyes and blew her nose. But the tears kept flowing.

"Calm down. There's a solution to this," Ned said.

"What solution? I'm going to go to jail," she sobbed.

"Well, maybe you don't have to," he said.

Suddenly she stopped crying. "What? I thought you said…"

Ned spoke to her in as priestly a tone as he could muster, "The corporation doesn't want to put you in jail. You made a mistake. We all make mistakes. I admit yours was a big one. They want this whole matter to go away."

"How?" she was puzzled.

"You're going to have to resign, of course, and give the money back," Ned said.

"I don't have any money. I spent it all."

"They've worked out a payment plan. It seems reasonable," Ned said.

"But I hardly make enough now. That's why I took the money in the first place," she said.

Ned thought for a moment, "Well, you can get a second job."

"Doing what?" she asked.

"There's a lot of things I bet you can do."

"But it's a lot of money to pay back," she lamented.

Ned cleared his throat, he was embarrassed by what he was going to propose, "I know of one job where you can make a lot of money on a regular basis," he said.

"What is it?" she inquired.

"You have a nice speaking voice. You can do phone sex at night. I understand it's quite lucrative."

She was taken aback, "Phone sex? How do you know about that?" her tone changed from fright and fear to disgust.

"I had a patient at my last hospital. He was having phone sex every day. He ran up a bill of four thousand dollars in one month. The only way we caught him was when the bill came. Every night he told the nurses he was talking to his mother," Ned shook his head, "...and they believed him."

Ned handed the document Lyle gave him and gave it to Sueann, "Take a look at it and sign it and this whole thing will be settled."

She started to read it then she looked at Ned, "I think maybe I should have a lawyer look at this."

Ned's Javert instantly returned, "Lawyer? Did you hear the part about them prosecuting you and jail? The first thing any lawyer you talk to is going to want is five or ten thousand dollars. You have that amount of cash handy?" Ned asked.

"No," she said.

"Then sign the damn paper so we can go back to Central City and you can clean out your desk and go home," Ned handed her a pen. She took it and signed the document.

Ned delivered the signed document to Saul. He received the obligatory thank you along with a handshake. Saul reminded Ned that getting this done would not be forgotten. As Ned shook Saul's hand he thought of the immortal words of Harry Truman commenting about Richard Nixon: "He's a no good dirty son-of-a-bitch."

Ned didn't think those words applied to Saul or Lyle, he was thinking about himself.

During the funeral like ride back to Central City Ned turned to Sueann. She was stone cold sober, "Why did you do it?" Ned asked.

She sat there for a long time before she responded, "It was too easy not to."

Ned didn't wait for Sueann to clean out her desk as he was supposed to. There was protocol about firing. The employee who was whacked was to be watched so they couldn't take anything that could hurt the corporation. They were then to hand over their keys and be escorted to the parking lot where their last act was to hand over their garage gate opener. The whole staff would be watching. It was a dignity dumping moment even for a thief like Sueann. Ned allowed her to just slip away. As for her taking documents that might be embarrassing to the corporation, anything she took would only open the door to her prosecution and Ned was sure the forensic accountant had the originals anyway. Ned slipped out of the facility before Sueann. He didn't want to explain anything. He didn't want to talk to anybody. He just wanted a beer and a pizza.

RYE AND A CHERRY

Four nights a week Ned took the 110 freeway out of downtown to his home in Pasadena. On Fridays he treated himself and went up Alvarado Street to the Glendale Freeway and got off in Eagle Rock where he ordered a pizza from a little joint, Casablanca. The sausage and pepper pizza, Ned's favorite, made there was acceptable but nothing like the pies he could get back in Rhode Island. But on this Friday night after the incident with Sueann, that drive up Alvarado was out of the way and Ned was in no mood. He took the 110 to South Pasadena and Bristol Farms. That was his favorite grocery market. He bought a frozen pizza and a six pack and a quart of Alden's double dark chocolate ice cream.

Since his divorce from wife-two, Katie, his social life was less than zero. He tried a few dating sights but they were scams. The best he could hope for on this Friday night was a good fight or a decent movie on HBO. It turned out the pizza tasted like cardboard and HBO didn't come to his rescue. Ned just ate most of the ice cream and went to bed.

On Saturday morning Ned got up early. His part in the terminating of Sueann pretty much kept him awake all night. He didn't like firing people. It damaged a little part of him every time he had to do it. Even though Sueann needed to be fired, Ned didn't like the way he was dragged into it. At first light Ned went for a three-mile run around the Rose Bowl. That run was a very popular spot to stretch ones' legs. There were dozens of people running, walking, pushing baby strollers or leading their dogs around this Pasadena landmark. And if Ned got lucky, he could run behind some in-shape young thing in tight short-shorts and watch her backside for the whole three miles. On this particular Saturday morning there were very few good-looking bottoms to look at so all Ned got was a workout.

Ned was, by nature, a morning person. He liked the quiet of the early dawn. It allowed him the solitude to think. Mostly, he thought about the mistakes he made and how he would have done things differently. But that was Ned being dishonest with himself. In the pit of his stomach he knew all the turns he made in life were conscious. There was no reason to blame anyone. He was right where he was at this minute because he allowed it to be that way. Yes, he knew some of his choices were at best stupid, but they were his choices. Going forward, what he wanted was to be a mench, a good guy, to his family and his friends. He knew his dedication to his job was pushing the bounds of unhealthy. More than one shrink told him that. But as Ned shaved every morning he knew his job was all he had that kept him from despair. And he knew when the day came that he had to give it up, he would go through the deepest emotional crisis of his life. But like most people, Ned kicked that can down the road. He hoped way down the road.

When Ned came back from his run he checked the sprinklers in his yard. He made sure the gates worked and then he hosed out the garbage pails. All things he hated to do. As he surveyed his property he saw there was a dead rat on the roof. "How did you get up there?" Ned asked the rat. Ned got the ladder out of the garage and removed the rodent's corpse.

Ned was just the opposite of his father and brother, John and Mike could fix anything and enjoyed tinkering around the house. When Katie and Ned broke up, she wanted a new life. Ned couldn't blame her so they came to an agreement. She signed the house over to Ned, and he gave her the equivalent amount in cash. In a way it was kind of Shakespearean. Ned was cash poor, but the thing he hated most, anything to do with having to maintain a property, rich.

After disposing of the rat, Ned dusted and vacuumed. He kept promising himself he'd hire a cleaning lady but when it got down to it, he was just too frugal to spend the hundred bucks a week to have somebody do the chores for him.

At about noon he called Rose and spent the usual five minutes finding out who died and how her bingo game was going. The highlight of his weekend would be the steak he'd barbecue and rest of the chocolate ice cream he didn't finish from his Friday night dinner. When he was done with his obligatory morning chores he went to Bristol Farms to buy his steak.

Bristol Farms is one of those specialty grocery stores where the produce and meats are the best and the prices are the highest. Ned got himself a rib-eye and decided to buy a more expensive than usual bottle of cabernet. After all, it was the weekend. Food was the one place Ned splurged. As he picked out a bottle from Napa Valley, he heard a woman talking. She was just steps away from him. She was on her cell. She was a beautiful black woman. Ned guessed in her forties. She had salt and pepper hair that shot out of her head in thousands of tiny, elongated curls. Her fire-engine red lipstick outlined a delicious mouth. Ned noticed she was smartly dressed for a Saturday morning in the grocery store.

"I'll get a bottle of Crown Royal and do I need anything else to make a Manhattan? Hello? Jane?" she looked at her cell phone. It had just died. "Shoot!" she blurted out.

Ned watched as she went over to a Bristol Farms' employee who was stocking wine onto a shelf.

"Can you help me, please?" she asked.

"Sure, what do you need?" the employee responded.

"Can you tell me…"

Just then the PA system blurted out… "Manny, please come to the manager's booth."

Manny, the employee the pretty black lady was talking to, responded instantly, "That's for me. Can you give me a minute and I promise I'll be right back and get you what you need." Manny left for the front of the store.

"I don't have a minute," she said as the employee disappeared out of the liquor department.

The woman looked around. She was obviously in a hurry. The only other person in the liquor department was Ned. "I wonder if you can help me. Do you know how to make a Manhattan? I hate to bother you but my battery just died," she said apologetically.

The woman held up her dead phone for Ned to see. As if proving she was telling the truth.

"See…"

"You use rye whiskey for Manhattans, and you need cherries and you also need bitters and sweet vermouth," Ned said to her.

"Not Crown Royal?" she asked.

"Purists use rye whiskey," Ned said.

"Are you a bartender?"

"No. I just know how to make a Manhattan," Ned said.

"Ok, thank you," she said.

There was that awkward moment when Ned wanted to say something else but didn't. He pushed his cart out of the liquor department and went on with his shopping.

That night after he consumed his steak and his cabernet, he finished off the last of the double dark chocolate ice cream. His social interaction involved watching a featherweight fight on HBO. The fight was boring. Ned liked to watch big men pound it out as they stood toe to toe. Watching featherweights go at it was like watching two flies trapped in a mason jar dancing around in circles trying to get out. Ned's mind wandered. He was sorry he didn't try and strike up a conversation with that good-looking black woman in Bristol Farms.

Maybe it would have come to nothing…but who knows? He wondered.

The following Monday, Ned drove to work a little early. The cute hooker who was a permanent fixture on the corner next to Central City waved to him. He smiled and waved back. He entered the parking garage. The two kitchen workers he caught drinking beer on his first day were there but drinking Coke instead. They greeted him pleasantly.

"Good morning, Mr. Ned," one of them said.

They he showed Ned the can of Coke. "See, Coke, no beer."

"Good morning. Coke is good. Pepsi is better."

Ned couldn't resist. One of the kitchen workers was caught flat footed by Ned's comment. "How's the kitchen today?" Ned asked.

"Everything is good," they both replied.

"Great!" Ned said.

Ned climbed the stairs and entered the hospital. Central City was light years better looking and smelling than it was when Ned first came to the facility. Ned walked through the lobby. The usual wheelchair suspects were there. "Good morning, everybody," Ned said.

None of the patients responded. Steven, the candy salesman managed a wave.

"Good morning, Jose."

He opened the reception window with his gloved hand. "Good morning, Boss."

Then he added pointing to a man sitting in the lobby. "That's Angel Sanchez. He's here from corporate."

"Angel? Come in," Ned said.

Ned entered his office with Angel Sanchez in tow.

"Sit down," Ned said, "What can I do for you?"

Angel sat down, "Saul sent me over. He said your Business Office Manager resigned. I'm going to fill in until you replace her."

"Wonderful!" Ned said.

"Go see Jose. He's the one wearing the yellow kitchen gloves."

"Yeah, I noticed that," Angel said a bit confused.

"He'll set you up," Ned said.

Angel left Ned's office.

This was going to be a good week. Ned thought to himself. Angel was a positive sign that corporate was paying back a little of the debt they owed him for the Sueann debacle. Out of the corner of his eye Ned watched Michael Weller, one of his patients, through the window. Weller drove his electric wheelchair out of the lobby and down the street.

I wonder where he goes every day? Ned asked himself.

Ned turned to his computer and started deleting the dozens of emails that filled his 'in- box.' Ned never even bothered to open them. The ones he had to read were from corporate. And there was one from his first ex-wife, Ann. He'd answer that one with a phone call. He punched in her number on his cellphone, "Hello Ann. It's Ned."

"Thank you for getting back to me so quickly."

"Sure, no problem. What can I do for you?"

"I had a little accident in the parking lot of Ralph's yesterday," she said concerned.

Ned cut her off, "Are you ok?"

“I’m fine. My car has a scratch and so does the other car. I couldn’t find the driver of the other car so I put a note on the windshield. I just wanted you to know,” she said not quite knowing what Ned’s response would be.

“Long as you’re ok. I’ll call the insurance company. Don’t worry about it,” he said.

“Oh, thank you! Thank you! I’ll let you go back to running your hospital.”

“Ok, Ann. I’ll call you soon.”

He hung up the phone.

Ann once said of Ned, “He’s a much better ex-husband than he ever was a husband.”

That statement was absolutely the truth. Ned went out of his way to be on good terms with both his ex’s. He never argued with them or held anything from them. He went out of his way to give them more than they asked for. He knew the reason he was divorced had nothing to do with them. It was his fault. They were both good wives. There’s a country song that has a lyric: ‘I need someone to cheat on.’ That was Ned’s motto through both his marriages. It’s not like he didn’t love his wives, he did, but Ned had this hole in his ego that they just couldn’t fill. So Ned kept trying to fill it with other women. Now he was alone. Most of the time, he preferred it that way. But being alone is being alone. And that meant steak for one and ice cream you don’t share.

PLASTIC CORDS HOLD THE MAYO

Benito, the maintenance super, came into Ned's office.

"Mr. Ned. I have this problem," he said quite concerned.

Benito took out his cell phone and showed Ned a picture of a frayed electrical cord. "This the wire in Juan Estrada's room," Benito said.

Ned looked at the picture, "Is that an extension cord?" he asked.

"Mr. Ned, the CNA say he chew the cord."

"Are you sure?"

"Well, that what she told me," Benito responded.

"Go and take everything that's attached to a cord out of the room now. And find a way to cover the electrical outlets," Ned instructed.

Benito left Ned's office. Ned picked up the phone and punched in Anthony's number.

"Yes."

"Anthony, get a one-on-one for Estrada. He's chewing the electrical cords in his room. Then come to stand-up."

"Ok," Anthony said.

Ned arrived at the stand-up meeting a few minutes late. The chatter that Ned heard just outside the conference room door stopped immediately when he entered the room. All Ned's department heads looked at him. Their faces radiated concern. He took his usual seat at the head of the conference table. He opened his agenda binder he had prepared for the meeting. Ned looked around the table. This morning even Violet showed up, but Violet wasn't there for the meeting, her spies at corporate had told her what happened with Milaney and Sueann, Violet was there to twist the truth to her advantage. When Ned saw her, he knew she was there to find a way to blame Ned for the firings. Firing two department heads is a big deal. The people in that room were hardly able to swallow the news about Milaney getting fired and now suddenly they heard about Sueann. Ned understood the vibe that was going through the room. They all wondered if Ned was the hatchet man for the corporation who was going to get rid of more of them.

"Well, you're a grim looking bunch today," Ned said trying to add a little levity into the meeting. It didn't work.

"Two of the people that have been here are gone. One of them was here for a long time. Some of us are concerned," Dylan said.

Ned wondered if he should skirt the issue of the terminations or take it head on. He decided to get right into it. He closed the agenda binder,

"Two department heads were let go. I'm responsible for one of them. The other was done by corporate. Milaney wasn't doing what was needed to turn this facility around. That was my call. The other was a case of violation of company policy. Don't ask me to get into the details 'cause it's nobody's business."

"There are all kinds of rumors floating around," Dylan said.

Ned cut him off, "I don't listen to rumors."

"You can understand that some of the people in this room are a little nervous," Violet interjected.

"If you do your job there's no reason to be," Ned said.

"How do we know that?" Violet asked, her voice filled with provocation.

"I wasn't hired to clean house. I was hired to rebuild it," Ned said.

Anthony entered the meeting. Ned used the moment to hopefully change the tone of the meeting.

"For those of you who haven't already met him this is Anthony, our new DSD."

Anthony didn't say anything he just nodded to the others gathered in the room. There was hardly a reaction. Since all the chairs were filled Anthony found a space to stand against the wall. Violet saw an opening to get a shot at Ned and keep the tension in the room high.

"Weren't you the DSD at Glen Haven? I heard you had some staff problems over there," Violet said.

"Yeah," Anthony answered.

Violet knew full well about the issues Anthony had at his other facility, her network of spies filled her in on the details the day Anthony arrived at Central City. The CNAs at Glen Haven repeatedly called corporate and complained that Anthony was following them around, trying to find a reason to fire them. It wasn't true, but Violet saw the opportunity to use it against Ned anyway.

Before Anthony answered Ned jumped into the conversation, "Corporate suggested Anthony for the DSD position here at Central City. I met with him and I agreed with their call. I believe he's going to be positive addition to our team."

"We'll see," Violet said with a defiant smirk.

"Bringing Anthony here was my call. I get to do that. Much as it annoys you, Violet, I'm the administrator."

Ned looked around the room at the faces of his department heads. What he saw was worry and concern. He decided to push past it and get on with the business of running Central City.

"Now that the soap opera portion of the meeting is over how about we get into the stats?" Ned said as he reopened his binder. "Freddie, how many Medicare do we have today?"

Realizing he had missed something important, Ned interrupted Freddie before he could even get started with the daily statistics. "Oh, Mr. Estrada is chewing the electrical cords in his room. Anthony did you put a CNA one-on-one with Mr. Estrada?"

Anthony gave Ned the thumbs up.

"Good," Ned turned to Violet.

"And Violet I want your nurses to check on Mr. Estrada every half hour until we get him out of here. I want the times they check on him noted. Put the original in the chart and bring me a copy."

Violet didn't respond to Ned's request. Ned prompted her a second time. "Violet, did you hear me?"

"Yes, I heard you," she snapped back. Then she added, "We wouldn't have to have to go through all this trouble with that patient if we never admitted him in the first place."

"That's true," Ned responded, "I'm sure you would have found a way to keep his bed empty."

"I think an empty bed is better than a suicidal patient," she insisted.

"Well, if you'd like to go out marketing with Dylan perhaps the two of you can bring back some better patients. How about a couple of knee or hip replacements for the rehab department? I'm confident you can find patients who won't chew the electrical cords."

Ned turned to Dylan, "Dylan, since you're his buddy, why don't you call Dr. Kovani and inform him we're going to send Mr. Estrada back to Rothman before he electrocutes himself. Tell the good doctor if he can get enough drugs into Mr. Estrada to stabilize him so he loses his appetite for electricity, we'll take him back."

Violet was incredulous upon hearing Ned's words, "You would take him back?" she said.

"As long as we can control him, yes, I'll take him back," Ned answered.

"That's a dangerous and a reckless thing to do," Violet angrily argued.

"Difficult patients in skilled nursing facilities are a fact of life," Ned said.

Violet was furious. "You're running this facility right into the ground!" she commented.

By now Violet would have established her dominance over the new administrator. But it was obvious Ned wasn't going to cower before her. She sat there as long as she could, her blood boiling. When she couldn't stand it any longer, she got up and stormed out of the meeting. The room was dead silent as they all watched Violet leave. All the department heads were pasty faced, as if they had just witnessed a hanging.

"Is it just me or does Violet just have a habit of leaving meetings early," Ned said.

After the rest of the department heads sighed in relief that the meeting didn't end with blood on the floor, the stand-up meeting dragged on. Ned went back to his agenda, "Ok Freddie, how about those Medicare numbers."

Freddie nervously blurted out the current stats as Ned looked around the room at his department heads. Ned was more concerned with how the people he was looking at would absorb the obvious war he was engaged in with Violet and the dismissal of Sueann and Milaney than the daily stats. He wondered about his staff's gut feelings. Who would they bet on? The safe bet was Violet. Ned knew the only reason Violet showed up at the meeting was she saw the chance to poison the well for him. He was sure Violet was busily spreading rumors that Milaney and Sueann's termination were all Ned's doing. She wanted to plant the seed of fear. Violet knew fear of losing a job was a big motivator. If she could get that seed to take root throughout the facility, what came out of the ground would be a big win for her. And now, in addition to the firings, Violet could crow about the suicidal patient. Violet could point out how dangerous those kinds of patients could be. No competent administrator would have allowed such a patient into Central City. Ned put the entire staff in danger. Ned was sure Violet would take every opportunity to exploit the Estrada situation. At some point, Ned knew in his heart, the only outcome with Violet would end with one of them being gone. But the people right in front of him, right now, would help determine that outcome. If he didn't win those hearts and minds, Ned knew he better polish up his resume and start looking for another job.

URBAN LEGEND

As Ned was walking toward his office, a few days after the clash with Violet during the stand-up meeting, he saw a group of CNAs hovering outside a patient's room. The room was occupied by a Mr. Park. He was an elderly Korean gentleman who was on hospice. Ned walked over to see what was happening. "What's going on?" Ned asked.

Carolina responded to Ned's question, "Dr. Tang is pulling maggots out of that guy's mouth."

"What!" Ned said shocked.

"Yeah, really," she said.

Ned pushed his way by the nurses and entered the room.

Carolina added some commentary. "That's because the charge nurses don't do shit around here."

Ned turned around and spoke to Carolina and the rest of the CNAs hovering outside the room.

"Don't you have patients to attend to? Go on, go take care of your patients," Ned said as he shooed them away.

"But watching this is more fun," Carolina said chuckling.

"Please go attend to your patients, especially you, Carolina!" Ned responded a little more forcefully.

The CNAs giggled as they went back to their assignments. Carolina couldn't refrain from getting in one last dig, "I'm telling you Mr. Ned, it's the charge nurses. God knows how many other patients have maggots."

"Carolina!" Ned yelled.

"Ok, I'm going," she responded.

Ned entered Mr. Park's room and walked over to the bed where Dr. Tang, a tall, thin Chinese man with an even thinner moustache was indeed using a tweezers to pluck maggots out of Mr. Park's mouth. Dr. Tang was the wound care specialist for Central City.

"Ah, that's a big one," Dr. Tang said as he pulled another maggot out and put it in a specimen cup on the bedside table. Mr. Park just lay there in a deep almost coma like sleep, his body the color of wax, his mouth open. His breath as shallow as it could be. His body was operating at a level to just be able to call him alive.

"How did they get in there?" Ned said. He could hardly believe his eyes.

"Patient sleeping with mouth open. Fly go in and lay eggs, pretty soon maggots. Look another big one," Tang said chuckling.

He held out a wiggling maggot trapped in the tweezers for Ned to see. Then the doctor dropped the wriggling worm into the specimen cup.

"I guess I don't see the humor in this," Ned responded.

"You think I do?" Tang responded.

"But sometime you must laugh. Old Chinese proverb…life is ridiculous."

Ned took a deep breath as if weighing the consequences he might be facing.

"Now I have to decide if I should report this to DHS," Ned lamented.

"I wouldn't. This happens now and then. Especially, with patients that are like this poor fellow. Usually maggots show up in wounds, but mouth just as good a place to lay eggs."

Ned moved his head trying for a better view of Park's mouth.

"The maggots not change anything," the doctor added as he handed Ned a flashlight. "Shine light in his mouth, please."

Ned complied. "This has never happened to me before," Ned said.

"You're lucky. Don't take so hard. I've seen before. Lots of times. Better mouth care. No more maggots."

You think I should check all the other patients? Ned asked.

"Not bad idea. Also, put better screens on windows. No flies, no maggots," the doctor responded.

Ned moved up close and peered into Mr. Park's mouth. "I've heard about maggots in patients' mouths but I thought it was an urban legend," Ned commented.

"Oh no," Dr. Tang said, "I've pulled maggots out of mouths in some of the best hospitals in LA."

"At least I'm in good company," Ned pointed to the specimen cup full of maggots. "Mind if I borrow that?"

"Sure, plenty more where they came from," the doctor chuckled.

Ned took the specimen cup and snapped on the lid. "I would appreciate it if you kept this whole insect thing in this room," Ned asked politely.

"Don't worry," Tang said with a smile.

Ned started to leave the room.

"Too bad," Dr.Tang said over his shoulder, "I was planning to share this experience at my next mahjong tournament."

Ned stopped, "You play mahjong? I thought only old Jewish ladies played mahjong."

Dr.Tang stopped digging in Mr. Park's mouth and looked at Ned, "Old Jewish ladies play too, huh?"

Ned left Mr. Park's room, with the specimen jar in his hand, and walked through the facility until he found Anthony. "Get all the CNAs and bring them to my office. Then I want the licensed nurses who treated Park next. Do it quietly," Ned said.

"Ok," Anthony responded.

Ned went to Violet's office. He didn't bother to knock. He turned the door knob but the door was locked. "Violet, I need to talk to you, would you let me in, please," Ned said.

A few seconds later she opened the door, then returned to her desk. "What do you need? I have a lot to do," she said curtly.

Ned entered her office. "I'm sorry to be the bearer of bad news but it seems every time I come to your office it's with another nursing problem," Ned said as he put the specimen cup full of maggots on Violet's desk. "These came out of Mr. Park's mouth. Do you remember Mr. Park? He's the hospice patient with the family that visits him every day. Luckily, one of these things didn't fall out of his mouth while they were here. I don't believe it was deliberate…," Ned said.

Violet cut Ned off, "I'll speak to the nurses. I'll take care of it. It won't happen again."

That's as close to an apology as Violet could manage. But even then, the words were delivered through clenched teeth.

"You seem to be treating this incident as if we gave a patient chocolate instead of strawberry ice cream. Violet, don't you see this incident as a major breach of protocol," Ned responded.

"It's unfortunate that it happened," she said.

"It's more than that. This is a direct result of your licensed nurses not following up with the CNAs. This would never have happened if they were doing their job," Ned said.

"They do their job. We never had these problems before you admitted such difficult patients. My nurses are stressed out. If you continue pushing them, they're all going to quit," Violet shot back.

Violet's subtle threat angered Ned, "Let them quit. And I'll report every last one of them to the Nursing Board. Starting with you!"

"Don't you threaten me," Violet counterpunched.

"It's not a threat. These nurses are required to take care of patients. It's not happening. At one time you may have been a good nurse, but that was long before I got here. You have let this place turn into a disgrace. Don't you have any pride left?" Ned turned and left Violet's office.

Anthony gathered the day shift CNAs in Ned's office. The rumor of the maggots was already throughout the facility. Ned was angry at his staff, but he managed to contain himself as he addressed the CNAs.

"We're here to talk about mouth care. I'm sure you all know what happened. It is at best disgusting. I won't get into names. But those nurses assigned to Mr. Park are going to be written up," Ned proclaimed.

"I don't have Mr. Park," Carolina said.

"I'm sure we're all delighted to know that," Ned commented.

"I just didn't want to get blamed by accident," she added.

"Mouth care is part of your job. I don't ever want to have this conversation again. If it becomes necessary I'm coming down on the guilty party with both feet."

Another CNA spoke up. "But what if the patient refuses?"

"Then you come back in fifteen minutes and try again, you bribe them with ice cream. But you find a way to get it done. Should another patient have anything that resembles bad breath the person responsible will be suspended and maybe, depending on my mood, termination. Anthony will give you the formal in-service on mouth care. Thank you. Now get back on the floor," Ned said.

The CNAs began to file out of Ned's office.

"Carolina stay," Ned said.

"Do you need me? Sippie asked.

"No, but thanks for asking."

When all the CNAs, but Carolina, were gone Ned closed the door. "Am I in trouble, Mr. Ned?" she asked.

"Aside from the fact you have a big mouth, no, I need your help," Ned said.

"Me? Why do you need my help?" she asked.

"I believe you know what's going on in this building before I do," he said.

"Can I have a red whip?" she pointed to the jar of red whip licorice Ned had on his desk.

"Go ahead," Ned said.

She dug her hand into the jar and pulled out a handful.

"You can have all you want. And how 'bout I throw in a raise, too?"Ned added.

"Sure. Why do you want to give me a raise?" she asked.

"Carolina, I need a person to keep me informed," he said.

"About what?" Carolina asked.

"What goes on in this hospital."

"What does that mean?"

"For Central City to become a really good skilled nursing facility, I need to catch issues before they become problems. Bad mouth care, an issue, becomes maggots, a problem, understand?" Ned responded.

"Sounds like you want me to become a snitch. I'm no snitch," she responded.

"What is it with snitch? I'm not a warden. This is a hospital," Ned said frustrated.

"I'm not asking you to rat out your friends just let me know when you see a problem so I can fix it, that's all."

"Why don't you ask, Sippie? I'm sure she would love to do it for you," Carolina remarked.

"Let's just say I think you're a better choice," Ned said. He dug in his pocket, pulled out a ten-dollar bill and extended it toward her.

"Go out and have lunch. Think about what I'm asking."

Carolina looked at the bill in Ned's hand for a moment. She knew if she took it on some level, she would be making a deal with what she perceived could be the devil. Finally, she took the ten.

"I'm not going to be a snitch," she warned.

"No, you're going to help make this the best hospital it can be," Ned added.

Ned opened the door. "Enjoy lunch," he said to her as she left the office.

Two LVNs were standing outside Ned's door. Azel was twenty-something and Erika was in her early thirties. They knew what was coming. They were in charge of Mr. Park. They were both embarrassed and had sheepish expressions on their faces. They filed into Ned's office. He closed the door behind them. "You are licensed nurses that were assigned to Park," Ned said.

They both nodded in agreement but never looked Ned in the eye.

"You have a greater responsibility than CNAs for keeping patients in this place cared for. Don't you?" Ned asked rhetorically.

"Yes," they both whimpered.

"And you do understand that responsibility extends to mouth care," Ned added.

Again, they whimpered another, "Yes."

"If you don't look after our patients properly and this happens again, I'm going to fire you. Do you both understand?" Ned said firmly.

"But Mr. Ned…" Erika tried to break into the conversation.

Ned trampled right over her. "Do you think there's anything you can say that will justify what happened today?" Ned asked.

"No," Erika responded.

In case you don't know it, if you don't take proper care of your patients it is abuse and that could mean loss of license. Did you hear what I just said?"

"Yes," they both meekly mumbled.

"You get away with a write-up this time, but never again. You are professionals. Act like it. Now get back to work," Ned instructed.

As the two nurses started to leave Ned added, "Violet said that some of you are unhappy. Maybe you were going to quit. If you want to quit, quit. But if you stay, you'll do your job. The days of this place being the armpit of the company are over."

A few minutes later Ned was in the lobby. He watched Estrada, the electrical cord eater, being wheeled out on a gurney. Dylan had done his job.

"Fuck you!" Estrada yelled at Ned as they wheeled him out the front door.

Ned didn't respond. Instead, he walked to Estrada's room to see if Estrada had left any parting gift like feces on the bed or a broken window. On the wall in letters about a foot-tall Estrada had written 'FOCK YOU' in black marker.

Not only was he suicidal, Ned thought, but he can't spell.

THE COUNTER ATTACK

Violet pulled her Camry into the parking lot at corporate headquarters. She stopped at the gate. The door to the attendant's smoke-filled cubicle slid open. A white cloud of smoke spilled out before Chang appeared out of the cloud. "Hello, Miss Violet," Chang said.

"Hello, Chang," she replied.

"You haven't been here for some time. It's good to see you. Here for a meeting?" he asked.

"Yes. I should be an hour or so," she responded.

Chang took a deep drag from his electric cigarette, "You can park right over there." He pointed to one of the spaces marked RESERVED.

"Thank you, Chang," she answered.

He disappeared back into the white smoke.

Violet parked her car, got out and walked with a deliberate step toward the bank of elevators. Unlike every other day, when she went to Central City, today she was dressed to the nines. A bright new dress, her hair and makeup as good as it could be. She pressed the call button to summon the elevator for the tenth floor. The elevator doors opened. She stepped in. The doors closed behind her.

Very few employees of the company were even allowed on the tenth floor. It was the equivalent of the Oval Office or the Pope's private residence. The fact that Violet was allowed there was a testimony to her status in the company. It didn't seem to matter that Central City was an economic dog or that recent surveys from the Department of Health were less than stellar, Violet was there at the beginning of the company and that mattered.

The elevator rose to the sixth floor and stopped. The doors opened and Jeanie, Lyle's assistant, stepped in. Jeanie was a bright looking thirty-something. She was wearing a dark pants suit. Her hair and make-up perfect. She pressed the button for the eighth floor. She was surprised to see Violet. "Oh, hi, Violet, how are you doing?" Jeanie asked.

Jeanie noticed that the button for the tenth floor was illuminated. Jeanie rarely went to the tenth floor and when she did, it was only to pick up something for Lyle, and then she would quickly descend back to the eighth floor where she belonged.

"Fine," Violet responded.

Violet knew that Jeanie was Lyle's assistant. And it was Lyle who put Ned in her hospital. Ned was the third administrator in a row that didn't work out for her. Violet viewed administrators, all of them, as annoyances. After all, the corporation ran skilled nursing facilities not skilled administrator facilities. As Violet saw it, administrators were just people that got in the way. Ned was just the latest administrator Lyle assigned to Violet's hospital. Or better put, Violet's kingdom. Perhaps, she thought, Lyle's judgment should be called into question. Perhaps, that should be mentioned in her meeting when she spoke to Mr. M. The elevator stopped on the eighth floor. The doors opened. Jeanie smiled and stepped out. "Have a nice day," Jeanie said.

"Thank you," she replied.

The elevator rose up smoothly from the eight to the tenth floor. The doors opened onto the inner sanctum of the corporation. There were only six offices on the entire floor. One of which, the one she was going to, was the biggest and holiest of all of them. It was the office of the founder, the ancient wise man who built the empire with his bare hands. A man so revered no one dare even utter his name. He was simply called: Mr. M.

Violet entered the reception area outside Mr. M's office. She was greeted by Edith, M's assistant.

"Hello, Violet, it'll be just a few minutes. He's thinking," Edith said.

Edith had been M's assistant for decades. She was upholstered without looking fat. She was smartly dressed with appropriately styled hair. She seemed at first glance to be European but was from Iowa. She was the perfect complement to the rare antiques and imported Oriental carpets that decorated M's outer office. The carpets and antiques were so rare and exquisite that upon M's ascension into heaven they were going to the Smithsonian. M had willed them to the Smithsonian and the Smithsonian was delighted to get them.

"Would you like a cup of coffee while you wait?" Edith asked.

"No thank you," Violet responded.

Down on the eighth floor Jeanie walked into Lyle's office. "Violet Tomas just went up to the tenth floor. Thought you might like to know," Jeanie said.

"Oh shit," Lyle groaned.

Lyle knew the only reason Violet was on the tenth floor was to complain about Ned. Lyle guessed Ned must have really put a stone in her shoe for Violet to come to corporate to complain about him. The other two administrators Lyle hired to run Central City simply ran away rather than stand up to her. She crushed them like she extinguished butts in an ashtray. The truth was, Lyle wanted Violet out. He would try anything to get rid of her. She was the old technology. Lyle wasn't sure she could even turn on a computer. She wasn't going to help bring Medicare into the facility. She wasn't going to help Lyle get Central City's profits up and allow him to claim another economic victory that he could parade in front of kingpins on the tenth floor. The corporation was funny that way. If you were grandfathered in, as Violet was, you could fail all day long and you were safe. But for the new people, like Lyle and Ned, it was all about the numbers. Lyle was always looking down the road. Someday, Mr. M would become the living God of the corporation, adored but unable to make the day to day decisions to keep the wheels turning. When that day came someone would really have to run the company. And Lyle envisioned himself to be that person. He saw himself up on the tenth floor in the biggest office in the corporation. But to get there, Lyle needed more economic victories. Violet was in his way. And to date, Lyle hadn't found the right person to put Violet down. So far, she had out drawn every gunfighter Lyle put up against her. Lyle had no idea if Ned was her match or not. Ned was a desperation hire. Only time would tell. Lyle wondered if Ned would even survive Violet's meeting with Mr. M.

A light blinked on Edith's phone. Edith smiled at Violet. "Mr. M will see you now," she said. Violet got up and walked to M's office. It was behind two massive wooden doors. As she approached the room the doors silently opened.

M's office was more church sanctuary than a place of business. Mr. M was seated behind a massive, dark oak desk. There was no clutter on the desk just a Mont Blanc fountain pen and a large, leather bound diary. Mr. M used that pen to write his thoughts in the diary. M didn't write frivolous notes or office memos. Just thoughts. And all of them were worthy of keeping for posterity. His office was dimly lighted. The glass windows of the modern steel structure that housed the office had been perfectly tinted so the bright exterior light would not glare and annoyingly reflect the California sun into M's space. The effect was the Los Angeles skyline on the other side of the glass looked like a large, perfectly exposed photograph.

There was a page from the original Guttenberg bible framed and placed on the wall. That page dominated the room. It was positioned and properly illuminated so it could not be missed. There were bookshelves with rare, ancient books, and in the middle of the room, a glass case with artifacts from the Middle Ages. There was a spare crown from the Holy Roman Emperor, Charlemagne, some of his various all occasion rings, and his be-jeweled broadsword.

M sat behind his oak desk in a large cathedra that came from the Vatican. M purchased the chair by out bidding a Russian oligarch when the word leaked out from the Jesuits in Rome that the Pope was having 'a yard sale.' The cathedra was originally in Notre Dame. Its first occupant was the Bishop of Paris who sat in it for the consecration of Notre Dame's altar in 1196. Rumor was M paid millions for that chair.

M was a gentleman in his late seventies. He had a full, beautifully trimmed beard. He wore a tailored dark suit and tie. The dark tie lay perfectly against his expensive, handmade white shirt. There were two large wooden chairs, also from the Middle Ages, placed before his desk. Violet sat down in one of them. She was comfortable enough in the presence of this modern-day king not to have to ask if she could sit.

"I want to talk to you about the new administrator in my hospital," she said.

Mr. M sat up higher in his chair. He folded his hands on the desk and leaned closer to Violet.

"He's causing a great deal of disruption," she then added, "I have my doubts if he will work out."

Mr. M sat there like the Sphinx.

Her audience with M complete, Violet got back on the elevator. The scowl she wore going up to the tenth floor was now replaced with a smile. Violet felt victorious. Soon, she felt, Ned would be gone. She took her cellphone out of her purse and called Central City.

"Good morning, Central City Convalescent, Jose speaking. How can I help you?"

"Jose, this is Violet. I won't be coming in today."

She ended the call and put the phone back in her purse.

The phone rang on Lyle's desk. "Yes."

It was Jeanie. "It's Edith."

"Shit," tumbled out of Lyle's mouth again. "Put her through."

Mr. M hadn't spoken on the phone directly to anyone below the tenth floor in years. That's not the way he ran his corporation. Like the God of the Bible, his words came through burning bushes or out of clouds. Edith was the burning bush that always spoke to Lyle.

"Good morning, Lyle, Mr. M wants you to make sure that everything is going well at Central City. There seems to be a problem with nursing," Edith said those words in as pleasant as voice as possible.

But Lyle understood that a problem with nursing was Ned. He was the only administrator that got any traction at Central City and now Violet wanted to get rid of him.

"I'll make sure everything over there runs as it should, Edith. Tell Mr. M I'll go over there and personally straighten things out," Lyle promised.

"I'm sure Mr. M will be glad to hear that. Good bye."

A profound sense of worry came over Lyle. The thought that kept running through his mind was Violet could end up taking him down along with Ned. She had been with M for thirty-years, Lyle had been there but one. To make matters worse, Lyle did not get along with Marilyn Fowler, the head of all nursing for the corporation. Marilyn was a staunch supporter of Violet. Making money was not Marilyn's concern, that was Lyle's problem. Her job was to keep the patients and her DONs happy.

Once a week Lyle, Marilyn and the other key players of the corporation would meet in the corporate conference room on the eighth floor and discuss the state of affairs. Mr. M would listen in from his office. If he heard something that he questioned, Edith would later call that individual who made the unfortunate comment with 'thoughts' Mr. M had on the subject. After Violet's visit to Mr. M, Ned would surely be discussed at the next conference room meeting. Lyle needed to be prepared for that discussion. What if Violet had convinced Mr. M that Ned should be dumped? Lyle thought to himself. I'm going to look like I don't know what I'm doing. He had already hired two people to run Central City and neither of them worked out. No matter how Lyle explained that to the people at the upcoming meeting, they would ultimately blame him for Ned's failure. After all, Lyle was the Vice President of Operations. It was his job to hire successful administrators. Ned was his third spin of the wheel Lyle had at Central City. And, now one of Marilyn's sacred cows was complaining that he wasn't working out either. Lyle sat at his desk thinking about his options. He really only had two ways to go. He could throw Ned to the wolves and look for a replacement or he could go up against Violet and gamble with his own career that Ned would succeed.

He picked up the phone on his desk and pressed the button for his assistant. "Jeanie, call Central City and tell Ned Russo to meet me for lunch."

CHURCHEE

Ned watched Ying Kang, the elderly Korean lady who grew fruit flies in her closet, roll her walker out of Central City. Ned got up and walked to the window to observe Kang. She saw Ned watching her through the window.

"Churchee," she said smiling at Ned, "Churchee."

Ned didn't really understand what she said so he just smiled and waved back at her. She rolled her walker down the sidewalk and out of Ned's sight. Ned had witnessed this woman leave and go somewhere almost every day. For some reason, it suddenly occurred to Ned that he had no idea where this woman was going or if she even had an 'out on pass' so she could leave the building.

Ned picked up the phone and pressed the button for station one.

"Yes," came the response from Linda, the charge nurse.

"Linda, can you please tell me if Ying Kang has an out on pass signed by her physician?" Ned asked.

"Yes, she does," Linda instantly responded.

"Are you sure?"

"Well, she goes out every day," the charge nurse responded.

"Just because she goes out every day doesn't mean... Can you please check her chart," Ned asked.

The charge nurse put Ned on hold. That awful elevator music that annoys everyone who as ever was put on hold played in Ned's ear until the charge nurse returned to the phone a few minutes later.

"You know, I can't actually find an out on pass for her," Linda said timidly.

Ned hung up the phone. He hurried out of his office. He went by the reception area and called to Jose as he was headed out the facility. "Have a CNA follow me," he said.

"Where are you going?" Jose called after him.

"After Ying Kang."

Ned ran out of the front on the facility. He looked up and down the street for Ying but she was gone. He decided to walk toward Alvarado Street. Since he visited her room and saw that she was farming fruit flies, Ned guessed she might be going to buy more bananas from the open-air vendors that lined that thoroughfare.

About thirty yards beyond Central City, on the way to Alvarado Street, Ned passed by a hole in the wall auto shop. The shop was probably a store at one time but some enterprising mechanic turned it into his repair business. There were half a dozen or so older cars parked in the small parking lot next to the auto shop. Mixed in between the sounds of pneumatic wrenches and the banging of hammers on metal, Ned heard music. It wasn't coming from the auto shop but was coming from an open door above. Ned stopped and listened. Odd, he thought. If there was going to be music he would have bet on Mexican Ranchero. But this music wasn't Mexican at all. It was Christian.

"Jesus loves me yes I know. Cause the Bible tells me so."

As Ned listened to the singing, he realized the spiritual's words had a definite Korean accent attached to them. Ned looked at the rusting iron fire escape that led to the second floor that and the source of the music. He started to connect the dots in his head. Suddenly, he shuddered at the thought that Ying Kang climbed those stairs with a walker to attend which he now realized was 'churchee.'

"Oh Jesus!" Ned gasped.

Ned dashed up the fire escape. The stairs rattled and shook as he climbed to the second floor and entered that open door. Just inside the open door was, to Ned's surprise, not a church, but a Mexican kitchen. It was staffed by three plump, older Mexican women. They were busily cooking five-gallon pots of frijoles and rice. In a room, just off the kitchen, a dozen or so hungry looking, probably undocumented, people saw Ned and suddenly freaked.

"Immagracion!" one of them blurted out.

The fear from that group spread through those waiting for their beans and rice like wild fire. A couple of the younger ones got up and ran for the door. Ned quickly realized he was the source of the group's anxiety. "No, no, no immagracion," Ned screamed. "I'm looking for one of my patients," he said trying to reassure the frightened residents that he was not a threat. They had no idea what he said. They sat there terrified. Another young man got up and ran for the fire escape.

"No. No immigration!" Ned repeated.

"Jesus loves me yes I know. Cause the Bible tells me so."

The singing led Ned down the hallway into a make-shift Korean church. There were folding chairs instead of pews and an altar made out of a five foot by three foot table. The altar was covered with a white bed sheet. There was a large wooden cross, made out of two by fours. A Korean man wearing a Dodger's shirt was leading a dozen or so believers as they marched in a circle around the room, chanting the Jesus loves me song. Among the marchers was Ying Kang pushing her walker. She smiled and stopped when she saw Ned. "You come churchee too," she said sporting a very pleased smile.

When Ned entered the 'church', the singing and marching stopped. The pastor went up to him. He, like Ying Kang, thought Ned was there to enjoy a bit of revivalism. The pastor used hand signals to urge Ned to join in the parade around the room, and of course, to sing. The pastor started the parade and singing again. "Jesus loves me..."

Ned cut him off, "No you don't understand," Ned tried to get the parade to stop.

The pastor and his followers behind him stopped like a car hitting an abutment...and so did the singing.

"Thank you. Thank you. Are you the pastor, here?" Ned asked.

The Korean man smiled. "Me pastor, me pastor," he responded.

Ned realized this guy's English was limited to the same amount of Korean Ned could speak...virtually zero.

"Ying Kang is a patient at the hospital," Ned pointed to Central City, "I have to take her back."

Ned did his best with a combination of hand gestures and limited use of words that he needed to get his point across.

"I know Kang patient at hospital," the pastor responded, "You take back?"

Ned was pleased that he had communicated with the pastor. "Yes," Ned responded smiling.

The pastor spoke to Kang in Korean. At first, she didn't seem to agree, then the pastor insisted that she go with Ned, and Kang seemed to agree.

"She go now," the pastor said.

"Thank you," Ned said shaking the pastor's hand.

The pastor smiled and bowed a lot and led Kang and Ned out of his church down the hallway past the Mexican kitchen and the frightened people waiting for their frijoles, and out onto the top landing of the rusty iron fire escape. That's when the situation got out of control.

"No!" Kang decided she didn't want to go back to Central City. She grabbed hold of the fire escape. The pastor argued with her in Korean and tried to pull her hand off the railing, but Kang bit the pastor's hand. The pastor screamed at her in Korean and Kang screamed back.

"Do you need some help, Ned? Do you want me to come up?" came Sippie's voice from the bottom of the fire escape.

When Ned saw Sippie all he could think was of all the CNAs in that hospital why, Jose, did you send her? Ned yelled down to Sippie, "No, stay there and hold the fire escape steady."

Sippie complied and took a firm grip on the fire escape.

Ned tried to pull Kang's hands free of the fire escape. She tried to bite him as well. But he was faster than the pastor and Kang's teeth never got to Ned's hand. Kang tightened her grip on the rusting iron railing. Ned suddenly realized if Kang fell off the fire escape and was killed he would probably go to prison. There was only one course of action that made sense. Ned called down to Sippie. "Sippie, call the fire department. Call 911."

She used her cell phone and called.

Ned, Kang and the pastor stood almost frozen in place waiting for the next shoe to drop. It did within a couple of minutes.

Sirens blared as the Fire Department came down the street and pulled into the small parking lot of the auto shop. When the fire engines parked, the remaining undocumented residents waiting for their beans and rice made a run for it. They scrambled out of the make-shift dining room and down the fire escape, pushing Ned, the pastor and Kang out of the way. The extra weight on the fire escape made it shake and rattle to the point Ned thought it was going to detach from the wall and most of them were going to be killed and he would serve life in prison rather than just five years for killing Kang. The undocumented residents reached the parking lot, and scattered in all directions. The ranking fire fighter, the fire captain who had given Ned aggravation during his last visit, watched the people scrambling.

"What the fuck is going on here?" the fire captain said.

Ned called down to the captain, "Up here."

The fire captain looked up and recognized Ned. "You again," he muttered.

Kang and the pastor were on the top of the fire escape. The captain started to climb the stairs. The rickety nature of the fire escape gave the captain pause. He stopped about three steps up, "Jesus, this fucking thing is coming down." He yelled up to Ned, "What the hell are you doing up there? Get those people down here and I mean right now!"

"Remember me? I'm the administrator from Central City."

"Yes, I remember you," the captain snarled.

Ned pointed to Ying Kang and yelled to the captain, "This woman is one of my patients. She won't come down."

"What do you mean she won't come down? Pull her off the goddamn railing," the captain ordered. The captain looked the situation over and then yelled to Ned, "What the fuck is she doing up there in the first place?"

"It's a long story," Ned yelled back.

The fire captain turned to his paramedics, "You two get up there and get that woman down here."

Then he turned back to Ned, "You know this doesn't look good, a woman on a walker climbing a fire escape."

"I know," Ned responded, "Believe me I know."

The paramedics climbed up the fire escape with the intention of dislodging Kang from her hold on the iron railing. Kang screamed at the paramedics, in Korean, as they climbed the stairs. She let go just long enough to throw her walker at them. The walker missed. She quickly reattached herself to the fire escape. Then she turned and continued shouting at the paramedics in Korean, and at Ned and the pastor. Whatever she screamed was inflammatory enough so the pastor began shouting back at her in Korean.

"What are you doing? You're supposed to be helping," Ned exasperatedly shouted at the pastor.

Ned tried again to pry Kang free from the fire escape but he just made matters worse. Kang sat down on the fire escape and wrapped her arms and her legs around the railing. She had the grip of an anaconda. The two paramedics arrived and tugged and pulled at her but couldn't pull her from the railing. Kang bit one of the paramedics.

"Jesus H. Christ!" the captain shouted.

"All right, two more of you get up there and pull that son-of-a-bitch down!"

Then the captain turned to Ned, "This is all your fault for letting her go up there in the first place. If one of my guy's gets hurt I'm going to make sure I take it out of your ass."

Two more fire fighters clambered up the rattling fire escape. The fire escape wobbled from the weight of all that were now on it. For a second everyone froze. They all were afraid the fire escape might pull out of the wall.

"Holy shit! Hurry up and get her down!" the captain yelled.

The two firefighters and the two paramedics regained their composure. With one mighty maneuver they managed to pull the screaming Kang off the fire escape. They quickly carried her Korean-screaming, flailing body, back down to the safety of the parking lot. Ned followed the fire fighters, paramedics and Kang. The paramedics, with the help of the fire fighters, quickly loaded Kang onto a gurney and strapped her in. The whole time Kang pulled at the gurney's restraints and kept screaming in Korean.

"Can you take her to the hospital?" Ned asked the fire captain.

"Are you fucking crazy? For what? She's in better shape than you are. Didn't you see it took four grown men to get her on that gurney?" the fire captain responded.

"But she's got serious mental problems," Ned pleaded.

"The only one with a problem here is you for letting her climb that fucking fire escape with a walker," the fire captain said.

"The woman is psychotic," Ned insisted.

"Oh, yeah, well, that's your opinion," the captain fired back, "She's your problem. You deal with it."

"Come on, won't you please help me," Ned pleaded.

"If I take her to the hospital, my next stop is going to be DHS," the captain pointed a finger in Ned's face, "And you're going to get your ass in a sling for patient dumping. That's a huge fine in this city."

"You're not going to help me, are you?" Ned said.

"She's your patient. I have other more important things to do. I'm going to condemn this fucking fire escape before it comes down and kills somebody."

Ned realized he had been defeated. "All right, bring her back," Ned said reluctantly. He wondered how he was going to control her once she got off the gurney in the lobby of Central City.

"Take this woman back to the nursing home," the captain ordered the men pushing the gurney. Then he turned his attention again to Ned, "And if I were you, I'd make goddamn sure she never climbs this or any other fire escape again. What the hell were you thinking?" the captain said incredulously.

Rather than get into a discussion with this city official who knew nothing about managing patients with mental problems Ned decided to try and solve the problem he was going to have when Kang got back to Central City.

"Sippie," Ned said, "stay with her one-on-one."

"Anything for you Ned," she responded.

"And Sippie, please stop calling me Ned."

Sippie followed the fire fighters pushing the gurney back to the hospital. Then Ned took out his cell phone and called Dylan.

Dylan was driving when he answered his cellphone, "Yeah, Ned…"

"Dylan, call Kovani. Tell him we're sending Kang over. Tell him Kang needs a psychotropic cocktail to calm her down. I don't want her back, but tell him I promise to take her if he can't get rid of her any place else."

"Got it," Dylan responded.

"And Dylan, plead with Kovani I've got to get rid of her. I can't go through this again," Ned said.

"Go through what?" Dylan asked.

The phone rang in Jose's reception cubicle. He answered it with his latex-gloved hand.

"Good morning…" Jose suddenly wondered for a moment if it was still morning. He checked his watch. "It is! Central City, this is Jose how can I direct your call?"

"Jose, this is Jeanie."

"Jeanie who?"

"Jeanie from corporate."

"Oh, hi Jeanie, what can I do for you?" Jose cheerfully blurted back.

"Tell Ned, Lyle wants to meet him for lunch."

"Where?" Jose asked.

"Taylor's Steak House, at one," Jeanie said.

"Right now, he's chasing a patient down the street but I'm sure he'll be back by then."

EATING WITH A SHARK

Ned pulled his SUV into the parking lot of Taylor's Steak House. The parking attendant walked up to the driver's side door. Ned handed him the key. The attendant had a moustache like Salvador Dali's. Ned stepped out of his car, the attendant ripped off a parking receipt and handed it to Ned. "Enjoy your lunch, senor," the attendant said with a flare as if he actually meant it.

"Thanks."

But Ned was worried if the lunch would be enjoyable or if Lyle was going to give him a belly full of indigestion. He knew Violet was gunning for him and the 'let's have lunch' from Lyle could only be bad news.

Taylor's was one of those 1950's Frank Sinatra kind of places. Red leather booths, hostesses and waitresses with big hair and bigger breasts stuffed into half-buttoned, bright white shirts.

Ned entered the restaurant and had to wait for his eyes to adjust before he could see. When Ned's eyes adjusted a pretty hostess was smiling at him. "Party of two, Ellis," Ned said.

"You're the first to arrive. Would you like to be seated or would you rather wait at the bar?" the hostess politely asked.

"I think I'd like to sit down. I spent this morning on a fire escape," Ned responded.

The hostess led Ned to a booth at the far end of the restaurant. Within seconds the waitress showed up, "Hi, I'm Gwen. I'll be serving you today. Can I get you a drink while you wait?" After the morning he had just endured with Kang, Ned really wanted a Grey Goose Martini but he wondered what kind of a signal that would send to Lyle. Ned decided he didn't want Lyle to see him drinking on their first business lunch.

"Just bring me a sparkling water with a piece of lemon."

She smiled and disappeared back toward the bar.

Ned knew he wasn't going to get fired. Corporations don't waste a lunch on someone they're going to dump. They send Human Resources, hand that person who is going to be termed a check, and ask for their keys. The excuse HR gives the victim is always the same, it's not working out, or that senior management is going in another direction. Ned loved that one. Ned often wondered what other direction a skilled nursing facility corporation could go. Were they going to convert the SNF into a veterinary clinic? And they now need administrators with animal husbandry backgrounds. He felt the cleanest way to fire somebody would be to train a parrot that would do the firing. The victim would come to work on the appointed day to find the parrot perched on his or her desk. Then the parrot would squawk "You're fired." Then poop on the victim's desk. There would be a banker's box filled with the victim's belongings, next to the fresh parrot droppings, with a note that read: LEAVE YOUR KEYS AND GET OUT!

The door to Taylor's opened. Lyle entered the restaurant. There, standing in the doorway was either Ned's savior or his nemesis. Ned wouldn't know until lunch was finished.

Lyle, like Ned, had to wait a few seconds while his eyes adjusted to the darkness of his surroundings. The hostess approached Lyle. They exchanged a few pleasantries and then she led him to the booth where Ned was waiting for him. Lyle sat down across from Ned.

"Are you hungry? I'm starved," Lyle said.

"I could eat," Ned responded.

Lyle settled into the booth. "How's it going at Central City?" he said cheerfully.

"You tell me?" Ned responded. He did his best to hide the nervousness.

The waitress reappeared with Ned's sparkling water and put it in front of him.

"What the fuck is that?" Lyle indicated Ned sparkling water.

"I don't know about you, but I need a real drink," Lyle said.

"What can I bring you?" the waitress asked.

"A vodka Martini, straight up," Lyle responded.

Lyle pointed to Ned's sparkling water, "Are you sure that's what you want? I thought you were a guy with balls."

"Am I going to need something stiffer?" Ned asked.

"You never know," Lyle responded.

Ned turned to the waitress, "Then I'll tell you what. Bring me a Grey Goose martini, very dry, with three Sicilian olives."

"Sicilian olives?" Lyle questioned.

"They have a slightly less briney taste. They give a whole new dimension to the vodka's flavor," Ned responded with authority.

"In that case I'll have what he's having," Lyle said to the waitress.

"I don't know if we have those olives," the waitress said.

Ned cut her off, "Then we'll settle for whatever you have."

The waitress smiled and headed for the bar.

"Okay, now that you know I watch the Food Channel, tell me, how bad is it?" Ned inquired.

"Bad enough. Your DON went to see Mr. M to complain about you. That's a record. Usually it takes a few months before she starts complaining. She wants your head on a spike. It seems you're upsetting her applecart. You're making all her nurses unhappy. But I think we can get through it," Lyle said.

"Why do you think that?" Ned asked.

"Because you're not fired already," Lyle responded matter-of-factly.

"That's reassuring," Ned said.

"The only reason you're not gone are the numbers. I stuck my neck out for you," Lyle said.

"Thank you," Ned said.

"Don't thank me yet, I'm only going to stick it out so far," Lyle said. "Why can't you get along with her? That would make my life so much easier," then Lyle added as an aside, "Not that you should be different than any other administrator I've sent over there. She hates them all," Lyle commented.

"Would it surprise you to know Violet doesn't like Medicare, too much additional paperwork, too much work in general. She's old and tired, Lyle. She's had it too easy for too long," Ned said.

"Well, I'm sorry about that," Lyle said facetiously. "Frankly, I don't give a shit about her or her nurses. They're all a bunch of slackers who've spent years sitting around growing their fat asses," Lyle said.

"I wouldn't have put it quite like that," Ned added.

Lyle went on thinking out loud, "The question is how to get rid of her? I have been toying with offering her another facility but then all I'm doing is moving the problem."

"That would be wonderful if you could get her to move," Ned added.

"I'm just jerking off with that idea. She isn't going to move. She is so safe there and she knows it."

"Violet bucks me every step of the way," Ned said.

"I'm not surprised. You're going to have to tiptoe around her for now. When it comes to Violet I'm dealing with a serious political situation. Your DON has a powerful ally at corporate, Marilyn Fowler. She's the head of all nursing. She protects her nurses like they were made of gold. Getting around her isn't going to be easy," Lyle said.

"I'm trying to work with her, Lyle, but from the first minute we met it was all downhill. Now when Violet sees me, she sneers and leaves. I heard she comes to the building after I leave to see if she can send my new admits back," Ned said.

"Like I said, you're going to have to hang in there. I have to work on it from my end. I have to chip away at her upstairs."

"And if you don't mind me asking, how are you going to do that?" Ned inquired.

"Actually, you're going to do it," Lyle said sporting a wide smile, "The key, my friend, is going to be your performance. What's going to keep you alive is more Medicare."

"Always show me the money, right?" Ned responded.

"Always," Lyle said, "But I'm betting you can do it. The last two admins I sent over there had no balls. Violet ate them for lunch. But I just feel it in my bones that you're different. Please don't disappoint me."

"I have no intention of letting you or me down," Ned added.

Suddenly, Ned knew this was going to be a good lunch. Lyle was on his side, at least for now. Strategically, Ned knew this was the opportunity to chum the water and get the shark he was having lunch with into a feeding frenzy. Ned leaned in toward Lyle, "I can get you a lot more Medicare."

"How much more?" Lyle asked.

"Twenty-thirty percent…easy. Maybe more. We're getting the inquires."

"That much?" Lyle said like a kid drooling over a banana split.

"I know I can do it," Ned said confidently.

"Do what it takes," Lyle said enthusiastically.

"They're all going to be psych. That's the niche that needs to be filled. That's where the Medicare is I can funnel into Central City."

"I don't give a shit what they are as long as they're Medicare," Lyle said.

"Also, I want to add a few new docs to the panel. It'll cost, but I know a couple of guys that need the help and they in turn will help me."

"Go for it," Lyle said.

"Be prepared. Violet is going to moan that every new patient I bring in is going to be too dangerous," Ned said.

"I don't care. Just get the numbers up," Lyle said.

"I'm going to need help with the staff. They're not ready for a psych building," Ned warned.

"I'll clear the money for some special training. That'll look like you're patient oriented," Lyle said.

"I am patient oriented. That's why I asked you for the help," Ned said.

"Just make sure you're also profit oriented," Lyle added.

The waitress arrived with the two Martinis. She set the drinks down on the table.

"Turns out we do have Sicilian olives. The bartender was impressed you asked for them," she looked at Ned, "He said you must be a man with discriminating taste."

Lyle picked up his Martini, "Here's to more Medicare."

Ned picked up his drink. They clinked glasses. Ned sipped the Martini. It was warm as it passed down his throat.

"You gentlemen know what you want for lunch?" the waitress asked.

"Yes, a new DON," Ned responded.

SOME GUYS NEVER LEARN

Now that Lyle had given Ned the Papal Blessing to bring in more psych patients to Central City, Ned implemented the plan he hoped would work.

After lunch, Ned drove directly from Taylor's across town to East LA. On the way there, he made a call to one of his old colleagues. Like Ned, this doctor had recently transitioned from the tony Westside to a far less desirable part of Los Angeles. Ned was banking on the fact that this doctor's current circumstance would play into Ned's plan for success.

LA Hospital, in East LA, was one of the older hospitals in the City of Angels. At one time it was a primary care facility for the city. It had a sterling reputation. But that was a long time ago. Now it was one of the only sources of medical care for indigent patients in one of the poorest neighborhoods of Los Angeles. The hospital was in the heart of Chicano gang turf. It was crime and drug infested. The land of lowriders and Virgin Marys' in those upright bathtubs that were displayed in the front yards of pastel colored houses that dotted the east side of town. But it was also home to the best burrito restaurant in all of LA, El Tepeyac. Ned had been going there since he moved from Rhode Island. He found out about the place from the cop who gave him his first speeding ticket in California. Ned loved the fact that the burritos were so big the NFL could have used them for footballs. And they were so delicious Angelenos were willing to dodge the drive-by shootings just to get one of their giant flour wrapped delights.

Ned pulled his SUV into the hospital parking lot and parked right by the front entrance. He walked into the lobby. There were murals on the walls painted in the thirties when the hospital was built. They depicted the hard working citizens of East Los Angeles. But the murals needed tending like everything else in this place.

In the lobby, patients were sitting in chairs chatting with family members in Spanish. A couple of kids were chasing each other. A janitor slowly mopped a section of the floor. Ned crossed the lobby to the bank of elevators. Two of the three had a sign hanging on the door reading 'Out of Order.' A bell rang, and the door to the functioning elevator opened. Ned stepped in and pressed the button to the sixth floor and to the offices of Dr. Benjamin Gross. The elevator rose to the sixth floor and stopped with a jolt. The door opened and Ned stepped out. A short walk down the corridor and Ned was at his destination.

Dr. Gross's offices were well appointed. The office furniture was one of the few things left to him after a very messy divorce. Ned went up to the window. A pretty twenty-something receptionist slid open the glass panel and smiled at Ned. "Can I help you?" she said.

"Ned Russo. I'm here to see Dr. Gross."

Ned knew Dr. Gross when he ran Sea Breeze. He did business with him but Ned always considered the doctor a bit of a flake. Not that he was a bad physician but that he had too many other things that got in the way of healing the sick, like banging cute CNAs in every hospital where he had privileges and in every skilled nursing facility that he visited. Not that he was the only doctor who banged nurses, but he was so obvious about his extra-curricular activities that it always made the higher-ups in the hospitals where he had privileges very nervous.

"Oh, yes," the girl said. "He told me you were coming. Have a seat. He'll be right with you."

The waiting room had a couch and three chairs. Ned sat down on the couch next to a portly, middle-aged Hispanic woman. She maneuvered her gelatinous body further down the couch, as far away from Ned as she could go. Ned smiled at the Hispanic lady who now looked more uncomfortable than when Ned first sat down. Ned looked over at the receptionist behind the glass panel. Dr. Gross always had young, good looking girls in his office.

It was common knowledge throughout the hospital community that Dr. Gross's proclivity for the younger girls was always at the core of his problems. The gossip floating around the LA medical community was the good doctor had gotten one of his pretty receptionists pregnant. She then filed a paternity suit. She sued the doctor and the hospital where they were both working. There was a big settlement and an ugly divorce, and of course the scandal. Other hospitals got wind of what happened and decided they wanted to avoid that kind of problem. That's how Dr. Gross ended up in the barrio.

"The doctor will see you now," the receptionist announced.

Another young, pretty girl opened the door to back offices. She smiled and led Ned down the hall to Dr. Gross' office. When Ned entered, the doctor got up from behind his desk to greet him. "Ned, how are you doing?" Dr. Gross said sporting a grand smile. Then he extended his hand across the desk. "Good to see you buddy," he said enthusiastically.

"Good to see you too, Doc," Ned responded.

"I heard you're running a facility in Koreatown," the doctor said.

"Yeah, it's closer to my house," Ned said. Then Ned added, "I see you haven't lost your eye for pretty office help."

"It gives me something to look at," Doctor Gross said with a smirk.

And knowing you, something more than to look at…some guys never learn, Ned thought.

Dr. Benjamin Gross was a good-looking man in his forties. He was well dressed. He wore expensive French cuff shirts and diamond studded cufflinks. He drove a Bentley convertible. Ned wondered if his ex was driving the Bentley now. The outward appearance the doctor presented was more like a plastic surgeon in Beverly Hills who went to Oscar parties than a physician in East LA tending to the poor.

"What can I do for you?" the doctor asked.

"Actually, it's what can I do for you. You need any patients?" Ned asked.

"Can never have enough patients. Something's got to pay for all this," Dr. Gross said wryly.

"Good! We have the beginning of a renewed relationship. I have what you need and you have what I need," Ned said.

"Oh? What's that?" Doctor Gross asked.

Ned dangled the bait in the face of the fish he was trying to hook. "I'll guarantee you at least ten new patients in the next couple of months. And if things work out I'll put you on my physicians' panel."

"If you're looking for Medicare, I don't get much around here. Everything is HMO or straight medical," Dr. Gross explained.

"I'm not looking for patients," Ned responded.

"That's a first," The doctor was surprised by Ned's comment, "What do you need?"

"What I need from you is an open door into LA Hospital. When I need to get a problem patient out of my facility, I need you to have a bed for them," Ned said.

"That won't be a problem," the doctor said.

"One more thing. I need you to show up and complete your paperwork on a regular basis."

"Sure," Gross said confidently.

"Well, if you remember, it was a bit of a problem at Sea Breeze," Ned said couching his words as best he could. "I really need you to come, Ben. I don't need my nurses bustin' my chops about they can't get you to the facility."

"That won't happen again. Promise. The world has changed a lot since Santa Monica," the Doctor said apologetically.

"I heard," Ned said.

"And if I get any Medicare, you'll be the first I call," the doctor added.

Ned thought the promises of the good doctor hadn't changed. He was one of those physicians who promised a lot but delivered very little.

"I appreciate the offer. I'm always looking for more Medicare and if you get one, I'd love you to send it my way. But what I really need from you is to help me get problem patients out.

"I understand," the doctor said.

"When I call you it's because I'm shipping a patient to the ER here and I need you to admit them. That's what I'll be paying for," Ned said.

Dr. Gross thought about it for only a few seconds. "There's no reason why we can't do a lot of business again, Ned."

"Like I said, things go the way I think they will, in a couple of months, I'll put you on the panel." Ned dangled more money in front of the doctor. "You can always use a few bucks can't you?"

Now it was Ned's turn to pad the truth, "I've got a big budget for panel docs and I'd love to give you some of it." Ned smiled. He was guessing that Dr. Gross was probably up to his neck in debt and the chance to make easy money was something he couldn't pass up.

"No problem. I'll be there whenever you need me," the doctor responded.

I hope so, Ned thought to himself. Ned was gambling that the doctor's divorce cost him a bundle and that now he had to pay a lot more attention to his business. Ned stood and extended his hand to the doctor. "You'll be hearing from me, Doc," Ned said as he left the office.

Ned left Dr. Gross and went back to the bank of elevators and pressed the 'down" button. The door on the elevator opened. The elevator was filthy. Ned decided to take the stairs back to the lobby.

It occurred to Ned as he was driving back to Central City that gambling was a great deal of how he was now conducting business. He knew he was building a house of cards. He knew that one good stiff breeze and he'd be out of a job again. Yes, there would probably be another facility to run but with each time he got fired and had to move, the pay was getting less and less, the hospitals were getting more and more difficult, and he was getting older. He wanted Central City to work. If there was to be a next move, Ned would be the one who wanted to make it.

THE LUCKIEST BURRITO

As Ned drove through East LA on his way back to Central City he realized he was on Evergreen Avenue. Ned remembered El Tepeyac was but a few blocks away. It had been forever since he last had one of their burritos. "You have to celebrate the little victories," Ned said aloud.

He decided to reward himself for bringing Doctor Gross on board. He turned his SUV around went down about a mile. He was lucky and found a place to park out in front of the restaurant.

Back during his first marriage, Ned and Ann would often get up early on a Sunday morning drive across town to split a Torta de Guacamole Burrito, an egg omelet with guacamole and beans wrapped in a flour tortilla. They loved it! Ned walked into El Tepeyac and ordered a Carne Asada Burrito to go. His purchase made, Ned tucked his football size burrito safely into front seat next to him. Seconds later, he got a whiff of his soon to be consumed dinner and decided to extend his victory celebration by blowing off work and going home. Hell, it was almost time to quit for the day anyway.

As a foodie, Ned knew if you're going to eat a burrito you'd better have a six-pack of Mexican beer, lots of chips, and plenty of salsa to go with it. When he got back to South Pasadena, Ned pulled into Bristol Farms. He grabbed a basket and picked up the beer, chips and salsa and a few other items. He splurged on a couple of quarts of McConnell's Whiskey Pecan Pralines ice cream. His shopping complete, Ned rolled his cart toward the front of the store and the check-out counters. As he was going down one of the aisles, he saw the same good-looking black woman to whom he gave the Manhattan recipe. Ned remembered he was sorry he didn't strike up a conversation with her when he had the chance. So, he decided to throw caution to the wind. He rolled his cart up next to hers. "How did the Manhattans come out?" Ned asked politely.

At first she didn't recognize him, "What?"

"The Manhattans. Remember rye whiskey instead of Crown Royal?" Ned reminded her.

It took a second before she remembered him. "Oh, hi, fine. Everybody thought I knew so much about making the cocktail because I knew about the rye whiskey. My friends were very impressed. Thank you," she responded smiling at Ned.

He saw that she didn't have a wedding ring. He noticed the contents of her cart. She had a frozen pizza and a bag of apples. He speculated, and hoped, that she was dining alone. "Did you just start shopping or are you finished?" he asked.

"I'm almost finished," she started to push her cart.

"I don't want you to think I'm being forward or anything."

She stopped.

"But I guess I am being forward, so please excuse me." Ned felt a little embarrassed and awkward. Striking up a conversation with a woman in a grocery store was not Ned's style. "I had a pretty good day at work. Um…It's a long story but I was in East LA and as a reward for my success I picked up a burrito from El Tepeyac…"

"My God…," she said interrupting him, "Is that place is still open? I haven't been there in years."

"Oh yes. It's still open. I didn't get the five-pound Manuel Special but I did get a Carne Asada Burrito. It's waiting to be eaten on my front seat. And you know how big they are," Ned said.

Ned illustrated the football size of the burrito with his hands. "And I hate to eat alone. So, ah…would you like to share it with me?" Ned timidly asked, "I'll even throw in a beer and chips." He added pointing to the six pack of Corona and the bag of chips his cart, "And dessert. McConnell's is very good ice cream."

She smiled. She liked what she knew of Ned but that wasn't much. "I don't know…," she responded. "I'm not in the habit of eating with strange men."

"I can appreciate that. I'm not in the habit of asking ladies out in the grocery store but I was really sorry I didn't ask you your name last time and it's serendipity that I got to see you again, so I figured I better take my shot." Ned extended his hand to the woman, "I'm Ned Russo. And I'm not strange. I'm completely trustworthy. I'm in the medical field."

"So was Doctor Jekyll," she quickly interjected.

Ned chuckled, "Ah… I see your point," he added whimsically.

"The offer is tempting but I have a lot of work to do," she said smiling.

Before she could turn Ned down completely, he made a second proposal. "Tell you what. There's a restaurant in the back here at Bristol Farms. If I can buy us a table I'll get the burrito and we'll eat here. That way you don't have to worry about Mr. Hyde showing up for dessert."

"Are they going to let you do that? After all it is a restaurant," she said.

"I'm going to do my best to convince them," Ned responded.

As she thought about Ned's proposal…

Ned added, "You eat with me and you won't have the pizza box to clean up. Then you can do your work. I'm actually offering you a time saving proposition."

"First, see if they'll let us eat your food in their restaurant," she said.

Ned went to the restaurant at the back of Bristol Farms. The place had a few patrons but most of the tables were empty. He went up to the only waitress.

"Can I help you," she asked.

Ned dug in his pocket and pulled out his cash. He peeled off a twenty and held it out to the waitress, "How would you like to make a twenty dollar tip?"

"Sure. What do I have to do?"

"Absolutely nothing," Ned responded.

Ned and his dinner date had a table in the middle of the nearly empty restaurant. Ned cut the football size burrito in half. He had already opened two Coronas from the six-pack he purchased. His date took a sip from hers. "I remembered they were big. But I forgot how big," she said.

As he was putting half the burrito on her plate, Ned realized he didn't know her name. He stopped, holding her half of the burrito in mid-air, "I don't know your name. What do I call you?" Ned set the burrito down on her plate.

"Lenore," she answered, "Lenore Waincott."

"Lenore, huh, the only other Lenore I know is in Edgar Allen Poe's poem."

"I was named after my aunt. I'm surprised you read Poe. I didn't think he was still popular," she responded.

"I don't know if he is. I read a lot. I was into Poe when I was a kid. Now I read mostly biographies. How about you?" Ned asked.

"I read a trashy novel from time to time. I don't have time for anything else. Who has the most impressive biography you ever read?" she asked.

"Hmmm..." Ned thought for a moment. He took a bite of his burrito and a swallow of his beer.

"Einstein, Washington, even LBJ, all very impressive men."

"No women?" she asked.

"I read a book about the founding mothers once, Dolly Madison, Martha Washington, that group. Ok, back to the original question, most impressive person. I'm going to have to go with Abe Lincoln," Ned responded.

"Lincoln, why?" she asked.

"Think about what he did. Think about problems he had to solve. The country was torn apart five minutes after he became President. He had to fight a war, end slavery. These were not easy things to do. And..." Ned spoke passionately, "...and in the middle of all this he even had the foresight to build the transcontinental railroad. The man was a combination of Moses, FDR and Eisenhower. That's a tough act to follow."

"I guess you're right. You're different than most doctors I know," Lenore said.

"That's because I'm not a doctor. I'm a hospital administrator," Ned said.

"You talk like you should have been a history teacher," she added.

"No. Babysitting teenagers is not my idea of a good time. Besides, the way history is taught is all wrong. History is people, not places and dates. The more you look at history the more you realize all that changes in the world are the clothes and technology. People have been the same forever. That's what makes history vibrant," Ned answered.

"That's a very interesting perspective," she said.

"And what is it you do?" Ned asked her.

"I'm a public defender with LA County," she responded.

"I'm impressed. I heard you guys are over worked. Not unlike hospital administrators. And on top of that, you never get the really notorious cases, is that true?" Ned asked.

"Yes, all of us are very over worked. And yes, generally, we get the run of the mill stabbings and hold-ups. If you commit a really good crime the celebrity lawyers come out of the woodwork and immediately take over," she answered.

"What was your most interesting case?" Ned asked.

"Haven't had it yet. But I'll let you know when I do," Lenore said.

"Every couple of years I get called for jury duty. I hate it, pulls me away from the hospital. Somebody told me to get out of jury duty to tell the court the defendant must be guilty of something otherwise he wouldn't be on trial," Ned said.

"Sorry, won't work. I've heard way better than that. Besides it's your civic duty," she said.

"Yeah, I know. Next time you need a juror call me. I'll sit on your jury," Ned said.

"That will get you excused," she smiled.

The burrito dinner went on for about an hour, including dessert. The waitress kept Ned's ice cream in the freezer, Ned gave her another five. Lenore talked about her job. Ned talked about his. They talked about their personal lives. She was divorced. She was married to her job. No kids. Ned was struck with her beauty and her intelligence. By the end of the burrito, the chips, the beer, and of course the McConnell's they both secretly decided their interlude was worth it.

"This has been great, but I need to go home now and get ready for court tomorrow," she said.

"Anything interesting?" Ned asked.

"A homeless guy went into rob a liquor store. He threatened to defecate on the floor if the cashier didn't give him money."

"Did he? Defecate on the floor, that is?" Ned asked.

"Yes," she said.

"He sounds like one of my patients," Ned commented.

"I'm going to plead him out. See if I can get him into a rehab program," Lenore said.

"Is there a shitters' anonymous? Sorry, I couldn't resist," Ned said with a chuckle.

"That's all right. I wondered the same thing," she said.

Ned walked Lenore out to the Bristol Farms parking lot. "Thank you, for letting me share my burrito with you," Ned said.

"I got a history lesson and you were right I didn't have to clean up the pizza box," she said.

"Who knows maybe you'd like to do it again sometime," Ned said.

"Maybe," she said with a smile. She dug through her purse then handed him her card. "Call me at work. Leave a message. It's the best way to reach me. I'm always in court or in jail."

"Jail!" Ned proclaimed.

"That's where I get most of my clients," she said.

"I get a lot of mine there too," Ned said.

A few minutes later, Ned was driving home. He looked over at the remainder of the McConnell's ice cream he and Lenore hadn't gotten to at their chance dinner. He was glad he had ginned up the courage to talk to her and was already hoping there would be a next encounter when his cell phone rang. It was Central City. At this time of night, it could only be trouble.

"Hello," Ned answered.

"Mr. Ned, its Benito. We have the problem."

"What is it?" Ned responded.

Benito was in the lobby restroom. He was wearing rubber boots and standing in water. The toilet bowl and tank were smashed. The shards of white porcelain scattered all over the restroom floor. A fountain of water was shooting up from what was left of the toilet's innards.

"One of the patients, he broke the toilet in the lobby," Benito said apologetically.

"What do you mean, broke the toilet?" Ned asked.

"He take the top of the tank, you know the cover for the water and he smash it against the bowl. He make a big mess. Water everywhere. And the bowl is broke. I need to get a new toilet." Benito said.

"No way you can save it?" Ned asked.

"I no think so, Mr. Ned." Benito responded.

"All right. When can you get the new one installed?" Ned sighed.

"I go to Home Depot. I have a new toilet for you by nine the clock in the morning."

"Ok. You know who did it?" Ned asked.

"I no know. Maybe the charge nurse can tell you."

Ned knew asking a charge nurse anything was a waste of time. Their stock answer for everything was always, "I don't know." But Ned would go through the drill anyway. Who knows, maybe this time he would get lucky and somebody would actually say they saw something.

"I'll see you in the morning," Ned frustratedly answered.

He dumped his cell phone onto the passenger seat. Then he chuckled remembering what the grizzled old administrator once told him years before: "Someday run a pysch facility. I promise you you'll never have a dull moment."

NEW JIMMY CHOO'S

Karen Stoble pulled her shining new BMW up to an apartment in front of the projects somewhere in South LA. She checked the address on her cell phone hoping she was at the wrong place. She wasn't. She was reluctant to get out of her car in this neighborhood but there was a hospice patient waiting to be signed up. And at the end of the day, she was about signing up patients. She had gotten the 'lead' from Ensi a discharge planner at California Hospital. This patient wasn't actually in California Hospital but was being taken there by ambulance at least once a week. The patient was costing the hospital a lot of money and the best solution for everyone, including the patient, was hospice. Since Ensi gave Karen a lot of patients Karen felt obligated to make the effort and visit this very sick patient and do her best to sign her up. Unfortunately, this patient lived in a part of LA Karen had never dreamed she would ever see, let alone have to visit.

Karen walked up to the front door. She noticed Christmas lights were still up in the front window, although Christmas was long over. There was a group of teenage boys making suggestive remarks about her and her car. She tried to ignore them as best she could, but she was uncomfortable. Karen knocked on the door to the apartment. A rather fat black man came to the door. He opened it just enough to see who was on the other side, "Yah…?" He took one look at Karen and wondered what in hell this white bitch was doing in this neighborhood.

"Hello. My name is Karen Stoble. Ensi from California Hospital told me that she spoke to you about hospice." Karen handed the man her card through the narrow opening he had allowed in the door.

The man turned his head back inside the apartment, "There's some white woman here to talk about hospice? You know anything about this?"

"Yes, I do. Let her in," came the words attached to a very hoarse female voice.

The man stepped aside and opened the door. Karen entered the apartment.

Karen's first instinct was to turn and run back to her car and get the hell out of Dodge, but she sucked it up and entered the apartment. The apartment smelled horrible. It was so dirty that Karen had a hard time placing her foot on the floor. Inside, an obese black woman, Shaquon Golden, was hooked up to an oxygen tank. She was sitting in a ratted out recliner. Next to it was a TV tray table. On the tray was an opened bag of chips. In the woman's hand was a quart sized bottle of malt liquor. Also, on the tray table, was a large ashtray overflowing with cigarette butts. About two packs worth. Shaquon looked terrible. Her once mahogany skin was now the color of tallow. In front of her was a very big screen TV. Blaring from it was Let's Make a Deal. Karen scanned the apartment. To say it was filthy was being kind. She could see into the kitchen. Dishes and takeout buckets of the Colonel filled the sink. There were roaches scurrying across the kitchen floor. There was a large kitchen garbage container filled to over flowing with empty malt liquor cans. Bits of food dotted the floor.

"Come on in, hon," Shaquon said. She moved her oxygen mask to the top of her head so she could light up another cigarette, "Why don't you sit down."

Karen looked around the room for a clean place to sit. There really wasn't any. The only available sitting space was on a cat-hair covered couch. If Karen chose to sit there she would have to share it with a twenty pound tom cat. The tom was perched in the middle of couch. The cat had his hind leg up in the air and was licking his balls. Karen decided there was no way she was going to put her three hundred dollar dress on that couch or anywhere else in that apartment.

"That's all right. I've been driving for hours. I prefer to stand," she said.

"Suit yourself, honey," Shaquon said.

Behind the couch, was the largest fish tank Karen had ever seen outside of a sushi restaurant. Instead of fish, the aquarium was filled with clothes. The glass of the aquarium hadn't been cleaned and there was residue on it from the former fish residents. The clothes were not neatly folded but seemingly just poured into the tank.

Shaquon took a drag from her newly lighted cigarette. "The last time I was in the hospital Ensi told me you'd be coming by to talk about me going into a nursing home."

"Ensi feels then you'll be more comfortable there. You'll get round the clock care," Karen said.

Shaquon took another deep drag from her cigarette. Before she finished inhaling she began to cough. The coughing went on until she took a large swallow of the malt liquor. The coughing stopped. "I only have one question," Shaquon said.

"Sure," Karen said, "What is it?"

"Can I smoke there?"

Karen got back in her BMW and drove away from that apartment as fast as she could. She called Ned. He was in his office working on his computer. Her name appeared on Ned's cell. Ned answered, "Angel of Death, how's it going?"

"I'm sending you a female hospice patient, Shaquon Golden. She has lung cancer. I give her a few months. I'll get you the higher rate for this one. She's going to need some extra work," Karen said.

"Is she going to be trouble?' Ned asked.

"I don't think so. She's just messy," Karen said.

"Ok, thanks for the head's up," Ned said.

As she was talking to Ned, Karen pulled her BMW in front of a row of homeless peoples' tents on the side of the street. She pulled off her shoes and tossed them out the window at a homeless woman who was sweeping her section of the sidewalk. The homeless woman picked up the shoes and smiled at Karen. She smiled back and pushed her shoeless foot on the gas pedal and drove away, "You have no idea what I had to do to sign this one up. Be prepared to buy her lots of cigarettes."

"I thought you said she had lung cancer," Ned said.

"The cigarettes were they only way I could close the deal," then she added, "Oh, by the way you owe me a pair of shoes, Jimmy Choo's."

"Did you have to give the woman shoes too?" Ned asked.

"No, the place was so filthy I can't imagine ever wearing those shoes again. I just threw them out the window and you're going to replace them. And Ned, I really liked those shoes," Karen added sighing to herself.

"How am I supposed to expense a pair of shoes?" Ned asked.

"Not shoes, Jimmy Choos," Karen quickly responded. "I don't know but that's your problem," she said. Then she added, "And be prepared for Lyle to shit when he sees the bill."

A CHILDREN'S TOILET

Benito came into Ned's office, "Mr. Ned, let me show you something."

He led Ned into the restroom where he had just installed a new toilet, "What you think?"

Ned examined the newly installed toilet. Ned studied the bowl from every angle. The toilet was about half the size of what would be considered a normal-size toilet. "Where did you get it, in the children's department?" Ned asked.

"Mr. Ned, the purchase order from the corporate said I have to buy this kind," Benito responded.

"Look how small it is. Any decent sized person sitting on that thing is going to be like an elephant sitting on a piano stool. Did you tell them it was small?" Ned asked.

"Yes, I tell them. Maybe they read the number wrong. I know it's small but what can I do?" Benito added.

"Hope you never have to use it," Ned said as he walked back to his office. Sharon entered with another empty bottle of cheap vodka. "Let me guess. Shelia Moran again," Ned said.

"This one was under her bed. This one…" Sharon took a full pint of vodka and placed it on Ned's desk, "…was in her closet."

"How is she getting the booze in here?" Ned asked.

"I think its Michael Weller. I've seen Shelia give him money," she commented.

"Weller, huh…now what I have to do is catch him," Ned said.

Ned waited like a duck hunter in a blind for Michael Weller to return from his daily wheelchair jaunt away from Central City. As he was approaching the facility, Ned got up from his chair and went to his window. Ned watched closely as Weller made the turn from the city sidewalk toward the lobby door. As he proceeded onto Central City property, he slowed his electric wheelchair just a bit as he passed by a clump of bushes. Then he drove his electric wheelchair into the facility, passed Ned's office, and on toward the smoker's patio. When Weller was out of sight, Ned went outside and looked in the bushes where Weller had slowed down. There it was, stuffed in between the branches, another new pint of cheap vodka. Ned took the pint and went onto the smokers' patio where Shelia and Michael were having a cigarette. "I believe this is yours," Ned said to Shelia. Ned opened the bottle and poured its contents into the patio drain. Shelia watched. The expression on her face was that of a little kid who just had her ice cream cone snatched out of her hand by the neighbor's dog.

"Mr. Weller, your bootlegging business has been shut down. You will be searched every time you come into the facility. Should you be caught again, I'm going to kick you into the street," Ned said tossing the empty bottle into the trash.

Ned got back to his office and called Dylan. He was out of Central City visiting hospital discharge planners. "Dylan," Ned said, "I want you to go to LA Hospital meet Dr. Benjamin Gross. He's up on the sixth floor. Introduce yourself. He and I just made a deal. Tell him I want to send him Shelia Moran for lab work. She's been drinking at least a pint of vodka every day. Tell him to hold her for three days and then get rid of her. I don't want her back," Ned said.

"Ok," Dylan responded. Ned ended the call. Suddenly, Ned heard shouts of terror.

"Help me! Help me! I'm being kidnapped!"

The shouts were coming from the lobby. Ned immediately went to see what was going on. He opened his door to see Minerva Whiting, a woman deep into her eighties, Minerva was blind in one eye so it had that hazy white look. The other eye was bright blue. Her hair was dull grey, long and wild. Minerva looked like a witch. She was strapped onto a gurney. Two ambulance attendants were holding her so she couldn't accidentally fall off the gurney.

"Help me! Help me! I'm being kidnapped!" Minerva shouted as often as she could gather the breath to get the words out. "Help me! Help me!" Minerva howled again.

Ned went up to the gurney, "What's the matter, Minerva?"

"Can't you see, you dumb shit. They're kidnapping me!" Minerva fired back at Ned.

Casey Flynn, the ADON, was part of the entourage that was guiding Minerva and the gurney toward the front door. There was an ambulance waiting in the street.

"Why is Minerva on that gurney?" Ned asked Casey.

"Minerva just bit off her roommate's toe," Casey said dead pan.

"Ah, that explains it," Ned said. "Please, tell me you're kidding?" Ned added incredulously.

"No, she really did. We put the toe on ice to see if the hospital can sew it back on," Casey said.

"Of course, you did. Well, that's a first for me," Ned lamented.

"What's that?" Casey asked.

"Cannibalism," Ned responded.

With sirens blaring, the paramedics pulled up next to the ambulance that was about to take Minerva out to the psych hospital. The ambulance crew loaded Minerva into their vehicle.

"Help, me! Help me! I'm being kidnapped!" were the last words Minerva said as the ambulance door was closed behind her. The ambulance drove away.

Grant came up to Ned, "I've already started the SOC 341," Grant said.

"Good. This one will be tough to explain to DHS. I can hear it now. One of my patients tried to eat another patient's toe. And why would that be, the DHS would ask. Aren't you feeding them enough protein?" Ned said.

An LVN pushed an ancient little black lady, Parthenia Jones, into the lobby. She was sitting up in her wheelchair. Parthenia was the woman who just had her toe bitten off. She was surprisingly calm considering the size of the blood stained dressing wrapping her foot and the ordeal she had just endured. On her lap was her toe. It was in a clear plastic, zip lock bag full of ice.

"Parthenia, are you ok?" Ned asked.

"Oh, I'm fine," Parthenia answered.

"Are you in pain?" Ned asked.

"No, but I have to go to the bathroom," she said.

"We gave her a nice big shot of morphine, she won't feel a thing for hours," Casey said.

"These nice men will take you to the bathroom after they sew your toe back on," Ned said to Parthenia.

"Oh, that's nice," she said smiling at Ned.

The paramedics took Parthenia's vital signs, lifted her out of her wheelchair and put her on a gurney.

"Bye, bye," Parthenia waved to everybody in the lobby.

"Bye, Parthenia," the group gathered and waved back to her.

Then the paramedics casually loaded her into the back of their ambulance. They drove away, sirens blaring.

The lobby was suddenly filled with staff that had heard but wanted to see what had happened. Mostly, the staff chuckled in amazement. It was just another day in Central City.

"Ok everybody, back to work. The excitement's over," Ned said to the onlookers.

"I hope," he muttered to himself.

"Why did Minerva do it?" Ned asked Casey.

"She said she was hungry?" Casey responded.

"Hungry? I think when I do the paperwork for the DHS I'll put down that Minerva's responsible party is Hannibal Lector."

ALL BASKETBALL PLAYERS AREN'T IN THE NBA

Corky Carr had a short career as a pro in the NBA. He had all the makings of one of the best. He was over seven feet tall, great hands good footwork. That is until his knees, and soon after his career, went south. When the pain in his knees started the team doctor put him on pain killers. He never got off. Now in his forties, his body was a wreck. By the time he got to Central City, all the drugs had pretty much melted his brain away too. He was one of Ned's the 'deal' patients. He was part of a package, two Medicare for one problem, Corky. Violet hated the fact that he was in Central City. He was too young and too dangerous.

Corky was in the lobby when his grunts were a signal he was building toward rage. Jose watched from his reception cubicle and decided, before Corky became uncontrollable, he better call Ned.

"Mr. Ned, come to the lobby, stat!"

When Ned got to the lobby Corky was being followed by three LVNs trying to calm him down. The nurses looked like Huey, Dewey and Louie trying to calm Uncle Donald down from one of his tirades. Corky walked in circles around the lobby. The nurses followed. The more he circled, the more worked up he became. The more worked up Corky became, the farther back the LVNs stayed.

"Mr. Corky, how about we get you some ice cream?" One LVN pleaded as sympathetically as she could.

"I ain't no fuckin' baby. Don't talk to me like I'm a fuckin' baby," Corky screamed back.

At this point all the LVNs who were previously scared, were now terrified. Corky looked like he was just about to hit one of them when Ned quickly stepped between him and the LVNs.

"Whoa, Corky, calm down," Ned said to the giant man standing in front of him.

"You gonna offer me some ice cream too, like I'm a fuckin' baby. I ain't no fuckin' baby!" Corky's fists were now clenched and ready to strike. Corky loomed over Ned just inches from Ned's face.

"No," Ned responded in a normal tone, "You're not a baby."

Ned turned to the LVNs, "You can go back to the floor. Corky will stay with me."

"Violet has already put in the call to have Corky removed from the facility. She told us to stay with him until the ambulance got here," one of the LVNs sheepishly responded to Ned.

"Well, you go turn that order off, Corky is going to be fine," Ned said.

The LVNs didn't know what to do. They stood in the lobby like confused sheep. One of them tried to explain. "But…"

Ned cut her off, "Cancel the order for removal. Now go." The he added, "You have Corky's meds?"

"No," she answered. "I'll go get them."

The LVN took the opportunity to get away from the situation. She raced down the hallway toward the med cart.

"How about you and I go for a walk?" Ned asked Corky.

"Where?" Corky responded.

Ned spoke to Corky nonchalantly as if he were asking a friend to go for a stroll on a spring day.

"Around the block. Just to get out of here," Ned said as he took a few steps toward the door.

At first Corky just stood there in the middle of the lobby, his fists were still clenched.

"Come on, let's go for a walk," Ned pleasantly urged Corky for a second time.

"Mind if I tag along?" Casey asked. Then she added, "I need a cigarette anyway. I'll get Corky's meds and be right behind you."

"Yeah, that's a great idea," Ned said to Casey.

"We'll head down to 7-11," Ned turned back to Corky, "I'll buy you a soda."

Ned opened the lobby door and stepped out. Corky stood there in the lobby deciding whether he would follow Ned. Finally, he did.

Ned and Corky walked down the hill toward the 7-11.

"Don't you want to say something to me?" Corky asked.

"No, not really," Ned responded. Then he added, "You want to say anything to me?"

"You really gonna buy me a soda?" Corky asked.

"Yes," Ned smiled.

"Everyone thinks I'm stupid. I'm not stupid. I went to college," Corky said.

"Where did you go," Ned asked.

"Michigan," Corky responded proudly.

"Did you get drafted right after you graduated?" Ned asked.

"Yeah, by the Pistons," Corky said. A smile appeared on his face. His demeanor was visibly calmer.

They got to 7-11. "You have a seat," Ned said indicating the bench in front of the store, "I'll get you a soda. What kind you want?"

“Coke,” Corky responded.

“You want anything else?” Ned asked.

“No.”

Ned went into the store and returned with a Coke for Corky and bottled water for himself. He sat down next to Corky. Ned handed Corky his Coke, “I wasn’t a Pistons fan. I’m from Rhode Island.”

“Celtics, right?” Corky said with a smile.

“All the way,” Ned responded.

Casey crossed the parking lot in front of the 7-11 and walked over to Ned and Corky. “Mind if I join you,” Casey asked.

“Move over a little bit, Corky. Let Casey sit down,” Ned said.

Corky and Ned moved down the bench a bit so Casey could fit with them. She sat down and lit up a cigarette.

“Did you bring Corky’s meds?” Ned asked Casey.

She held out small cup containing a number of pills.

“Are you going to take those?” Ned asked Corky.

Without responding, Corky took the cup from Casey and poured the meds down his throat. He washed them down with a mouth full of Coke. Then he turned to Casey, “You know you shouldn’t smoke.”

“I know,” Casey responded. “I’ve been quitting for years.”

“Those things will kill ya,” Corky said.

“You’re probably right,” Casey said to Corky as she took another drag from her cigarette.

When the trio got back to Central City Ned turned to Corky, “What do you want to do now?”

“I think I’ll take a nap,” Corky responded.

The meds were already beginning to take effect.

“I wish I could take a nap,” Ned said to Corky. Then he added, “You going to go to your room?”

“Yeah,” Corky said.

“You need any help?” Ned asked.

“No, I’ll be fine.”

Corky shuffled down the hallway toward his room. “Thanks for the Coke.” Corky said to Ned over his shoulder.

“I was impressed the way you handled that situation,” Casey said to Ned.

Ned stopped and turned to Casey, “It seemed like the logical thing to do. Would you have shipped him out?”

Casey thought about her answer, “No. I think Violet acted a little hasty.”

“So do I. Corky didn’t need to be transferred to a psych ward. He needed to be managed. Isn’t that what we’re supposed to do here?” Ned asked.

Ned went to his office. Casey followed him. She closed the door behind her, "I've been thinking about what you said."

"Oh, I say a lot of things," Ned responded, "Which gem of wisdom are you speaking about?"

"Helping to change the culture around here," Casey responded.

"Oh, that one, and have you come to a decision about our conversation?"

Ned waited for her response. He was secretly hoping she was about to join his team.

"I think you're a good administrator. You're definitely a rarity around here," Casey said.

"I don't know any other way to do this job," Ned interjected.

"I think it's more than that. I think you care," Casey said.

"I've succeeded to pull the wool over your eyes," Ned smirked. Then he added sarcastically, "Truth is I'm at Central City for the big bucks."

"Me too," Casey said with a smile, "With the hours we put in, we could both probably make more money at Starbucks with a whole lot less headaches," she said.

"Actually, my dream job is shift manager at In-And-Out-Burger. I just love their fries," Ned said.

"I know the culture around here has to change. But don't be too hard on Violet," Casey said.

"Why not, it seems she has definitely forgotten why she became a nurse. Remember, 'do no harm.' Isn't that nursing one-o-one?" Ned asked.

"She used to be a good nurse. But she has seen a dozen administrators come and go through this place. None of them cared."

"That's no excuse," Ned said.

"I know. But after years of seeing Central City turned into a stepping stone for administrators she's lost heart. Like Violet, I've seen administrators come make a mess and leave. You're different. I know that. I don't think Violet understands you."

"Well, Casey, let me tell you how the world works. They've got a stopwatch on me at corporate. I either deliver or I'm gone. And I don't have but a few stops left in me. I don't have the luxury of waiting for Violet to come around and realize I have the Mother Teresa gene," Ned said.

"I understand. I'll do what I can to help you," she said.

"That's music to my ears," Ned said with a smile.

Then Ned held out his hand to Casey. "I look forward to working with you," Ned smiled. Casey shook Ned's hand. "Now I'm going to go have an argument with Violet over Corky," Ned said.

Ned walked down the hall to Violet's office. He knocked on her door. "Violet, I'd like to talk with you, please."

"It's open," she replied.

Ned entered. Violet was sitting at her tiny desk talking on her cellphone. Her conversation stopped. "I hope the nurses told you I canceled the transfer order for Corky Carr."

"I'll call you back," Violet said into her phone. She ended the call and put the phone on the desk.

"What that patient needed was a little bit of understanding not to be locked up," Ned said.

"He needed to be removed. I made that decision based on the safety of the other patients in this facility," Violet responded.

"You made that decision based on your convenience, not what was best for the patient," Ned said.

"He belongs in a psych ward not a skilled nursing facility," she said.

"The situation was handled correctly," Ned said forcefully.

"That's your opinion not mine," Violet said defiantly.

"He took his medication and has calmed down."

"This time," she said.

"All we have is this time. I'm going to try and work with you, Violet, I want your cooperation, you will certainly get mine, but I can just feel you're going to fight me every step of the way," Ned said.

"Then why don't you leave," she blurted out.

"The next time you try and transfer someone out of here for behavior, you check with me first," Then he added, "You can go to corporate and cry to anybody you want. But as long as my license is hanging on the wall, much as you hate it, I run this facility."

Ned left Violet's office. On his way, the anger he held in control with Violet came out, Ned kicked over a hamper full of dirty linen. He was shocked at his own outburst. The noise of the hamper hitting the floor turned the heads of both surprised patients and nurses.

"Just having a bad day, that's all," Ned apologized.

WHEN IS FOOD NOT FOOD

When Minerva decided to bite off her roommate's toe, Ned fully expected a visit from the Department of Health. The morning it happened it came in the guise of Candy Mintz. When she came walking into Central City, Ned knew he had trouble.

"Mr. Ned, line ten. Mr. Ned, line ten."

There was no line ten. That was the alarm Jose announced over the PA to warn the staff that the DHS was in Central City. Ned looked to his monitors to see who the DHS was throwing up against him.

Ms. Candy Mintz was short. To compensate, she wore six-inch black stiletto heels that clip-clopped on the floor as she walked. She was smartly dressed, in all black. The only bit of color was her white ID badge from the Department of Health. She was dragging a wheeled briefcase. Her makeup was Goth-white with black lipstick and matching black nail polish. All she was missing were leathery black wings. Ned wondered if she was a Punk Zombie who got into nursing because of the easy access to the blood supply. By the way she strutted across the lobby, Ned could tell she was here to beat the tar out of him and Central City.

Jose intercepted her in the lobby then steered her to Ned's office.

"This is Candy Mintz from the Department of Health." Jose said reading the name off her name badge. Then he added, "Oh, Candy Mintz, I get it."

Ms. Mintz grimaced but didn't comment.

"Thank you, Jose," Ned said.

Jose left Ned's office. "I bet you get that all the time," Ned said.

"Only from certain kinds of people," Ms. Mintz said with as much annoyance as she could put into those few words.

"What can I do for you?" Ned asked as she sat down.

"I'm here to look into the toe biting incident that you self-reported," she said.

"Ah, yes, I figured you folks would be here to investigate. It was definitely an unusual occurrence," Ned said.

"Where can I work?" she asked.

"I'll put you in the Media Room," Ned responded.

Ms. Mintz opened her briefcase and removed a notebook. She opened it. "And have the charts of Minerva Whiting and Parthenia Jones brought to me," she said as she got up.

"I'll have somebody bring them to you," Ned said.

She started to walk out of Ned's office. "Don't you need me to show you where the Media Room is?" Ned asked.

"I'll find it," she clip-clopped out of Ned's office.

Ned picked up the phone and called Jose, "Jose, get the DHS settled in the Media Room and then have Freddie bring her the charts for Whiting and Jones. And no more comments about her name, please," Ned put down the phone. Ned thought for a second and then he punched in Casey's number.

"Yes," Casey answered.

"The DHS is here for Parthenia's toe chewing incident. Can you baby sit her?" Ned asked.

"Sure. But she just went into the kitchen," Casey reported to Ned.

"Why did she go into the kitchen?" Ned asked.

"You'll have to ask her," Casey responded.

To be on the safe side, Ned decided to follow Ms. Mintz just in case she found something not to her liking, he would be there to, hopefully, explain it away.

When Ned arrived in the dietary department, Ms. Mintz was already grilling Calvin, the cook.

"What's the temperature that has to be maintained in a refrigerator?"

"Ah…" the cook grunted as he searched his brain for the answer.

Ned rightly guessed Calvin had no idea, even though he had been drilled on it at least a thousand times. Since he was standing behind Candy, and out of her line of sight, Ned decided to help the cook. He held up four fingers.

"Four," Calvin smiled and blurted out.

Ned quickly made a 'T' with his hands.

"Four – T," Calvin quickly added and then repeated, "Forty degrees."

Ms. Mintz turned around to see Ned standing behind her feigning a lack of interest in her question to Calvin. His hands were already down by his side. She gave Ned a dirty look as if she knew he was coaching the cook, but couldn't prove it. Ned just stood there, oozing innocence. She resumed her inspection. She took a little flashlight out of her black bag.

Ned knew this was an escalation of trouble. She used her flashlight to illuminate the out of the way nooks and crannies in the kitchen. She wanted to find something…anything, Luckily, Ned had the kitchen deep-cleaned a few days before. He was beginning to feel he may have dodged a bullet. Then Ms. Mintz walked by the spice rack. She took another two steps passed it, then stopped. She stepped back and looked a little harder at the rack's contents. She removed a half empty bottle of red food coloring. The date the bottle was opened was three years ago. The 'best used by date' was two and a half years ago. She looked through the other bottles of food coloring on the rack. They were all pretty much in the same shape as the one she was holding. She turned to the cook, "Do you use this food coloring?"

"Yeah," Calvin cook answered proudly.

"And these others as well?"

"Yes, we use the red one to make icing to decorate cakes. I use the brown one to make the gravy browner. Mr. Ned showed us how," Calvin responded.

"Did you know every one of these bottles is out of date?" she asked him.

"They are?" Calvin responded quite shocked. Panic set in. He looked over to Ned for help.

Candy turned to Ned, "Since you use these products in a variety of foods you serve to all the patients and every one of these bottles is out of date…you are putting the whole population of this facility in jeopardy. And have been for who knows how long. You could have killed your patients with this product."

"Are you kidding?" Ned blurted out.

"I'm going to call my supervisor and if she agrees, I'm going to call an immediate jeopardy."

The leathery winged creature had found her prey…Ned's kitchen.

"Immediate jeopardy! What are you talking about?" Ned said incredulously.

"I'm talking about the fact this kitchen has been using out dated products," she said.

Ms. Mintz pointed to a sheet cake with pink frosting that was on the work table. She turned again to the cook, "Are you going to serve that cake for desert?" she asked.

"Yeah…" Calvin sheepishly answered.

"And did you use the food coloring to make the pink icing for that cake?"

Calvin was afraid to answer. He turned to Ned for help.

"I'm sure he did," Ned said.

"You don't know that cake won't kill half the population in this facility," Ms. Mintz said scolding Ned.

"That can't happen!" Ned said to Ms. Mintz

"Why not?" she snapped back.

"Food coloring isn't food!" Ned responded.

"Of course it is," Ms. Mintz said with utter confidence.

She held the bottle of the red food coloring up to Ned, "See…F-O-O-D coloring."

Ned quickly retuned her volley, "Food coloring is an inert product. Like salt, which comes from the ocean where it can be floating around for thousands of years or from a mine deep underground where it could be sleeping there for millions of years."

"This isn't salt," she said.

She turned the bottle to the 'best used by date' printed on it, "It says so right here...best used by. Salt doesn't have a date."

"Best used by only means if you go over the date the red will become a bit pinker. That's all. There is no protein in that bottle, it can't go bad," Ned insisted.

"I disagree," she said with a smirk.

"You are wrong. But I'll tell you what, Ms. Mintz, why don't you make your phone call and then go to the Media Room and investigate the toe chewing incident. And I'll prove to you food coloring is not food. And by the way, you'll discover Parthenia's toe was successfully sewed back on. Her foot looks a little Frankenstein-ish but it works just fine. If you don't mind, I'll borrow that bottle." Ned snatched the bottle of food coloring from Ms. Mintz. He turned and left her in the kitchen.

Ned went back to his office. He read the label on the bottle and found the name and a phone number of the manufacturer. Ned wasted no time and called the company. A female voice answered, "Gilfor food products, how may I direct you call?"

"I need to talk to somebody in charge of the food coloring. Maybe a chemist?"

"That will be the research department. I'll connect you."

Within a moment Ned was talking to a chemist. Ned explained who he was and his predicament. "...and if this woman from the Department of Health Services issues me an immediate jeopardy, I can get shut down or at best get stuck with a hefty fine. Can you help me?" Ned asked.

"That's a first. This woman is really an idiot, isn't she? I'll fax you the chemical components of our food coloring. That should prove your point. Food coloring could be a hundred years old and never hurt you," the chemist said.

"I tried to tell her that but it did no good. And if you don't mind, could you write a note on your letterhead explaining your credentials. That will also help," Ned said.

"Give me about half an hour and I'll fax it to you," the chemist said.

Freddie was in the Media Room with Candy Mintz. He was nervously trying to point out the necessary sections in Parthenia and Minerva's charts that would prove that Central City was not responsible for the toe biting because the incident was unforeseen and therefore unavoidable.

Those two words, unforeseen and unavoidable, Ned put in every letter he wrote to DHS. They were the equivalent of the accused standing before a judge pleading 'not guilty.'

Ms. Mintz was meticulously going through Minerva's chart. She wanted to find a reason Central City was responsible for Minerva biting off Parthenia's toe.

"On the day of the incident," Mintz said, "I see that Minerva didn't receive a snack. In the dietary notes it points out she wanted hot dogs every day at lunch. It also points out she has dementia and is nearly blind. Do you think it's possible that since the facility did not provide her a snack on the day of the incident, she mistook her roommate's toe for a Vienna sausage?" Mintz asked.

Freddie buckled. The question was too idiotic for him to answer. He began to sweat.

"I suppose it's possible," he nervously responded.

While Freddie was being interrogated in the Media Room, Ned was waiting by the fax machine in Jose's cubicle.

"Do you think Ms. Candy Bar is going to give us an IJ? She looks like such a roaring bitch." Jose said.

"Mintz not Bar. I'm sure she'd like to," Ned commented.

After what seemed like forever, the fax machine spit out the pages from the food coloring chemist that would save Ned's facility from a severe penalty. Ned read the document, "Ah, there it was in black and white, food coloring is not food,"

Ned made a few copies of the chemist's fax and marched it down to the Media Room.

When he got there, Ms. Mintz was interviewing Parthenia. She was sitting in her wheelchair. Her foot wrapped in a bandage.

"Oh, hi Parthenia," Ned said as he entered the room.

"Do you know who this is?" Ms. Mintz asked her.

"I think he's my son," Parthenia looked at Ned, "Are you my son?"

"No, honey I'm not," Ned gently responded.

"Are you sure? You look like my son," Parthenia said.

"I'm absolutely sure," Ned said.

"I have to go to the bathroom. Can you take me to the bathroom?"

Ned looked to Ms. Mintz, "Are you finished with her?"

"Yes, she can go," Ms. Mintz said.

Ned rolled Parthenia out into the hallway. He stopped a passing CNA, Carolina.

"Please take Parthenia to the bathroom," Ned instructed.

"She always has to go to the bathroom," Carolina said having a little fun at Ned's expense.

"Please take her to the bathroom," Ned repeated.

"Anything for you, Ned," she responded in her best Sippie voice. Ned bared his teeth like an angry dog at Carolina, "Take her to the bathroom, now!"

Carolina wheeled Parthenia down the hallway and to the comfort of her familiar toilet seat.

Ned went back into the Media Room. He handed a copy of the chemist's fax to Candy Mintz.

"This is for you, and you can have another for your supervisor."

Candy read the report. Even though it showed conclusively that Ned was right, she wasn't about to give in. "I'll show this to my supervisor," she said, "...she'll make the final decision." She put the two reports in her rolling suitcase.

"Does that mean you're not going to call an immediate jeopardy?" Ned asked.

"Not at this time," Ms. Mintz replied.

Ned knew he had won.

Then Mintz re-opened Minerva Whiting's chart. "You transferred Minerva Whiting?" she asked.

"We sent her to the hospital. I called her doctor and told him we're not going to take her back. I think you can understand why. I don't want to explain why she chewed off another limb." Ned said.

"And what steps are you going to take to prevent this from happening again?" Ms. Mintz asked.

Ned loved that kind of question. It was the kind of standard question every investigator asked every time they came to a facility for any reason at all. It must have been written on the first page of the Department of Health's question guide to annoy administrator and SNF staff. But Ned was ready, "As soon as the incident took place, I formed an Appendage Biting Committee. We are going to give an in-service to the staff. The purpose of which is to alert them to the warning signs of a possible biter. Then we're going to pass out something to model fingers and toes, I haven't figured out what that is exactly, but I'm toying with lady fingers. We're going to instruct all the patients explaining what NOT to do should they get the urge to bite off any part of their neighbor's body. And as a final precaution we are also in the process of isolating the potential biters in the facility to see if any of them are having significant weight loss. If so, we will adjust their diet to bring them back to their ideal body weight. We will in-service the staff quarterly to insure they are aware of the warning signs of an impending appendage chewing incident. All this will be outlined in the 2567 I'm sure you'll be sending me," Ned flashed a broad smile to Candy.

That was the most impudent mouth full of words Ned could think of to respond to her absurd question. Ms. Mintz knew she was being zoomed and was not amused. "Do you have a Policy and Procedure on patient to patient biting?" she asked through clenched teeth.

"No, but I will send a recommendation to our consultants to implement one. Will there be anything else I can help you with?" Ned asked.

"You'll be contacted with our decision," Ms. Mintz snarled.

Then she stood up. The interview was over. Ned accompanied her out of the facility.

METHANE

A few hours later as Ned was making rounds, Anthony suddenly came running by him. He was holding an ice pack. Anthony ducked into one of the rooms. Ned knew something was up so he followed his DSD. There, sitting on the bed was Sippie, her head was tilted back. The front of her scrubs splattered with blood. She was holding a towel against her nose. Anthony applied the ice pack to her face. "Hold onto this," Anthony said to her.

She took the ice pack and held it against her nose. Carolina and Cynthia, the RN supervisor, were keeping two wheelchair bound patients, a very elderly white gentlemen, Mr. Ramsey, and a black gentleman, Mr. Miles, apart. Ned quickly surveyed the room to assess what had happened. His bleeding employee was his first concern. "Sippie, are you all right? What happened?" Ned asked. She removed the ice pack from her nose long enough to answer. "I'm fine, Ned," she said as she returned the ice pack to her nose.

"You don't look fine," Ned responded.

"Mr. Ramsey and his roommate started to get into it. Sippie got in the middle of it and took one on the nose," Anthony said.

"Ouch! Why don't we get her to the clinic? Get her nose checked out," Ned said to Anthony.

"I don't think I can drive, will you take me, Ned?" Sippie asked.

Even in her damaged condition Sippie couldn't help but try to get her boss alone.

"Oh, please..." Carolina grumbled under her breath.

"I have too many fires to put out here, Sippie, but I'll get somebody to run you over there."

"I'll take her," Anthony replied.

"Why don't you take me to the goddamn clinic?" Mr. Miles shouted at Ned, "I'll do anything to get out of this shithole. You people are trying to kill me!"

"Why would we want to kill you, Mr. Miles? We hardly know you," Ned questioned.

"Did Oswald know Kennedy? That didn't stop him, did it?" Miles asked.

"I'm glad you've elevated yourself to presidential standing, Mr. Miles, but I think your analogy is way off base," Ned responded.

"Of course, you do. That's because you're in on it. Hell, you're probably the fucking ring leader," Miles responded.

"Be that as it may, what exactly is your problem, Mr. Miles?" Ned asked.

Mr. Miles was a paranoid schizophrenic and prone to outbursts and seizures. He was wearing a padded, bright blue helmet in case he fell out of his wheelchair and banged his head on the floor, which he often did. When he wasn't splayed out on the floor like a murder victim, he was writing letters to various government officials expounding his latest conspiracy theories.

"He's my goddamn problem," Miles said stabbing a finger at Mr. Ramsey. "He farts all goddamn day! This goddamn room smells like fart, awful, terrible, fart, all day long. And I'm goddamn sick of it!" Miles screamed nearly falling out of his wheelchair.

Mr. Ramsey was a dementia patient. He simply smiled back at Miles. He was either glad he was able to foul the air in the room, or he didn't have a clue what he was doing.

"Is Mr. Ramsey having some digestive issues?" Ned asked Cynthia.

"Mr. Ramsey has been passing gas since he was admitted. He could easily fill a large O-2 tank everyday if he wanted to," Cynthia said calmly.

"Has it always been bad enough to start fights?" Ned asked.

"No, this is relatively new," Cynthia responded.

Cynthia was an older RN. She had been through it all and was used to patient on patient behavioral interaction. It didn't rattle her in the least.

"Why don't we get a gastroenterologist to take a look at him?" Ned suggested.

"That will take a while to set up. Getting a specialist to come down here is difficult," Cynthia said.

"Why don't we work on it anyway," Ned suggested.

"We can all be dead by then," Miles added.

Carolina grimaced and waved her hand in front of her nose, "He just cut another one."

"See! See! What did I tell you!" Miles screamed out.

"You people put something in his food, some kind of bacterial agent that he can fart out and kill everybody in this place."

"Why would we do that? If I let him kill off all my patients how would I defraud Medicare?" Ned responded wryly.

The foul smell reached Ned's nose. He grimaced, "Oh boy! Did Mr. Ramsey eat the ass off a skunk recently?"

Everyone in the room, but Ramsey, covered their nose with their hand. Ramsey just sat in his wheelchair and smiled obliviously.

"Open the window," Ned said.

Carolina opened the window and complained. "It won't help. I swear to God. His farts are like the worst in the world," Carolina stayed by the window and breathed in the outside air.

Anthony was holding his hand over his nose. "Let's go to the clinic now. Come on," Anthony said as he helped Sippie up and they left the room.

"Mr. Ramsey, I can now fully appreciate your concern as to the air quality in this room," Ned said. He turned to Cynthia, "Why don't we see if we can move Mr. Ramsey or Mr. Miles, and why don't we at least get some labs done on Mr. Ramsey, pronto. Perhaps, some creature got into his system and died there."

"I don't want to move. I want to get the fuck out of here! And kill this son-of-a-bitch!" Miles screamed. Then he took another swing at Ramsey but the punch connected with only the foul air in the room.

"Mr. Miles, I'm willing to give you another room. I agree it stinks in here. Help me help you," Ned said.

"I don't want another goddamn room! I want out of this place!" Miles screamed.

"And where are you going to go?" Ned said trying to reason with his patient.

"I don't care! Anywhere but here!"

"Mr. Miles we can't just let you go into the street. We are obligated to find you a place to go. And that will take some time," Ned said.

"I know my rights. I'm leaving. Today! And you can't stop me!" Miles screamed.

"Mr. Miles you're being unreasonable," Ned said.

"Move your goddamn fat ass," Miles said to Cynthia as he struggled to get his wheelchair out of the room and into the hallway.

"What do you want to do with him?" Cynthia said indicating Mr. Miles.

"See what you can do for Ramsey's insides. Can't we feed him charcoal or something like that? I'll take care of Mr. Miles," Ned said.

Ned followed Miles down the hallway toward the front door. As Miles rolled himself toward the lobby, he screamed obscenities at everyone he passed. "Fuck you! Fuck all of you!"

Ned was right behind him trying to soothe over Miles' outbursts, "It's all right Mr. Miles is upset, that's all."

When Mr. Miles got to lobby, he wheeled himself over to the front door. He pressed the pad that opened the electric door. The door opened. Freedom was but a few feet away. Mr. Miles then tried to wheel himself out of the facility but Ned grabbed Miles' wheelchair and stopped it from moving. "Let go of my goddamn wheelchair," Miles screamed at Ned.

He tried to power his wheelchair away from Ned but Miles didn't have the strength to break Ned's grasp, "I said let go of my goddamn wheelchair."

"It's not your wheelchair it's mine," Ned said, "...as you may or may not recall when you came into this facility, you came in with a hospital gown and nothing else. I'm willing to give you the clothes you're wearing but the wheelchair stays. Oh, and I think I'll take back the blue helmet too. They're very expensive. The next time you fall on the sidewalk you can crack your head open. You won't be my patient anymore that means you won't be my problem," Ned said confidently.

"I'll crawl bare ass into the street if I have to," Miles said as he struggled to get out of the wheelchair. The only thing that held him back was a seat belt.

Ned was now faced with a conundrum, if he held Miles in the facility against his will, Miles was sure to get more agitated. Perhaps, another CNA would end up taking one on the nose. If he let Miles crawl out of his wheelchair onto the sidewalk, Ned ran the risk of a fall with injury. Ned suddenly saw himself trying to explain to the DHS his thinking behind that particular strategy.

"Ok, Mr. Miles, I'm going to let you borrow my wheelchair and helmet until you get up to the corner," Ned said.

"You're goddamn right you are! I know my rights! I'm going to call my lawyer and he's going to sue your goddamn ass off," Miles screamed.

"That will be fine, Mr. Miles," Ned said condescendingly.

Ned loosened his grip on the wheelchair and Miles was able to roll his wheelchair out the front door. Ned followed Miles out onto the sidewalk. Once Miles got outside the facility, he became confused. He really didn't know where he was.

"Now what, Mr. Miles, where are you going to go?" Ned asked.

Miles looked around. Nothing was recognizable to him. "I'm going to go back to my apartment," he responded defiantly.

"Miles, you don't have an apartment in LA. You came from Fresno and that's two hundred miles from here." Ned indicated the direction toward Fresno. "It's that way, north. Fresno is way on the other side of those mountains."

Jennifer, a black female CNA walked out of the facility and up to Ned.

"Jennifer, why don't you walk with Mr. Miles up to the corner. When you get there help him onto the curb. And bring back my wheelchair and the helmet."

Then Ned spoke to Miles, "I'm sure you'll be able to hitch a ride to Fresno from there. That corner looks like a very good spot for hitchhikers." As Miles assessed the journey, he was about to undertake, a lot of the acid that fueled his anger was already draining out of him.

"Good luck, Mr. Miles," Ned said to him as he gave a wink to Jennifer. She smiled back at him. "Ok, Mr. Miles, here we go," she said as she escorted Mr. Miles on his trek up the slight hill to the corner.

As Miles contemplated the trip up the long steady hill, Ned leaned and whispered in Jennifer's ear, "Let him do most of the work getting up that hill. In fact, let him do all the work."

Ned took a ten dollar bill out of his pocket. "When you get to the top, he'll be exhausted." Ned handed her the ten. "Buy him a soda and get one for yourself. By the time you get back we'll have his room changed and his problem with Ramsey will be over."

She smiled at Ned. "Ok, Mr. Miles, let's go," Jennifer encouragingly said to Miles.

Miles struggled to propel the wheelchair up the hill. He huffed and puffed like the little engine that could. Jennifer followed. "That's great keep rolling that wheelchair, you're doing fine," Jennifer said encouragingly.

Almost immediately, Miles was grunting as the wheelchair moved very slowly up the incline. Ned, knowing how the eventual outcome of his strategy would turn out, went back inside the facility and returned to his office. He picked up his phone and called Eileen.

"Yes…," she said.

"Eileen, please transfer Mr. Miles to the other side of the building. I don't want him to have another run in with Ramsey," Ned said to her.

"I'll put Ramsey in eleven. The roommate there is quiet," she responded.

"The guy in eleven, does his nose work?" Ned asked.

"What? I don't know," she responded totally confused by Ned's question.

"Never mind, thanks," Ned hung up the phone.

Eileen was someone Ned could trust. She knew everything about Central City. Before he made the call to her Ned knew she would be able to handle the room change problem for him and she did. Ned leaned back in his chair and scanned the security monitors. For the moment, Central City was at peace.

Ned began to go through the emails on his computer. About halfway through ads from podiatrists wanting patients, offers from various healthcare gurus proclaiming sure fire ways to solve every nursing home problem, to the dozens of edicts from the corporate office, Ned took a breath. He looked over at the stack of papers that needed addressing. He knew if he gave up his home in Pasadena and moved into his office, he would still never catch up with his work load. Over the years, Ned had taught himself to celebrate the victories, even the little ones. He decided that overall the Miles issue was a success. Yes, there was Sippie's bloody nose, hopefully it wasn't broken, but this was the perfect place to give himself an at-a-boy. Ned knew exactly the treat he wanted. He took out his cellphone and called Lenore. He got her cellphone message: "This is Lenore Wainscott with the Los Angeles County Public Defender's Office. If this is an emergency call 911. Otherwise please leave a message and I'll get back to you within twenty-four hours," then the familiar beep.

"Lenore, this is Ned Russo. I'm in the mood for whole fried catfish from Shiro's. How 'bout you? Say seven? Let me know."

Ned got a text from Lenore within minutes. 'Seven is perfect. See you there.'

He went back to shuffling paper and answering emails. At one point, he as looked up at his surveillance monitors, he saw Jennifer and Mr. Miles in the dining room.

"Back already, huh? That didn't take long," Ned said aloud.

Ned had guessed right. Jennifer had returned with Mr. Miles who had forgotten about the incident with Mr. Ramsey and was currently enjoying a game of dominoes with another patient. Ned knew Miles would no longer have to endure Mr. Ramsey's gastronomical problems. The issue, as Ned was concerned, definitely fit into the small victory category. Ned watched the monitor as Mr. Miles beat his opponent. Miles' threw his arms into the air as if he had just won Olympic Gold rather than a game of nursing home dominoes. Ned got out of the chair and went into the dining room. He wanted to thank Jennifer for helping solve the Miles problem in person. Ned walked up behind her and tapped Jennifer on the shoulder. "Thank you for helping me with Miles," Ned said with a big smile.

"I was glad to help," she responded. Jennifer suddenly remembered, "Oh..." she dug into the pocket of her scrubs and produced the change from the ten Ned had given her at the beginning of Mr. Miles' short journey into freedom. "Here, Mr. Miles ran out of gas halfway up the hill. We never got to the corner. I pushed him the rest of the way to the store and bought him a coke. And I bought one for me too." Jennifer tried to hand Ned the change.

"You keep it," Ned said, "Save it for the next time Mr. Miles decides he needs to return to Fresno."

Ned smiled as walked back to his office. He felt good that he had just given his CNA a little reward for doing a good job. He liked doing that. Instead of going back to his computer, Ned decided to get a bit of fresh air and take a walk. As he was going out the lobby door he waved to Jose. "I'll be back in ten minutes."

Ned went down the block and turned toward Alvarado Street. He walked over by the auto repair shop where the rescue of Ying Kang took place. Ned stopped and listened to the Korean accented spiritual that came out of the open door at the top of that rickety fire escape. "Jesus loves me yes I know, cause the Bible tells me so."

"Churchee" Ned muttered aloud. And then he laughed, "Churchee."

Later that afternoon, as Ned drove out of the parking lot, he saw Shelia Moran on a gurney being loaded into an ambulance. Dr. Gross had come through for him. Ned reflected for a moment about the contradictions in everyday logic he had to face being an administrator of a psych facility. It was lunacy. Then he realized of course it was lunacy. Ned laughed.

DINNER BUT NO DANCING

Ned went home. He worked out on the heavy bag, ran a few miles, took a hot shower and then a serious nap. About six he woke up tried on three or four clothing combinations before he decided on a Brooks Brothers button down white shirt, light colored V-neck sweater and his most expensive dark slacks. The last part of his presentation to Lenore was a splash of his best cologne. Ned wanted to impress her. Now ready, he drove to Shiro's.

The whole fried catfish at Shiro's was, Ned believed, the best he ever tasted. Shiro's during the week was a quiet little restaurant in South Pasadena. That's why Ned liked it. He heard enough screaming and noise at Central City that by the end of the day, Ned needed mellower surroundings. Ned was already seated at a table by the front window when Lenore came in. She looked beautiful. Ned stood up. She walked over to him. He kissed her on the cheek.

"You are a knockout. You know that?" he said to her.

She smiled, "Aren't you a charmer."

"I call'm as I see'm. I took a chance on ordering dinner and I threw in Grey Goose martinis. I hope that was all right?" Ned asked seeking her approval.

"I'm sure it will be fine," she said.

"Oh good, I'm trying to impress you. How am I doing?" Ned asked.

"I'm more impressed by the second," she said with a smile.

The waiter brought the martinis to the table. Lenore sipped her cocktail. "This is good…and strong."

Ned could see that Lenore was a bit overwhelmed by the drink. "If it's too strong…" Ned said.

"No, no it's fine. I'm just not much of a drinker.

"You're obviously a brilliant woman, college educated with a law degree. Didn't you get blasted now and then in college or after you passed the bar?"

"I was a good girl in school. But I did get drunk once at a Dodger game. I was trying to keep up with my date. I had too many beers and Dodger dogs and vomited all over myself. That was the last time I ever saw him. That kind of cured me of the drinking thing."

"That guy was a fool. One little unladylike episode…You didn't vomit in his car, did you?

"No, I didn't vomit in his car, but I think I got a little on him."

"That's' worse," Ned said jokingly.

"He didn't look too happy when it happened," she said.

"Well, the good news is you're hanging around with a bad influence now. I'm going to make it my goal to corrupt some of your good girl habits."

"I've got bad habits," she smiled and answered defiantly.

"Oh, yeah, what are they? Name one," Ned asked.

"I work too hard," Lenore quickly said.

"That's not a bad habit. This is America. Everybody works too hard. You have to just to keep your head above water."

"That's true. I'm sure I have other ones. I just can't think of any right now," she said.

"Ah, that's the Grey Goose talking, it's already working," he said.

The waiter, a smiling man in his twenties, arrived with the platter of catfish. He placed their dinner on the table.

"Ooh, look at that," Ned said eyeing the feast before them. "You eat on that side and I'll eat this one. And don't forget the ginger. It's those little sliced things between the meat," Ned said teasing her again.

"I know what the ginger is," she said pulling off a piece of the fish with her chopsticks.

"I just wanted to make sure. I'm not completely off base here. I mean you didn't know about rye in a Manhattan."

"Thanks to you, it will always be rye in my Manhattans from now on," she said then added as an aside, "If I ever drink one again."

"I don't have that problem. But when I do drink, I like the good stuff. In fact, I like the good stuff in every aspect of my life. That's why we're here. You're a beautiful, charming woman and I wanted to get to know you better."

"Aren't you a silver-tongued devil," she said with a smile.

"You know that's a Kris Kristofferson song," Ned said.

"Who, never heard of him."

"Kris wrote and sings songs about the heart," Ned suddenly sang the beginning of another Kristofferson song. "Lovin' her was easier than anything I'll ever do again."

"Don't know that one," Lenore said.

"How about this one," Ned began to sing again. "Take the ribbon from your hair…"

Lenore sang the next line.

"…Shake it loose and let it fall," that's a pretty song. I thought Bob Dylan wrote it," Lenore said.

"No, it was Kris. Alcohol, music, I have a lot to teach you, counselor," he said jokingly.

She smiled at him. "Long as you do it over Grey Goose and catfish."

"Tell you what, your next lesson will be at my house for dinner, I'll cook" Ned said.

"Sounds like I'm in for a treat."

"Honey, you have no idea."

CONSIDER IT A GIFT

Ned's phone rang. It was Jose. "Boss, there's a guy on the line who says he's the administrator of Fountain Gardens."

"Put him through…" Ned took the call, "Ned Russo."

"Ned, my name is Dave Longo. I'm the administrator of Fountain Gardens, around the corner from you."

"I know your building. Good morning. What can I do for you?"

Fountain Gardens was a tiny part of the biggest chain of nursing homes in California. The owner was rumored to have ties to the Russian and Israeli Mafia.

"How 'bout you let me buy you lunch today? You know Bestia?" Dave asked.

"Oh, yeah, I know it."

"See you there at noon."

When Ned first came to LA it was not really considered a fine dining paradise. But over the years that changed. Now there were scores of restaurants that rivaled the best in the country. Bestia was definitely one of those. Ned got there early. Since he wasn't eating with his boss, he ordered a Grey Goose martini. And he decided to go with an appetizer, the veal tartare. Dave arrived a few minutes after the veal. Though they had never met, Ned was able to spot him the second he walked into the restaurant. Blonde hair receding, fifty pounds overweight, expensive suite that was so shiny it looked like it was made out of chrome. He had a gaudy pinkie ring you could see across the room. He definitely looked like one of the goombas Ned grew up with back in Providence. He came right to Ned's table and saw the tartare. He pointed to it and went into a Godfather accent.

"Try the veal. It's the best in the city!" Dave laughed at his own joke.

"I agree. Sit down," Ned said.

Dave sat down and adjusted his chair so he would be closer to Ned when time came to talk turkey. The waitress arrived. Before she could ask, Dave pointed to Ned's drink.

"Bring me one of these. And bring us a Margherita pizza and the salami thing," Dave turned to Ned, "You ok with this?"

"Keep going," Ned responded.

He turned back to the waitress, "That's a start. When we want more I'll let you know."

The waitress left.

Dave got right into the usual small talk. He touched all the bases, family, wives, the Lakers, back East. Dave was from Jersey. By the time the pizza came, Dave got the conversation to where he wanted it to be.

"So, how's your Medicare?" Dave asked.

"You know. There's never enough," Ned responded.

"True. But the guys I work for have figured a way to increase the odds on the Medicare."

"Oh, how's that?"

Ned knew where the conversation was going but he decided to play it a bit dense.

"We have a large number of SNFs and co-operative docs so we can move patients around. We use up the days here, we move the patient there. The system stays healthy that way. You know what I mean?" Dave explained.

Ned knew exactly what Dave meant. They cheated.

"Sounds great. What does that have to do with me?" Ned asked.

"I bet you have some dead wood at your place you'd like to get rid of," Dave said.

Ned cut him off. "So, you'll take them as long as they have a Medicare card, active or inactive, right?"

"Right," Dave responded with a chuckle.

"What's in it for me?" Ned asked.

"You get rid of a bad patient, a bed that opens up. I put a thousand in your pocket for every one you send me. Consider it a gift," Dave said smiling.

There it was, sitting right next to him eating pizza, graft. In the past, Ned had been offered a few bucks to do a favor or two. But this was the big time. Ned knew he could pick up fifteen or twenty 'K' a year under the table for doing what he had to do anyway. It was obviously tempting. The way it worked for Dave was simple. He got a Medicare patient that he stored in one of his sister facilities until the Medicare days regenerated. Then he got one of his docs, who was in their system, to come up with some reason for the patient to go to the hospital and made sure the patient stayed there for three days. The qualifying stay in place, the discharge planner, who was also on the payroll, returned the patient to Dave, a new Medicare, worth plenty. For the out lay of a few bucks, Dave got the return of thousands. Not a bad deal. The only trouble with this arrangement...it was all illegal. If the State or the Feds found out you were part of that system, you could lose your license and possibly acquire an orange jump suit. And Ned knew he didn't look that good in orange.

An espresso and a chocolate dolci behind them, Ned and Dave left Bestia. Dave had gone fishing. Now all Ned had to do was figure out how to eat the bait off the hook without getting caught.

Overnight Ned pondered how he could benefit from Dave's proposal without getting his hand stuck in the cookie jar. The next morning, when Ned got to work, he ran his idea by Ed Denning, the corporate legal counsel. Ed was blue suit, USC law, very conservative. Ned knew if he could get his idea by this guy he would be saved from the State or the Feds.

When Ned called, Ed was driving to work in his Jaguar.

"Ed Denning," he said answering his cell phone.

"Good morning, Ed, Ned Russo at Central City. I have a question for you."

"Shoot," Ed said.

"I know I can take money from a family member or say an ambulance company as a donation towards a facility party. Is there a limit to the amount I can take?" Ned asked.

"I guess it depends on the size of the party. If an ambulance company wanted to give every patient in the building a gift card, that could get pretty pricey. But it could be justified. I would keep a list of who got a card just in case there were questions," Ed said.

"What if it were a staff party?" Ned asked.

"What do you have about a hundred and thirty or so employees? You could go to around two grand without raising any eyebrows," Ed speculated.

"That's what I needed to know, thanks Ed."

The conversation complete Ned hung up the phone. Then he called Carolina, his opinionated CNA, over the intercom. "Carolina, please come to my office," Ned's voice echoed through the facility.

A few moments later Carolina was standing in Ned's doorway. "Am I in trouble?" she asked.

"Why do you always ask me that? Should you be?" Ned responded.

"Never, I'm your best CNA. You know that," she said smiling.

"Yes, sometimes that's true. But right now, I want to know about your husband's taco truck."

"How did you know about the truck?" she asked.

"I know a lot of things," he said.

Ned made it his business to know a little bit about his employees' lives. So, Ned found out about birthdays and little league games and where their sons or daughters were accepted to college.

"It's not totally his truck. He just owns a little piece of it," she said.

"I want you to call him," Ned said.

"Why?" she asked.

"I want to know what it'll cost me to hire his truck to provide lunch for the staff," Ned said.

His conversation with Carolina finished, Ned went to Grant Carrillo's office.

"Do we have any used-up Medicare that we need to transfer out of here?" Ned asked.

"There's a couple that I'm working on. I just need to find them a place to go so we have a safe transfer."

"I have a place for them to go, Fountain Gardens. Do you know Dave Longo? He's the administrator over there. He's looking for anyone with a Medicare card, days or not," Ned said.

"That makes my job a lot easier," Grant responded.

"Get a list. Get it over to him. Then work out the transfers."

"How did you accomplish this?" Grant asked.

"I got lucky," Ned responded.

Within a few weeks the deal had been completed. Fountain Gardens had three of Ned's former Medicare patients, and Dylan had three open beds which he quickly filled with new Medicare patients. Ned's bottom line got a bit blacker. Everyone was a winner. Carolina's husband got a 'bump' from his partners for delivering a big lunch at Central City. And all of it was clean and above board. Dave paid for the taco truck and Ned never took a dime.

With fliers posted all around the facility and plenty of word of mouth spreading the news, on the day of the 'Taco Truck Appreciation Lunch' employees, patients and family members alike turned out for the event. Ned became an instant hero. Latrina Watkins, the woman who asked Ned about her mother's leg, was even there getting her free lunch. Most of the staff came up to thank Ned for his generosity. Violet didn't attend the gathering. She had one of her henchmen tell Ned she had too much paperwork to do. Ned forced a smile and said he understood. What he really understood was Violet giving him the finger once more.

Casey came up to Ned and handed him a fish taco plate. "Here, I noticed you haven't had anything to eat."

"I've been so busy being thanked I forgot," Ned said.

Ned took a healthy bite out of the taco. "This is good," he said.

"I don't think most administrators would have done this for the staff," Casey said.

"Oh, I don't know," Ned said.

"I do. Fountain Gardens has a reputation for buying Medicare. I think most administrators would have taken advantage of the situation."

"I did," Ned responded by pointing to the taco truck.

Even Dave Longo dropped by for a couple of tacos. He walked over to Ned, "What a great idea this was. Me, I would have taken the envelope. But if this is what makes you happy, I'm happy," Dave said.

"This makes me happy," Ned said.

"Who knows? You keep sending me patients and by Christmas I'll come over here dressed like Santa and give everybody a toy."

Ned poked Dave in the stomach. "Another few pounds and you will be Santa."

They both laughed.

THE LETTUCE GOES IN THE FRONT

Ned opened his email. There was an 'invitation' from Jeanie, Lyle's assistant, asking him to be part of a lip-sync contest that would be held in a few weeks at Whittier Narrows Recreation Center. Ned knew all invitations from corporations are veiled orders. Nobody who doesn't want to lose their job decides not to be part of whatever it is the corporation is hosting. Since Central City was part of the downtown region, Ned was placed on their team. Included in the email was the time and location of the first rehearsal. The theme of the event was 'A Mexican Holiday.'

"What is this about?" Ned wondered aloud.

All the corporations where Ned had worked previously held some form of corporate retreats. Some companies took their staffs away for a long weekend to a resort like Cancun or Tahoe. Others had a day at Disneyland or Knott's Berry Farm. Most corporations planned theses interludes, whether at some exotic location or just in town, was to show their appreciation for all the hard work the administrators and DONs were giving the company. These, soon to be on Facebook 'selfie moments', allowed the grunts who actually did the heavy lifting for the company to hobnob with the senior corporate staff. All corporations seemed to like putting on these kumbayah moments. They felt they were team building. In truth, most administrators and DONs would have preferred a few days off with pay or maybe a nice Starbuck's gift card.

Often motivational speakers would be brought in at these soirees to pump up the enthusiasm of the attendees. These speakers would always give some version of the 'Win one for the Gipper' speech. And, of course, the Gipper would be the corporation. Generally, the information theses wan-a-be Tony Robbins imparted was broad and non-specific. It was as useful as the wisdom that can be derived out of a stale fortune cookie from a cheap Chinese restaurant.

There were four rehearsals scheduled for Ned's group. Ned found a legitimate way to avoid them all. In reality, he was busy making money for the corporation. On the day of the contest, Ned showed up early. He felt perhaps he could smooth over his lack of rehearsal participation with a little stage hand help. He put out chairs and was an extra body that put up the Mexican themed mural that served as the backdrop where the performances by all the regions would take place.

Within an hour, the parking lot filled with administrators and DONs. They sauntered over to the picnic tables where a breakfast of Mexican pastries and coffee was available. Someone had even piped in a local Mexican radio station through an amplifier for that added touch. There were a few DONs that were exempt from coming. They were the queen dowagers of the corporation. They were either too old or too powerful to need to put in an appearance. Violet was counted among that group. The motivational speaker was a former nursing home administrator. His specialty was speaking to the healthcare industry. He was already working the crowd prepping them for his upcoming informational bonanza that would take place right after the performances.

When all the administrators and DONs from the downtown region arrived, Susan Bally, a DON at another facility, and the lip-sync director for the downtown region, called to all that were now gathered, "All members of downtown region please gather by the port-a-potty for one last rehearsal."

Ned, along with the other members of the downtown region dance troupe, made his way over to the port-a-potty. He was handed a taco costume by Susan. "You're going to be one of the Dancing Tacos in the last row. The Enchilada Mamas will be in front of the Tacos and the Big Burrito will be out front lip-synching La Cucaracha," Susan said all this with a straight face as she was slipping into her enchilada. She handed Ned four sheets of paper with the dance steps printed on each page.

"This woman is really serious about this thing," Ned muttered to himself as he looked through the pages. There were enough different steps in the Tacos' routine that would have given the dancers in Swan Lake a run for their money. Ned realized trying to learn the complicated steps, turns and arm movements that the Dancing Tacos had to perform in the next five or ten minutes, was a fool's errand. He decided on a different tact. Rather than looking like a complete fool who didn't know what he was doing, he decided to play a complete fool who didn't know what he was doing. His first step was to put his taco costume on backwards. Seeing Ned putting the taco on backwards, Susan immediately instructed Ned on the proper wearing of his taco costume. "The lettuce goes in the front," she said.

"Oh, I usually eat tacos from the back that's why I put it on this way," Ned responded.

The look on Susan's face was pure confusion. But there was no time for her to react. The music for 'La Cucaracha' came up and the downtown region danced its way in front of the Mexican mural. Even though Ned was in the last row he managed to be so out of step with the other dancers that it actually looked planned. It could be argued that dancing Mexican food is funny enough on its own but Ned's clowning added an extra layer of comedy to the downtown region's presentation.

When all the regions danced and lip-synced their way into corporate history, the motivational speaker grabbed a mike and made his entrance in front of the mural. "Weren't all the regions just fabuloso! Come on, everybody give yourself a big hand!"

The motivational speaker led the clapping and clapped the loudest. He walked the crowd encouraging more and louder clapping. When the clapping began to die down, he launched into his spiel. He spoke with the same kind of overblown enthusiasm as a barker selling the newest set of non-stick cookware at a county fair. But Ned was ready for him. Fortunately for Ned, Susan had created an agenda for the Mexican Holiday and the motivational speaker. So, at the appointed time, Ned sent a text to Dylan informing him he was out of the taco costume and needed to be summoned. "Sorry, DHS just walked in, got to go," Ned sadly announced to Susan.

Of course, Ned was broken hearted he wouldn't be able to stay to absorb the words of wisdom from the motivational speaker, but duty called and Ned had to return to the facility. He apologetically left the festivities and went back to Pasadena.

THE LITTLE TOILET THAT COULD

Central City had been without a Dietary Services Supervisor since Ned arrived there. It was a god-send when HR sent over Effie Peppers to hopefully fill the open slot of DSS, Ned saw her as a welcomed relief. Her credentials seemed impeccable. She had learned her trade in the US Army. She rose to a respectable NCO (non-commissioned officer) rank during her over twenty years served in the military.

The day Ned met her she was wearing a conservative but stylish pants suit. She was a black woman in her late forties. She had a voice like a cheese grater. Ned met her at the end of a set of rounds as he walked back to his office. Effie was waiting for him in the lobby. When she saw him coming, she got up from her seat and walked up to him.

"Ned Russo," she stated.

"Yes," Ned replied.

"I'm Effie Peppers. Carlos from HR sent me over here to meet you. I'm supposed to talk to you about the open DSS spot," she extended her hand to him.

Ned smiled, "Great. Let's go into my office," Ned shook her hand. She had the grip of a good ol' boy from Texas.

When they entered Ned's office, Ned was surprised to see that Benito had delivered a new high -backed desk chair. "Look at that!" Ned said pleased. He sat in the chair. He adjusted it up and down. He rolled it back and forth. "And it doesn't even squeak," Ned said to Effie.

"That's good, I guess," she responded.

"The chair, it's a long story. Now tell me about you," Ned said.

"I spent two tours in Iraq, cooking for the General. He liked my food so much he brought me with him to his next command," she said.

"I like that. If you could make a General happy, I'm sure you'll be able to satisfy this bunch," Ned said.

"I can do a good job for you."

"I want you to know this is a tough building. Iraq will seem like a walk in the dietary park next to this place. I'll stand behind any decision you make. What I want is not to have to think about the kitchen. I want the food to look good and taste better."

"I've been doing that for over twenty years," Effie responded confidently.

"Then we're going to get along just fine," Ned said smiling.

While Ned was interviewing Effie, a drama was unfolding with one of Ned's residents. Janice Haniff was a very heavy woman. That is the kind way to say she was morbidly obese. She could waddle around, but needed to lose a ton of weight. At the particular moment, Ned was interviewing Effie Peppers, Janice needed to use her bathroom, but the housekeeping department was cleaning it. She decided to use the gender neutral bathroom in the lobby. To fit her bulk on the children's sized toilet Benito had installed in the lobby, and complete her business, she realized she had to raise the seat and sit directly on the porcelain bowl. That was a big mistake. She was just the right size to slide into the bowl just enough to create a tight seal and get stuck like a cork inside a wine bottle. After a number of attempts to extricate herself from the toilet, she decided she needed assistance. "Help! Help!" Janice called out from the bathroom.

From his receptionist cubicle, Jose heard the cries for help. At first, he couldn't identify where the cries were coming from, but he followed the sound and ended up at the door of the restroom.

"Help!" Janice called out again.

To be sure of the origin of the sound, Jose put his ear to the door of the bathroom.

Janice let out another cry, "Help…anybody help."

"Are you all right?" Jose asked through the restroom door.

"No, I'm stuck," Janice answered.

Not understanding 'stuck' in relation to a toilet Jose asked, "Did you fall down?"

"No, I'm stuck in the toilet," Janice yelled through the door.

Jose wondered how anyone could be stuck in a toilet, "Stay right there I'll get help."

He went to Ned's office and opened his door. He was still interviewing Effie.

"Sorry to interrupt but there's a woman stuck in the toilet."

"What?" Ned said.

"Somebody's calling for help…I think its Janice Haniff," Jose said.

"Excuse me for a minute," Ned said to Effie.

"No, I've got to see this for myself," Effie responded.

Ned and Effie followed Jose to the restroom. Ned leaned in next to the door.

"Hi, this is Ned, what's going on?"

"I'm stuck in the toilet," Janice responded.

Ned tried the door but it was locked. "Can you open the door?" Ned asked.

"If I could open the door I wouldn't be stuck, now would I?" she responded condescendingly.

"You're right. Sorry," Ned said apologetically.

Ned turned to Effie, "I'm usually not this stupid."

Ned spoke to Jose, "Get Benito."

Within minutes, Jose had gotten Benito and he had used his key to unlock the restroom door. Ned opened the door. Sure enough, Janice was sitting *in* the toilet.

Ned quickly assessed the situation.

"Ok, Janice we're going to pull you out," Ned said as he grabbed one of her arms. "Benito grab the other arm."

Benito took hold of her other arm. Ned and Benito tried to pull Janice out of the toilet. But, because of her weight and the vacuum seal she created, she wouldn't budge. All she did was cry out in pain, "Stop! Stop! You're hurting me! Goddamnit stop!"

"She stuck pretty good," Benito said.

Effie decided to try and help solve the problem, "If you tell me where the kitchen is, I'll get some oil. We can pour it around the edge of her ass and maybe that'll loosen her up enough to pull her out," Effie suggested.

"It's worth a try," Ned agreed. Ned turned to Janice, "This ok with you?"

"All right. Anything to get me off this toilet," she reluctantly responded.

Benito led Effie to the kitchen. Effie asked the cook for a cup of cooking oil. He obliged. They returned to the restroom and Effie poured the oil where Janice met the porcelain.

"All right let's try it again," Ned said.

Ned and Benito each took one of Janice's arms. "Ready. Pull."

The second try didn't fare any better than the first. Janice cried out in pain again. She didn't move an inch. "Stop! Stop!" she howled.

"Now what?" Jose asked.

Ned stood there thinking. Then he turned to Benito.

"Turn the water off bring a hammer. We'll break the toilet off. It's too small anyway."

"No, you won't," Janice protested.

"I don't know that we have another choice," Ned responded to Janice.

"Call 911, if you idiots can't figure out what to do maybe they can," Janice growled.

Ned turned to Jose, "Ok, call 911. Benito turn the water off."

Benito reached down below Janice's big bottom and shut off the water to the toilet.

"Now we'll see if the fire department can do any better," Ned said.

Two fire trucks pulled up in front of Central City. The first fire fighter to enter the facility was the fire captain Ned had encountered before. Ned saw him and realized he was about to enter the facility. "Oh brother, not him again," Ned muttered.

The captain came into the lobby looked around, then sauntered up to Ned. "I understand somebody's stuck in a toilet?" the captain said not really believing the words he just spoke. "Is that true?" he added incredulously.

Ned pointed to Janice. Not that she needed an introduction, but Janice announced her predicament to the captain, "I'm the one who's stuck."

The captain turned to Ned, "Why don't you just pull her out?"

"We tried. But we couldn't get her to budge," Ned answered.

Then the captain spoke to Ned with distain. "Are you shitting me? You called the Los Angeles fucking Fire Department over here to pull a woman's ass out of a toilet? What have you got a bunch of sissies working here? Don't you know we have better things to do?"

The captain turned to two of his fire fighters. "All right pull her ass out of there."

Two fire fighters attempted to grab Janice's arms. But she resisted, "Don't you touch me!" Janice screamed.

The two fire fighters backed off and looked to the captain for guidance.

"Lady, you want to get off that fuckin' toilet or not?" the captain said to Janice.

"Now pull her out of there," the captain ordered his men a second time.

"You're not going to have those goons break my arms. Find another way," Janice responded growling at the captain.

The captain stood there temporarily defeated by Janice.

"You have some kind of saw that'll cut through the porcelain?" Ned interjected into the standoff.

"Yeah, we've got a saw that will cut through anything," the captain announced.

"Why don't we use it on the toilet?" Ned suggested.

The captain thought for a moment then turned to one of the fire fighters, "Go get the sawzall."

One of the fire fighters went to the fire truck and returned with a rather impressive tool. The sawzall was a large, reciprocating saw. It could indeed cut though anything. The fire department used it to cut crash victims out of their crushed cars.

Janice viewed the saw and suddenly wondered if getting off the toilet was worth having that machine inches from her bottom. "Are you sure you won't hurt me with that thing?" she asked.

“Don’t worry this man is a professional. He has never killed anybody while he was saving their life,” the fire captain said trying to reassure Janice.

The fire fighter got down on the restroom floor and went to work on the toilet. The saw shrieked, but that blade made easy work cutting through the toilet just below Janice’s bottom. Now Janice was free from the toilet but her ass had a porcelain ring attached to it.

“Why don’t you take her to the hospital and let them remove that last piece of the toilet,” Ned said to the captain.

Reluctantly, the captain conceded. He ordered his men to remove Janice from Central City. “All right get her on a gurney,” the captain ordered.

Janice was loaded face down on a gurney. Her big bottom, with the remaining part of the toilet attached to it pointed skyward. Carolina was thoughtful enough to toss a blanket over Janice’s bottom as she went out of the lobby door.

The fire fighters returned the sawzall to its place in the fire truck. They loaded Janice into the ambulance and drove away. The captain was the last one out of Central City. As he was leaving, he turned to Ned. He needed to get in the last word, “I don’t like you. This is the second time you fucked up and I had to fix it. I swear to Christ I’m going to find a way to nail your ass the next time I have to come here on some bullshit call,” he walked out of the facility.

Ned turned to Benito, “Get another toilet, pronto. And make sure it’s for an adult.” Then he turned to Effie. “Still want to work here?”

“Are you kidding? I love a challenge and I can see this place is full of them. I’m in,” she said.

Violet was quietly standing in the far corner of the lobby. She had watched the paramedics haul Janice out on a gurney but she said or did nothing to help. All the incident did was to make her angrier at Ned. This current debacle added another layer to her growing resentment. Janice was another of Ned’s Medicare deals. And Violet was sick and tired of everything Ned was doing. Violet believed Ned was turning Central City, her hospital, into a circus. Violet knew that as long as Ned was the administrator, she would have to put up with difficult patients. This incident was just another reason for Violet to hate everything about Ned. The days of Central City being the sleepy nonprofit center that Violet was used to, were gone.

As Ned led Effie back to his office, he saw Violet standing in the lobby. Without saying a word to him Violet went back to her office. She took out her cell phone and called her best ally at corporate, Marilyn Fowler. Violet had gone to Mr. M and was still waiting for the outcome of that meeting. Now she would go to her ally, the head of all nursing, the second most powerful person in the company.

Marilyn Fowler, and the entourage she always travelled with, two nurses, were at another of the corporate's skilled nursing facilities. They were inspecting the nursing department at that hospital when Violet's call came through on Marilyn's cell phone. Marilyn saw that the call was from Violet, "Yes Violet, what can I do for you?" Marilyn asked.

Violet was furious. It came through in her voice as she spoke, "I've worked for this company a long time. Marilyn, I'm getting to the point where I don't want to come here anymore. This place is becoming unbearable. I didn't become a nurse to work in this kind of environment."

"Calm down. What's the problem?" Marilyn asked.

"I'm not going to calm down. You know what the problem is, that arrogant asshole administrator, Ned Russo." Violet pushed out Ned's name through her clenched teeth. Then she played her ace. "I'm getting to the point of quitting. I don't want to leave you or Mr. M, but Marilyn, I can't take this much longer."

There was a long silence before Marilyn spoke. She knew she had to pick her words carefully.

"You know we all think highly of you, Violet. You are more than just a long term employee of this company. You are part of its soul. I promise I will help get this issue resolved."

"When?" Violet demanded.

"Soon, I promise," Marilyn ended the call.

Marilyn wasn't pleased. She had hoped the hostility between Violet and Ned would end given time, but she now she realized the management problem at Central City was intractable. Marilyn knew if she didn't step in the issue would come to an unfortunate conclusion. Violet had just played her strongest card. The fact that she threw in the histrionics just amplified the threat of 'I'm going to quit.' would make everyone at corporate straighten up in their expensive leather chairs. Finding experienced DONs to work in skilled nursing facilities was like finding another lost city in the Amazon jungle. Violet was sure Marilyn would tell Mr. M and that news would filter down throughout the key people in the corporation. Violet knew the obvious discussion among those people would be who was more important to the ongoing success of the corporation another administrator that could be easily replaced or a proven, loyal DON. Her trump card played, Violet knew should anyone from corporate call to mollify her, the best demonstration of her resolve was to walk off the job. She picked up her bag and went home to wait for the next shoe to drop.

DISICIPLINE

It was lunchtime. The way lunch works in a nursing facility is the CNAs bring the patients into the dining room. At Central City three CNAs and a charge nurse are always assigned to the dining room to insure some semblance of order and safety. Someone in the kitchen announces lunch is ready. The patients' trays come out of the kitchen on a rack. A charge nurse is positioned to inspect the patients' trays. Once the trays on that rack are checked by the charge nurse, they would then be rolled into the dining room where the assigned CNAs would distribute whatever was being served to the eager bib wearing patients. The process was time tested and worked. That is if all the players were in position.

"CNAs assigned to the dining room please come now. Trays are coming out," the voice of Sonia, the charge nurse assigned to tray inspection that day, blared over the PA system.

Two of the CNAs came when they were called. On this day, however, the kitchen delivered lunch about fifteen minutes early. The third CNA who was assigned to help was busy achieving orgasm in Benito's maintenance shop and didn't hear Sonia's call.

Sonia took up her position outside the kitchen door. The door opened and the first rack containing ten trays of the vulcanized beef stew rolled out. Sonia inspected each tray to be sure that each resident received the correct meal. Satisfied, Sonia pushed it to Paula Alcala, an older CNA who rolled it into the dining room. Unfortunately, only one other CNA was waiting to distribute the trays to the patients, and that meant slower meal distribution. Down one-third of the tray distribution work force, the process of orderly feeding of the patients was greatly impaired, which meant problems.

Paula began complaining, "Where's Tameka? She's supposed to be here. There's too much for us to do."

Between racks of trays, Sonia called out on the PA again, "Tameka, please come to the dining room. Trays are out."

Minutes passed. More trays were distributed without Tameka's help. Some of the unfed patients were getting agitated. That was the recipe for a potential patient on patient problem.

"Where's my food?" was heard echoing throughout the dining room.

Not getting their own trays, a few patients decided to eat their tablemate's lunch rather than wait for their tray to be served. This put more stress on the situation. In addition to serving the food, Paula and

Nelly, another CNA, had to preserve peace between the residents. Paula got angrier by the minute. "Where the hell is she?" Paula said loudly.

"This is not fair. She never comes when she is supposed to," Nelly added.

The kitchen continued rolling out trays. Sonia continued inspecting them and pushing them toward the dining room. Paula and Nelly did their best but got further and further behind. When most of the trays were distributed, Tameka finally appeared in the dining room. Paula was feeding one of the patients.

"Where the fuck have you been?" Paula screamed.

Realizing she was late, and caught off guard, the best Tameka could come up with was a lame excuse, "I was busy," she screamed back.

It did not go un-noticed by Paula that Tameka's wig was slightly askew and her scrubs, which were neatly pressed earlier that day, were now wrinkled. And there was a large wet spot on the front of Tameka's scarlet scrubs.

"Oh, yeah, busy doing what, fucking Benito!" Paula shouted.

"None of your goddamn business," Tameka shouted back.

"Since you were too busy to help us, you can finish feeding the patients by yourself," Paula shouted. Then she threw the spoon full of pureed stew she was about to feed a patient down into the plate instead of into the open mouth of the poor patient who was waiting to eat it. Furious, Paula left the patient and stormed out of the dining room.

"I ain't gonna do this by myself," proclaimed Tameka. She followed Paula out of the dining room. Sonia did nothing but stand there frozen in place like a deer in headlights. Nelly, kept on feeding her patient while muttering a variety of Spanish curse words all targeted at Tameka, one of which was pendejo.

Ned was in Jose's cubicle when Anthony stuck his head in, "We have a problem."

"What is it?" Ned asked.

"Two CNAs were screaming at each other in the dining room. Then they walked out leaving the patients alone."

Ned sighed in frustration, "Where was the charge nurse?"

Anthony shook his head, "She was useless."

"Is everything ok in there? Ned asked.

"It is now. I pulled a couple of nurses off the floor and put them in the dining room," Anthony responded.

"When did this happen?

"About five minutes ago."

Ned and Anthony went to Ned's office. He re-wound the dining room security camera to the incident. There, on the screen, the ugly truth was replayed for Ned and Anthony. "Get those two CNAs in here," Ned ordered.

Within minutes Anthony marched Paula and Tameka into Ned's office. Ned did not invite them to sit down. Anthony closed the door behind them.

"Take a look at this," Ned ordered his CNAs. Then he pointed to the security camera screen and played the incident back for Paula and Tameka. Ned leaned back in his chair and addressed his two employees, "You want to tell me why you walked off your assignment and abandoned those patients?" Ned asked sternly.

Paula was the first to answer, "She didn't come to her assignment like she was supposed to. She left us with all the trays and all the feeders."

"I told you I was busy," Tameka sassed.

"That's bullshit!" Paula fired back.

"Busy doing what?" Ned asked.

"I was busy with a patient." Tameka toned it down quite a bit when she responded to Ned.

"Which patient?" Ned asked.

"Twenty-seven 'C'…I think," Tameka responded.

"You think?" Ned asked skeptically.

Paula interjected, "She was with Benito. She goes down there every day. People see her down there. Why don't you look on the camera and you can see for yourself?"

"Please don't tell me how to conduct this interview," Ned said to Paula.

"I was told the two of you were screaming at each other in the dining room before you both walked out. Is that true?"

"She started it," Tameka said.

"Fuck you, bitch!" came flying out of Paula's mouth.

Tameka quickly moved toward Paula. It was obvious that in the next second hair pulling was about to take place. Luckily, Anthony was quicker than Tameka and got between the two women before a punch could be thrown or the hair pulling could start.

"Are you kidding me? You think this is the WWF?" Ned was completely taken aback by the CNAs' behavior. "Both of you are suspended. Clock out and go home!" Ned yelled.

"I don't give a shit if you suspend me or not," Tameka defiantly said to Ned.

Ned got very angry, but he managed to control his rage, "I'd keep my mouth shut if I were you. You're just digging the hole deeper for yourself."

"Yeah, well that's too bad. I don't give a shit. You're nothing but a racist stickin' up for the Hispanics," Tameka said.

"Get them out of here before I do something stupid," Ned barked at Anthony.

“Let’s go,” Anthony said as he led the two CNAs out of Ned’s office. He led them to the time clock and then to the parking garage. They both got in their cars and drove away. Anthony returned to Ned’s office, “They’re gone.”

Ned had rewound the security camera that looked down the hallway in the basement. One of the doors off that hallway was the entrance to Benito’s maintenance shop. “Look at this.”

Ned said as he pressed the ‘forward’ icon on the security screen. Out of Benito’s shop came Tameka. She was tying the string that held up her scrubs. Her wig was disheveled and there was a large wet spot on the front of her scarlet pants.

“Now we know which patient she was busy with,” Anthony smirked.

“Yep, we sure do!” Ned said.

“By the way, Tameka quit,” Anthony said in matter-of-fact monotone.

“Good, saves me the trouble of firing her,” Ned said.

“What are you going to do about Benito?” Anthony asked.

“I’ve been wondering about that. Benito is a sticky wicket,” Ned said to Anthony.

“He’s worked for the company almost from the beginning,” Anthony said.

“I know,” Ned responded.

“You know he’s the handy man for Mr. M at his house,” Anthony added.

“I know that too,” Ned said.

“I guess I would tell you to be careful,” Anthony warned.

“Your advice is well appreciated,” Ned said.

“There are certain people in this company that are untouchable,” Anthony said.

Ned interjected, “And you’re telling me he’s one of them.”

“I’m telling you you’re not,” Anthony added.

“I think I have a solution,” Ned smiled at Anthony.

About a half hour later Jose called Ned. He picked up the phone, “Yes, Jose.”

“It’s Paula. She’s crying and she wants to talk to you.”

“Ok, put her through.”

Jose put the call through. Ned answered without a drop of sympathy in his voice, “What do you want, Paula?”

“Mr. Ned, I’m sorry. I promise I’ll never do that again,” she said sobbing, “I don’t want to lose my job.”

“I accept your apology. But you’re still suspended. If you ever walk out on the patients again, I will terminate you and turn your license into Sacramento for job abandonment. Do you clearly understand what I just said?”

“I promise. I’ll never walk out of the dining room again,” Paula said still sobbing.

“And you will control your temper and always act professionally.”

“Yes, I will,” she responded.

“I’ll see you in a couple of days,” Ned hung up the phone.

THE ELECTRONIC VASECTOMY

The next morning a befuddled Benito came into Ned's office, "Ah, Mr. Ned."

"Yes, Benito, how are you doing today?" Ned said with a cheery smile.

"Fine, fine... But I have the question. There's a man, Henry, he put the camera in my shop. Henry make the install, he say you want put it there? I ask him maybe he make a mistake. He say no."

"Let's take a look," Ned said. He used his mouse that was attached to the monitors to have the shot of Benito's shop fill the entire screen. The video installer Henry was looking into the camera making final adjustments. Ned pressed the button on his phone to engage the PA system. "Henry, how's it coming?" Ned's voice blared throughout the facility.

Henry gave a 'thumbs-up' into the camera.

Ned turned back to Benito, "That's beautiful. I think we're in business, Benito."

"Maybe it's no a good idea," Benito suggested.

Ned cut him off, "Benito, with a camera in your shop I could see when you were down there. It would save me all that looking for you. It's a time saver. It's a very good idea, don't you think?" Ned enthusiastically smiled at Benito.

"Maybe... I no know...," Benito eked out a timid response.

"Well, tell you what, we'll try it for a while and if it doesn't work out we can always remove the camera. That's fair," Ned said.

"Ah...ok."

Benito had run out of arguments to save his privacy. As he left the office he turned back to Ned.

"How long you want to keep the camera in my shop?"

"I don't know. It's an experiment. Let's see how it works. Then we can decide," Ned said flashing a big smile at Benito.

Benito nodded and left the office.

"Ah..." Benito tried one last time to say something but didn't, he knew he had lost the battle.

"Ok...I see you later," Benito said.

"No, I'll see you later," Ned said as he pointed to the camera monitors.

Ned had just taken away Benito's romantic hide-a-way and they both knew it.

THE BELL TOLLS FOR THEE

Dylan came into Ned's office, "Dr. Kovani has a Medicare for us 100 days."

"How bad is he?" Ned responded.

"You know. He's one of Kovani's. He's has the usual pysch issues," Dylan responded.

"That means he's bad. You have the paperwork?" Ned asked.

"If we can get a couple of weeks out of him, he'll be worth it. Then if he doesn't run away, I'll get rid of him." Dylan said handing Ned the patient's history. Ned read the profile. It was long and checkered. The patient was Gregor Ragasin. He was forty-seven years old, and schizophrenic. College educated with lots of behavior problems. He was big man with an electric wheelchair. He had a long history of bouncing from facility to facility. He rarely stayed in one place more than a month. There was a lot of reasons for Ned to say 'no' and only one to say 'yes' to this patient, Medicare. Ned knew this admission would give Violet another opportunity to complain to corporate about the patients he admitted. But Ned was going to bet that Gregor would help give Central City a better than expected profitable month. Ned threw caution to the wind, "All right, tell Kovani to send him over."

The day Mr. Ragasin arrived at Central City Ned was dealing with a small problem. He was walking the facility doing rounds when he saw one of his patients, Daisy Charles, trying to wiggle out of her wheelchair. Daisy was a lady in her nineties and for the most part, a problem-free patient. She was the old woman who spat on Ned's Ralph Lauren suit on his first day at Central City.

"Daisy, what's the matter?" Ned asked.

"My coochie-coo itches," she responded.

Without knowing the exact location of a coochie-coo Ned surmised from the wiggling that Daisy's genital area was giving her the problem. He turned and saw that Sippie was close by. Sippie would have been Ned's last choice, because of her constant sexual innuendos, but she was logistically available. He called to her, "Sippie, can you help me? Daisy is having a problem."

"Anything for you, Ned."

Ned pretended not to hear Sippie's slip-up. "Let's get her to her room and check her out," Ned said.

Sippie rolled Daisy to her room. She assisted her onto her bed and closed the privacy curtain. She then loosened Daisy's pants and examined her 'coochie-coo,' Sippie giggled. Then she spoke to Ned, who was waiting on the other side of the privacy curtain, "I think you should see this," she said.

Ned drew back the curtain. There, coming out of Daisy's backside was half of a nursing glove. The other half was inside Daisy's rectum. "You've got to be kidding me," was all Ned could get out.

"What do you want me to do?" Sippie asked.

"Take it out!" Ned exclaimed.

Sippie gently removed the glove from Daisy's rectum. Ned turned and left Daisy's room. He marched to Anthony's office.

"One of the nurses left a glove in Daisy's backside. See if you can figure out who it was. Then write him or her up, please."

"You really mean in her ass?" Anthony asked jokingly.

"Yes, I really mean in her ass," Ned said as he turned and walked back toward his office.

"Ok, and I'll give an in-service on proper disposal of gloves," Anthony chuckled.

"Only in this place would something like that be necessary!" Ned said over his shoulder.

On the way back to his office Vicky, the charge nurse, came up to Ned. "Mr. Bell has passed away," she said.

Vicky led Ned to Mr. Bell's room. The nurses had covered him with a sheet. There were four empty pizza boxes on his bedside table and the TV was on.

"Get rid of those boxes and turn off the TV," Ned said.

Vicky complied and said, "Well, he's in a better place now."

"I wonder if he'll be any thinner when he gets there," Ned commented.

When the mortuary people came to take Mr. Bell away, they discovered they didn't have a gurney big enough to accommodate his body. They had to call the paramedics who have a special bariatric gurney for just such occasions. Alerted to the problem, the paramedics arrived with the oversized gurney in an oversized truck. The nursing staff led the paramedics to Mr. Bell's room. The removal entourage worked to get Mr. Bell's remains onto the oversized gurney.

"We're going to have to take him out the front door. That's where the truck is," the lead paramedic said to Ned.

"Can't you just move the truck into the alley? I don't want all the patients to see a dead body go out the front door," Ned said.

"No. We need the curb for the lift gate. This guy's nothin' but dead weight, the lead paramedic said.

"That's obvious," Ned said.

"If the gurney fails it will take a forklift to get him into the truck," the paramedic continued.

"It's not going to fail, these things don't fail," Ned said.

"With a guy this big, it's possible. If it were to happen, you know some guy with a camera will be here and you'll end up on the five o'clock news," the paramedic responded.

Ned was unfortunately able to see the logic in the paramedic's thinking. "Ok, take him out the front, but make it quick," Ned said reluctantly.

Mr. Bell's body was rolled through the lobby. Some of the patients that were there looked on in stunned silence. Some of them, the patients' who still had some ability to reason, like Steven, the candy man, knew what was happening. They knew they were looking at their own future. One day that's how they would leave, on a gurney covered with a dark piece of cloth. The oversized paramedic truck was backed perpendicular to the curb so that the lift gate could rest on it. With the lift gate lowered, the paramedics struggled but managed with much grunting, to get Mr. Bell into the truck. The doors on the truck were slammed shut and Mr. Bell was driven away. The patients gathered in the lobby watched. Their faces sober, their voices silent. Ned felt sorry for his patients. He wanted to take away their pain as quickly as possible.

"All right, who wants ice cream?" Ned announced.

Steven was the first to respond. He struggled but managed to get out the word.

"Chocolate."

THE MAD MONK

Dylan entered Ned's office. "Kovani just gave us two more Medicare," he said.

"That's three! How did you do that?" Ned asked.

"A bottle of Grey Goose and three real Cohibas."

'How did you get real Cuban cigars?" Ned asked.

"I have a connection," Dylan said with an impish smile.

"Are they really real Cubans or the ones produced in the Dominican Republic?"

"No, these are the real thing. Cost me fifty a piece."

"Expense it. Call it physician gifts. And get one for me."

"Already did," Dylan said. He took the Cohiba out of a leather cigar holder and handed it to Ned. "If you weren't going to smoke it, I was," Dylan added.

Ned lifted the cigar to his nose and breathed in the aroma of this, one of the world's finest cigars.

"I've only had one of these in my whole life," Ned said breathing in the aroma again.

"Now I have to get a really good bottle of cognac to accompany this beauty," Ned said.

Dylan handed Ned the leather cigar holder. He carefully returned the Cohiba into the holder.

"Next month buy him another one of these and make sure you get one for you and me."

Ned made rounds. As he was walking through the hospital, he wondered about the perfect setting to enjoy his Cohiba. He took out his cellphone and called Lenore. He got her voice mail.

"Lenore, this is your favorite hospital administrator. I have become the beneficiary of something very special. I'd like to share it with you. How's Saturday around sunset. My backyard."

Ned finished with making rounds. He got back to his office as the ambulance bringing Gregor Ragasin pulled up in front of Central City. Gregor was the first of Kovani's three Medicares. The moment the attendants took Gregor out of the giant ambulance Ned realized he was in for trouble. Gregor was big. Like six-five, three hundred plus pounds big. The ambulance itself looked more like it was designed to haul broken vehicles more than broken people. What really sent a shiver through Ned was the second truck that pulled up and unloaded Gregor's motorized wheelchair. Like Gregor, it was massive. It was more small car than big wheelchair.

Ned called Jose, "Jose, find Dylan. Get him over here, please." Ned hung up without waiting for a response.

Gregor got off the gurney on the sidewalk. He settled into his wheelchair and drove into the lobby of Central City. Ned was waiting for him. When Gregor got to the middle of the lobby, he stopped and made a three hundred sixty degree turn.

"Oh, not again," Ned muttered to himself.

Experience taught Ned electric wheelchairs were inherently bad in a skilled nursing facility. No matter how good the driver, accidents happen. Feet get run over. Drivers plow into walls.

Gregor was wearing two bed sheets with holes cut in their centers to make a sort of double poncho. Around his neck hung a string of large wooden beads and a second leather string attached to a leather pouch. The pouch was stuffed full of something.

One of the ambulance attendants followed him into the facility. Ned greeted Gregor with a smile.

"Welcome to Central City."

Ned was trying to do his best to deal with what he knew was going to be a bad situation.

Gregor looked up at Ned and said nothing. The ambulance attendants came up to Ned. "What room?"

It only took seconds for the rumor mill to announce the arrival of this giant new patient. A few CNAs and Eileen, from MDS, had come to the lobby. "Room thirty, bed A," Eileen said to the attendant.

"I'll find it," Gregor said. He engaged the throttle on his wheelchair. The whir from the chair's electric motor filled the lobby. It was reminiscent of a jet engine. Gregor drove his wheelchair, at full speed, out of the lobby and down the hallway.

"Did you hear the motor on that thing? I never heard one that loud before," Ned said to Eileen.

Her face said it all…despair. "Maybe you can ask him not to drive so fast," she said.

"Yeah, I'll do that." Ned's delivery echoed Eileen's despair.

"Well, maybe he won't be so bad," Eileen hoped.

"Eileen, you and I have been in this business a long time. You know that patient is going to make us put two feet in one shoe," Ned responded.

"Maybe if we can control him for a little while…all we need is eight days so we can get a decent payment," Eileen said. She was trying to put a good face on what she knew was going to be a difficult situation.

"I'll figure something out. We'll manage," Ned said.

The ambulance attendant handed paperwork to Eileen. She signed it.

"Good luck. You're going to need it," the attendant said to Eileen and Ned. The attendant left in a hurry almost fleeing before Ned could change his mind and order them to load Gregor back into the giant ambulance and get him off the property.

Getting Gregor back into the ambulance was Ned's first thought but he knew that would burn the relationship with Dr. Kovani. No, Ned would have to find a way to get through the necessary days with Gregor before he could get rid of him. Rather than leave the handling of this patient to his staff, Ned decided to personally take charge of Mr. Gregor Ragasin.

Ned followed his new patient down the hall to his room. When Ned entered Gregor's room, he was examining his bed. "This isn't a bariatric bed," Gregor growled.

"I'll get you one from our warehouse. It'll be here in a few hours," Ned responded.

"It better be or I'm calling the state. And while you're at it, get me a new mattress."

Dylan entered the room. He had been warned about Gregor by Jose and was trying to 'make-nice.' "Hey man, you need a pack of cigarettes? I'll get you whatever you want."

"I don't smoke. And if any of these people in here smoke get them out. I can't stand that cigarette smell."

"How about some clothes?" Dylan asked.

"These are my clothes," Gregor responded pointing to his sheets.

Ned spoke in his most diplomatic tone. "Dylan, maybe Mr. Ragasin is hungry."

Ned turned to Gregor. "Are you hungry? You want something from the kitchen?"

"No. I'm sure the food here sucks. Order me a large vegetarian pizza."

Ned had been down this road with difficult patients before. Ned knew he was being tested. Eight days or not, if he didn't draw a line in the sand somewhere Gregor's demands would simply escalate. Ned decided to draw the line right down the middle of the pizza.

"We don't normally order pizza for our patients. We have a perfectly suitable kitchen. I'm sure they will be able to get you something you want."

"I'm not," Gregor responded.

"Why don't I get somebody from the kitchen to come and talk to you. We have an extensive list of food options…" Ned was cut off by Gregor.

"No! I told you I want a vegetarian pizza."

"Mr. Ragasin, why don't you give our kitchen a try?" Ned was doing his best to negotiate with his new patient.

“No, I want a fuckin’ pizza,” Gregor angrily responded.

“There’s a myriad of reasons we don’t order food for our patients. A lot of them have to do with dietary restrictions,” Ned said diplomatically.

“I don’t have any restrictions,” Gregor fired back.

Gregor suddenly erupted into rage. He pounded the bed with his fist then ripped the bedspread off the bed and threw it on the floor. Gregor was throwing a tantrum like a two year old that didn’t get his way.

“You’re not meeting my needs,” Gregor screamed.

Ah…here we go. This guy has been here five minutes and we’re not meeting his needs, Ned thought to himself. Ned realized Gregor was demonstrating the tactics of a professional nursing home patient. These were patients who knew the system very well and played it to their advantage. The “you’re not meeting my needs” line was the threat Gregor was throwing in Ned’s face. The implication was that Gregor would be calling the DHS and filing a complaint against Central City. He probably used that threat often to get what he demanded. And it probably worked. The last thing any administrator wanted was the DHS investigating a patient complaint. The DHS operates under the Napoleonic code, guilty until proven innocent. Or what has come to be known as ‘the customer is always right’ even if they display the foulest dispositions and are dead wrong.

“I want a fucking pizza. And I want it now! Are you going to get it for me or am I going to get it myself? And while I’m out, I’ll call the DHS.”

“No problem. I’ll get it,” Dylan said seeing the fire spreading. He decided to put it out himself.

“That’ll be about fifteen dollars,” Ned said.

Dylan had just given Gregor the round but Ned was determined he was not going to lose the entire fight.

“What?” Gregor said quite surprised.

“That’s about what a good pizza cost around here. And I’m sure you want a good pizza, Right? Oh, by the way you want jalapenos on that pizza?” Ned said.

“You’re too fuckin’ cheap to buy me a pizza,” Gregor said surprised his threat didn’t work.

Ned stood there silent as a statue.

“Fine, you cheap bastard. I’ll pay for it myself,” Gregor said.

He opened the leather pouch that was hanging from his neck. In it was money. Lots of money rolled up into a toilet paper roll of bills. Twenties, tens, even hundreds.

“DHS is going to hear about this,” Gregor said.

Ned and Dylan saw the roll of cash and looked at each other. Gregor peeled a twenty dollar bill off the roll and tossed it on the bed. “And I want to see the receipt. I want to make sure you fucks don't steal any of my money. And no fucking tip for the asshole who brings it here either!"

"Mr. Ragasin you have what looks like a large amount of cash. I suggest you put it in the safe in the business office," Ned said.

"Why, so you people can steal it?" he replied.

Ned assessed Gregor's anger could easily become violence. He decided the better course of action, at this moment in their relationship, was to back-off rather than confront this new obviously volatile patient.

"Mr. Ragasin, this is a hospital not a hotel. I'm an administrator not a concierge."

Ned picked up the twenty and turned to Dylan, "Let's order Mr. Ragasin his vegetarian pizza."

"Now get out. I'm going to pray." Gregor closed his eyes and folded his hands across his chest and began to chant. "Ommmmmm…"

Ned led Dylan out of the room.

"That's a large pizza, you assholes!" Gregor called after them.

As they were walking down the hallway Dylan turned to Ned, "Did you see that wad of cash in that pouch?"

"How could I miss it? When you give him his pizza make sure you present him with the admission packet, point out that we're only responsible for fifty dollars. Tell Mr. Ragasin that wad of cash around his neck will easily pay for some CNA's retirement ranch in Mexico. Tell him again we strongly suggest we put his money in the business office safe," Ned said.

"You think he's going to go for that?' Dylan asked.

"No, he's not going to go for anything. He's not even going to sign the admission packet. But go through the drill anyway. And make sure you have someone else with you as a witness. In fact, have two people with you," Ned said.

As Dylan was walking away, Ned called to him. "And remind me to kill you later this week for bringing that son-of-a-bitch in here…that is if he doesn't kill me first."

"I think that's a distinct possibility. Did you see how mad that bastard got? How are we going to get rid of him? You want me to call Kovani?" Dylan asked.

"No, not yet, we do too much business with him. I don't want to screw that up unless we absolutely have to," Ned said.

"You know that prick is going to make every nurse in here piss blood," Dylan said.

"I know." Ned thought for a bit. "But Dylan, every Achilles has a heel. I think I already know where Mr. Ragasin's is. I hope we can control him for eight days. If all it takes is pizza, we'll be ok. But if not, I'll go after him."

"This is going to be a long eight days," Dylan said.

A MODERN USE OF TRAVEL BAGS

Casey, the ADON, came into Ned's office. She looked unhappy. "I think we have a problem. The new patient in twenty-one 'A' is claiming abuse."

"Didn't she just get here? We didn't have time to abuse her, did we? What's the patient's name?" Ned asked.

"Doreen Sankie. She's very alert," Casey said.

"Sankie? That's another one of Kovani's patients," Ned remarked.

"It is," Casey responded.

They left Ned's office and went to see Ms. Sankie.

When they entered Ms. Sankie's room she was awake. The head of the bed was at a forty-five degree angle propping her up. She was a younger patient, in her forties. She was wearing blue jeans and a black t-shirt. What looked like a purple duffle bag full of clothes was also on the bed down below her knees.

"Who are you?" Sankie said to Ned.

"I'm the administrator."

"I was abused and I'm not going to tolerate it," Sankie said.

"Do you know who abused you?" Ned asked.

"No, I was sleeping. It was dark. I just felt someone slapping me," she replied.

"Ms. Sankie, I don't mean to question you, but why would someone just slap you for no reason?" Ned asked.

"I don't know. I want you to send me back to the hospital," Sankie ordered.

"The phlebotomist was here earlier. She said she tapped her arm looking for a vein," Casey said to Ned.

"That's a lie! She abused me," Sankie screamed.

"Ms. Sankie, the phlebotomist doesn't even know you. Why would she risk going to jail? Isn't it possible she was just trying to draw your blood? That's not exactly abuse. She was just doing her job," Ned tried to explain.

As he was trying to settle the abuse issue with Ms. Sankie, Ned noticed she had a suprapubic catheter and a colostomy bag. This was a woman with a lot of medical issues, Ned thought. He hadn't seen her chart but since she was another one of Kovani's patients, Ned knew she also had psych issues to boot. Then Ned noticed something very odd about the duffle bag lying on her bed. It wasn't full of clothes, *she was in it*. Then Ned realized Ms. Sankie had both her legs amputated from the mid-thigh. What was really strange was Ms. Sankie, or what was left of her, was sticking out of the top of this purple duffle bag. In all his years in healthcare Ned had never seen a patient coming out of what had to be a specially designed travel accessory for one's lack of appendages. Ned suddenly got the feeling he was talking to a ventriloquist's dummy that somehow came to life, got sick, and ended up in Central City.

"It is abuse to me! Now I want to go back to the hospital," Sankie screamed.

"Doctor Kovani discharged you out of the hospital, to here. I'm afraid they won't take you back without a legitimate reason. I want to go back to the hospital isn't a reason," Ned explained.

"Then find another hospital," Sankie yelled.

"I called the hospitals you suggested earlier. None of them will accept you," Casey said.

"Then call Arizona," Sankie demanded.

"Arizona? You mean the state of or every hospital in the state?" Ned asked.

"I don't care. Just call!" she screamed.

"And after I call every hospital in Arizona, then what, Utah? Ms. Sankie, I'm not going to do that. Now, can't we come to some sort of an agreement?" Ned asked.

"No! I want out of this place!" she screamed.

"Well, this isn't jail. You're welcome to leave anytime you want," Ned pointed toward the front door, "The door's that way."

"You know I can't go by myself," she said.

"Yes, I do. For the time being, you and I are stuck with each other. If you really want to get out of here, you'll be co-operative. A month or so down the road, I'll find you a place where you'll be happy. I'll call the administrator of your new home and tell him what a wonderful patient you are."

Ms. Sankie thought about what Ned said. Ned learned a long time ago when selling something, anything, he who talks last loses.

"I don't want anybody to bother me at night. No blood draw. No diaper change. I have a colostomy bag and a catheter for fuck's sake," Sankie said.

Ned knew he had won, "I'll have a sign put over your bed within an hour. I'll make sure nobody bothers you. I promise it won't happen again. And, with your permission, I'll tell the rehab people to put you on the schedule."

"And you need to be seen by the wound doctor and the treatment nurse, too," Casey turned to Ned.

"She has a couple of stage three wounds on her sacral area."

"And the wound doc and treatment nurse," Ned added.

Wounds in a nursing home were like ants at a picnic. Fighting them was a constant battle.

Sankie thought about Ned's proposal. "Ok," she said.

"Thank you," Ned responded.

Ned and Casey left Sankie's room.

"I really like the way you handle difficult patients," Casey said.

"You're not bucking for a raise are you?" Ned asked with a smile.

"No, I know I'll never get one," Casey said.

Later that morning an ambulance arrived with a new patient. She was black woman about sixty and was wearing a hospital gown and had no other belongings with her. Her hair was matted and she had no teeth. The attendants wheeled her into the lobby.

Ned greeted her, "Good morning."

He picked up the paperwork that accompanied her and quickly scanned it. "Ginger, from Good Sam," then Ned looked up at Ginger, "Hi, I'm Ned."

She gave Ned the once over and decided she liked what she saw, "Hello. My you are a handsome man." Ginger extended her hand to him.

Ned took her hand, "I'm going to see your stay here is extra special."

"And so gracious too," Ginger was instantly taken with Ned.

"I don't see any clothes. Did she come with any?" Ned asked the attendants.

"No clothes. Just her," the attendant said.

"I think they're still at the hospital," Ginger added.

"I'll see that we get you a couple of outfits. In the meantime, I'll have somebody call Good Sam and find out about your clothes. What color outfits would you like, Ginger?" Ned asked.

"Oh, red, I look really good in red," Ginger replied through a toothless smile.

"Red it'll be," Ned responded.

"If I can get a shower and somebody can work on my hair I'll come back to see you," Ginger promised.

"I look forward to it," Ned said smiling.

"I'll even put my teeth in, if I can find them," Ginger added.

One of the attendants held up a clear plastic baggie with Ginger's dentures in it. "That's the one thing that made it from the hospital."

"Then I'll definitely be back to see you soon, Mr. Administrator," Ginger said.

"I can't wait, Ginger," Ned said. Then he added speaking to the attendants. "Take Ginger to station two. They'll help you."

Ned was feeling pretty good. He was two for two with patient interactions this morning. He decided to give himself a reward. He took out his cell phone and called Katie. She answered.

"This is a surprise. How's the kimchi?" Katie asked.

"Very funny. You want to have lunch? I owe you one," Ned said.

"What do you have in mind?" she asked.

"I feel like a burger," Ned said.

"Our usual place?" she asked.

"That's exactly what I had in mind," Ned said.

THE HAPPIEST PLACE ON EARTH

If you live in Los Angeles, most people believe the happiest place on Earth is down the five-freeway to Anaheim, Disneyland. But Ned believed it was much closer to home. The place that put the biggest smile on Ned's face was the Grand Central Market. The Market was located in the shadow of City Hall. It was a microcosm of everything Ned came to love about LA. It was noisy and crowded and there was no place to even turn around without bumping into somebody of a different culture. The Market had dozens of stalls that sold every kind of exotic food imaginable. There was Mexican cactus candy, Swedish potato sausage, fifty dollar a pound cheese from some mountains in Europe no one never heard of, to trotters which, Ned surmised, was an interesting way to disguise pig's feet. Many of the stalls were illuminated by large, bright neon signs. Every time Ned visited the Market, he imagined he was on a narrow street in a scene from some old black and white movie that was set in some far off mysterious Asian city. Belcampos, the premier butcher shop in Grand Central, was Ned's favorite place to buy meat in all of LA. It's where he went for his osso bucco or guanciale so he could make pasta carbonara the way his grandmother back in Providence taught him. But today he was going there to have a burger with his ex.

As Ned maneuvered his way through the multitudes in the Market, he saw Katie and their daughter, Amelie. They were waiting for him under Belcampos neon sign. Ned was surprised and delighted to see Amelie. He adored his daughter. He pushed his way through the crowd and grabbed his daughter and gave her a big hug. Nothing could have made him happier. Amelie's looks favored Ned's side of the family. Her hair was dark, her skin flawless and her smile bright. At twenty she was like a Georgia peach in July, sweet and at the peak of her beauty.

"What are you doing here? You're not ditching school are you?" Ned jokingly asked.

"No, I was at Mom's doing laundry," Amelie said.

"How's school?" Ned asked.

"Oh, it's fine. I haven't had a Belcampo's burger in forever," Amelie said.

All the counter stools at this the Mecca of burger emporiums were filled, but Ned had brought his family to Belcampo's many times and he knew many of the employees. He called to Pete, one of the butchers, "Pete!"

Ned called over the head of a Japanese tourist seated at the counter, who was eating his way through a Belcampo's special burger. Pete looked up and recognized Ned and his family. Ned held up three fingers.

"Three burgers, medium, fries and Cokes. I'll be at the end of the bar," Ned said.

Ned indicated a place he knew Pete would recognize as Ned's place. Pete gave him the thumbs up acknowledging his order. Ned towed Katie and Amelie through the crowd to the end of Belcampo's stall where there was a short piece of chest-high counter space that was unused. It was just out of the way enough to enjoy a standing-burger without the multitudes bumping into you.

"Have you gone to see your grandmother lately?" Ned asked.

"Last week," Amelie responded.

"How is she?" Ned asked.

"Complaining you don't come to see her," she said.

"If I moved in over there, she'd complain I wasn't there enough," Ned said.

In a few minutes, Pete delivered what Ned believed to be the best burgers in LA. Ned, Katie and Amelie wasted no time and immediately dove into their lunch.

"I love this place," Ned said. Then he added, "It's so alive, so completely different from my job. That's why I come here to remind myself there is life outside of a nursing home."

Ned grabbed a French fry off Katie's plate.

"Hey, that's mine," she said.

"They are good, aren't they? I've had a pretty good day at work. I convinced a woman whose amputated legs were stuffed into a suitcase not to file abuse charges against the facility, and I had a woman with no teeth come on to me."

"Oh, Daddy, that's awful," Amelie said.

"No, that's your father's way of trying to make me jealous," Katie said.

"Is it working?" Ned asked Katie.

"Not really."

"Actually, I'd rather entice whole women with their own teeth," Ned said to Amelie.

"Daddy, why didn't you become a lawyer like Uncle Mike?" Amelie asked.

"I've asked myself that question every day since I got into healthcare," Ned answered.

"It's not too late to change careers you know," Amelie said.

"Let's get you through college first then we'll worry about me," Ned responded.

Pete came back to check on them, "Everything ok?"

"Great, as usual," Ned responded.

"Can I get you anything else?" Pete asked.

"Give Katie a couple of pounds of hamburger patties," Ned said.

"I don't need hamburger patties," Katie said.

"Yes, you do. When Amelie comes over to do her laundry you'll have something good to feed her. You can get your own buns. And make sure their brioche," Ned said winking at his ex.

THE ARRIVAL OF THE QUEEN

The following day Ned got to work early. As was his habit, the first thing he did was check his email. As he was deleting the scores of junk mail cluttering his in-box, on the monitor he noticed Violet arrived at the facility much earlier than usual. Ned watched as she parked her car and went directly to her office. "Not like her at all. Wonder what she's up to," Ned thought aloud.

Most mornings, before Violet would disappear into her closet-sized office, she liked to talk to a few of the nurses to complain about what she considered to be Ned's latest disasters. But not today.

About half an hour later a large black SUV pulled up in front of Central City. Ned watched the monitor as the driver and front passenger got out of the vehicle. They were two chunky ladies in pant suits. They opened the rear door for the passenger. The woman that got out was stylishly dressed. She was wearing large opaque sun glasses. The scene looked like a foreign dignitary arriving at the White House. Ned wondered who had just arrived and what did they want. He watched as the cameras tracked the three women. They came through the lobby toward his office. The woman with the sunglasses stood in the doorway to Ned's office, "I'm Marilyn Fowler. I'm here to have a meeting with Violet, then I'd like to speak with you. Please be here so we can talk later," she said.

"Sure," Ned responded with a smile.

She turned and left. Ned watched Marilyn as she walked down the hallway toward Violet's office. Her two traveling companions followed her. Ned returned to the security cameras. At one point, Marilyn stopped and pointed to her companions. They separated and went into patients' rooms. Ned watched as Marilyn continued then she disappeared into Violet's office.

Violet was pleased when Marilyn arrived. She knew she had won a round in her battle with Ned. "The reason I came by, Violet, is to demonstrate how solid my support is for you," Marilyn said.

"I really appreciate that, Marilyn. I've given my heart and soul to this facility," Violet responded.

"And believe me. That carries a lot of weight with Mr. M," Marilyn confirmed.

Violet smiled confidently and the two got down to the subject at hand, Ned.

"I believe we are at the point where you have to make a decision about how this facility is going to operate," Violet said.

"That's why I'm here," Marilyn responded.

Central City was coming alive for another day. Ned was watching all of it on the monitors. CNAs were cleaning up breakfast trays. Other CNAs were starting their shower routine. Licensed nurses were doing their med pass. Some of the CNAs stopped by Ned's office and greeted him with a smile and a "good morning" while they loaded their pockets with the candy he always had available. Sippie, as was her custom, stopped by to give Ned a special, personalized good morning. It was never for the candy.

Lucy, one of the licensed nurses came into Ned's office. Lucy was a nurse Ned learned he could trust. She was the prototype of all the seasoned nurses Ned had come to know at all the hospitals where he had worked. Late forties, a little overweight. She was dependable and didn't participate in the various dramas that were always swirling around the facility.

"Ms. Flowers is in Mr. Imo's room trying to give him an erection," Lucy said.

"Can you get her out of there, please," Ned said.

"We already did, but Mr. Ned, she's doing that almost every day. It's very frustrating," Lucy added.

"I know, Lucy, I need a big favor. Look at the monitor," Ned pointed to the screen.

Marilyn's henchwomen were going from room to room.

"You see those two women wandering the halls? They're spies from corporate. They don't need to see Ms. Flower's mode of affection for Mr. Imo or any other of the unique things that go on here at Central City. You understand?" Ned asked.

"Yes, I'll take care of it," Lucy said.

"Thank you, Lucy."

She left Ned's office.

Ned couldn't take his eyes off the monitors. The last time he paid such attention to a TV he was watching OJ's slow speed pursuit. Ned watched as Marilyn's companions went in and out of the patients' rooms. Lucy periodically would show up and direct one of them to see one of Central City's better patients. When they would emerge from the room, Lucy would then look up at a security camera and give a secretive 'thumbs-up' to Ned.

"Thank you, Lucy," Ned muttered.

As Ned watched, one by one the department heads arrived. Instead of making another set of rounds, as was his usual routine, today Ned stayed in his office his eyes glued to the monitor. Eventually, Marilyn Fowler came out of Violet's office and walked back to see Ned.

“Would you like a cup of coffee?” Ned asked trying to be cheerful.

“No. Let me come right to the point,” Marilyn said.

“Violet has been the DON here a long time. I trust her. You two aren’t getting along. That’s a bigger problem for you than for Violet. Maybe you should listen to her, especially when it comes to what kind of patients you are admitting.”

Ned knew that was code for Violet had better be part of the admissions process. Marilyn took off her sunglasses and looked right into Ned’s eyes. “I have confidence you two can work this out,” she said.

The threat couldn’t be more obvious. Marilyn turned and left Ned’s office without saying goodbye.

Sure we can, Ned thought. Violet will make sure the Medicare goes in the toilet, Ned will get whacked and life will return to normal…for Violet.

Ned got up and followed Marilyn into the lobby. Marilyn’s two companions were waiting for her by the entrance. Suddenly, Gregor Ragasin came shooting by on his electric wheelchair. Marilyn had to quickly step back to avoid being hit by him. Without saying a word, Gregor continued out the front door. Marilyn looked at Ned. If looks could kill, Ned would be feeling his fatal heart attack beginning at that instant.

Marilyn and her entourage left Central City. Her two companions assisted her back into the large SUV and they drove away. With Marilyn gone, Ned went back into his office. A few moments later there was a knock on Ned’s open door. It was Casey.

“Can I come in?” she asked.

“Yes, of course,” Ned responded.

Casey sat down. “Marilyn Fowler’s visit is no small thing. You need to pay attention to what she said. I can’t remember the last time she was here. I bet it’s been years. But I do remember after she left, they changed administrators.”

“That bad, huh? I get the feeling you’re trying to look after me,” Ned said.

“Like I said before, I think you’re different. You’re good for this facility. I’d like you to stay. That means Marilyn can’t become your enemy or she will get rid of you,” Casey warned.

“I’ll do my best to keep from getting fired,” Ned said.

“I hope so,” Casey said as she left Ned’s office.

“Oh, Casey…” Casey stopped and turned to Ned.

“Can you see that Lucy gets a gift card. She helped me out this morning with Marylin’s bodyguards.” Ned said.

Ned sat down and thought about the events that just transpired. He decided he needed to make a call. He picked up his cell phone and punched in Lyle’s number.

"Ned, how's Central City today?" Lyle asked in his politician's tone.

"Just want to give you a heads-up. Marilyn Fowler paid us a visit this morning. She had a private meeting with my favorite DON. After seeing Violet, she came to my office to threaten me. I imagine she'll go back to corporate and tell them what a terrible job I'm doing."

"What did she say to you?" Lyle asked.

"That I better get along with Violet," Ned replied.

"Or else…" Lyle interjected.

"In so many words, yeah," Ned said.

"Ok. Thanks for the info. I'll make sure she doesn't blindside me…or you. You're doing a great job over there. Nobody else has even come close to what you're doing. Keep your Medicare up. At the end of the day, all Violet's bitching and warnings from Fowler will fall on deaf ears if you have a strong bottom line. You understand?" Lyle asked.

"Yes," Ned answered.

"Good," Lyle hung up.

Ned tossed his phone onto the desk. "Keep your Medicare up," Ned uttered Lyle's words. "That's the magic. It's just that easy," Ned mumbled.

If it were that easy, Ned knew he would still be in Santa Monica. But then Ned was aware that the Medicare tree out in front of Central City only had fruit like Gregor Ragasin hanging from its branches. That was the rub. To keep Lyle happy was to keep Marilyn and Violet unhappy. The thing that made Ned more uncomfortable was that yes, the Medicare was important, but equally important was the fact that Ned's fate would be determined not only by what he did or didn't accomplish but by the outcome of the political war that would take place at corporate between Lyle and Marilyn.

BOTTOM FEEDER'S EXTORTION

Marie, a bright, perky, thirty-something physical therapist, at Central City came marching into Ned's office. She was exasperated. "Mr. Ragasin refuses to participate in his therapy. I tried to explain to him if he didn't participate, we would have to take him off Medicare, but he was unreasonable. He refuses to listen. Maybe you can talk to him?"

Suddenly, there came a thump, thumping sound down the hallway. It sounded like the giant Jack upset in the nursery rhyme. The thumping got closer and closer to Ned's office.

"What the hell is that?" Ned muttered.

Gregor Ragasin entered Ned's office and pointed a sausage sized finger at Marie, "This woman is an idiot! She doesn't know a fucking thing about rehab. I refuse to go anymore. In fact, I'm calling Medicare and turning this fucking facility in for fraud!"

Ned stayed cool, "Would you like to sit down, Mr. Ragasin. I'm not sure the chair will hold you but…"

"Fuck you!" Ragasin fired back.

"Marie, you can go," Ned said to his young therapist. Then he turned to Ragasin, "If you would be kind enough to let her get by, I would appreciate it."

Ragasin moved aside just enough to allow Marie to squeeze by him and out of Ned's office.

"Mr. Ragasin, I was hoping we could come to an accommodation, at least for a little while, but I'm beginning to realize that's not going to happen."

"That's because this place is a shit hole. And I'm not going to take it. I know the regulations," Gregor screamed back at Ned.

"I'm sure you do. Perhaps, you would be happier at another facility? If you would like to go, I'll be happy to accommodate you," Ned said with a fake smile.

"I'll move to the Broad Street Motel. You pay for a month's rent and give me fifteen hundred for my trouble and I'll be gone today. Otherwise I'm going to call the fucking Health Department every day until they close this dump down," Gregor warned.

Ned leaned back in his chair. Now he had this guy pegged. He flashed a broad smile and wagged his finger at Ragasin. "Ah, now we get right down to it, don't we?" Ned said.

Mr. Ragasin was a shakedown artist. Fifteen hundred and a month's rent. Now Ned knew how Ragasin acquired that roll of cash hanging around his neck. Blackmail. Ned was sure Gregor scared the hair off most of the administrators' heads he came up against. And after ten minutes of fretted worrying how to get him out of their buildings, most administrators would cave in and jump at the chance of ridding themselves of this monster. As for money, any administrator worth his weight in dirt knew the money could be buried in the operational costs of their facility seven ways from Sunday. Mr. Ragasin might have been possessed by a schizophrenic personality, he might be prone to wild outbursts of rage, but he had his shakedown act down cold.

Ned smiled at the hulk in his doorway, "Let me think about it, Mr. Ragasin."

"You think about it. But the next time I see you the price goes up," Ragasin threatened.

Gregor turned and left Ned's office. He thumped, thumped his way back down the hall.

Ned watched on the monitor as Ragasin disappeared into his room.

Ned zeroed in on another part of the monitor. He saw Benito was in his shop. Ned picked up his phone and called Benito. "Yes, Mr. Ned," he answered.

"Benito, what do you know about electric wheelchairs?"

THE BLIND ROMEO

The third part of Dr. Kovani's hat trick arrived at Central City. His name was Pedro Sanchez. Ned watched from his office window as Pedro was taken out of the ambulance. Pedro was in a wheelchair. He was holding a white stick that was folded and on his lap. Pedro looked to be fifty-something. He had a three day growth of beard and stained clothes. A second attendant carrying a suitcase followed Pedro into the facility. The attendant wheeled this blind man into the lobby. Pedro put his white stick together and stood up out of the wheelchair. Pedro immediately started to swing his white stick about. There were about ten other patients in the lobby including Steven who, as usual, was selling his candy.

Most blind people seem to navigate with the white stick by sweeping it in a narrow pattern just off the surface of where they are walking. Mr. Sanchez operated his stick as if it were radar. Instead of feeling the area where he was about to step, Pedro's sweeps were low, high, and in the middle of the air in front of him. It was as if his white stick was a fire hose and he was trying to put out a blazing fire before him.

"Please, don't swing that stick like that," Ned said.

Left and right the white stick cut through the air in the lobby. In seconds, his stick hit wheelchairs and walls and nearly took the nose off one of the patients. Unfortunately, Ned's warning was too late for Steven's bucket of candy. The white stick hit the bucket knocking it right out of Steven's hand. Mars Bars, Snickers, Kit Kats, were suddenly all over the floor. It was as if Pedro had hit a piñata and it broke open. Some of the other wheelchair bound patients who were fixtures sitting in the lobby, and hadn't moved in years, were suddenly scrambling to gather what sweet treasures Pedro had released from Steven's candy stash.

"Hey! That's mine," Steven slowly screamed unintelligibly.

Some of the patients ate the sugary treats immediately while others stuffed as much of the candy as they could into their pockets. It was obvious Steven's candy sales for the day would plummet.

"Stop!" Steven mumbled at his fellow patients.

Ned, although the damage was done, grabbed the white stick away from Pedro. He picked up the bucket and began to gather what candy he could off the floor and return it to Steven's bucket. But the numbers were against him. Ned realized the other patients in the lobby were eating most of Steven's inventory. "Jose, could you help me, please," Ned said.

Jose came out from the reception area. He took the bucket from Ned and gathered up as much of the candy as he could. But his gathering was hindered by his thick, rubber gloves.

Even though Ned removed his stick Pedro continued to 'feel' the space around him with his outstretched arms. Pedro's groping hands somehow managed to find Jose's backside. Pedro smiled as Jose jumped and let out a scream. Ned decided to curtail Pedro's game of blind man's bluff through the lobby. He grabbed hold of Pedro's arm putting a halt to the disturbance he was causing. "Mr. Sanchez, you're hitting people. Please stop," Ned said.

"Where's my stick?" Pedro grumbled.

"I have it. I'll give it back when we get to your room," Ned replied.

Ned turned to the attendant, "Why don't you bring his wheelchair and his bag to his room."

He's in twenty-two A," Jose said.

Ned led Pedro down the hallway. When they passed Ms. Flowers' room, Pedro got a whiff of her aftershave. He stopped and sniffed the air like a dog that just picked up the overwhelming scent of something he liked. "What's that?" Pedro asked.

"That's Ms. Flowers," Ned said.

"Did you say Ms. Flowers?" Pedro asked.

"Yes," Ned responded.

Pedro sniffed again. "But isn't that Old Spice aftershave?" Pedro remarked.

"Yes, it is. She decided it's a scent she's very fond of."

Ned tugged Pedro along, "Your room is right over here."

He led Pedro into what was to be his new home at Central City. Pedro looked around.

"Where's the television?" he asked.

Ned was flummoxed. First, that Pedro looked around the room and second, that he asked about a device he couldn't theoretically see. "Television? Wouldn't you rather have a radio or maybe a CD player?" Ned asked.

"No, I like to watch TV," Pedro answered. "And make sure it gets ESPN."

"Ah-huh," Ned responded.

Ned realized Pedro's 'blindness' was his way of getting what he wanted.

"Ok, I'll have a TV brought in here. And luckily for you I believe our cable package does include ESPN," Ned said. "Anything else?"

"Yeah, what did you say the name of that woman was who had on the aftershave?"

"Ms. Flowers. She's a very nice lady but she has some difficulties. Be friendly, but I'd kind of stay clear of her for the most part," Ned gently warned.

Pedro didn't respond.

Sippie entered Pedro's room. "Hi, my name is Sippie. I'm going to be your nurse," she said to Pedro.

"Ah, Mr. Sanchez, you are a lucky man," Ned said. "Sippie is one of our best nurses."

Pedro could see enough of Sippie's shapely body to entice him to want to cop a feel. He immediately went into his blind man act. He reached out as if trying to find where she was and somehow, by sheer luck, he managed to find her thigh. He gave it a quick squeeze. Sippie jumped back.

"Careful, you don't want to damage your nurse," Ned said.

"Will you be the one giving me a shower?" Pedro asked.

"Twice a week," Sippie responded.

"What if I want more?" he asked.

"We can arrange that," Ned said.

"Oh, that's very good," Pedro smiled.

Ned left Pedro's room. He signaled to Sippie to follow him into the hallway. "Be careful of that one. He's a touchy-feely kind of guy if you get my meaning," Ned warned.

"I wish you were," she responded to Ned with a big smile.

Ned pretended not to hear her comment.

Ned had been around the block enough times and seen enough horny patients to realize Pedro was a Lothario disguising himself as a poor blind man. Ned hoped he was wrong about Pedro but he knew he would have to err on the side of caution and to keep an eye on him.

"Mr. Ned to station three. Mr. Ned to station three," Jose's voice echoed over the PA system.

Ned was never summoned for something pleasant or because the corporation arrived with an award of some kind. It was always trouble.

The charge nurse at station three, Erika Ha, was all upset. She was a tiny Asian girl that weighed maybe ninety pounds soaking wet. She was easily knocked out of her nursing routine by the slightest abnormal behavior by a patient, and there were plenty at Central City. She unfortunately was now stuck with Gregor Ragasin. His bulk and abusive behavior kept her in a constant state of anxiety. "Mr. Ned," she said as Ned approached the station, "I'm sorry to bother you, but Mr. Ragasin has turned his bed sideways and he won't turn it back."

"Turned his bed?" Ned questioned.

"Yes, sideways. I told him but he won't turn it back."

Erika was as much afraid of Ned's reaction that she couldn't control her patient, as she was of Ragasin's behavior.

"I'll take care of it," Ned said as he marched to Ragasin's room.

Mr. Ragasin's bed was turned perpendicular to the other beds in his room. Since it was the first bed in the room it blocked the entrance. Ragasin was sitting in his electric wheelchair eyes closed, hands clasped, head bowed, chanting. "Ommmmm…" came a low steady tone out of Ragasin's throat.

"Mr. Ragasin, I need to speak with you, please," Ned said.

"Can't you see I'm praying?" Ragasin answered as he gave out another throaty "Ommmm…"

"You can pray after I talk with you," Ned responded.

"That's a violation of my religious preference," he answered.

"I'm here to talk about the violation to the city's fire law preference," Ned said.

Ragasin opened his eyes and looked at Ned. "What do you want?" he asked.

"You can't block the door with your bed," Ned stated.

"The feng shui in this room is all wrong. I need the bed to go this way so I can maximize the flow of energy for my rehabilitation," Ragasin said.

"I'm sorry but the flow of energy is going to be interrupted because I'm going to have the bed turned back the way it was. That's the fire department's feng shui," Ned said.

Ned turned to Erika who was hiding behind the doorway to Ragasin's room.

"Erika…"

She peeked her head around the doorway, "Yes…"

"I'm going to call Benito and have him turn this bed back the right way. Let me know if Mr. Ragasin's urges as an interior decorator return," Ned said.

"Then I'm going to move it again," Ragasin said defiantly.

"Then I'll move it back again. And if we keep playing this stupid game I'll have the bed screwed into the floor if I have to." Ned turned and left Ragasin's room.

As he was walking back to his office, Ned took out his cell phone and called Benito.

"Hello," Benito answered.

"Do you remember we talked about the electric wheelchair?" Ned asked.

"Yes," Benito responded.

"Go to Ragasin's room and move the bed back the way it's supposed to be. And then come to my office," Ned said. He ended the call.

As Ned was about to enter his office, he found Ginger, the toothless lady, waiting for him in the lobby. She was sitting in the chair closest to his office door. She was wearing a red dress Sharon had found for her at the Salvation Army store. Her legs were crossed and the dress was pulled up all the way to her mid-thigh. Her hair was combed. She had on makeup and most importantly she had her dentures in. She flashed a big smile at Ned. Her gleaming white dentures made her look twenty years younger. "What do you think?" she asked Ned.

"Ginger, if I weren't the administrator of this hospital, I'd ask you out dancing," Ned responded playfully.

"Don't let that stop you," she said coyly.

"Unfortunately, it has to," Ned said.

Ginger signaled for Ned to come in close so she could whisper in his ear. He accommodated her request. "You stay late one night I'll take my teeth out and give you the best blow job you ever had in your life," she said.

"Ginger, there are laws against such things," Ned said.

"I won't tell," Ginger said.

"Tell you what. I'll think about it but that's all I'm going to do," Ned responded.

"If you change your mind…," she said.

"I know where to find you," he responded.

Ned closed his office. He wanted to get home and get ready for his dinner guest.

FIDEL WOULD BE JEALOUS

Ned had just closed the oven to check on the osso bucco when Lenore rang the doorbell.

"It's open. Come in," Ned called to Lenore.

She walked into the kitchen. She saw Ned was wearing a Jonathan Club apron.

"I'm impressed. You're a member of the Jonathan Club," she commented.

The Jonathan Club was a long time social gathering place for the elite of Los Angeles. It had been around since 1895. If you were anyone of stature, or wanted to be, and were willing to put up the hefty entrance fee, and of course were nominated by someone of importance, you too could become a member. If Ned were the CEO of Huntington Hospital instead of the Administrator of Central City, he might have been invited to join.

"No," Ned said. "I went to a charity event there once and managed to steal this." Ned tugged at the apron. "That's as close as I ever got to being a member," he added.

"I'm still impressed," she said. "I was never even invited to a charity event there."

"The food there was spectacular but not as good as what you'll be eating tonight," Ned said.

Ned took the osso bucco out of the oven and placed it on top of the stove to rest.

"What can I do to help?" she asked.

"Hand me the plates. They're in that oven," Ned indicated the counter top oven. "Be careful. They're hot," Ned gently warned.

Lenore took a kitchen towel off the counter, removed the two plates and placed them on the counter. He ladled a bed of polenta and a portion of roasted tomatoes, he got from pans on the stove, and put them onto each plate. He divided the veal shank and finished the plate with a garnish. He used a kitchen towel to pick up the finished plates. "Ok, right this way," Ned said to his Lenore.

Ned led Lenore out through the French doors in his living room out to the patio. The table was meticulously set with the wine already poured and the candles lit.

"Now I am impressed," she said.

"What would have happened if I were late?" she asked.

"The osso bucco would have been ruined. But, I was hoping you wouldn't be," Ned responded.

They sat and ate and drank a bottle of Barolo. They giggled and laughed about their jobs. During the espresso Ned served at the end of the meal, the sound of a band rehearsing seemed to drift in over Ned's rooftop.

"What's that?" she asked.

"It's coming from the Rose Bowl. There's a concert there this weekend," he answered.

"I'll bet you get to hear every concert that plays down there, and for free," Lenore commented.

"Concerts, football games, but the best is Fourth of July fireworks. I can sit right here and watch the whole show in my underwear. Now I have that special surprise for you," Ned said.

Ned went back into his house and returned with a tray. On it were two brandy snifters, a bottle of Remy Martin XO, the Cohiba Dylan had gotten, a cigar cutter, and Ned's cigar ashtray and match holder. Ned poured the Remy, clipped the end of the Cohiba and handed the cigar to Lenore.

"What do you want me to do with that thing?" she asked rhetorically.

"It's not a thing, it's a Cohiba. It's fifty dollars worth of cigar. I'm giving you the honor of the first puff," Ned said.

"I'm supposed to be happy about that?" she asked.

"Go on. You'll see how wonderful it is," Ned said.

Lenore gingerly put the cigar in her mouth. Ned struck a wooden match and put the flame to the end of the Cuban cigar. "Now slowly turn the cigar and puff," he said.

She followed his instructions.

"That's right," Ned said.

Lenore got a bit too much smoke and started to cough.

"Drink some of the cognac," Ned instructed.

She did, and eventually the coughing stopped. "I don't care how much it cost. That's awful," she said. She made a disgruntled face and handed Ned the Cohiba, "Thanks for the honor of the first puff, but I think I'll pass on the rest of the cigar," she said.

"Pity, you're missing one of the truly great pleasures in life," Ned took the Cohiba and began to smoke it.

The dinner ended. The wine gone. The cigar smoked. The evening was over. Ned walked Lenore to her car. He opened her door. "Thank you for a lovely evening. Everything was wonderful…but the cigar," she said.

There was a brief moment when they just looked at each other. Then they kissed. Not passionately but gently.

“I’d like to do it again, how about the fireworks show on the Fourth of July,” Ned said.

“Ok, but promise me no cigars,” she said.

“No cigars, but I’ll think of something equally as wonderful,” Ned said.

She got in her car. Ned watched her drive away.

Ned cleaned up the kitchen. Took a shower and went to bed. As was his usual custom he would put on the TV close his eyes and fall asleep to CNN and whatever bad news dominated the airwaves that day. But tonight, he didn’t turn the TV on. He closed his eyes and went to sleep thinking about the night he had just spent with Lenore.

BIG BAD JOHN

Gregor Ragasin always woke up early. He would climb onto his electric wheelchair and take himself out of the facility and go get a breakfast burrito from the local Taco Bell which was about a block from the facility. This had become his daily routine. The burrito would hold him over until breakfast was served at Central City. Then he would eat again, complain about the food not being fit for consumption, burp, fart loudly, and then begin to torture the staff with his outlandish demands.

But today would be different. Gregor got out of bed, slipped into his double poncho outfit, put his roll of money around his neck and stomped out of his room. He unplugged his electric wheelchair from the wall socket and climbed aboard. He engaged the forward drive on his wheelchair but the chair didn't budge. Gregor tried again and again to get his wheelchair operational but it never moved. Gregor got off the wheelchair, did a complete check of the battery and the wiring, and saw nothing wrong. It became obvious to him the chair's malfunction was due to sabotage. Gregor's schizophrenia took over. He went from mean-hearted bastard to crazed lunatic. "That son-of-a-bitch! That fucking son-of-a-bitch!" Gregor screamed.

Gregor was suddenly out of control. He punched a hole in the wall. He stomped down the hallway screaming obscenities. He turned over hampers. He punched another hole in the wall.

Nurses came running from all directions.

"Mr. Ragasin! What are you doing? Stop!" the charge nurse, Erika, yelled at him.

She realized she was trying to convince a madman to act rationally. It didn't even slow him down. Two CNAs came running down the hallway. When they saw it was Gregor, they stopped and stayed a safe distance away from him.

"Please, Mr. Ragasin, stop!" Erika yelled.

Ragasin turned and started to stomp toward her. Terrified, she turned and ran as fast as she could down the hall away from him.

"I'm going to kill that son-of-a-bitch!" That was Gregor's mantra as he turned from Erika and continued stomping his way down the hallway toward Ned's office. Anything Gregor could pull off the wall got pulled. Anything in his path was smashed or overturned. Other nurses saw what was happening but were smart enough to observe from a safe distance. Nobody attempted to stop him. The crashing and yelling got patients up and out of their beds. They went to their doorways to see what was happening, but the CNAs quickly intercepted them and pulled them back into their rooms and out of Ragasin's wrath. One of the CNAs, Carolina, used her cell phone to call Ned. He was in his car driving to work.

"Good morning," Ned said with a cheer in his voice.

"Mr. Ned, This is Carolina. Mr. Ragasin is smashing the building."

"Call the police. Now!" Ned quickly responded.

Carolina immediately followed Ned's instruction and called.

"911 emergency."

"Send some cops over to Central City right away. One of the patients has gone crazy!" Carolina pleaded.

Gregor yelled and smashed his way down the hall, screaming all the way to Ned's door. He punched a hole right through the administrator sign. He then went to work on the rest of the door smashing it with his fists. "Come out of there you son-of-a-bitch!" he screamed over and over.

Another charge nurse tried to calm Gregor down. "Mr. Ragasin, Mr. Ned's not here. Please calm down."

Gregor turned to the charge nurse, "I'm going to kill that bastard!"

Gregor picked up a small chair that was in the lobby and smashed it against the floor. Pieces of the chair flew everywhere.

The charge nurse ran for cover. Panicked, she called Ned.

He answered, "I know Ragasin is going crazy. Carolina just called me."

"Mr. Ned, now he's in the lobby, and he just smashed a chair."

Ragasin picked up a potted palm tree and smashed it against the lobby floor. "...and now he just smashed the palm tree," she added.

"Stay out of his way! And keep everybody away from him," Ned said.

Ned ended the call with the charge nurse and then he called the PET team. He wisely had put their number on his speed dial.

The Psychiatric Emergency Teams (PET) were mobile units from psychiatric hospitals whose job it is to remove patients from situations where they are either a danger to others or themselves. Ned knew Gregor's rampage would definitely qualify for a removal.

When he thought about what was unfolding, an impish smile appeared on Ned's face. He turned into the parking area. He didn't particularly hurry. As he was climbing the back stairs, he heard the sirens. In addition to the PET Team his staff had wisely called the cops. The sirens announced the arrival of the police. Rampart Division was home to some of the toughest cops in Los Angeles.

Ned and two cops from Rampart entered the lobby at about the same time. One of the cops was very young, he looked like he was just out of high school and the other was an LAPD corporal and looked like he had some seasoning. Gregor picked up another chair. He was about to throw it against the floor when he realized that the cops had entered the lobby. He was smart enough and in control enough not to get into a brawl with the police. Gregor's rampage suddenly stopped.

"That son-of-a-bitch broke my wheelchair!" Gregor pointed at Ned and yelled to the two cops.

The corporal held his hand up to Gregor. "I want you to stay still. Don't move. You understand? And put that chair down," The cop's voice was calm but demanding.

Gregor carefully put the chair back on the floor. The cops looked around the lobby and surveyed the damage. "Now I want you to sit in that chair," the corporal ordered.

Gregor wisely obeyed the corporal's order.

The corporal looked to Ned, "You in charge?"

"Yes," Ned responded.

"That son-of-a-bitch broke my wheelchair," Gregor repeated.

"I called the PET team. They should be here anytime now. They need to take him to a psych hospital and hold him for observation," Ned said.

Ned's plan was to get Gregor out and call Dr. Kovani or Dr. Gross to be sure Mr. Ragasin would be transferred to another facility and never darken the door of Central City again.

"Fuck you! I'm not going!" Gregor yelled at Ned.

"As you can plainly see, Mr. Ragasin is out of control," Ned calmly said to the officers.

"Fuck you!" Gregor yelled as he started to come up out of the chair.

"Sit down!" the corporal yelled at Gregor.

Gregor responded but it was obvious that he was so agitated he would explode any second. He could hardly keep himself in the chair. He balled his fist and pounded the chair's arm until it broke off.

The Rampart Division police were used to psychotic, out of control individuals. After all, Central City was full of homeless people and in one of the most crime-infested neighborhoods in LA. These cops were used to dealing with the mentally ill. What made this situation a little different was Gregor's bulk and his level of agitation. This, the cops knew from experience, only amplified the danger. The corporal radioed for backup.

Jose watched, wide-eyed, from the safety of his receptionist cubicle. Ned tapped on the cubicle glass. Jose was too frightened to open the sliding glass panel.

"Yes," he said through the glass.

"Jose, open the damn glass," Ned said.

He slid open the glass panel just enough to satisfy Ned's demand. "Tell the staff to keep everybody out of the lobby," he said.

Jose picked up his phone and made the announcement over the PA. "Attention all staff and residents, please stay out of the lobby until the cops take Mr. Ragasin out of Central City."

"Jose!" Ned yelled.

"That's a HIPAA violation," Gregor screamed.

The corporal pointed at Gregor, "You shut up!"

"Oh, I'm sorry, I wasn't supposed to say Mr. Ragasin's name, was I?" Jose said over the PA.

Frustrated, Ned sighed. The damage was done. Ragasin's right to privacy was violated but the message was clear.

Casey, the ADON, and Anthony, the DSD, were sharp enough to quickly organize the CNAs and department heads and cordon off the lobby. No one would be allowed there until this situation was under control. Violet, as usual, didn't help but watched from a safe distance. Now it was a Mexican standoff. The cops in one part of the lobby carefully watching Ragasin, and Ragasin in the other part of the lobby taking apart the chair he was sitting in piece by piece.

As the minutes ticked by, Gregor's level of agitation heightened. Ned was quietly waiting for the next act of this drama to unfold. That would be when the PET team arrived.

The PET team arrived before the police backup. It consisted of two smaller than average females, neither of each weighed over one hundred pounds. The idea that they would be able to muscle Ragasin onto the gurney they brought with them defied logic.

"You're the PET team? You have to be kidding me. You see that guy smashing the chair. That's who you're here to get," Ned said.

The PET Team leader walked over to Gregor. "Sir, we're here to take you to the hospital. Would you please get on the gurney," the smaller of the two females said politely.

"I'm not going. You can't make me," Gregor defiantly yelled.

The leader of the PET team turned and spoke to Ned, "I don't know that's there's anything we can do if he won't get on the gurney."

"You see the smashed chair and the palm tree on the floor. How do you think it got there? Please, you need to get this guy out. It's obvious he's dangerous," Ned said.

"I'm sorry. If he won't go willingly there's nothing we can do," the PET team leader said.

Ned knew the absurd reality of the thinking behind that logic was predicated on the belief that allowed a completely schizophrenic patient to self-determine if he should be allowed to take drugs that would control his out of control behavior. Ned suddenly began to worry that his plan to remove Gregor from the facility was in jeopardy. His last hope was the police backup.

"I'm not going," Gregor stated again.

But even a blind pig occasionally finds an acorn. Ned's acorn arrived on the back of an LAPD motorcycle. Ned was expecting two or three squad cars full of cops. The LAPD had their own patient extraction team. The extraction team cops were well trained and used to dealing with the mentally ill. But what came to Ned's rescue was only the one giant police officer. Big Bad John was the nickname given to him by his fellow officers at Rampart Division. This giant, black police officer dismounted his bike and walked into the facility. He was the size of the biggest lineman in the NFL. He stood in the lobby doorway, his helmet on, dark glasses covering his eyes, gleaming motorcycle boots, black leather gloves. Attached to his belt were a gun, taser and what looked like and extra-large baton. Just the sight of him could make the knees on any would be tough guy watery.

"What the fuck is going on here?" John's deep, thunderous voice rumbled through the lobby.

Ragasin, who up to this point was acting agitated and defiant, suddenly calmed at the sight of this officer. Big Bad John looked around the lobby before he spoke to Gregor, "Are you the problem?" John's grumbled baritone register seem to rattle the lobby windows.

"I'm not going!" Ragasin ginned up the courage to proclaim, although there was a hint of a quiver in his voice. Then he added, "I know my rights. You can't make me."

That giant, black police officer looked over to the corporal.

"We need to remove this guy before he hurts somebody," the corporal said.

Ned sighed with relief. "Thank God," Ned muttered.

Big Bad John looked at the damage in the lobby before he walked slowly and deliberately over to Ragasin, "Did you do this?" Big Bad John asked Ragasin as he indicated the damage in the lobby.

Ragasin pointed to Ned, "He broke my wheelchair."

"That has nothing to do with it," the giant cop said. Then he turned to Ned, "What do you want to do here?"

"He needs to go to the psych hospital for an evaluation," Ned responded.

"I told you I'm not going!" Ragasin yelled at Ned.

Big John took his baton out from his utility belt. It looked even bigger and more menacing than when it was in its holder. Then that giant, black officer tapped the baton into his gloved hand. The implication was obvious. The next place the baton would land was going to be on Ragasin. Big Bad John leaned in close and spoke to Gregor, "Now, I want you to get your fat ass on that gurney. If you don't, I'm going to beat every ounce of shit out of your body." To emphasize his point, Big John beat the baton harder into his own hand.

It didn't take long even for Gregor Ragasin to determine the gurney was a far better choice than the baton. Even in his crazed state, Gregor Ragasin could visualize the outcome if he decided to go up against the giant standing before him. He got out of the chair as fast as he could and stomped his way across the lobby and climbed onto the PET Team's gurney. The PET Team ladies quickly strapped him in before he could change his mind.

Ned thought to himself. That's all it took…one giant policeman and the threat of a beating to end Ragasin's mayhem at Central City. Thank you, LAPD, and Big Bad John.

Ned was pleased. The day was starting off well. A smile appeared on Ned's face. As Ragasin was being wheeled out to the ambulance he yelled to Ned, "I'm not finished with you, you bastard. I'm calling the Health Department and tell them what you did. I'm going to sue your ass off. I'm going to own this place! And you better not lose my wheelchair." Ragasin's verbal threats continued. The PET ladies had a hard time loading Ragasin into their ambulance but with help from the two cops and CNAs, Ragasin was safely locked away. When the ambulance door closed behind him all that could be heard were Ragasin's muffled rantings. The attendants got in the ambulance and drove Ragasin away.

The giant, black policeman took another look around the lobby and left the facility without saying another word.

"Can I have your card? For the report," The corporal asked of Ned.

"No problem," Ned said. "And I need yours as well."

Ned called to Jose. "Jose, give this nice officer a card, please." He opened the glass panel with his kitchen-gloved hand and gave the police officer Ned's card. The corporal turned to Ned. "What's with the gloves?"

"It's a long story," Ned responded.

The corporal and his high school looking partner left the facility. Normalcy, as best as it could be described at Central City, returned. Ned, still standing in the lobby, enjoyed a moment of peace as he watched the ending to the Ragasin drama.

Dylan came up to Ned, "Did you see how fast he got on the gurney? I didn't think he could move like that," Dylan commented.

"I told you he had an Achilles heel," Ned responded wryly.

"You sly dog," Dylan said.

"Call Kovani tell him Ragasin is gone. He has plenty of Medicare left so Kovani won't have a problem dumping him off on some other administrator. If he balks call Dr. Gross. And then go by the Honey Baked Ham store and buy the biggest ham they've got for the Rampart Division cops. Deliver it with a big bow and thanks from us. You know we'll be using them again," Ned said smiling at Dylan.

"You got that right," Dylan said.

Ned took out his cell phone and called Benito.

"Hello," Benito said.

"You better come up here there's a lot of work to do," Ned said, then he turned to Dylan, "Do me a favor, get somebody to help get Ragasin's wheelchair downstairs. I'm sure somebody will be calling to pick it up soon. Make sure Benito gets it running again."

Ned left the lobby and went to his office. He leaned back in his office chair it began to creak.

"Not again," Ned exclaimed. He got out of the chair and rocked it back and forth. The creaking continued. He opened the lower desk drawer looking for the can of WD-40 Benito had given him. Then Ned stopped, "No, today's is a good day, the hell with the squeak."

Ned was satisfied that he had solved the Ragasin problem, but didn't like the fact he had lost a Medicare. After all was said and done, Ned was able to rid himself of Gregor without losing a lot of blood. Yes, it would cost Ned a few bucks in repairs but that was far cheaper than the chaos Ragasin would have brought to the facility and cost Ned in the long run. For as smart as Ragasin thought he was, Ned was smarter. Ragasin rode around on his Achilles heel. Ned wondered how many other administrators Gregor had terrorized, and would terrorize in the future. And yet, the answer to the Ragasin removal would stare each administrator in the face from the moment they met him. But, Ned wondered, how many administrators would have the balls to do what he did. After all, 'adjusting' a patient's wheelchair was a drastic step and if discovered by the Department of Health could have proven to put Ned into a very sticky situation. Weighing it all, Ned felt pushing the envelope was well worth it.

BLIND MAN'S BLUFF

A few days later, Ned was on the phone answering a complaint from a relative. It was a regular part of his job. Some relatives would call up screaming about everything from bad food to purposefully trying to kill Grandma once or twice a week. Today, the person on the other end of the line, Arlene Weathers, was the daughter of one of his longtime patients, Ruth Anderson. Arlene was screaming so loudly Ned held the phone away from his ear but was clearly able to hear the woman.

"Why was that man wearing my mother's dress?" Arlene screamed.

"The gentleman you're talking about is incapable of rational thinking," Ned calmly said.

"I don't care! Isn't your staff supposed to prevent things like this from happening?" Arlene screamed.

"Yes, and I truly apologize," Ned said.

"Some strange man was wearing my mother's favorite dress. Do you know how that made her feel?" Arlene angrily asked.

"I can't even imagine," Ned said.

"That's all you can say. You can't even imagine. I want to know how that man got my mother's dress? Is he a transvestite or something? What kind of people do you admit into that place? How do I know my mother is safe with that guy running around in your hospital in women's clothes?" Arlene screamed angrily.

"Ms. Weathers, I promise you that gentleman is harmless. He has dementia. He's a longtime resident here. He just borrows things from other patients from time to time and tries them on," Ned said.

"My mother's dress? The man is over six feet tall. My mother is hardly five feet. He was wearing her dress for a scarf," she screamed.

Lost, borrowed, or stolen the disappearance of articles of clothing are a given in many skilled nursing facilities. It was especially true in Central City. There are a thousand reasons why. But the result is always the same, angry patients, angry relatives, and lots of complaints.

"Ms. Weathers, I will replace the dress," Ned promised.

"You're damn right you will. How do I know you'll keep that man out of my mother's closet?"

Anthony, the DSD, knocked on Ned's door then opened it. He stuck his head into Ned's office and indicated the TV monitors. He spoke quietly as not to interfere with Ned's phone call.

"I need to rewind the cameras," Anthony said.

Ned nodded for him to go ahead and rewind the camera while continuing his phone call. "I will do everything I can to make sure the gentleman in question never takes another piece of your mother's clothing," Ned said to Arlene.

Anthony operated the mouse and clicked the computer instructions. The computer rewound the cameras in the facility to a few minutes before. Anthony then zeroed in on one of the multi-happenings that had just taken place in the facility. He clicked the picture he was looking for and the picture filled the entire monitor. "You better look at this," Anthony said.

The picture was of the dining room. There, on the screen, was Ms. Flowers sitting at a table by herself. She was just looking out the window at the smokers on the smokers' patio. At another table twenty feet away was Pedro Sanchez. He was flipping through an old, dog-eared Playboy Magazine. He unfolded the Playmate of the Month and held it up to get a good look at Playmate's various feminine charms.

"Pretty good for a blind guy, huh?" Anthony commented wryly.

Ned began to take serious interest in what was happening in the dining room. Ms. Weathers continued to rant at Ned. He put the phone down on the desk and fully turned his attention to what was happening on the monitor. "Ms. Weathers," Ned said leaning into the phone on his desk, "I promise I will do my utmost to guarantee that no one ever wears another of your mother's dresses. I'm sorry but I need to go now," In the middle of Arlene's rant, Ned hung up the phone.

Ned studied the monitor. After getting enough stimulation from the Playmate's picture, Pedro looked over at Ms. Flowers. Maybe it was a whiff of Ms. Flowers' aftershave that propelled Pedro's next actions. He got up from the table where he was sitting and walked over and sat by Ms. Flowers.

"Watch closely," Anthony said.

Pedro looked around the room. Satisfied, he lifted up Ms. Flowers' shirt and began fondling her breasts.

"Whoops!" Ned exclaimed.

"I thought he was blind," Anthony said chuckling.

"Not so blind he couldn't find her breasts," Ned commented.

"Wait there's more," Anthony said smirking.

After stroking Ms. Flowers' breasts, Pedro decided he wanted more. He leaned over and began to suckle Ms. Flowers. A second later, a CNA, Carolina, interceded. She ran into the picture and separated Pedro from Ms. Flowers. Another CNA entered the picture. She led Pedro out of the room. Ms. Flowers attempted to follow Pedro but Carolina kept her in the dining room.

"Play it again. I want to be sure I saw what I saw," Ned said.

"You did," Anthony said. He rewound the images and played them again for Ned.

"What do you want to do?" Anthony asked.

"Tell Grant to do a SOC 341. You call the cops. Have a CNA put Pedro in his room and stay with our Don Juan, and bring me his face sheet."

Anthony executed Ned's instructions. Within minutes the same police duo that came to Central City on the Ragasin call arrived from Rampart Division. Jose led them into Ned's office.

"Good morning, officers, nice to see you again," Ned said.

"You have an abuse situation?" the corporal asked.

"One of my male patients, Mr. Sanchez, got a little randy and touched one of my female patients, Ms. Flowers. He's sentient and has capacity; she's demented. That is sexual abuse. If you would be kind enough to please remove him from the facility, I would be grateful. This is the gentleman in question." Ned handed the officers Pedro's face sheet. The corporal scanned the information.

Pedro's face sheet clearly pointed out he was mentally capable of understanding the world around him. That meant the second he touched Ms. Flowers he committed a crime…Elder Abuse. If Pedro had been schizophrenic or demented the police would have been polite, but unless there was blood on the floor, they would not have removed Pedro from the facility.

Ned operated the computer and played the incident for the officers. They watched silently as Pedro touched and suckled Ms. Flowers.

"Want to see it again?" Ned asked.

The officers looked at each other. They exchanged some silent police communication.

"No, where is he?" the corporal asked.

"He's in his room. I'll take you there," Ned said as he led the police duo to Pedro's room. Sippie, was standing guard in the doorway assuring Pedro couldn't flee. Pedro was sitting on the bed. His roommate, Mr. Harmon, a crusty, old black man with a catheter and a portable urine bag attached to his belt, was in the second bed watching TV.

"Mr. Harmon, I wonder if you would excuse us for a few minutes. These nice officers would like to talk to Pedro," Ned said. Ned gestured to Sippie to get Harmon out of the room.

"I hope you're going to arrest his ass," Harmon said to the officers. "All he does is jerk-off all day and night. I'm sick of looking at his dick."

"Come on, Mr. Harmon." Sippie said. "Let's go see what they're doing in the dining room. I think Harmonica Mike is here today."

"That asshole! I don't give a shit about him or his fuckin' dog," Harmon said.

Sippie helped him out of bed, into his wheelchair and then pushed him out of the room. When she was out of hearing range, the corporal turned to Pedro, "Mr. Sanchez, did you improperly touch a woman in the dining room?" the corporal rhetorically asked.

In addition to instantly reverting to total blindness, Pedro suddenly became stone deaf. He reached out in front of him grabbing the air. "What…what did you say?" Pedro moved his head around as if trying to find the origin of the sound.

"We're going to take you with us," the corporal said.

"Huh? What did you say?" Pedro was laying it on as thick as he could.

The corporal gestured to his partner. The two cops stood Pedro up. They cuffed him and led him out of the room.

"Don't forget his white stick?" Ned said.

The younger officer got Pedro's white stick off the bed and took it with him.

"He's going to need it to get around in his cell," Ned said.

"Where are you taking me?" Pedro asked. "I'm blind. You can't take me to jail."

Pedro protested his removal the entire time he was being led out of Central City. He was safely tucked into the back of the police car and driven away.

On the way back to his office, Ned stopped off to see Ms. Sankie. Marie, the therapist was working her arms. Her legs were neatly tucked into her purple suitcase.

"Hi!" Sankie said enthusiastically to Ned.

"How's it going?" Ned responded.

"Great! My therapy is progressing. As soon as I get these wounds on my ass healed, Marie says I'll be able to move back into my van," she said.

"That's wonderful," Ned said as he gave Sankie the 'thumbs-up.' He left her and walked down the hallway. Life is absurd, Ned thought. A woman who keeps what's left of her legs in a suitcase, who lives in a van which is why she developed wounds on her backside to begin with and the reason she was in nursing facility, can't wait to get back to her old life…and maybe develop some new wounds. Ned chuckled aloud.

Ned walked by the dining room. There was a group of his patients, some awake, some asleep, some paying attention, some having a good time, and others just looking out the window. They were all just sitting in their wheelchairs watching 'Harmonica Mike and his Dancing Dog' perform. Mike was in his eighties, the dog was even older. Mike and his dog had seen better days. Mike wore a suit with frayed cuffs, the dog had bald spots here and there. Mr. Harmon was in the dining room and he had already fallen asleep. Harmonica Mike was belting out 'I've Been

Workin' on the Railroad" on his harmonica while his dog was up on his two hind legs slowly going around in a circle. Ned wondered which was more bored, some of his patients, or the dog. In a far off corner of his mind he could hear the Nitty Gritty Dirt Band…

"I knew a man Bojangles and he danced for you. In worn out shoes. Silver hair, a ragged shirt and baggy pants. The old soft shoe. He jumped so high. He jumped so high. Then he'd lightly touched down. Mr. Bojangles, Mr. Bojangles, Mr. Bojangles…Dance."

Yes, Ned thought, life if definitely absurd.

As Ned watched Mike, the dog, and his patients in the dining room he thought of his father, John.

"Promise me, you'll never put me in a nursing home, no matter what," his father would often say.

"You were right, Pop. You were so right," Ned muttered aloud.

Ned headed back to his office. He sat in his squeaky chair and went through the emails that were piled up in his computer. One was an apologetic few words from Dr. Kovani. He thanked Ned for taking Ragasin and understood why he needed to 'transfer' him to another facility. The good doctor promised there would be other patients. Kovani and Central City were locked in a symbiotic relationship. They were like the rhinoceros and that bird that perches on that ancient herbivore's back. The rhino provides lunch and the bird provides pest control. At the end of the day, Ned figured Kovani's hat trick was one-one and one. Ragasin was a loss, Pedro Sanchez was a push and Sankie would turn out to be profitable. If Ned could bat a .333 with every doctor he did business with he would end up in Administrator's Hall of Fame.

MASQUERADE

"Sharon, Activities, please come to my office," Ned said over PA system.

A few minutes later, Sharon walked to Ned's office. "Yes?" she said wondering why she was summoned.

"Sharon, I've been thinking. While Harmonica Mike and his mangy dog were mesmerizing, perhaps we could shake things up with our activities. Maybe make things, I don't know, more interactive," Ned said.

"How? You know all they want to do is play bingo?" Sharon said.

"Sharon, think outside the box," Ned said.

"What box? What are you talking about?" Sharon was befuddled.

"I want to do something different," Ned said.

"Like what?" Sharon asked.

Ned thought for a moment then he blurted out, "I don't know, different. Why don't we have a costume party? Yeah, a costume party."

"A what?" Sharon seemed even more befuddled.

"We'll get a cake and ice cream…" Ned said.

"You mean I'll get a cake and ice cream," Sharon responded with a hint of protest in her voice.

"Ok, you'll get a cake and ice cream," Ned kept right on going. "I'll put up prizes for the best patient and staff member costume. Think of it from the patient's point of view. They don't have to see scrubs for one whole day," Ned said.

"But Halloween don't come until October," Sharon said.

"We'll do another one in October. Sharon, come on, get in the spirit of things. I'll even get you a costume," Ned pleaded.

"What kind of costume?" she asked.

"You can come as a stripper. Big ear rings, pink feather boa. You can wear it home. Your husband will love it!" Ned said.

"He's lucky I come home at all," Sharon said wryly.

"You'll look great in pasties. And with a little practice you could do the whole propeller thing." Ned mimicked spinning chest propellers with his fingers. "Come on Sharon, we've got to do something besides BINGO!" Ned said desperately.

"Well, how do you want to do this?" she asked reluctantly.

The following week, colorful flyers were posted. The buzz of a seventy-five dollar first prize, with a second and third money prize, for the best staff and patient costume managed to excite the whole facility.

Even the housekeepers decided to join in. One secretly told Ned she was coming as 'Bob the Builder.'

Ned felt the excitement growing in Central City and he decided to double the prize money. The few skeptics now felt the tug of greed and climbed on board. Who was coming as what was all the staff talked about for days.

Sharon made a trip to the ninety-nine cent store and purchased lots of art supplies for the patients' costumes. Fuzzy cotton for beards and wigs, construction paper for crowns, beads, lots of beads, false noses and glasses...anything that could be turned into a costume. For once, reluctant as she normally was, this time Sharon put a bit of creativity into Ned's plan.

Ned decided that he was going to lead from the front on this. After all, this was his idea. He wanted to make as big a splash at the costume party as he could. Not that he was looking to win a prize. Ned had a rule that department heads could never win anything. But the point was to please the patients and do a little team building with his staff.

Ned went to a costume shop he knew of in Glendale. It was a rental company the studios used to outfit extras in background shots. They had every conceivable period of history covered. As Ned walked between the hundreds of racks of garments, all he had to do was decide who he wanted to become. He toyed with the idea of becoming a Roman Emperor but decided he wasn't imperious enough to pull that off. Then he thought about becoming President Lincoln, but he decided he wasn't tall enough to pull the Lincoln thing off either. Then after searching through dozens of racks, he found what he was looking for, the perfect outfit that displayed power, taste and love.

The day of the costume party Central City looked more like the Masquerade sequence from Phantom of the Opera than a skilled nursing facility. Everyone, staff and patients alike, wore some sort of a costume. 'Bob the Builder' was cleaning rooms. Superheroes ranging from Batman to Wonder Woman were passing meds. The whole kitchen staff sported vampire fangs and covered themselves in a combination of red food coloring mixed with cornstarch. This was their idea of fake blood. Every patient suddenly had a cotton beard or false nose and glasses, some of the women patients wore witch hats and long paper mache noses. In keeping with the spirit of the day, Effie, the dietary super, changed the breakfast menu to feature 'Mystery Eggs.' They were the same eggs that she served every other day, but the garnish was a little sugar-free cookie that looked like the Lone Ranger's mask.

The whole atmosphere in Central City was lighter and more fun, which is saying a whole lot for a skilled nursing facility. Dylan came as a giant hotdog. Sharon dressed up in a 1920's Flapper outfit and around ten in the morning she channeled Bessie Smith. She set up the portable microphone in the dining room and sang 'Nobody Knows You When You're Down and Out' to the patients. As she sang, Sharon didn't exactly spin pasties but she shook her breasts and her booty. Both patients and staff howled with delighted laugher. Even Benito, who, at first, 'poo-pooed' the idea of a costume party, got in the spirit. Ned had rightly surmised Benito was still pissed at him for putting a camera in his office. That camera severely cramped Benito's amorous adventures. But on the day of the party, Benito showed up as a violin playing mariachi, which was what he was every weekend. And to prove the violin wasn't just a prop, Benito played a selection from the mariachi favorite hits songbook. Everyone participated but Violet. She was content to stay in her office and condemn the whole event as silly and unprofessional.

Ned came to work later than usual on the day of the costume party. He wanted breakfast and med pass to be over and most of the patients up so nothing could lessen the effect of his arrival. Instead of coming up the back stairs of Central City as he usually did every morning, Ned made his grand entrance through the lobby. Ned the administrator was, for today, Pope Ned the First. He spared no expense to assume Papal presence. He came completely decked out. He sported a Pope's miter and carried a scepter staff. He even wore knock-offs of Pope Benedict's red velvet slippers. If Ned had gone downtown to Our Lady of the Angels Cathedral, he might just have pulled off a surprise Papal visit. Ned's entrance into Central City brought the first squeals of laughter from Jose. He was wearing a full-on Hazmat suit. In his case, the Hazmat suit wasn't a costume as much as it was actual protective gear. Jose alerted the rest of the staff of Ned's arrival over the PA system,

"Attention everyone, we are indeed fortunate to have a special guest in Central City. Guess who? Pope Ned is in the building!" Immediately staff and patients came to see the Pope. Ned walked through the lobby as his employees and patients cheered and clapped. He blessed them all and headed down the hallway. He made rounds waving like, well the Pope, as he walked along. Nurses and patients alike came out from behind their med carts or from their rooms to see the 'visitor' from the Vatican. Giggling and clapping followed and a few of the dimmer patients thought Ned was actually the Pope and asked him for a blessing. He, of course, kindly obliged.

It seemed the patients were calmed by the appearance of all these oddly dressed people in the building. There were no fights between patients, that in and of itself was a minor miracle. Showers were given without protests. Meds were passed and nobody spit the pills back in the nurses' faces. No plates of food were thrown on the floor and none of the patients tried to run away. The day was going along wonderfully. Steven, the candy salesman, won the best patient costume. Sharon helped him fabricate the muscles to transform him from a wheelchair bound stroke victim into Arnold Schwarzenegger's 'Conan the Barbarian.' The best staff costume prize went to Martha Gonzales. She was a CNA who dressed up like Celia Cruz the Cuban chanteuse. She wore a big sparkly dress, a blue wig and came to work in 'brown face.' When Martha's sang Celia's version of 'Oye Como Va' to the crowd gathered in the dining room, she assured herself of first prize.

But no matter how brightly the sun is shining, sometimes a cloud will show up and rain on everything. The cloud that blew over Central City on the day of the costume party came in the form of Candy Mintz from the DHS. She was in her usual all black out fit and dragging her black wheeled-briefcase. She was wearing her too tall, black high heels that clip-clopped down the hall. And, of course, she was in her Kabuki–like, Goth make-up. Candy was there to answer Arlene Weather's complaint about a male patient wearing her mother's dress. When she entered the lobby, Jose sounded the alarm over the PA system, "Mr. Ned, line ten. Mr. Ned, line ten."

Suddenly, the party balloon that was Central City that day began to lose air.

"DHS, why are they here?" Ned muttered aloud.

Ned left the festivities in the dining room and hurried back toward his office. Candy intercepted him as he entered the lobby.

"I'm here on a family member complaint. Why are you dressed like that?" she asked.

"We're having a costume party today," Ned answered.

Candy seemed puzzled, "Why? It's not Halloween. It's not even October."

"I just wanted to shake things up around here. You know, add a little fun," Ned answered. "By the way," he added, "...we're giving out cash prizes for the best costumes. Would you like to try for a prize? I'll bend the rules and let you enter. You can come as Marilyn Manson," Ned said smiling.

"Very funny," Candy replied with a snarl. Then she added, "I want to see your policy and procedure on laundry distribution and personal clothing."

"We don't have one, any more than we have a policy and procedure for rainy day activities. They're the same as sunny day activities," Ned responded.

"How do you keep track of the patients' clothes?" she asked.

"We have the family members or CNAs write the patients' name in the collar or waistband if it's pants," Ned said.

During Ned's interrogation, Martha, AKA Celia Cruz, came out of the dining room. She was pushing Hattie Oaks in her wheelchair. Hattie had a bag of potato chips on her lap and was chain eating them. Martha was still wearing the blue wig and brown face when she rolled Hattie by

Candy and Ned. Candy saw Martha's 'brown face' and stopped her. "Why are you in black face? Don't you know that's racially offensive?" Candy asked.

"It's not black it's brown and it has nothing to do with race. She dressed up like Celia Cruz," Ned said.

"Who? I don't care who she pretending to be, black face is offensive," Candy's voice became louder and more annoyed.

"It's not black. It's brown," Ned repeated as Martha nodded in agreement.

"All right it's brown. But it's still a racial stereotype and its offensive!" Candy insisted.

Hattie turned her head to Martha. "Who is this fucking bitch?" Hattie said pointing at Candy.

Then Hattie turned to Candy. "What's your problem, bitch? You got white paint all over your fuckin' face. That's offensive to me. Besides I like her black face."

"It's brown, Hattie!" Ned interjected.

"Take me to my room. I have to take a shit," Hattie said.

"Martha, please take Hattie to her room," Ned said as he gestured for Martha to move Hattie along. As Martha rolled Hattie down the hallway Hattie called to Ned, "You get me some more potato chips. And get that white-faced bitch outta my fuckin' house."

"I'm going to call my supervisor about this. We have enough racial problems in this city without you adding to them," Candy threatened.

"There is absolutely no racial anything going on here. You are way out of line, Ms. Mintz," Ned said.

"We'll see about that," she responded.

"Let me remind you about the last time you went down a rabbit hole…remember the food coloring business?" Ned asked.

Ned could see there was a moment when Candy blanched as she thought about looking like a fool to her peers possibly for a second time.

"I think this is a totally different situation," she said as she tried to cover her rising feelings of uncertainty.

Ned could see Candy was wavering. Perhaps, she could still remember the sting to her ego over the food coloring embarrassment. Ned had to quickly find a way to give her an 'out' that would allow her some dignity. He remembered Sun Tzu, and especially the passage about giving your enemy a place to retreat. Ned knew he would be dealing with Candy many times in the future and he didn't want to piss her off but so much.

"Tell you what, Ms. Mintz, why don't you think about the brown face for a bit? Maybe consult the ACLU or the NAACP. Ask about Celia Cruz. I'll see if I can find you one of her CDs. You might like it. In the meantime, you're here to answer a complaint about Ms. Anderson's dress that was being worn by Stanley Tolland. Very understandable issue. No racial anything there. I have already promised to replace the dress and will create a care plan to supply Stanley dresses of his own. Why don't I put you up in the Media Room and I'll have their charts brought to you. What do you think?" Ned smiled at Candy.

Candy thought about it for a few seconds. She was able to justify Ned's proposal, "I'll make a few calls to see if you violated something with the black face..."

"Brown face," Ned said cutting her off.

"In the meantime, bring me the charts." Candy said as she clip-clopped down the hallway toward the Media Room.

Ned felt he had won the round with Candy. The Celia Cruz thing would get lost in the discussion that would keep Stanley out of Ruth's dresses. Ned knew there would be others run-ins with Ms. Mintz and maybe next time he wouldn't be so lucky. As she walked down the hall Ned gave her his papal blessing.

What the hell, Ned thought to himself, can't hurt.

A SAFE TRANSFER

The following morning Central City got back to normal. There was yelling, screaming and the usual bad looking scrubs. Ned went to his office and opened his email.

Within minutes, Ned's desk phone rang. He answered it, "Yes, Jose."

"It's DHS on line two," she said.

Ned picked up the call. "Ned Russo. Can I help you?"

"This is Myla Childs with the Department of Health in Sacramento. I'm calling about Pedro Sanchez. I understand he was a former patient of yours," the woman said.

"That's right. But he's no longer here," Ned responded.

"That's what I'm calling about. I want to make sure he had a safe transfer. His family called. They were concerned it wasn't," she said.

"Couldn't be safer, he was taken out of here by the police," Ned said.

"The police! Why?" Ms. Childs asked.

"He sexually abused another patient. I followed our protocol and called the police and they arrested him."

"How can you be sure it was a safe transfer?" she asked.

"Ms. Childs, perhaps you didn't understand what I said. He sexually molested another patient, a demented old lady. That's a crime. I called the police and they arrested him and he was removed from the facility. It was a perfectly safe transfer," Ned said reassuringly.

"I understand all that, but you're still responsible for a safe transfer. That means you need to insure that Mr. Sanchez was transferred to a safe environment that can meet his needs. Can you tell me where they took him?" she asked.

Ned was quickly becoming frustrated with this moron in Sacramento.

"I can't be sure but I assume they took him to Twin Towers," Ned responded.

"And is that another skilled nursing facility?" she asked.

"No, it's the Los Angeles County jail. And as far as meeting his needs, I understand the baloney sandwiches are quite good. The beds are a little hard but that is offset by the interesting new people he'll meet. Now, if you want to know more about how Mr. Sanchez is doing, why don't you call the activities director at Twin Towers, if they have one, and I'm sure they can provide you with a report on Mr. Sanchez's bingo game performance. Thank you for your concern. Hope the weather is not too hot in Sacramento, goodbye," Ned said as he hung up the phone.

Ned could only wonder who the state was hiring to work at DHS. He decided to give himself a breather by doing a set of rounds. He poked his head into a few rooms asked the patients how they were doing. Then went to the kitchen to see what was on the menu. It was chicken…again. Patients in a nursing home eat so much chicken and turkey it was amazing they didn't sprout feathers. He picked up three bags of potato chips for Hattie. When he stopped by her room, she was screaming at her CNA.

"Don't touch me you fat fucking bitch."

"Hattie, are you being a bad girl?" Ned asked.

"This fat bitch won't leave me alone," Hattie yelled.

"She won't let me change her," the CNA responded.

"I don't need to be changed," Hattie proclaimed.

"She's soaked," the CNA said.

Ned dangled the three bags of potato chips in front of Hattie. "These are for you," Ned said.

Hattie reached out for the chips. Ned pulled the bags back just out of her reach.

"After you get changed," Ned added.

"I don't want to be changed," Hattie asked.

"You're wet and you need to be changed," Ned said. He wiggled the chips in front of the old lady. "Come on, Hattie, you know you want these," He wiggled the bags again.

Ned knew Hattie's potato chip addiction would override her need to sit in a wet diaper.

"All right, this fat bitch can change me," Hattie reluctantly said.

Ned handed the chips to the CNA. He turned and left the room. As he did he called out to Hattie.

"Thank you, Hattie. You be a good girl and I'll bring you more chips later."

"Hey…" Hattie called to Ned.

Ned stopped at turned around to see the old woman. "Yes, Hattie."

"I forgot to tell you I just got accepted into USC," she said.

"Well, isn't that nice," Ned said.

"You think I'm full of shit, don't you?" Hattie said.

Then she took a letter out of her bedside table and showed a letter at Ned. "Look at this. It's my acceptance letter."

Ned's curiosity got the best of him. He took the letter from her and read it. "It says here you've donated your body to USC Med School."

"I always wanted to go to USC. Now I'm going to be a Trojan forever! How the fuck do you like that!"

"Hattie, I am impressed. If you don't mind, I'm going to make a copy of this letter and put it in your chart. And as a gift to you, I'm going to have the original framed and we'll put it right by your bed."

"I think you're not nearly as big an asshole as people in this dump think you are," she said.

"Thank you, Hattie." Ned said as he walked back toward his office.

Hattie's final arrangements at USC brought back a moment in his past that made him chuckle.

Every year Ned would make an annual pilgrimage back to the homeland in Rhode Island. Ned came to call this journey 'the punishment tour.' To soften the blow, he always went during the summer. That way he could take advantage of one of the things he loved best about Rhode Island, the beach. Summer in Rhode Island was spectacular. The Atlantic, fishing, lobster, there was no end to how much those summers away from the nursing home business soothed Ned's soul. It helped make up for Rose treating Ned like he was twelve every time he came home. It was customary as part of the punishment tour that Ned would have to stay in his old room at his parent's house. When Amelie was old enough, Ned and Katie would send her back for a couple of weeks. Ned's two wives never understood why they couldn't stay at a hotel at the beach like adults and soon gave up going with Ned on the annual pilgrimage. They didn't understand how Rose would gnaw at Ned like a beaver chewing through a log with comments like… "Well, if my house isn't good enough…" or "Go ahead stay in a hotel. You know how much this will hurt your father?" Rather than start out each visit with an explanation of different lodging accommodations Ned just gave in. Every night while Ned was in town, Rose commanded Mike and his family to come over for dinner. The menu during all those hot sticky summer nights was always the same; red-sauce pasta with sausage and meatballs, or roast turkey. Where Rose could even buy a turkey in August to roast was a mystery to everyone.

On one of these dinner occasions John decided his final arrangements had to be made before Ned went back to California. Funeral arrangements and red sauce don't exactly mix but John and Rose would not be deterred. John had even called the local funeral home and made an appointment. The next day instead of going fishing like he had planned, Ned and Mike went to Solarno's Funeral Home to complete the business of John and Rose's pre-passing. Mr. Solarno was old school, black suit, black tie, black carnation. Ned wondered where Salerno got a black carnation. Solarno's funeral parlor smelled like an over-ripe florist shop. He went on in great detail about knowing John and Rose for years since they were all members of the same church and were all members of the Italian American Club. Solarno promised…

"When the time comes, which, God willing, isn't for many years, I promise John and Rose will look twenty years younger as they lay there in the viewing room."

Ned could only wonder why dead people looking twenty years younger was a selling point, dead is dead, but then he really didn't understand the whole idea of a funeral anyway. Solarno took Ned and Mike and showed them his three 'viewing rooms.' In one of the rooms there was a closed coffin surrounded with flowers.

"This room will seat fifty. Your mother and father have lots of friends. There will be a crowd just from the Italian American Club. I suggest we go with this room so everyone can be seated," Solarno urged.

"Does this one cost more?" Mike asked.

Mike was naturally tight. He had the first buck he ever made. Unlike Ned who found money to be a bit like mercury…tough to hold in your hand.

"It costs a little more but believe me your parents will need the seating," Solarno cautioned.

Of course, this viewing room was the biggest and the most costly. Underneath all the concern about how many members of the Italian American Club would come for the viewing, Solarno was just another version of a car salesman hawking his most expensive wares.

"Is somebody in there?" Mike asked indicating the coffin at the front of the room.

"Yes, that's Mrs. Picerno. Her viewing will be later today. She's was a member of the Club too. I wouldn't be surprised if your mother and father come by to pay their respects," Solarno responded.

"They'll probably come right after we finish the turkey," Ned said.

Then Solarno took Ned and Mike downstairs to the casket department. There were as many as a dozen caskets on display. Some of the caskets had liners that were just white. Others had with scenes, like a man fly fishing in a mountain stream, another was a depiction of Heaven's gates opening and a smiling Jesus welcoming the person in the casket into heaven. In a third casket there was a scene of a family picnic. To complete that scene, Solarno had a barbeque set up next to the casket with two rubber steaks on the grill.

"I almost understand the pictures in the caskets, but why do you have a barbeque?" Mike asked.

"We're getting into theme funerals. They're very popular in California. We can design almost anything you want. I recently did a circus theme and brought in a stuffed lion next to the casket. The family thought it was great," Solarno said.

"I'll bet," Ned said as he looked askance at his brother.

Solarno stopped his tour in front of two powder blue caskets.

"Since we are making the arrangements for both John and Rose, I can give you a really good deal on these caskets."

In unison Ned and Mike said, "BLUE!"

"They were special ordered. But the people who ordered them unfortunately were lost in a mudslide on a trip to Peru. Their bodies were never recovered. Shame. The caskets have a hundred year leak proof guarantee," Solarno added.

Ned and Mike looked at each other not really knowing how to respond.

Always the lawyer, Mike asked, "How would we know if they leaked in say ninety years?"

"Even if they don't leak, I don't think Mexican wedding blue caskets is what my parents had in mind," Ned said. Then he added, "Something a little more traditional would be fine. And I don't think they need scenes either."

"Unless you have one of a woman cooking red sauce," Mike added.

The deal for Rose and John's final arrangements was concluded. They would spend eternity in conventional mahogany colored caskets without scenes or a theme. But Ned and Mike did pop for the fifty-seat viewing room.

Later that night, and at a revival of another inappropriately heavy summer dinner, John asked the obvious question, "So, how did it go at the funeral parlor today?"

Every time Ned thought about John asking that question, from all those years ago it always made him laugh.

GREEN STAMPS

Ned's cell phone vibrated in his pocket. He pulled the phone out and looked at the screen. It was a call from Carlos in HR.

"Hello, Carlos. What can I do for you?"

"I've been getting calls from CNAs complaining about Anthony," he said.

"Has he been molesting anybody?" Ned asked facetiously.

"Not exactly. He's just being Anthony and following them around. They feel he's spying on them," Carlos responded.

"Isn't that his job?" Ned asked.

"I suppose, but he lays it on a little thick. He acts more like a cop than a DSD. He needs a little more carrot and a little less stick," Carlos said.

"Anthony told me the CNAs were going to call you and complain about this," Ned said.

"Why don't you nip it in the bud so it doesn't get upstairs. You with me, buddy?"

"I'll take care of it," Ned said.

"If you need any help…" Carlos added.

"I know, I'll call you," Ned ended the call.

"At least I'm going to try and take care of it," Ned thought aloud.

Ned thought about Carlos's words. "Nip it in the bud…"

That was Carlos's way of reminding Ned that the corporation didn't want to give the CNAs an excuse to think about the union.

'The union' was the bane of the corporation's existence. The union had far too many demands, rules, shop stewards, etc. The union would come into a facility and sell the idea that they would protect their members from guys like Anthony. Ned knew he had to tread carefully. If Central City became a union building, corporate would blame him. He had dealt with a union building earlier in his career. What he did was follow the Godfather's advice. "Keep your friends close and your enemies closer." Ned wasn't that afraid of dealing with the union. He knew that Laker tickets and lunches at the right restaurants would soften even the most strident shop steward's attitude.

Ned thought long and hard about how he would attack this HR problem without damaging Anthony's credibility, yet making sure Anthony was able to do his job properly and at the same time giving the CNAs a win. This was a conundrum for sure. That night Ned brought the problem home with him. He worked out on the heavy bag. His hands occupied his mind was free to think.

The following day he called Anthony into his office. "Close the door. Come in and sit down," Ned said.

Anthony followed Ned's instructions.

"As you predicted, some of the CNAs are calling corporate complaining about you," Ned said.

"I figured," Anthony responded.

"What we're going to do is spin their complaints to our advantage," Ned said smiling.

"How?" Anthony asked.

"You know what green stamps are?" Ned asked.

"No."

"A million years ago when you went to the grocery store they would give you green stamps. The more you spent, the more stamps you got. After you saved up enough stamps you could turn the stamps in for a set of dishes. The whole system was based on the illusion of free stuff. Most people bought more than they really needed so they could get more green stamps so they could get a cheap set of dishes they didn't need anyway," Ned said.

"People really got sucked into that?" Anthony chuckled.

"By the millions. People thought they were getting something for nothing," Ned said.

"Really," Anthony said amazed.

"We're going to do a version of the same thing here. It won't be dishes and it will involve a little bit of extra record keeping on your part," Ned said.

"That's ok," Anthony said.

"Your job is to set up an in service meeting for all nurses. Make sure there's plenty of pizza there," Ned said.

The meeting with Anthony over, Ned went to find Casey. She was in a patient's room hanging an IV bag.

"Did you know the nurses have been complaining about Anthony to corporate?" Ned asked.

"No, some have complained to me. I didn't know they called corporate" Then she added, "I tried to explain to the nurses that Anthony was just doing his job," Casey said.

"I've been working on something that might help calm the CNAs down," Ned said.

He laid out his scheme to Casey. She told him she would help to sell it to the nurses. Then Ned went to nursing station-one looking for the person he considered his most influential CNA.

"Where's Carolina?" Ned asked the charge nurse.

"She's on break. She usually goes onto the patio," the charge nurse responded.

Ned walked onto the non smokers' patio. Carolina was sitting at one of the tables munching Cheetos as she was busily texting away on her phone. Ned sat next to her.

"You know, those things will make you fat," Ned said as he reached into her bag of Cheetos and grabbed a few for himself.

"My husband likes me a little meaty. He said only dogs like bones," Carolina responded.

"He has a point," Ned responded as he took a few more Cheetos.

"Am I in trouble?" she asked.

"No, I need your help."

"Again? Mr. Ned, why don't you ask Sippie?" she said with a coy smile.

"I don't need that kind of help," Ned responded.

"What kind do you need?" she asked.

"I'm going to introduce an incentive plan for the nurses. What I need is buy-in from the CNAs. That's why I'm coming to you," Ned said.

"Me?" Carolina seemed confused.

"The nurses look up to you. If you get on board, that will go a long way to the plan's success."

"Oh yeah, what's the, what did you call it…the incentive?" she asked.

"Something I promise everyone, including you, will love," Ned said with a deep mellow, seductive tone.

"What is it?" Carolina asked.

"Make sure you're at the in service and love what you hear. Help me sell my idea to the other CNAs. You do that and you'll be on my team. That's going to buy you a lot of points with me," Ned smiled at Carolina the way the Devil smiles at every man he bargains with for their soul.

A few days later all the nurses, both licensed and CNAs, were gathered on the non-smokers' patio. Anthony had done his job well and almost every nurse that worked at Central City was present. Casey and Carolina were sitting up front. There was plenty of pizza to go around. The nurses were all in a good mood. Casey had spread the word before the in service that Ned was going to offer the nurses some sort of a bonus plan. Carolina fueled that same fire to the CNAs. The mood at the in service was as if Jeff Bezos was going to unveil his latest drone distribution plan to the gathering at Amazon. There was excitement in the air. When Ned stepped out onto the patio even Violet was lurking nearby to see what Ned was up to.

"Good afternoon everyone, thank you for coming. I hope you're enjoying the pizza," Ned said.

There were thanks and claps of approval as Ned went into his sales pitch. "All of you work very hard. I believe you should be rewarded for that hard work. So how would all of you like a day off with pay?"

At first there was stunned silence. Then Ned's words sank in. There were giggles and a few laughs and lots of cheers, but all the nurses thought Ned was teasing them.

"I'm not kidding. Do your job professionally and I'll give you a day off with pay."

The nurses were quiet. Some were skeptical. Ned let his words sink in before he continued. "Some of you are wondering, what's the catch. There is no catch. If there are no call offs, no coming to work late, no write ups, no cell phones or ear buds during patient care. Give Central City happy, clean, patients. I'll give you a day off with pay every quarter! Think about it. That's almost a whole week of extra paid vacation a year!"

At first there was stunned silence.

"Pass these out," Ned handed flyers to Carolina.

The flyers detailed the rules Ned had outlined to all the nurses at the meeting. Then Ned 'closed.'

"To help you get your day off with pay, Anthony will be there to see that you succeed. He will be here to guide you and make sure bed baths are properly given, med pass is correct. Anthony is here to help you. Ask him if you have questions or are unsure about any part of your job. That's what he's here for, so use him," Ned said.

Casey stood up and faced the nurses. "I've been a nurse for a long time and I can tell you no administrator has ever done this for the staff," Casey said. Then she smiled at Ned.

Casey, the trusted ally of all the nurses, had just driven home the run that Ned was counting on to win over the nurses. Suddenly, the nurses were a twitter with excitement. Jeff Bezos himself couldn't have presented Ned's plan any better. Ned's idea was a roaring success. Then to lay in one more layer to seal the deal Ned added, "And, to sweeten that day off just a bit more, all those who get their day off with pay, their names go into a hat and I pick one out and that person gets an additional hundred dollars."

The nurses went wild. They cheered and clapped. Their enthusiasm was overflowing. Suddenly, the idea of Anthony following them around wouldn't seem so odious. He was the conduit to that set of 'free dishes.' Ned also knew, and it turned out he was right, that the calls to HR would dry up. The possibility of Central City becoming a union shop would disappear from the thoughts of the nurses. Ned knew the odds that dozens of his nurses would drain the resources of the facility while they basked at the beach on their paid day off were only slightly better than winning the California lottery. Just to be safe, Ned would make sure a nurse or two would be a winner every quarter. He wanted to keep the carrot in place. That's why regardless how astronomical the odds Ned, like so many others, played the lottery every week.

FIREWORKS

It was good to have the Fourth of July off. Ned needed it. He had been putting in extra hours every day at Central City and he was bone tired. He had hoped he would sleep in but he woke up at his usual time, the crack of dawn. He blew off the run he had planned and instead cleaned his house. He was expecting Lenore that evening. She was coming over later for dinner and the fireworks show at the Rose Bowl. He wanted the evening to be perfect.

After he dusted, vacuumed and changed the sheets on his bed, he went out to see his back yard. He decided that's where they would eat. He cleaned off his patio furniture, got a vase out of the garage and placed it on the table. He would pick up flowers at Bristol Farms later. Ned surveyed the dining table but felt after they had eaten, they needed a more comfortable venue to view the fireworks. They would be exploding over Ned's house and the best viewing would be in the middle of his backyard. He thought about moving two lawn chairs to the middle of the yard but quickly came to the conclusion that he didn't have the right seating for fireworks viewing.

When he finished getting his house ready, Ned drove to Fishbeck's, a patio furnishings store in Pasadena. They were having a blow-out Fourth of July Spectacular Sale. Arriving at the store, Ned was surprised to see how many people were shopping. He thought he'd have the place to himself but he was wrong. There was a Black Friday atmosphere as shoppers looked over and sat on the odd pieces of patio furniture that had their prices slashed. Ned combed through the bargains until he found a double chaise lounge. It was lacquered bright-white with a dark blue cushion that would comfortably fit two people. It was just what Ned had in mind. He arranged to have it delivered that afternoon.

His next stop was Bristol Farms for scallops and linguine. He also picked a bottle of fruity Italian wine, peaches to roast for dessert, ice cream to put them on and lastly red, white and blue flowers for the table. When his house, the table, the dinner, the wine, and the chaise were set up, he called Central City. He kept his fingers crossed that there were no disasters or potential disasters brewing that would intrude on his evening. The RN Super told Ned there were no call-offs and so far, all the patients were safe. Ned un-crossed his fingers, sighed in relief, and then took a nap.

By the time Lenore came over, about seven thirty, the peaches he had marinated in the balsamic vinegar were on the grill, the scallops were at the perfect temperature to be sautéed, the wine was chilled, the water for the pasta was boiling and the flowers were in the vase waiting for dinner on the table. Lenore rang the doorbell.

"It's open," Ned yelled from the kitchen.

She let herself in and made her way to the kitchen. She was wearing a pair of tan shorts and a gauzy white top.

"I know you told me not to but I brought a bottle of wine anyway. I was always told you never go to a party without a little something," she said.

Ned stopped what he was doing to look at her. He realized he had never seen her legs before. They were long, slim and beautiful.

"Thank you. Put it in the fridge. Wow, you look stunning. And look at those legs," he said.

She was a bit embarrassed by what he said. "Oh, stop. They're just legs," she commented.

"No, they're way better than just legs."

She walked over to the stove where Ned was preparing to drop the pasta into the boiling water.

"What can I do to help?" she asked.

"Pour us a glass of wine."

She removed the chilled bottle of the wine and two glasses and poured them each a glass. She handed one to Ned. He held his glass up. "To us…and America of course."

They clinked glasses.

Lenore sipped her wine. "Hmm…Oh, that's good!"

"That's just the beginning of the goodness," Ned said sporting a broad smile.

When the pasta was al dente and the scallops were perfectly browned, Ned removed the scallops and put the pasta into the scallop pan. A few flips of the pasta so it would acquire the drippings and then Ned gently plated it. Then the scallops were arranged on top of the pasta followed by a garnish of fresh parsley to complete the dish. He handed his completed masterpiece to Lenore.

"That looks delicious. Is it an old family recipe?" she asked.

"No. I got it right out of Bon Appetite," Ned responded.

They went out to the patio and sat at the table. Lenore realized there was a tablespoon as part of her setting. She picked up the spoon, "I want to warn you I've never been very good at twirling spaghetti."

"Then watch closely," Ned demonstrated how to twirl linguine for her, "Spoon in this hand, fork in that hand now grab some linguine with the fork. Now put it on the spoon and twirl."

She followed his instructions and had a twirled forkful of pasta.

"Bravo," he said.

She put the pasta in her mouth.

"You are now officially Italian."

They finished the pasta and scallops and the bottle of wine and the bottle Lenore brought. They were both a little tipsy. They giggled and laughed and listened to the band playing 'You're a Grand Ole Flag' in the Rose Bowl warming up for the fireworks show, Ned served the balsamic roasted peaches topped with vanilla bean ice cream for dessert. Ned and Lenore had already taken up residence on the new chaise.

"I never would have thought vinegar and peaches would go together," she said.

"But they do, don't they?" he responded.

"You're really an amazing cook," she said.

"It's a great stress reliever and it tastes good too," Ned responded.

As darkness set in, the fireworks over the Rose Bowl began. There was a flash of green light as a rocket shot into the sky. There was a whistle as the rocket climbed high above Pasadena. Suddenly, there was a burst of green light as the rocket exploded sending out hundreds of green streamers that filled the night. And then a loud BOOM cracked like thunder. Another whistle, another blast and a red rocket exploded. Boom and another, boom and another and another…

Lenore moved in close to Ned. He reached down and laid his hand on her smooth, taffy colored leg. That touch shot through both their bodies like a bolt of pleasure. They were both overcome. It's as if they had been waiting for this moment since they met. They embraced and kissed. Their kiss was deep and long. Their hands suddenly began exploring each other's body. With each new sensation their passion grew. Their hearts raced. They gave in to their desire. With fireworks bursting overhead, Ned and Lenore made love on Ned's white lacquered chaise. The climax came for all of them, Lenore, Ned, and the fireworks show at the Rose Bowl. It was all truly spectacular.

They moved from the chaise to Ned's bed where they made love again. They stayed together until the first rays of light peeked through the darkness of that summer's night.

In the early light of dawn, he brought Lenore to her car, kissed her gently and watched her drive away. After she left, Ned went back to bed and held the pillow her head rested upon moments before close to his face. He wanted to savor every molecule of her presence she had left behind.

A CHANGING OF THE GUARD

The next morning Ned came to work early. When Ned drove by the front of Central City he saw that the paramedics and a fire truck were parked in front of the facility. He didn't really think anything of it. The Fire Department and Central City were constantly in business. He pulled under the building and parked in his usual spot. When he got to the top of the stairs, Eileen was waiting for him. Her eyes were swollen and filled with tears. He instantly knew there was something terribly wrong.

"What's the matter?" he asked.

"Mr. Ned, I have some very bad news. Casey is dead," she said.

The shock of such news went through Ned's whole body as if he had been struck by lightning.

"Dead?" Ned muttered. He heard what Eileen said but he didn't want to believe it.

"I think she had a heart attack. When she came to work this morning, she greeted me like she always does then she went out to have a cigarette. One of the housekeepers found her," Eileen sadly explained.

Ned walked over to where the paramedics were standing over Casey. She was still on the ground. Her eyes were open and she had a look of surprise on her face.

There must have been that instant when you knew, Ned thought.

"I'm so sorry, Casey," Ned softly said to her. Then tears began to stream down Ned's face.

"There's nothing more we can do here. Do you have an empty bed where we can put her?" one of the paramedics asked.

"I don't know, probably…" Ned said. His mind at that moment was unable to process what was happening.

"Yes, bring her to room eight," Eileen said.

It seemed at that moment everything and everyone in Central City was paralyzed. The building, usually full of noise, was quiet. The staff all seemed stunned and unable to speak. The patients usually loud and moving about seemed to vanish from Ned's consciousness. A profound sadness permeated the pores of the entire facility.

The paramedics gently placed Casey's body on the gurney. They covered her with a sheet and pushed the gurney into the facility. Ned was left alone standing in the place where Casey died. It was her private smoking spot. The ashtray she used was filled and there was an empty airline sized bottle of vodka on the sidewalk. Ned stood there for a moment, unable to move, then he walked to room eight.

Casey was in the room by herself. A sheet covered her body. The privacy curtains were drawn and the lights were off. Ned stayed for a moment out of respect for her then, he left her.

Ned stopped by the reception cubicle. Jose was crying.

"Can you call corporate? Ned asked. "Tell them what happened. I just can't do it right now," Ned said his voice cracking.

Jose held back what tears he had left, "Yes, I'll do it."

Ned went into his office closed the door, sat in his chair and stared out the window. He was trying to make sense out of what happened but couldn't.

Later that morning, the mortuary people came and transferred Casey from the bed onto their gurney. They covered her with a purple shroud. Ned and most of the staff accompanied her body out to the hearse. No one said anything. There was some crying but mostly just the stunned silence of shock. When the hearse pulled away from the curb, it suddenly hit Ned that he would never see Casey again.

The rest of the day was a blur. People came by from corporate, Marilyn Fowler and her entourage, Lyle, Carlos, Ed Denning. They were all as shocked as Ned and the staff at Central City. They offered their sympathy. They went around to the staff to see if there was anything they could do. There wasn't. Central City functioned that day, but just barely.

Eventually all the corporate people left. Ned sat in his office staring out the window until the shift changed at three o'clock. Ned brought them all, nurses, housekeepers, kitchen staff into dining room and gave them awful news. By then most had already heard. They were all devastated.

Ned waited for the police to come to fill out the necessary paperwork and then Ned drove home. He called Katie and told her what happened. She asked if he needed her. He thanked her but at that moment Ned needed to be alone.

When he was able, Ned contacted Casey's sister. She asked if Ned would help her arrange for Casey to be cremated and her ashes shipped back to Maine. Ned complied.

The following morning at the stand-up meeting, no one could speak. The grief was a blanket that covered everyone. All the department heads were there with the exception of Violet. Ned arrived at the meeting late. He was carrying a brown paper bag.

"I'd like to say good morning but it's not. This is a very sad day for all of us," he said.

Ned emptied the contents of the bag on the Media Room table. There were a dozen airline sized bottles of vodka.

"Pass these out," he said.

All the department heads took a bottle. Ned took one, unscrewed the cap and held it up, "I know this is against company policy, but today I'm going to make an exception. This is for you Casey. You will be missed." Ned took a swallow from the tiny bottle of vodka. The other followed Ned's lead.

"Meeting is adjourned," Ned said.

He decided he wasn't going to stay at Central City today, it would have to function without him. Ned went home. He worked out on the heavy bag. He sat in a chair and stared blankly at television the rest of the day, until the emotional exhaustion forced him to sleep.

A few days later, Ned packed up Casey's things from her office. All of Casey's life at Central City would fit into a box that Ned would send to Casey's sister. He took special care to wrap Casey's framed nursing degree. In that box Ned included a letter he wrote praising Casey and adding how much of a loss she would be not only to the facility, but to him personally. When the task was completed and the box sealed, Ned looked at the lifeless room that a few short days ago was her office. When the shock of her death was gone the sense of her loss became a reality. Her office, once the heartbeat for the staff at Central City, was now just an empty room with a box fill of memories sitting on a desk.

Ned got through the rest of the day. While Ned was driving home his cellphone alerted him there was a text from Lyle. The text read: 'How are you doing? Ned, I know this is perhaps a bad time to do this, but I've been wondering if you had somebody in mind to fill Casey's position. We need to move on this before Fowler does.' Ned threw the phone down on the seat. He knew for as inappropriate the timing of the text was, Lyle was right.

When he got home, the first thing he did was make himself a martini. He drank it in the backyard where he and Lenore ate scallops and watched fireworks. He looked at the white lacquered chaise where they made love. Then he thought about how to answer Lyle's text. He knew politically the replacement for Casey would be crucial in his ongoing struggle with Violet. He thought about what he wanted and more importantly how this decision would impact his success at Central City. He thought how he would miss Casey and what a good nurse she was. He thought about how angry he was at her for dying. He thought about who could fill her shoes. He felt guilty he could have such thoughts. He thought about all this before he called Lyle an hour later.

"Ned, how are you doing?" Lyle voice was restrained.

"Given the circumstances I'm hanging in there," Ned responded.

"You get my text?" Lyle knew Ned had received it.

"Yeah," Ned responded.

"I'm sorry about the timing, but if we don't move quickly..." Lyle said.

"I understand," Ned said cutting him off.

"Is there anybody at Central City?" Lyle asked.

"No, we need to go outside the facility," Ned said.

"Do you have anybody in mind?" Lyle asked.

"There's somebody, I haven't talked to her yet," Ned responded.

"Who?" Lyle asked.

"Her name is Usha Patel. I worked with her a few years ago. We keep in touch," Ned said.

"Why don't you contact her," Lyle said.

"I will," Ned responded.

"See if she's interested. Then get me her resume. But get on this right away or you're going to be stuck with someone who's loyal to Violet not to you. Marilyn will see to that," Lyle warned.

Ned ended the call.

The following afternoon Ned called Usha.

"Boss, how good it is to hear from you!" she said in her high squeaky voice that was layered over a thick Indian accent.

Usha always called Ned 'Boss.' Usha was a bit older than Ned. She was an elegant, wispy woman with long black and silver hair that she kept neatly tied into a single thick braid.

Ned worked with Usha in a skilled nursing facility in Culver City. In that time, he came to believe she was what every nurse was supposed to be. Usha was dedicated. She believed her patients came first and it was the job of her nurses to keep them well and happy. She was the kind of nurse that was always on-the-floor. She checked patients, went over charts and corrected problems on the spot. She was nothing like Violet. Her demanding attitude put some nurses off but Ned was always impressed with her effectiveness. In the three years they worked together they became fast friends. When Ned left that facility, they stayed in close touch. They would have lunch or dinner three or four times a year and always sent each other Christmas greetings.

"How would you like to cook some Indian food for me again?" Ned asked.

"That would be wonderful," she responded.

"Are you still looking to get out of being a consultant?" Ned asked.

"It's a lot of driving. Too much, Boss," Usha said.

"You want to come to work for me again?" Ned responded.

"I would love it!" she excitedly said.

"I need to warn you, it's a complicated situation," Ned responded.

"As long as it pays well. You know I don't come cheap. I have to drive all over the place but these people pay me top dollar," she said.

"If I can make this work, I'll pay you what you want but you have to promise to bring me Indian food at least two times a week," Ned chuckled.

"It will be like old times," she said.

"We need to get together and talk about this right away. I have a long story to tell you. Oh, and send me your resume, right away," Ned said.

When Ned received Usha's resume, he quickly sent it on to Lyle. Lyle was impressed with Usha's credentials. She was completely qualified to be a DON of Central City or any other facility in the corporate family.

Lyle called Ned. "I thought we were looking to replace an ADON?" Lyle asked.

"I'm looking beyond that. She's the best nurse I know," Ned responded.

"She's going to be expensive. That's going to be a hard sell upstairs," Lyle warned.

Ned didn't answer. He left the ball in Lyle's court. There was a moment of silence before Lyle spoke, "Let me see what I can do."

After considering how to make the Usha deal work, Lyle realized there was an opportunity at hand. He presented Usha's resume to Mr. M along with a prospectus he believed would improve a constant need at the corporation: the shortage of qualified DONs.

Lyle's proposal addressed the fact that DONs turned over almost as fast as administrators. The difference was that qualified DONs were far fewer in number. The loss of a DON left a facility vulnerable. On so many levels they were more important than administrators. Lyle argued in his prospectus establishing a reserve DON bench could give the corporation an opportunity to observe a prospective DON's ability and give the newly recruited DONs time to adjust to the corporation's culture without the down time of a learning curve. A DON would always be ready when needed. In a nursing market where good DONs were as difficult to find as hen's teeth, this experiment, Lyle's prospectus argued, was well worth trying.

Not only did Lyle send a copy of his prospectus to the tenth floor but he felt he had come up with a winning strategy so he sent one to Marilyn Fowler's office as well. Lyle felt his argument was strong enough that he could take on Marilyn and win. Marilyn countered Lyle's argument by writing a memo of her own to Mr. M. The basis of her counter argument was Lyle, VP of Operations, should not be involved in the hiring of nursing staff, claiming Operations didn't have the expertise necessary to hire senior nursing staff.

Within a week, Lyle and Marilyn were summoned to the conference room by Edith. As usual, there was only a speaker on the table with Edith's voice mouthing Mr. M's thoughts.

"Mr. M is willing to allow Operations to hire all senior staff, even senior nursing staff, provided the individuals are properly vetted. Mr. M agrees with Lyle that noting the turnover in DONs, it seems wise to always have a tested DON in reserve."

M's decision did not go down easily for Marilyn. She didn't like losing.

Edith went on to say, "This will be a pilot program and Mr. M knows that Lyle will consult with you, Marilyn, as part of the vetting process for all senior nursing staff positions."

Mr. M had carefully threaded the needle to give both his top vice presidents a taste of success. But the lion's share went to Operations. Lyle had won big. But he was shrewd enough not to gloat. If Lyle's experiment worked, it would become the new hiring policy for the corporation. If he could control hiring at Central City, he could control it at all the other facilities as well. The balance of power at corporate would shift a bit from Marilyn and move in Lyle's direction.

Ned was making rounds at Central City when Lyle phoned him with the news of his success.

"Ok. Make the deal with Usha," Lyle told Ned.

"And what about the money?" Ned asked.

"I'm going to give her what she wants. You've got maybe six months to make this work or I'm going to move her to another building as the DON."

"Fair enough," Ned responded.

The following day Usha and Ned met for a celebratory lunch at Pacific Dining Car.

"You're here as the result of a tragedy. My ADON suddenly died on me. She was loved by everyone in the facility. I'm not going to kid you, Usha, you're walking into a hornet's nest, but I'm going to support every decision you make," Ned said.

"Thank you, Boss," she responded.

"The biggest problem you're going to face is the DON, Violet. She is going to be gunning for you the minute you walk in the facility. She hates me and that means she's going to hate you," Ned warned.

"That doesn't frighten me. I've been up against some very tough cookies before," Usha said.

"As I recall you're a pretty tough cookie yourself. It's good to be working with you again," Ned said.

Usha gave her notice and finished up her business with the Orange County group. After a few days off, Usha arrived for her first day of work at Central City. The welcoming took place in Ned's office. Usha, as promised, brought Ned lunch, chicken tikka marsala, homemade naan and jasmine rice.

"Your new home is down the hall. It's actually a nicer office than mine. But if you need anything, like a new chair or something, just let me know," Ned said.

"I'm sure it will be fine. You know I'm mostly on the floor," she responded.

All during his conversation with Usha, Ned kept turning his attention to the monitors. He was waiting for Violet to arrive. Finally, he saw Violet's car pull into the parking lot, "Guess who just got to work?"

"Oh, boy, I have butterflies," Usha said.

"I thought you were a tough cookie," Ned said.

"No, that's what you said not me," Usha responded.

"Are you ready to meet the DON?" Ned asked.

"Of course," Usha said with a quiver of nervousness in her voice.

"Don't worry she won't be nearly as mad at you as she will be at me," Ned said.

Ned picked up the phone and called Jose. "Jose, call Violet for me."

"She's not here yet," Jose said.

"She just arrived," Ned said.

"How do you know?" Jose asked.

"I watched her drive into the parking lot. Jose, can you just call her and tell her to please come to my office." Ned hung up the phone and turned to Usha. "If I didn't believe that guy had a good heart, I would have fired him a long time ago. You'll see that he's a little strange but he'll grow on you," Ned added.

"You don't think Violet will cut my tires, do you?" Usha asked.

"No, but she may cut mine," Ned responded.

In Ned's tenure as an administrator the preferred revenge tactic employed by a disgruntled worker was tire slashing. That's why Ned had two of the facility's security cameras trained on his car. Should he need a new set of Goodyears he would know exactly where to send the bill.

In short order there was a knock on Ned's door. "Come in," Ned said.

Violet entered. She knew Usha was starting work today because Marilyn Fowler had kept her informed. Violet was seething, but she did her best not to show it. She somehow managed to push out a fake smile.

Ned stood up to greet her, "Good morning, Violet."

Violet ignored Ned and spoke directly to Usha. "So, are you my new ADON?" Violet asked, as impolitely as she could.

"Yes, she is. Violet, this is Usha Patel," Ned responded.

"I'm glad to meet you, Violet," Usha said as she held out her hand to Violet. Violet didn't take it. Usha pretended she didn't notice.

"Please, sit down, Violet," Ned said.

Violet sat down next to Usha, but spoke directly to Ned. "You know I had a couple of my nurses in mind for this position. I'm disappointed you didn't give me an opportunity to present them to you," Violet said.

"You should have said something, Violet. It wasn't a secret this facility needs an ADON," Ned responded.

"I guess I didn't know you were in such a hurry to replace Casey," she responded.

"The ADON at Central City was an immediate necessity. You know that. You knew about the position, and you are being consulted now. That's why you're in the room," Ned said.

"I don't believe an introduction to the new ADON is a consultation," Violet added.

Violet understood clearly Ned had pulled an end-run on her. She knew Ned had managed to steal a piece of her domain and she couldn't stand it. Violet sat back in her chair and turned back to attack Usha. She knew she had to work with this person, for the moment, but she was already plotting to get rid of her. Violet smiled at Usha the way the Evil Queen smiled at Sleeping Beauty as she handed her the poison apple. "So, Usha is it? Where do you live?" Violet asked.

"Long Beach," Usha replied.

"Coming up here every day, won't that be a long drive for you?" Violet asked.

"No, I'm used to traveling. I listen to books on CD when I drive. It's quite relaxing. I have lots of CDs and if you like, I can lend you some," Usha responded.

Violet ignored Usha's offer. "I can see by your age you're not just out of nursing school, or are you?" Violet asked.

"Heavens no. I've been an RN, my gosh, for over thirty years," Usha replied.

"Thirty years. That's impressive. Being an ADON is a very demanding job," Violet said.

"Oh, yes, I agree," Usha concurred.

"This is a very difficult facility. Do you think you're up for the long hours this job is going to demand?" Violet asked.

"I understand the job quite well and I'm ready for it," Usha responded.

"You've been an ADON before?" Violet asked.

"No, I've never been an ADON," Usha answered.

"Then why do you think you can do this job?" Violet asked.

Then Usha dropped a bomb on Violet. "I've been a DON for most of my nursing career so I understand fully the duties of an ADON. I've hired quite a few of them," Usha said.

Suddenly, the color drained from Violet's face. Her pink cheeks went ashen. She could not speak. For a second she sat there stunned as if she had been hit in the head with a hammer. She languished in that space between confusion and pain. For a micro-second the shock of those words shut down Violet's mind. When reason returned to her, Violet realized she had been set up by Ned. The woman sitting across from her wasn't there to assist her, she was there to replace her. When Violet fully regained her wits a second or two later, she got up, said nothing, and left the room.

Usha turned to Ned. "What happened?"

"I'm not sure. But whatever it was, it wasn't good," Ned replied.

Violet walked down the hall toward her office. She moved almost blindly. Her mind raced in all directions looking for a way to solve this problem and get rid of Usha and that bastard Ned. Almost unable to realize where she was going, Violet slammed into an old man in a wheelchair nearly throwing him to the floor. "Watch out!" the old man yelled.

"Excuse me," Violet managed to say to the old man as she went by him. She didn't even stop to see if he was injured. Violet got to her office and slammed the door behind her. At first, she stood there frightened like a deer in headlights.

"What to do? What to do? What to do?" she said aloud over and over. Violet took a deep breath. Then her mind cleared. The panic subsided. She realized the answer to her trouble was sitting on her desk. She would go to the one person who had been there for her during every problem she ever encountered, Marilyn Fowler. Marilyn had always been there for her. No matter what, Marilyn had come to her rescue. Violet believed she would be there again. Through the infinite variety of administrators that came to Central City…Marilyn was always there. She picked up her cellphone and called who she knew would be her savior. "Hello, Marilyn," Violet's voice couldn't disguise her fear.

"Yes, Violet," Marilyn answered.

Even with those two simple words, Violet could hear there was something off in Marilyn's tone.

"Marilyn, do you know what's going on over here?" Violet asked sharply.

"Are you talking about the new ADON?" Marilyn asked. She knew perfectly well what Violet was talking about but at that moment Marilyn wanted to side-step the issue.

"She's not the new ADON. That bastard brought her in to replace me!" Violet screamed.

"That's not going to happen," Marilyn said.

But the tone in Marilyn's voice was conciliatory rather than reassuring.

"I want you to get rid of her. Get rid of her now!" Violet screamed.

"Violet, you're being overly dramatic," Marilyn said.

"No I'm not! You won't have to come here every day and deal with them, I will!" Violet screamed.

"Violet, you need to calm down. Why don't you go home and think about all this rationally. You're the DON and will remain the DON," Marilyn said doing her best to take the worry out of Violet.

But Marilyn's weak reassurance did not calm Violet. Desperate, Violet worsened the situation by proposing a threat. "I have thought about it. If you won't help me, I'm going to see Mr. M," Violet threatened.

There was a long pause before Marilyn answered, "I wouldn't do that if I were you," her voice was suddenly icy cold. Then she added, "This matter has been decided. Now I'm telling you to go home and calm down."

It became clear to Violet she had been sacrificed. All the loyal years she had given selflessly to the corporation suddenly had no value. She felt violated and stupid. Violet realized she had lost everything. She was so angry she couldn't speak.

"Go home, Violet. Take a few days off. You need it. Everything will look different after you've rested. I'll talk to you tomorrow," Marilyn said as she ended the call.

Violet dropped the cellphone on the desk. Her emotions climbed back on a roller coaster that plunged her down to the steepest, darkest part of her psyche. She was overcome with fear. She was completely alone. There were no other allies to turn to. She wanted to call Mr. M, but what if she called and Edith wouldn't put her through? What if Mr. M wouldn't take her call? That thought was horrifying. She had given the corporation her whole life and now that she needed them, they were turning their back to her. Violet screamed like a tortured soul being dragged to hell. The fear suddenly became rage. She picked up the cellphone and hurled it against the wall. It broke apart. She swept the contents of her desk top to the floor. She grabbed the statue of Baby Jesus and threw it against the wall. It shattered into pieces. She pulled her desk drawers out and tossed them. She kicked and punched the wall. Then she turned the anger on herself. Violet began to punch herself in her face. She opened her lip and bloodied her nose.

Two CNAs heard the screaming and came out of patient's rooms to see what was happening. An LVN pushing a med cart in the hallway outside Violet's door heard the screaming and crashing. The LVN went to the door. "Violet, are you all right?" she asked.

Violet threw open the door to her office. She ran by the LVN into the hallway screaming and punching herself in the face. Blood splattered against the wall. The CNAs that witnessed her actions stood frozen not able to process what they were seeing.

"Violet!" the shocked LVN called to her.

Violet kicked the LVN's medcart.

"Go get Anthony!" the LVN screamed at the CNAs.

One of the CNAs ran toward Anthony's office.

Violet turned her rage to an encased fire extinguisher hanging on the wall. She punched the glass panel shielding the fire extinguisher. It shattered. The shattered glass cut her hand. Violet then pulled the fire extinguisher out from its mooring and threw it on the floor. It rattled down the hallway. Her cut hand began to splatter blood against the wall. Patients came out of their rooms. Nurses came running down the hall. What they were all witnessing was unspeakable.

Jose came bursting into Ned's office. His face was flushed his eyes wide with fear. Ned and Usha looked up at him. "You better come right now. Violet is having a nervous breakdown!" he announced in a confused, panicked voice.

The three of them ran from Ned's office down the hallway toward the sound of Violet's screaming. Three nurses and Anthony were gathered around Violet. They were holding her. She calmed down. Her thrashing stopped. The nurses and Anthony gently laid her on the floor. The rage in her expended, Violet began to sob. Anthony bandaged Violet's bleeding hand. Another nurse tended to her bloodied face.

The LVN who was pushing the medcart when Violet's episode all began was now down on the floor with Violet gently stroking her head. "It's going to be all right," she said as reassuringly as she could. Violet stopped sobbing. She seemed to regain a bit of composure. She looked up. Standing over her were patients and co-workers. They all looked on as Violet lay there on the hallway floor. Violet could see Ned and Usha in the back of that frightened and dismayed group. Ned and Usha were as shocked as the rest. Their faces bleached of color. Ned looked like he had just seen a person being killed. Violet began to regain some semblance of sanity. She looked around and realized what had happened. She realized her career was destroyed. She was broken and humiliated. Violet's crying became uncontrollable.

Eileen handed the syringe to Anthony.

"This will help," Eileen said to Violet.

Anthony injected the contents of the syringe into Violet's arm. She didn't seem to notice. In seconds the medicine in the syringe began to numb Violet. A CNA gently tucked a pillow behind Violet's head.

"Did somebody call 911?" Ned asked.

"They're coming," Eileen answered.

Violet seemed for a second to regain her composure. She tried to get up. "I can get up now. I'm better," Violet said.

"Please Violet, stay there," Ned said softly.

For as much venom as Ned harbored for Violet, at this moment as she lay there on that floor, broken, he felt compassion for his defeated enemy.

"I think it's best if you go to the hospital," Eileen said doing her best to comfort her old friend.

"No, I'm better. Help me get up," Violet said.

Anthony and the LVN gently pushed against Violet's futile attempt to get up. But the drug pumping through her veins was completing its work. Violet made one last attempt to get up then gave into the reality of her situation and the drug. She calmly relaxed. She rested her head on the pillow and closed her eyes.

The paramedics arrived. They knelt down next to Violet and began to take her vital signs.

"What happened?" the paramedic asked.

"She had a breakdown," Anthony responded.

"What happened to her hand?" the paramedic asked.

"She cut it when she punched the glass for the fire extinguisher," Anthony said. Then he added,

"I gave her one milligram of Ativan."

"How are you feeling?" the paramedic asked Violet.

Violet didn't respond.

Two other paramedics entered the lobby. They were pushing a gurney. Usha called to them, "Come this way."

The paramedics pushed the gurney over to Violet.

"We're going to need some information," a paramedic asked.

"Can somebody go to her office and see if she has a purse, and bring it here, please," Usha ordered. One of the CNAs ran to Violet's office.

The changing of the guard had taken place.

"Let's get her on the gurney," the lead paramedic ordered.

"Be gentle with her," Usha ordered.

Violet was placed on the gurney.

"Where are you taking her?" Usha asked.

"Good Sam," the lead paramedic responded.

In that moment of crisis, Usha had taken over the reins of Central City.

The paramedics wheeled the gurney, with Violet on it, down the hallway toward the lobby. The CNA who ran to get Violet's purse handed it to one of the paramedics. The paramedic placed it on the gurney next to Violet. The gurney went out the front door.

"Can somebody call her family, please?" Usha asked.

"I'll do it," Eileen answered.

It seemed all the noise and constant clutter of patients, staff and activity that was Central City suddenly stopped and held its breath as the paramedics lifted Violet and pushed her into the back of the ambulance. The siren blared. The ambulance drove away. Violet was gone.

The following morning Usha knocked on Ned's door then came in.

"That poor woman, I hope she's all right," Usha said.

"I hope she is too," Ned said then he added, "For as much as I wanted to get rid of her I never envisioned this is how it would happen."

“That’s because you have a good heart, Boss. I know you. You pretend to be a tough guy but you are as soft as a marshmallow,” Usha said.

“Don’t let anybody know that. It’ll destroy my image around here,” Ned responded.

“What happens now, Boss? Do you think they will send another DON?” Usha asked.

“No, I don’t,” Ned responded, “What I think is your tenure as ADON is over. And you are now the new DON.”

BETTER USE OF A COPIER

It was one of those mornings when Ned woke up before four. He hated those mornings. He had less of them since Usha became the DON but they still shortened his night's sleep from time to time. Ned felt like an aging bear that had to get up during his hibernation to urinate. He was in a foul mood. He looked at his cell phone. It was three-forty-two. "Shit," he grumbled.

Ned tried for five minutes to go back to sleep but he knew it was a fools' errand. When he woke up, he was up. He decided to go to work and stop by Angel Donuts and pick up a treat for the NOC shift. He showered, got dressed and headed to work before five.

NOC shift were those members of the nursing staff that held the hospital together from eleven at night until seven in the morning. It was the easiest shift in terms of patient duties and needs but the hardest for normal human beings that were used to sleeping at night. Ned did not make a habit of showing up in the middle of the night for fear that he would find most of his NOC shift staff asleep. Sleeping NOC shift nurses was a common problem at all nursing facilities.

Ned pulled into the parking lot of Angel Donuts.

"Hey, man, got any spare change?" one of the homeless that lived outside the donut shop asked Ned. He dug into his pocket and pulled out a dollar and handed it to the homeless man.

"You want a donut?" Ned asked as he walked into the store. The girl behind the counter recognized Ned. "You early today," she commented in a thick Thai accent.

"Couldn't sleep. Give me two dozen donuts. Mix them up. And give that guy outside one with a cup of coffee," Ned said.

The girl boxed his purchase and put an apple fritter in a separate bag as a treat for Ned. "This for you," the girl said.

"Thanks."

He slipped a couple of dollars into the tip jar. Ned left the store and passed by the homeless man.

"I got you a donut and a coffee, enjoy. She'll take care of you," Ned said pointing to the counter girl. The homeless man said nothing then entered the store.

Ned placed the donuts on the passenger seat and then drove off.

As he was turning into Central City's underground parking garage, Ned saw the same young black girl leaning against the side of the building he had seen many times before. Ned could see that she was cold. He wondered how a young pretty girl could end up in her situation. She waved to him and smiled. He lowered the passenger side window. "You want an apple fritter?" he asked. Before she could answer Ned held out the bagged apple fritter to the girl. "These are my favorite," Ned said.

The girl didn't say anything.

"Come on take it. You look hungry."

She took the fritter from Ned. "Thank you," the girl responded.

He handed one of his business cards to her, "If you ever decide to change professions, come and see me."

Ned smiled at the girl. She smiled back. He drove into parking garage. But instead of what should have been the quiet of a sleeping hospital the parking garage was filled with the blaring sound of trumpets, violins and guitars. "What is that?" he muttered aloud. It took Ned about three notes to realize it was mariachi music. The music was loud enough to seep down from the hospital through the concrete floor into the parking garage. Ned quickly got out of his car, grabbed the donuts and his briefcase and followed the very loud music up the back stairs into the hospital to a room by nursing station three. Yo, the Korean RN in charge, ran up to him. She was in in her early thirties and new to LA. She was in a panic. "Mr. Ned, very strange patient in twenty-seven play music so loud. Won't stop," she said.

Rather than ask the obvious question to his RN supervisor, why didn't you just turn the music down? Ned decided to simply handle the situation himself. He handed Yo his briefcase and the donuts. "Here, put this in my office. Give the donuts out to the staff. Save me a chocolate one with the sprinkles," he gently ordered. "Oh, and Yo make a pot of coffee, please."

Ned walked to room twenty-seven. He was surprised by what greeted him. There, sitting in a wheelchair in the doorway to his room was Israel Gonzales. He had a boom box on his lap. It was the source of the blaring Mariachi music. As Ned approached Mr. Gonzales, he couldn't help but notice that Mr. Gonzales was wearing a sparkly black skirt with a brightly colored, also sparkly, flowery top. Since most designers didn't fabricate their female creations around a weightlifter's build, the outfit was ridiculously tight. The dress would have looked good on a slim woman but it looked absurd on a buff, newly released prison inmate which is what Mr. Gonzales was. In addition to his spectacular build, Israel sported a thick black moustache that had bright red lipstick smudged on it and on his lips below. Mr. Gonzales' muscled legs were encased in fishnet hose. Ned saw that Gonzales was not wearing any shoes.

"Couldn't you find any pumps to go with that outfit?" Ned commented.

“What…?” Was the only response Gonzales could get out of his lipstick-smudged mouth.

Mr. Israel Gonzales was one of Dylan’s Medicare deals. Dylan had engineered a connection that gave him a first look at the freshly out of prison population who needed some form of therapy. Usually it was for drug rehab. They all came from Dr. Kovani. It was a profitable situation for Central City. But most of these patients were very scary looking. They had hard bodies covered in prison tattoos and faces with squinty eyes. Theirs’ weren’t the most friendly of looks but considering where this group of patients had just come from, it probably served them well in their former surroundings especially if they were cross dressers like Mr. Gonzales.

Mr. Gonzales had, in the short time he was at Central City, found a way to terrify almost all of the nurses. And the nurses on the NOC shift were especially fearful of him. The idea that this brute wore woman’s clothing and smudged lipstick made him even more likely to be an axe-swinging monster out of a slasher movie. To Ned, the thuggish behavior and attempted-Vogue look actually softened the chances that this guy would use violence as a means to an end. What he saw sitting before him was one psychologically damaged individual.

Mr. Gonzales took a swallow of cheap vodka, the kind that comes in a plastic bottle. He was clearly muy borracho…very drunk. Ned started with the obvious. “Can you turn the music down, please?” Ned asked.

“Who the fuck are you?” Gonzales muttered.

“I’m the administrator. We met when you first came here but you were sober and dressed differently. People are trying to sleep. Can you turn the music down?” Ned said again a little more forcefully.

“Fuck’em, I like this music,” Gonzales said.

“I do too on Cinco de Mayo. Now turn the music down,” Ned repeated.

“I been to prison eighteen times,” Gonzales warned.

“I wouldn’t put that on my resume if I were you. It’s obvious politeness is not working so let me try and get through to you another way. If you don’t turn the music down I’m going to take that boom box downstairs into the garage and smash it into little ity-bity pieces.” Ned held up his fingers to give Gonzales the approximate size of each piece. “Each piece about this big,” he said.

Mr. Gonzales looked Ned straight in the eye. Then, with a show of bravado, he tried to get out of his wheelchair. “I ain’t going to take that shit from you,” Gonzales said. But he was too drunk to manage getting up. He could also see that Ned was not intimidated in the least by Gonzales’ jailhouse history or his threatening facial expressions. The administrator and the cross-dresser glared at each other until Gonzales backed down. “Can I have a cigarette?” Gonzales asked.

"Turn the music down first," Ned responded.

Mr. Gonzales fumbled with dials on the boom box until he found the volume. He complied with Ned's wishes. Not only did he turn the music down he turned it off.

"Thank you. Mr. Gonzales, may I have the bottle of vodka?" Ned demanded.

"It's mine. I paid for it," Gonzales replied.

"I'm sure you did, but you should have saved your money for Coke or cigarettes."

Ned suddenly snatched the bottle of vodka out of Gonzales' hand with the speed of a magician pulling a tablecloth off a table while leaving the table settings in place. Ned was so deft removing that bottle Gonzales checked his now empty hand to see what had happen.

"Now, Mr. Gonzales, why are you acting like a jerk?" Ned asked as he tossed the vodka bottle into trash compartment of a nearby house keeper's cart.

"That bitch disrespected me," Gonzales answered indicating Yo, the RN supervisor. She was cautiously standing a safe distance away preparing an IV for another patient.

"Mr. Gonzales, you're an ex-con wearing a dress with red lipstick scribbled all over your moustache. You do understand you're not exactly set up for respect."

"Why, because I have a dress on? My girlfriend likes me in a dress. That bitch disrespected me. That's all," Gonzales growled.

"I agree, your choice of garments should have nothing to do with the way you are treated, but the notion that one human being should respect another comes out of their actions not simply their demands, or in your case couture. Respect isn't Halloween candy. You don't simply ring a doorbell and people drop some respect into a bag you're holding."

Ned started to walk toward his office. Then he added, "I'm going to get you and me a cup of coffee. You need one and I want one. Now you go back in your room and put on some male clothes or a dress that comes in your size. When you sober up in an hour or so come to my office and we'll talk about how you're going to become a model patient. Or we'll talk about the alternative."

"What's that?" Gonzales asked.

"Throwing your ass in the street," Ned said.

Ned looked for Yo to tell her the immediate danger with Mr. Gonzales was now over. He saw that she was in Jose's receptionist cubicle. He entered the receptionist area and saw Yo placing a full IV bag that would soon be pumped into someone's veins on the copying machine. She engaged the copier the copier's light ran across the IV bag.

"What are you doing?" Ned asked.

"Warming medicine. It too cold," she responded.

"On the copying machine?" Ned asked.

"Temperature just right," she responded.

The copying machine spit out a copy of the IV fluid bag.

"How do you know it's not cooking the meds inside?" Ned asked.

Yo took the copy of the IV bag out of the copier and handed it to Ned. "For you," she giggled then she added. "This no problem. We warm IVs in Korea like this every day."

"You always warm the IVs on the copier?" Ned asked.

"Just cold ones," she responded.

SOMETIMES SHIT JUST HAPPENS

While Mr. Gonzales, unique in so many ways, was really just part of the circus parade that travelled down the main street of Central City every day. In Ned's tenure there, he had become a grizzled veteran of running one of the toughest skilled nursing facilities west of the Rockies. He had seen almost everything and solved almost every kind of patient problem. Dealing with the patients was easy for Ned. He just put on his administrator's hat, applied a little street savvy and acted accordingly. But dealing with his staff was different. Some of these people Ned had come to appreciate and love in the same way that soldiers in a combat zone come to protect one another. He had bought them lunch. Lent them money he knew he would never get back, been with them when they laughed and cried. He organized baby showers and helped with the paperwork that sent their dead relatives back to where ever they came from for burial. He created a position in Central City for one of his CNAs who had been shot in a drive-by until she was able to resume her normal duties back on the floor. Dealing with his staff, especially the ones he had grown so fond of became a deeply personal experience that touched his heart in a way that couldn't be covered by any administrator's hat.

Ned was in his office shopping on the internet for a 'little something' for Amelie. Ned was a terrible gift giver. He inherited that gene from Rose. She bought him gifts like shoes. There were so many variables with shoes that as a gift they seemed odd and impractical. Ned's default gift position was always a gift card. But he wanted to buy something more personal than that for his daughter. Anthony and Usha came into Ned's office. He could see that they were both wearing grim faces. Anthony closed the door behind them. The internet shopping came to an abrupt end.

"What is it?" Ned said expecting a problem.

"Boss, we have an abuse situation," Usha said.

"Are you sure?"

"I'm afraid so. There are witnesses," Usha said.

"What happened?" Ned asked.

"One of the nurses threw water on Paul Stockwell," Anthony said pointing to the monitors. "Let me show you."

Ned rolled his squeaky chair back far enough for Anthony to get to the computer and rewind it to the incident that took place a few minutes before. There was Paul Stockwell, along with three nurses surrounding him, a couple of nurses sitting at the station charting and a few patients looking on.

Stockwell was an old, demented, verbally abusive patient. He was striking out and cursing at nurses standing around him. For the most part, the nurses were smart enough to stay just out of Stockwell's striking range. It was obvious they were attempting to calm him down. Yet, regardless of what the nurses did to soothe his unspecified anger, Mr. Stockwell continued acting out. Stockwell could be seen mouthing screams at the nurses surrounding him. Then he took a swing at one of the nurses. The blow missed. One of the nurses, Brenda Easton, left the group surrounding Mr. Stockwell and went to the sink in the nurse's station. She filled a plastic cup with water returned to Mr. Stockwell and threw the water right in Stockwell's face.

Brenda Easton was a twenty three year old girl right out of the projects. Ned liked her from the start. He could see that she could be so much more than where she came from. All she needed was a chance. And Ned wanted to give it to her.

"Oh, Jesus, Brenda! Why did you do that?" Ned exclaimed out of frustration. Then he added, "What about Stockwell, is he all right?"

"He's fine. He can't even remember how he got wet," Anthony answered.

"Where is she?" Ned asked.

"She's sitting in the lobby," Anthony said.

"Bring her in here," Ned responded.

Anthony opened the door to Ned's office and called out into the lobby, "Brenda."

Brenda entered Ned's office. She seemed stunned.

"Sit down, Brenda," Ned said to her.

She followed his instructions.

"Why did you do it?" he asked.

"I don't know, Mr. Ned. I just couldn't take it anymore. I knew what I did was wrong, but I been puttin' up with that foul ol' man for months and I just couldn't take it one more minute."

The room went silent. Ned closed his eyes and rubbed his forehead. He was trying to contain his own anger. Finally, Ned's frustration got the best of him. "Brenda you're one of my best nurses. What possessed you..."

"I'm sorry, Mr. Ned, sometimes shit just happens," she responded. Tears began to roll down her cheeks.

Ned grabbed the box of tissues he kept on the bookcase. He pulled out a handful of tissues and handed them to Brenda. "I want you to go to bathroom, wash your face and sit in the lobby. I want to think about this," Ned said.

"I'm really sorry, Mr. Ned."

"I know, but Lady Macbeth said it a long time ago, what's done cannot be undone. Now do what I told you."

Brenda left Ned's office.

Ned stewed in his thoughts for a moment. "If I call corporate they're going to term her. If I write it up and report to DHS she's going to lose her license. She's twenty-something years old with a kid, no husband, no chance at anything but this job. Every time I talk to her she wanted to know about becoming an LVN. Her life will go in the toilet. Do you know anyone who never made a mistake? I don't."

Ned looked over to Usha. She knew Ned had decided what he was going to do. She smiled at him.

"I want this thing to go away. I'm not going to ruin her life over four ounces of water, Ned said. Then he turned to Anthony, "I want you to write her up. Then suspend her for a day. After she signs the write up make sure you lose it. I don't want it in her file."

Usha smiled she was pleased with Ned's decision. She turned to Anthony, "See I told you he was as soft as a marshmallow."

Anthony turned to Ned, "What about Lady Macbeth?"

"She didn't have the opportunity to erase the tape…I do," Ned answered.

WHEN THE MAN COMES AROUND

"Mr. Ned, pick up line ten. Mr. Ned, line ten." Jose's voice blared out over Central City's PA system. The DHS was about to enter Central City. Ned looked up at the monitors. He saw three people at the front door of the facility. He immediately recognized two of the trio. The first was Candy Mintz. She was in her usual Goth outfit and white kabuki makeup. The second was Felix Campo. Ned and Felix had a run in over missing narcotics once. Felix always wore a scowl and had the disposition of an angry porcupine. He was in his late thirties but looked much older. He was balding but rather than go for that totally bald, macho look, Felix did that comb-over thing. As if those last twenty-five hairs that went from ear to ear were going to matter. Ned didn't recognize the third member of the group. She was Filipina about fifty. She was appropriately dressed in an Ann Taylor business suit, high heels and a stylish haircut. She was carrying a Louie Vuitton bag, the real thing, not a knock-off she picked up at a swap meet.

Ned went out into the lobby to greet his DHS guests.

"Good afternoon, Miss Mintz, Felix, and, I'm sorry I don't know your name," Ned extended his hand to his unknown guest. She took it. "I'm Nancy Suva," she said.

If you guys are here for the Christmas party, I'm sorry but you missed it by a few months," Ned said. Then he flashed them a big smile. They didn't see the humor in Ned's little joke.

"We're here for your annual survey," Nancy said.

"Somehow I had the feeling that's what it was. I know you need a space to operate so I'm going to put you folks up in the Media Room. Follow me."

As soon as Ned led the three surveyors down the hallway, Jose quickly went through the facility and quietly brought the department heads to Ned's office.

"Ok, you guys know what to do. Mr. Ned is counting on us," Jose said.

The department heads left Ned's office and split up in different directions. Their job was to stay ahead of the surveyors and clean up any potential problem they saw. They efficiently and quietly spoke to all the line staff, from RNs to house keepers. The message Jose gave was the same to all of them, "Don't be nervous. Don't wear gloves in the hallway. And do whatever it takes to keep the patients calm. And never say I don't know."

Nobody who worked at Central City wanted to fail the survey. A failed survey meant the DHS would come back in twenty-three days and do it all over again. And if, God forbid, there was a second failure, that could mean the facility would not be able to accept any new patients. For the time the DHS was in Central City, the whole staff was on their best behavior. The food would taste better. The rooms would be cleaner. The CNAs would check their patients three times as often to make sure not a one would walk around with a load in their pants. The licensed nurses would try and do everything correctly. In general, the patients would be happier which made for a much better survey. For the few days a year, during the annual survey, Central City would look and act just like it promised in their brochure.

Ned led his Health Department guests to the Media Room. He opened the door for them.

"Would you folks like water, coffee, tea?" Ned asked.

"Water would be fine. We'll be ready for the entrance conference in about ten minutes," Nancy announced.

"Who would you like to attend?" Ned asked.

"You and the DON," she said.

All Ned could think was thank God the DON was Usha and not Violet. "See you in about ten minutes," Ned said.

The mechanics of the annual survey were straight forward, the Department of Health descended on a facility like the flying monkeys from the Wizard of Oz. They stuck flashlights into every nook and cranny in the facility. They grilled every employee trying to get them to say something stupid or just plain wrong so they could come back at the administrator with a problem. To boot, the nursing home industry was governed by a massive number of regulations that were second only in strictness and compliance to the Atomic Energy Commission. In nursing homes, most of the employees spoke English as a second language and they understood the regulations about as well as a first grader understands Einstein's 'Theory of Relativity.' Ned had always said if the DHS wanted to, the surveyors could easily close every SNF in America with a fifteen minute walk through. But if they did, what would they do with all those old, sick, crazy people? That was the one thing SNFs had going for them: volume.

Ned left the Media Room. He found Grant, Dylan and Eileen making rounds. "Stay close but not too close to the surveyors. Do rounds but don't be obvious. I don't want them to think we're worried. Stay cool. Do your best to prop up the new nurses. They'll be the most nervous," Ned said.

"We know, don't worry," Grant responded.

Ned started to walk toward his office. "We get through this and I'll buy you the best lunch you've had in a year," Ned promised.

After giving the DHS survey members fifteen minutes instead of the ten they asked for, Usha and Ned attended the Entrance Conference. Nancy Suva formally introduced herself.

"I'm the team leader for this survey," she said as she handed her card to Ned and Usha. "We are planning to exit in four days, provided there are no major problems, of course," Nancy added.

"Well, I certainly hope there won't be," Ned said.

"We will do our best," Usha added.

Nancy handed Usha a list of documents to produce. Some of the documents were to be turned over within the first hour, others the following day and the last group on the day of the exit. Of course, that was providing there was an exit rather than an extension of the survey.

"I need today's census. Any questions?" Nancy asked.

"No, this isn't our first dance with you folks. We'll take care of everything you need," Ned said.

"You can put this in the front window," Felix said as he handed Ned the sign that proclaimed to all that entered that Central City was in its annual survey.

Ned and Usha left the Media Room. "It's your show from here on, Usha," Ned whispered to his DON.

"Don't worry, Boss. I have everything under control," Usha said with confidence.

Since she came to Central City, Usha had begun prepping her nurses for the coming survey. She drilled them and she felt they, for the most part, were ready. Ned went back to his office and waited. It was too late with DHS in the facility to fix the big things. This was game day, as Julius Caesar said as he was about to cross the Rubicon, 'The die is cast.'

The surveyors left the Media Room and started their survey. Candy went to the kitchen, Felix began to interview staff and Nancy started to talk to patients. Ned sat in his office. He leaned back in his squeaky chair and watched the survey unfold on his monitors. From his very first days as an administrator, Ned learned that surveyors watched to see how confident the administrator was in their facility. If the survey was 'business as usual' the administrator was back to his office shopping on the internet. That gave the surveyors a degree of confidence that the SNF was probably in passable shape. But if the administrator paced the halls making rounds the whole time, the surveyors smelled blood in the water.

Ned picked up his phone to call Lyle. The whole time he watched the monitors and every move made by the three government invaders.

"How's it going, Ned?"

"DHS just walked in. We're in survey,"

"They're early this year," Lyle commented.

"Yeah, about a month," Ned responded.

"You need anything?" Lyle asked.

"No, we can handle it," Ned said confidently.

"All right. Good luck," Lyle said.

"Thanks," Ned ended the call. "That's the last thing I want to do is call you with a problem," Ned muttered as he put the phone down on the desk. Ned leaned back in his squeaky chair and glued his eyes to the monitors. The success or failure of the facility was now up to his staff.

Candy Mintz walked into the kitchen. The staff continued with their duties as if she wasn't there. They were preparing lunch. Candy watched Mamook, the deaf dishwasher. He was running the last of the breakfast dishes through the dishwashing machine. Candy saw that Mamook checked the water temperature and the automatic soap dispenser. He was doing everything exactly right. Candy walked to the refrigerators and the freezers to see if the temperature logs were properly up to date. They were. She opened the doors to the refrigerator to see if the contents were shelved properly. Not one item was misplaced. She took a small flashlight out of her pocket and looked under the steam table and in the corners for dirt or pest droppings. There were none. The kitchen was clean. Effie was standing in the doorway of her office watching Candy's inspection. Candy looked over to her.

"Looks good," Candy said.

"Thank you." Effie responded.

Candy stopped by the cook, Calvin, to check to see that he was following proper procedure. He was wearing proper food handling gloves and had thermometers resting in the steam table. All the temperatures were right where they were supposed to be.

"What's for lunch today?" Candy asked Calvin.

"Pork chops with Southwest vegetables, and rice," Calvin responded.

Then Calvin lifted up a cover on a small container that was resting in the steam table. It held a dark brown sauce. He showed it to Candy. "And with this here sauce, I make a squiggle on the plate.

"A what?" Candy asked.

Calvin took a dinner plate and ladled a 'Z' of brown sauce on the plate. Just like Ned had shown him all those months earlier.

"The pork chop goes on top of the sauce." Calvin placed a pork chop on the brown sauce. "It looks good don't it?" Calvin said proudly.

"Yes, it does," Candy responded.

"You eat with your eyes before you eat the food, you know," Calvin proclaimed with a degree of certainty.

"Really?" Candy commented.

"Then we put a little piece of parsley on the plate too, for that added touch," Calvin said.

Candy looked over to the rack where the bottles of food coloring bottles were stored. She remembered the last time she was in the kitchen and its outcome. This time she decided not to check the bottles.

Felix walked into a patient's room. The privacy curtain was drawn. Felix moved the curtain aside and stepped next to a patient's bed. Carolina was giving an old and severely compromised patient a bed bath. The patient, Mr. Tamoyan, was bedbound and contracted. His hands were knotted into balls and legs were tucked into a fetal position. Carolina dipped a washcloth into a basin filled with warm soapy water. She gently washed the old gentleman from head to toe. The whole time Felix stood there like a cop watching her.

"How are you today, Mr. Tamoyan?" Carolina asked her patient in a soothing voice.

Mr. Tamoyan grunted out a few unintelligible words. Then he did his best to smile at Carolina.

As Carolina was washing Mr. Tamoyan, she seemed almost oblivious to the fact that Felix was standing but a few feet behind her. Felix was stone faced typing notes into his I-pad. Carolina took the time to clean Tamoyan's whole body. With every gentle stroke of the washcloth she reassured Mr. Tamoyan how well he was doing. When she was finished, she patted the man dry and then applied lotion to his body.

"What was in the washbasin?" Felix asked.

"Soap and warm water," she responded.

"Do a lot of your patients have bed sores?" Felix asked.

"None of my patients do," Carolina responded.

Felix made a few more notes on his I-Pad then left the room.

Nancy Suva was following Vicky, the LVN, during her med pass. Vicky was shaking like a leaf on the inside but she appeared steady as a rock as she passed her meds. She did everything correctly. Vicky checked the patient against the medication record, administered the correct dosage and watched to be sure the patient took the medication. Nancy watched Vicky. After Nancy had watched Vicky pass meds to four patients she turned and walked away without saying a word. Nancy walked by an elderly lady, Rose Bono, who was quietly sitting in her wheelchair.

"Hi, I'm Nancy. What's your name?" Nancy asked

"I'm Rose," she answered back cheerfully.

"Do you like it here?" Nancy asked.

"Oh, yes, it's very nice," Rose said.

"Do you like the food here?" she asked.

"They don't know how to make meatloaf worth a damn. They need to put bacon on it," Rose said.

Nancy entered notes in her computer.

"I tried to eat a Christmas bulb off the tree, you know," Rose said laughing aloud.

"I thought it was a pomegranate. But the nurses stopped me. I don't do that anymore," she added.

"Do the nurses treat you well? When you press the call light do they come right away?" Nancy asked.

"Oh yes. They come right away, usually within three hours or four hours," Rose said with a smile.

The first day of the survey ended after about five hours of the trio's investigation. Felix, Nancy and Candy silently slipped out of Central City without saying a word to anyone. Ned watched them leave on the monitors as they left the lobby. He picked up the desk phone and used the PA system.

"All department heads please come to my office now. Elvis has left the building," Ned said.

One by one the department heads arrived in Ned's office. Ned checked their faces to see if there were any worried looks. There weren't.

"Anyone have anything horrible to report?" Ned asked.

"That woman wasn't in the kitchen but a few minutes. She looked here and there but didn't say anything negative to me," Effie said.

"Nothing about the CNAs," Anthony added.

"What about the med pass or maintenance, any issues there?" Ned asked.

The rest of the department heads were silent.

"Ok, it looks like we got through day one without any shockers. All of you go home get a hot shower and a good night's sleep. Be back here ready to do it all over again first thing tomorrow," Ned said.

Ned followed his own advice. He stopped at Casablanca and bought a sausage pizza and drank a Coor's right out of the bottle. He called Katie. "I'm in survey," he said.

"Good luck. How do you feel about it?" she asked.

"We could have used a couple more weeks to get ready…but they're here," he said.

"You go through this every year. I'm sure you'll do fine. You always do," she answered.

"I hope so," he said. Then he added. "When this is over, why don't you play hooky from the bank and we go to Santa Barbara. I'll buy you a lobster roll," Ned suggested.

"I think that's a great idea," she said.

"I'll see you in four days if all goes well."

Ned ate, took a shower, watched some movie on HBO, and went to bed. He got up at four the next morning and went to back to work to face the surveyors for another day. The survey team was there before six-thirty. They gathered in the Media Room before they took to the floor.

Ned had Anthony get pastry and coffee from Porto's Restaurant. Porto's served some of the best tasting bakery goods in LA. Ned had Effie set a table with china cups and plates and as an added touch, a small bowl of flowers.

The survey team hit the floor for the breakfast service and the first med pass. Ned went to his office took up his position and watched the survey team on his monitors. All Ned's department heads got there before six. They all quietly made rounds and corrected the few mistakes they saw made by the nursing staff.

On the second day of the survey the investigators changed assignments. Felix followed the med pass. Nancy went to interview Grant in Social Services and Candy talked to patients. Ned knew Felix following the med pass was probably going to be the most dangerous part of the survey. Ned had a lot of nervous, new nurses that Felix would intimidate. All Ned could hope for was they wouldn't make some catastrophic mistake. Ned watched the monitor as Felix was shadowing one of his newest LVNs, Jane Kilton. She was in her twenties, a recent graduate of a local nursing school. She had been at Central City only a month. She was green and still learning the nursing ropes. This was her first survey. She was nervous and Ned could see that Felix was giving her a hard time.

"Come on, Felix, leave her alone," Ned muttered to himself as he watched the monitor.

Felix and Jane were looking through the Medication Administration Record.

The Medication Administration Record book or MAR was where all the information of a patient's medication was stored. It was the place where Seroquel (an antipsychotic) would be ordered by a doctor when a patient wandered the halls all night or saw dozens of cats coming out from under their bed. Just as important, the MAR recorded the day to day administration or the refusal of a patient to take their medication. The beauty of the MAR for the surveyors it was a guaranteed place there were always mistakes.

After a little head-shaking by Jane and finger-pointing by Felix, Jane opened the narcotics drawer. She pulled out a bubble pack of pills. Felix watched as Jane counted the pills in the pack in front of him.

"Something's wrong," Ned muttered.

Ned picked up his cell and called Usha. She was on the floor talking with a CNA.

"Yes, Boss," Usha said.

"You better get over to station two. Felix is grilling Jane about medication. The narcotics drawer is open and they're counting pills. Find out what's going on and get right back to me."

Ned finished the call and threw his phone on the desk. His eyes remained glued to the monitor. In less than a minute Usha had joined Felix and Jane on Ned's monitor. Felix turned to Usha and was explaining something. He took the bubble pack and placed it next to the Medication Administration Record book. Ned watched as Usha took the MAR and the bubble pack of pills and carried them toward Ned's office. Felix was right behind her.

Schedule Two medications (narcotics) were a big deal with the DHS and the Feds. If a facility couldn't account for all the narcotics that were supposed to be in the facility, the immediate assumption was some wanna-be Pablo Escobar was running a drug ring out of the hospital.

A few seconds later, Usha and Felix entered Ned's office. "Boss, we have a problem," Usha said.

"What is it?" Ned asked.

"There is no entry in the MAR for Mary Ferrera's Oxycodone," Usha said.

"The pills are gone but there's no record they were given to the patient," Felix added.

"How many doses are we talking about?" Ned asked.

"Fifteen tablets," Felix said.

Ned cringed. This was exactly the same situation when Felix busted Ned at the other facility. During that last run in with Felix Ned had to go through hoops to prove that he or his staff didn't take the narcotics in question. It turned out to be an error made at the pharmacy. It was as close as Ned had ever come to putting his license in jeopardy.

"Fifteen tablets, you're sure," Ned said in frustration. "May I see that please?" Ned asked indicating the MAR. Usha put the MAR on Ned's desk. He looked to where Jane should have signed her name proving that she gave the narcotics to the patient, but there was no signature.

Felix put the bubble pack on Ned's desk. Nearly half the pills were gone. "As you can see the narcotics are gone and not accounted for. This is a big problem," Felix said ominously.

"It sure is," Ned commented reluctantly.

But every now and then even a blind pig finds an acorn. As Ned was reading through the MAR searching for something that would vindicate the situation Felix saw Ned's watch. It was an Omega Speedmaster Professional.

"You have a moon watch," Felix said.

"What?" Ned was distracted from his search through the MAR.

"The Omega..." Felix said pointing to Ned's wrist.

"Yes..." Ned saw an opening, and deftly turned the conversation from narcotics onto watches,

"... it's the one Neil Armstrong wore when he walked on the moon," Ned commented.

"I know. I have one too. I just bought it." Felix proudly held up his wrist to display his moon watch.

Ned realized this was the first time he had ever seen Felix smile. Up to this point Ned wasn't sure he had teeth.

"I love the whole idea of space exploration," Felix added.

Ned felt Felix had just pulled back the curtain and given him a window into his personality. Instead of watching a ball game on TV while having a beer and pizza like a regular guy, Felix played video games and dusted his collection of Transformers. Ned sensed an opening that he hoped might neutralize the potential nemesis standing in his office. Ned knew with a few key strokes on his I-Pad, Felix could completely nuke Central City's survey. Ned hoped the moon watch was a chance to do the blood-brother thing with Felix and Ned wasn't going to pass it up. He instinctively knew right now was the moment. He knew he might not have a chance like this again. So, Ned decided to lay it on as thick as possible. "Me too! I don't remember how exactly but I got into one of NASA's website. They had astronaut stuff for sale. That's how I got this watch."

"Are you kidding!" Felix said mesmerized by what Ned had told him.

Ned unclasped the wristband on his watch and handed the watch to Felix. He examined Ned's watch then weighed it in his hand. "This came from NASA? I am impressed." Felix said.

"Yes!" Ned said enthusiastically.

"I love the fact they're so heavy," Felix said.

Ned kept shoveling the NASA baloney in Felix's direction. "This one might actually have been worn by an astronaut."

"Whoa…!" Felix said amazed.

I remember they even had a Mercury Astronaut flight suit for sale," Ned said.

"You mean the silver John Glenn suit with the helmet and everything?" Felix excitedly had swallowed the hook Ned had thrown before him.

"They had all kinds of stuff for sale. If you want I'll dig up the website and get it to you," Ned said.

"Oh, I'd like that!" Felix said with the same enthusiasm as a teenage boy about to feel his first tit from the girl in his wet dreams.

"I've got it at home. I'll get it to you," Ned promised.

All of it was a total lie. Ned bought the watch from a jeweler as a present to himself for having made it to forty.

"This watch is one of my prize possessions. I get a lot of comments about it all the time. You will too. Believe me," Ned said.

"I know, I do already," Felix said proudly.

As Ned continued to lie to Felix with tales of NASA and his moon watch, Usha quietly slipped out of Ned's office and got to Mary Ferrera.

Mary was wheelchair bound. Before Usha brought her back to Ned's office, she was sharp enough to find out if Mary had been given all her narcotic pills. Mary Ferrera was in her early sixties. She had been a drug user most of her life. At this point she was so addicted to opioids for a myriad of pains both real and imaginary that her doctors gave up trying to wean her off her high. But regardless of her addiction she was still sentient and in control of most of her faculties.

Usha brought Mary into Ned's office. While Felix was still admiring Ned's watch, Usha gave Ned a positive 'wink' and a smile. Usha wanted to signal Ned reassuring him that Mary wasn't going to be a problem.

"Hi, Mary," Ned said.

Usha pushed her wheelchair all the way into Ned's office. "How are you doing today?" he asked.

"Fine. Hey, can I have a cigarette?" she responded.

"Sure. First can we ask you a couple of questions?" Ned asked.

"What kind of questions," Mary responded.

"Mary, have the nurses ever forgotten to give you your pain meds?" Ned asked.

This was the moment of truth. A smile and wink from Usha aside, if Felix heard a complaint from Mary about her narcotics the survey was doomed.

"No, I know when I'm supposed to get it and I go right up to the nurse and ask for them," Mary responded.

"Are you sure the nurses never forgot to give you your medication," Felix asked.

"I'm sure. If they did I would go see Usha," Mary said.

"What about at night when Usha isn't here?" Felix inquired.

"They never missed giving me a pill. I wouldn't let them," Mary said.

"Are you sure?" Felix tried again.

"Yes, I'm sure. Why are you asking me all these questions?" Mary said forcefully.

"Thank you, Mary," Ned said.

"Can I have my cigarette now? And how about a couple of those red whips too," Mary asked.

Ned grabbed a hand full of red whips from the jar he had on his desk and he then opened his desk drawer and pulled two cigarettes out of the open pack he kept for his patients.

"Here you go, Mary," Ned said.

He handed her the candy and cigarettes. Mary took the cigarettes put one in her mouth and one behind her ear. She put the whips on her lap.

"I'll take you to the smoking patio," Usha answered.

Usha pushed Mary out of Ned's office.

"Thank you, Mary," Ned said.

Ned smiled as Usha closed the door to Ned's office behind her. Ned looked at Felix. "You need to know anything else? I think we're talking about a clerical error not missing narcotics. You agree?" Ned asked Felix.

The ball was now definitely in Felix's court. He had the power to let the narcotics issue end here or decide that more investigation was necessary. Felix handed Ned back his watch. He was quiet as he thought about what he was going to do.

"Unless the team leader disagrees, we'll call this a clerical error," Felix said.

"Thank you!" Ned said.

"There's still going to be a deficiency," Felix added.

"And there should be," Ned said agreeing with Felix.

"I'll have Usha give in services to all the licensed nurses emphasizing the importance of proper and accurate charting when it comes to narcotics. We'll include that in our 2567."

Ned knew if Felix presented it as a clerical error Nancy, the team leader, would probably not question his judgment. Ned guessed at worst, a clerical error for nursing would amount to a slap on the wrist for Central City as opposed to missing narcotics which would possibly bring DEA into the facility for a full scale investigation.

As Felix started to leave Ned's office he turned to Ned. "Don't forget to get me that website where you got the watch," Felix said.

"I'll have it by the end of the survey, promise," Ned said.

Ned breathed a sigh of relief. Whether Mary was telling the truth or not about her narcotics didn't matter. She said the right thing at the right time to the right person. Ned couldn't help but wonder if Usha had bought Mary off with a pack of Marboro Reds, Mary's favorite brand. Ned didn't care. When necessary, Ned knew at times the use of a bribe was the only way to get what he needed from a patient. But more importantly, Ned believed in his heart it really was a clerical error. He truly believed none of his nurses were stealing narcotics.

After everyone left his office, Ned went to Jose's cubicle. "Since you spend all day checking your Facebook page and shopping, I want you to see if you can find a website that sells astronaut stuff," Ned said.

"What kind of astronaut stuff?" she asked.

"All kinds. Go on the NASA website. I'm sure they have one. See if they have a gift shop or something. Or better still go on Craig's list and see if there is a retired astronaut selling his old helmet or something," Ned said.

The rest of the survey was basically a piece of cake. Oh, there were a couple of bumps in the road. Calvin tried to make a soufflé for dessert and to show the surveyors how good the food at Central City had become. The soufflé deflated when Mamook, the deaf dishwasher, slammed the oven door. He couldn't hear it but the puff came out of that soufflé like a fat man sitting on a whoopee cushion. Luckily, Effie was right there and quickly saved the day with frozen carrot cake that was in the freezer.

Then Steven, the facility's resident candy salesman, was constantly bugging the surveyors to buy some of his wares. Ned kept trying to shoo him away but he was persistent. When Nancy Suva finally gave in she gave Steven a ten dollar bill for a 'Milky Way' bar. He took the ten, gave her the Milky Way, and rolled away. But, next to the narcotics issue, the closest to a survey problem for Ned came with a patient named Laverne Toppins. She was a bi-polar schizophrenic, female patient who believed she was being held at Central City against her will. Laverne tried to use the grease from a hotdog and a stolen pack of matches to light her pillow on fire. She must have figured that in the confusion of the fire she could make her escape from the facility. She didn't count on the fact that it's tough getting grease out of a cold hotdog and the pillow being flame retardant. A quick thinking CNA removed Laverne and the pillow from the facility before the surveyors found out what Laverne was trying to do. Ned made a quick call to Dr. Gross and Laverne was whisked away to LA Hospital.

After four days, as promised, Nancy called Ned and Usha into the Media Room for the exit conference.

"I want to thank you and your staff for your hospitality," Nancy said.

"Especially the Porto's," Felix said as he flashed a big smile.

This was only the second time Ned had seen Felix's teeth.

Nancy handed Ned a ten dollar bill.

"This is for the coffee and the baked goods," she said.

It was in the regulations somewhere that surveyors couldn't accept 'gifts' that might be construed as a bribe. Ned had always wanted to meet the surveyor that could be 'bought' for a Raisin Danish.

"Why don't you keep it. I know Steven sold you one of his over-priced candy bars," Ned said.

"No, I think he was just being an entrepreneur. And I applaud the fact that you allow him to have something in his life beside these four walls and his wheelchair," she said as she smiled at Ned.

Then Nancy gave her closing remarks. "My findings are generally based on the overall feeling I get from the patients in a facility. With a few exceptions, the patients here are happy and well cared for. Your staff is friendly and attentive. That impressed me and the rest of the team. Of course, there are always a few things. The most serious deficiency we found was the clerical narcotics error..." Nancy said.

Ned wanted to get up and kiss Felix, but he stayed in his chair. He had dodged the narcotics bullet.

"...There are a few other minor things that will be outlined in the 2567. All of our findings will be reviewed by our supervisor. Are there any questions?" Nancy asked.

"No, just a comment, make sure you're the team that does our next survey," Ned said.

The surveyors chuckled.

Ned and Usha looked at each other and smiled. The exit conference ended. The survey team left and was gone for another year. Ned graciously walked them out the lobby door. Felix turned to Ned as they were leaving. "Thanks for the website. If I find something interesting, I'll let you know."

"Please do. I'd like to get some tiles off the Space Shuttle and make a coffee table out of them," Ned said.

"Oh, what a great idea," Felix said as he left Central City.

Two weeks later the 2567, the year's report card for Central City arrived. It was faxed to the facility. Jose pulled it out of the fax machine and immediately brought it to Ned. He stood over his shoulder as Ned scanned through it. He didn't bother reading the details he just counted the deficiencies, there were only nine, the worst of which, as promised, was the clerical nursing error.

"Thank you, Jesus!" Ned proclaimed.

Ned punched the PA button on his phone. "Attention all department heads, licensed nurses, CNAs, rehab, house keepers, laundry, maintenance and residents of Central City. The 2567 is here. We hit a home run. Thank you everybody. And start planning a victory party!" Ned hung up the phone.

A collective cheer echoed throughout the facility. Then Ned turned to Jose.

"Jose, tell Effie to break out the ice cream for everybody!"

"But it's eight o'clock in the morning," he responded.

"Then tell Effie to serve it as dessert for breakfast," Ned said smiling.

Ned had delivered for Lyle. He was making money for the corporation and the survey was a universe better than the over forty deficiencies Central City received the year before Ned took over the helm. It was even better than the State of California's average of thirteen deficiencies. Ned had managed to guide Central City through a blizzard of problems and arrive at a sunny day. He decided he would get up on the roof and do a little crowing to corporate. He picked up his cell and called Lyle.

"Ned, how's it going?" Lyle said with his familiar opening line and cheerfulness.

“I got the 2567, nine deficiencies,” Ned said boastfully.

“Way to go!” Lyle responded.

“Mr. M is going to love hearing this. Congratulations! Hey, let’s celebrate we’re due for another lunch anyway,” Lyle said.

“You’re damn right we are,” Ned said.

There would be no knot in Ned’s stomach at this upcoming lunch. And this time he wouldn’t be shy about ordering that Grey Goose martini. Ned was now a made man.

AN OFFER HE CAN'T REFUSE

Vicky La caught Ned in the hallway as he was doing rounds.

"Dr. Melville is at station two. He said he wants to see you," she said.

Ned followed Vicky over to station two. Dr. Melville was his usual scruffy self. He was sitting there scribbling his name to orders. There was a nurse next to him. Her job was to be sure the good doctor didn't miss any of the places he needed to sign in the charts. And there were plenty of them.

There were at least a dozen patients charts stacked up at the nursing station beside the doctor. The nurse would remove one chart as Dr. Melville finished signing it and place another in front of him. Each chart had dozens of little red arrows sticking out from each page indicating where Melville should sign his name, or more accurately his scribble. Melville was so adept at this procedure he could do it without even looking. Forget reading whatever he was signing. What doctor had the time? Melville went from page to page scribbling his name as illegible as possible next to the dozens of red arrows populating each chart.

"Good Doctor Melville," Ned said.

Melville looked up at Ned but hardly skipped a beat. He just kept right on scribbling.

"I heard you had a good survey," Melville said.

"Yes we did! I'd like to take the bows for it, but the staff deserves the credit," Ned responded.

"Then let's go to Langer's and celebrate my treat," Melville said.

"No, I insist, the corporation's buying," Ned responded.

"I only have a couple more charts…" Melville said.

"Sorry, Doctor Melville, ten more charts" said the nurse sitting next to him.

"That many?" Melville said to the nurse. Then he turned to Ned.

"If you're hungry, get a banana to hold you," Melville said.

Ned waited on the banana. Eventually, Melville finished and he and Ned went to Langer's.

The line waiting to get into Langer's was at least an hour long.

"How long do you think we'll have to wait?" Melville asked.

"Not long," Ned said. He took a stethoscope out of his jacket and draped it around his neck. Melville's scope was already in place. "Follow my lead," Ned said.

Ned and Melville walked to the front of the line. Ned pretended to take a cellphone call.

"Make sure the kid is prepped and ready. Good. I have Doctor Melville with me. He'll be assisting," Ned said loudly enough so that the first person in line, an old gentleman, could hear Ned's conversation. Ned finished the pretend call and turned to the old gentleman.

"My name is Doctor Russo. I just got a call from Good Sam. We've got a kid in the ER, car accident. They're prepping him now for surgery. We only have a few minutes. This is an emergency. You don't mind if we cut in front of you?"

"No, go ahead," the old gentleman said.

"Thanks," Ned smiled.

The Hostess opened the door and Ned and Melville entered Langer's. The old woman who was with the old gentleman turned to her companion, "Why did you let them go ahead of us?"

"They were doctors," he responded.

"Why? Because he said so? Sometimes you're such a putz." she grumbled at him.

All the booths were taken, but two seats at the counter had opened up.

"You want to wait for a booth or you can sit at the counter?" the hostess asked.

"We'll take the counter," Ned responded.

Ned and Melville squeezed in next to a couple of motorcycle cops on one side and Japanese tourists on the other. As they settled in, Ned tapped the Japanese tourist sitting next to him on the arm.

"Try the pastrami. It's the best in the city. When Benjamin Netanyahu comes to LA, this is where he eats," Ned said.

"Really!" The tourist said with the thickest of Japanese accents.

The Japanese tourist turned to the Japanese woman sitting next to him and told her (in Japanese) what Ned said. They were both very impressed. They smiled and bowed to Ned. The counterman appeared and stood in front of Ned and Doctor Melville.

Like most of the waiters at Langer's he wasn't pleasant. He held his stubby yellow pencil in hand ready to take their order. Langer's wasn't a place one lingered over the menu. One didn't ask the server about the specials of the day. There weren't any. It was a deli. You got pastrami and attitude.

"Two number nineteens, please," Ned said.

"And order of fries and a Doctor Brown's Cream Soda," Melville added. Then Melville turned to Ned, "No self-respecting Jew would order a sandwich at Langer's and not get a Doctor Brown's Cream Soda."

"Make it two," Ned said to the counterman.

The counterman scribbled the order on his pad and walked away.

"That was quite a trick you pulled outside. I had visions of starving to death waiting in that line," Melville said.

"I give it to you as a gift. Use it at any restaurant in LA. It'll work. I promise. Just make sure you have your stethoscope with you. That's the key," Ned said.

"Now that you had such a great survey, I'm sure your bosses are happy with you. Who knows, maybe they will give you a raise," Melville said.

"Why don't you call my boss and tell him that," Ned responded sardonically.

"What? Come on. They must think you are the Messiah. That facility has been the shits for years. I know," Melville said.

"They expect a good survey. I would only hear from them if I didn't get one," Ned responded.

"You make it sound like they don't treat you well?" Melville commented.

"It's not that they don't treat me well, it's that they don't treat anyone any better," Ned said.

"Listen, I know administrators change facilities like I change socks. I am positive, with that survey, you're the new, young Turk on the block," Melville said.

"I'm not so young," Ned responded.

"Compared to me, everybody's young," Melville said. Then he added, "Wait, you'll get offers to run other facilities."

"From who?" Ned sloughed off Melville's remark.

"From me. How would you like to come back to the West Side?" Melville asked.

"Why, are you opening a facility?" Ned asked facetiously.

"Are you crazy? I wouldn't get anywhere near owning one of these places. Besides you have to be rich. I'm not," Melville said.

"So why are you asking me?" Ned said.

"There's a ninety-nine bed facility. They need a new administrator," Melville said.

"What happened to the old one?" Ned asked.

"Not enough Medicare," Melville responded.

"Where have I heard that song before?" Ned said.

"The owners are bleeding money. They're thinking of taking psych patients," Melville said.

"There's plenty of them out there," Ned commented.

"Exactly! But I told them to find someone who knows the psych business first. Not everybody does. The first person I thought of was you," Melville said.

"I guess you just paid me a compliment," Ned commented.

"Listen, you have the experience and the contacts and now a good survey behind you. Believe me, if they're going to get into the psych business you're what they're looking for," Melville said.

"I think you're serious," Ned smiled.

"You think I'm a comedian? I'm a physician." I never make jokes. Of course I'm serious," Melville said.

"Wow. This is a shocker," Ned said.

"Why? I don't think so," Melville said.

"What about the money?" Ned asked.

"That's up to you and them. All I can say is they need somebody," Melville said.

"How do you know these people?" Ned asked.

"I'm the Medical Director. They came to me and asked if I knew someone. If you're interested I'm sure you can get the job," Melville said.

The counterman brought Ned and Melville their sandwiches, French fries and Doctor Brown sodas.

"Can I have ketchup for the fries?" Melville said to the counterman. Then he turned to Ned.

"Think about it. But don't think too long. These people are in a hurry," Melville said.

After lunch Ned returned to work and Melville went onto his next nursing home. When Ned got back to Central City, he called Usha into his office.

"Yes, Boss," Usha said as she entered his office.

"I got offered a job at lunch," Ned said.

"By who?" she responded surprised.

"Melville," Ned said.

"Are you going to take it?" she asked.

"I don't know. I haven't even had an interview yet," Ned said.

"You would get it, Boss. You're the best administrator I know," Usha said. Then she added "Make sure they give you more money. You are worth it."

"Right now it's table talk at lunch. We'll see. No matter what, it's nice to be considered," Ned said.

"If you take it, bring me with you," Usha said smiling.

"Of course, who else is going to make me Indian food?" he said.

The idea of a new job had both good and bad attached to it. There was the excitement of the 'new.' A new anything, new job, new car, new woman was exciting for a short time and then the honeymoon is over and the 'new' becomes routine. The Westside was certainly a better neighborhood than Koreatown. And Ned felt he could probably squeeze a few more dollars out of the situation. But the more money Ned squeezed in salary, the more Medicare his new employers were going to demand Ned bring into the facility. Melville would be a plus. Not only was he a good doctor, but he would be there for Ned in a pinch. But the best part of the offer for Ned was the feeling that he had options. He wouldn't take this job out of necessity but out of choice. There was a lot to think about.

TO BE OR NOT TO BE

Usha was the best DON Ned knew but she never would have made it as a CIA operative or a hitman for a crime family. She talked too much. Within a day of his lunch with Melville, the rumors were flying throughout Central City that Ned was offered a big job and he was leaving. The rumors ran the spectrum. One had Ned the administrator of a posh nursing home in Beverly Hills. This supposedly was the facility where the movie stars went to dry out or to die, depending on if they were old or just needed to kick some bad drug habit. The most rampant rumor, the one most of his staff believed, was that Ned had been offered the job of State Commissioner of Nursing Homes. This was a job, to Ned's knowledge, that didn't even exist. Ned did his best to squelch the rumors but to no avail. No one in the facility would believe Ned would turn down being with drugged out movie stars or the job of State Commissioner of Nursing Homes to stay at Central City. Carolina, without a doubt the boldest of his CNAs took the opportunity to ask Ned for a raise before he left. That's when Ned decided to give up on the denials.

On the second morning of the rampant rumors, Steven rolled his wheelchair into Ned's office, his bucket of candy on his lap.

"Good morning, Steven," Ned said.

"Good morning," Steven grunted back in his hardly intelligible grunts.

As was his practice Steven held out his bucket of goodies to Ned. "You want candy?" Steven garbled.

"Sure. Let's see what you have here."

Ned said as he rummaged through Steven's bucket. "I'll have a Snickers," Ned said.

Ned took a Snickers from the assortment. Then Ned reached in his pocket and removed a five-dollar bill. He held it out to Steven. It was the dance they had done so many times before.

"That's all I got Steven," Ned smiled.

He said those words like a dinner theater actor who has played a part so many times the line has become boringly rote. As was their ritual, Ned was prepared for Steven to take the five and simply rollaway. But he didn't. Steven didn't reach out for the bill. Instead, Steven uttered as best he could the words…"Please don't go." Steven sat there looking at Ned silently trying to convey his feeling. When he had given it his all, Steven struggled and turned his wheelchair around. He rolled out of Ned's office and disappeared down the hallway. Ned was awed by the gesture of this broken, helpless man.

On the way home that night Ned called Katie.

"Hi." Katie said enthusiastically from her car.

"You have beer in the fridge?" Ned asked.

"Don't I always," she responded.

"Good. I'll get us a pizza. I need to talk to you. Sausage ok?" Ned said.

"Sure, but can you get me some jalapenos on the side too?" Katie asked.

"Not a problem."

After he picked up the pizza and a little plastic container of jalapenos, Ned drove to Katie's condo. Parking was always tight there but Ned luckily found a place right in front of her building. The condo was an older edifice. At one time in the fifties it was a working factory. Then it transitioned into boutique stores until some slick developer converted it into very chic condos. All the units were big and had lots of glass, brick walls, wood floors and open ceilings that exposed beams and the ductwork. The units had wide open floor plans and were designed to feel like lofts in Soho. Katie's condo was decorated with furniture she had refinished and Roger Medearis' artwork she had collected through the years.

Ned rang the doorbell. Katie let him in. "You mind if we eat at the counter?" Katie asked.

"I was hoping you'd say that," Ned said with a smile.

Katie and Ned took up residence at her restaurant style, stainless steel counter. Ned opened the pizza box and handed Katie a slice. She popped the tops off two bottles of Coor's. Katie added a few jalapenos to her slice. "So, what is it you need to talk about?" she asked.

"I got offered another job," Ned said between bites.

"Congratulations, are you going to take it?" Katie asked.

"I don't know yet," Ned responded.

"That doesn't sound like you. Is it better than what you have in Koreatown?" Katie asked.

"Probably," Ned said without hesitation.

"Then what's the issue? Have you grown fond of Kimchi? she asked.

"Don't be a wiseguy," Ned responded.

"Then what's to think about?" Katie asked.

"I don't know. New bosses, new staff. The drive," Ned responded.

Katie took another bite of her pizza and a swallow of Coors. "Where is it?" she asked

"The Westside," Ned responded.

"You love the Westside. Oh, I know what's holding you back you'll be closer to Rose. She'll force you to come by every day," Katie sarcastically responded.

"So far I hadn't figured that into the equation," Ned responded sardonically.

"Yes, you have," she said smiling at him. Then she added, "You're here drinking my beer because your conflicted about leaving Camp Kimchi, aren't you?" Katie said.

"No. Why do you say that?"

"Because I've known you for thirty years…that's why."

Ned thought about what Katie said for a bit then dodged the issue.

"What do you have for dessert?" Ned asked.

"Ice cream," she responded.

"Chocolate?" Ned asked.

"Course,' she said.

The following morning as Ned was driving to work, he was on his cell phone calling Dr. Melville. He got Melville's recording. After the familiar 'beep,' Ned left his message.

"Doctor Melville, Its Ned. I'm calling to tell you I don't think I'm going to change jobs just yet. But thanks for the offer. I'll see you next time you're down here, come at lunchtime we'll go to Langer's again," Ned ended the call.

He got to work, parked and went to his office. Jose intercepted him in the lobby and followed him into his office. He had a very confused look on his face. Ned sensed there was a problem immediately. "What's the matter, Jose?" Ned asked.

"Mr. Ned…um…" Jose said stumbling to get the words out.

"Yes…" Ned responded.

Jose looked around Ned's office as if to see if anyone else was there. "There's a woman in the lobby. She's here to see you," he said.

"Ok. Who is it?" Ned asked.

Jose moved in closer to Ned raised his rubber gloved hand to whisper in his ear.

"It's the girl who hangs out at the corner. You know…the hooker. She said you gave her your card." Jose whispered. Jose then showed Ned the business card he gave the girl.

"I did," Ned responded.

"You did!" Jose responded incredulously.

"Yes, show her in," Ned said.

Jose was stunned by Ned's answer.

"In here?" Jose questioned Ned.

"Yes. Show her in here," Ned repeated.

Jose couldn't quite understand why, but he followed Ned's instructions. The pretty young black girl Ned had seen many times soliciting gentlemen outside the facility entered Ned's office. She was still wearing her 'work' clothes. The girl who entered Ned's office had a different demeanor from the hooker on the corner who asked Ned for a 'date' on his very first day at Central City. She was shy and reserved. She was obviously feeling awkward in this situation. She clutched her over the shoulder hand bag as if it would afford her some protection.

"Sit down," Ned said pleasantly.

The girl looked around the office then she sat in the empty chair across from Ned. She pulled her very short skirt down as if trying to lengthen it. When that wouldn't work she crossed her legs trying to look as ladylike as possible.

"I'm glad you decided to come in. What's your name?" Ned asked.

"Felicity," she responded.

"You know your name means happiness?" Ned said.

"No," she responded.

"What can I do for you?" Ned asked.

"You told me if I wanted a different job I could come and talk to you and maybe you could help me," she said.

"Yes I did. So are you thinking about a new career?" Ned asked.

"I'm thinkin' about it," she said as demurely as she could.

Ned could see the girl had a layer of heavy makeup hiding a bruise around her left eye.

"Are you all right?" Ned asked pointing to the girl's eye.

"Yeah. Oh, you mean this?" The girl indicated her bruised eye. "It was a accident?" she said.

Ned didn't believe her. He knew it probably came from one of her 'Johns' or her pimp.

"You sure everything is all right?" Ned asked.

"Yeah," She responded a second time.

"Ok," Ned said.

Ned gave the girl the dignity of accepting her answer.

"Felicity, do you know what we do here?" Ned asked.

"I think it's a hospital, right?" she responded tentatively.

"Yes it is. But it's a very special kind of hospital. It's called a skilled nursing facility. It's different from a hospital like Good Sam or California. Those are acute hospitals. If you get hurt or get sick you go there they fix you up and you go home. We have a lot of patients in here who are sick and will never get better and go home."

"That's sad," Felicity said.

"For a lot of our patients it's the last place they're ever going to be."

"Why?" she asked.

"A lot of our patients have no home to go to. A lot don't have any family. For those patients we become their family. To those patients we have a special responsibility. Their mother was there at the beginning of their lives, we're here at the end. If you want to change what you do and decide to come to work here what you'll need is a big, understanding heart. A lot of these patients are very difficult, but you have to be kind to them no matter how they treat you."

"That sounds hard," she commented.

"It is. And the pay won't equal the amount of work, or caring you put into this job. You won't be praised enough and at times you'll be criticized unfairly for what you do. Working here will be the hardest job you'll ever have. But, Felicity, there's one big reason to come to work here," Ned said. Then he paused.

"What is it?" she asked.

"What we do is really important," Ned said.

Ned leaned back in his squeaky chair. "If this sounds like something you might want to do, then I can help you," Ned smiled.

THE END

Made in the USA
Las Vegas, NV
17 May 2024

90046179R00184